Queen Bee
of Mimosa Branch

HAYWOOD SMITH

St. Martin's Paperbacks

QUEEN BEE OF MIMOSA BRANCH

Copyright © 2002 by Haywood Smith.
Excerpt from *The Red Hat Club* copyright © 2003 by Haywood Smith.

All rights reserved. No part of this book may be used or reproduced in any manner whatsoever without written permission except in the case of brief quotations embodied in critical articles or reviews. For information address St. Martin's Press, 175 Fifth Avenue, New York, NY 10010.

Library of Congress Catalog Card Number: 2002068363

ISBN: 0-312-98939-3

Printed in the United States of America

St. Martin's Press hardcover edition / October 2002
St. Martin's Paperbacks edition / October 2003

St. Martin's Paperbacks are published by St. Martin's Press, 175 Fifth Avenue, New York, NY 10010.

10 9 8 7 6 5 4 3 2 1

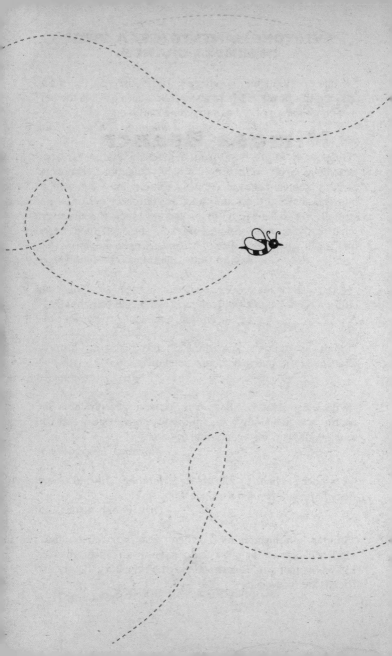

Dedication

This book is dedicated to my late, beloved father,
Jim Pritchett, Sr.,
who taught me much of acceptance, the joy of learning,
combustion engines, human frailty,
and true dignity and tolerance.
He shares that honor, as he shared everything else,
with my precious stepmother and friend,
Fancy Hinton Pritchett,
whose life is a lesson in grace, faith, love, true courage, and joy.
I love you, Redhead.

Acknowledgments

Special thanks are in order to St. Martin's Paperbacks Associate Publisher Jennifer Enderlin and Publisher Matthew Shear for allowing me to write in the voice and humor of my Southern heritage.

Heartfelt thanks go to my support network: my indispensable critique partner and dear friend, Betty Cothran, my inspiration and encourager, Deborah Smith, my precious sisters, Lisa Cross, Susan Carlsson, and Betsy Allen (in reverse alphabetical order this time), my mom, Anne Pritchett, for her wit, support, and wonderful, sharp pencil, and to my brother, for being a good brother and an even better man.

I am also more grateful than I can say to Georgia Romance Writers for their creative, emotional, and practical support over the past difficult years, especially Carmen Green and Carla Fredd, precious sisters in Christ.

Thanks, too, to Dr. Glen Havens at The Ark in Roswell, a real lifeboat. And my attorney, Alan Pilcher of Gainesville.

I am blessed, also, to have dear friends and gifted authors Kris Olson and Judy Swann in my life. I owe a deep debt of gratitude as well to Tom O., Mavis, DeAnna, Alice, Regina, Nita, Cathy, Wanda, Joy, Susan and Beldon, Elizabeth P., Monie, Susan, Joann, Martha, Annie, and all the good souls who have helped me find myself and fall in love with life.

Author's Note

One of my favorite quotes is "Fiction is the lie that tells the truth."

All my life, I've been fascinated by people's stories, their circumstances, their special mannerisms and personalities. I gathered them into a treasure chest of anecdotes, characters, events, and places, which I regularly retrieved to embellish with heightened drama and only a passing nod to accuracy. Now that I'm a writer, I continue to add to my trove even as I plunder my memories to create my own "lies that tell the truth." So the people, places, and events in this book are imaginary, even though some of them have been cobbled from the memories, news stories, local lore, and experiences in my treasure chest. They are not real—with the exceptions of my favorite priest, my brother, Jim Pritchett, and my favorite TV repairman, Wayne Burnette.

Another of my favorite quotes is "The smoothest and most convincing liar of all is memory." That's why I love writing fiction. I "get it right" whether I "get it right" or not, as long as I am true to the human condition.

Mimosa Branch and its occupants exist only in my over-active imagination, and—I hope—in yours. Over the past fifteen years, though, an awful lot of my friends have shared the heartache of betrayal and divorce, and the painstaking putting back together that must follow. Their stories were the inspiration for Linwood Scott's, but she is not any one person. She represents all those women, and her circumstances are common to far too many.

She's a lot more adventurous, bawdy, reckless, and irreverent than I am. We share only our affinity for old movies, our dark sense of humor, and our determination to make lemonade out of lemons. And, for the record, I have no tattoos on my body.

I hope my readers will laugh, cry, and grow with Lin. I did.

Chapter 1

I took the long way home that fateful midsummer day last July, maybe because I still couldn't quite believe what I was about to do.

I could still hear Miss Mamie—that's my mother; everybody calls her Miss Mamie, including my brother and me—telling me, on the eve of my wedding, that if I insisted on marrying Phil at nineteen, I shouldn't even *think* of turning up on her doorstep again. "You make your bed, you lie in it," she'd said with absolute conviction. (Miss Mamie says everything with absolute conviction.)

Yet here I was thirty years later, galled to my very soul that my family's dire predictions for my marriage had finally proven true. The phantom umbilicus that connected me to my mother had turned out to be a cosmic bungee cord, my fifty years of life one long, ludicrous leap that was rebounding at light-speed back to the womb, God help me.

So that Thursday, the day after the Fourth of July, I took the slow, scenic route through Mimosa Branch. Driving into the old business district, I was struck that my hometown seemed to have come up in the world at least as far as I had come down. Everything was fixed up, filled up, and decidedly suburban upscale, right down to the contemporary artists' warren in one of the old mill buildings.

Miss Mamie had told me all about the artists in her almost-daily phone updates. An equal-opportunity gossip, she belonged not only to the United Methodist Women, but also to the Baptist Women's Circle, so she got the scoop. She'd assured me the good ladies were doing their best to love these "offbeat transplants" in a Christian way, just as they tried to love "those Mexicans" who had flooded into the area and "snapped up" all the jobs at the poultry plant. But as to the artists, the good churchwomen of Mimosa Branch—Methodist, Baptist, Presbyterian, and even the Pentecostals—had been united at last by their common alarm about the New Age influence the interlopers had introduced to their conservative community. Worse still, several of the odd characters were from California, a point of origin surpassing even Florida in its capacity for alienating the locals.

I knew my mother would fill me in on all their subversive activities. Endlessly. Incessantly. In person.

Shuddering at the thought, I tried to concentrate on the brick storefronts that flanked Main Street. Gone were the FOR RENT signs and sad neglect. Like kudzu, Atlanta's suburban tentacles had invaded my hometown and cloaked it in green—the spending kind. And like kudzu, the blanket of green had certainly made things look better, at least on the surface. Whether it was really an improvement, though, remained to be seen. The decay was still there under kudzu; you just couldn't see it.

Yep. Things had definitely changed. I passed the nude painting Miss Mamie had told me "blared right out on Main Street." Galleries now replaced all but a single law office of the dozen that once practiced here. I'd always wondered how so many lawyers could stay in business in a town of 3000 that wasn't a county seat. Apparently, they couldn't. But then again, this was no longer a sleepy little town of 3000.

Even the people on the sidewalks looked different. Where were the fat women? Mimosa Branch had always had the state's highest per capita ratio of fat women. I wondered if one of those California artists had gotten the city to enact that same secret ordinance they had in Beverly Hills and Brentwood, banning fat people from coming out in public.

My thirty extra pounds smarted in outrage.

The one comforting presence downtown was Chief Parker's Drugs, which had defiantly held on to its ugly aluminum awning and faded fifties commercial tackiness through three owners and the insurgence of trendy bistros, boutiques, and galleries. "NEVER CLOSED TO THE SICK" was still painted on the front windows above the store's number and old Doc Owens's home phone. The place stuck out like a sore thumb among its trendy new neighbors.

Mimosa Branch, trendy. I still couldn't believe it. Seeing the tastefully quaint renovations in subdued merchants'-association-approved coordinated colors, I felt like I was looking at a movie set.

How long had it been since I'd come here last? I thought back. Not since the year I'd dragged Miss Mamie on that cultural exchange to France . . . '91. Cripes. Ten years. I was moving back to a place I hadn't even seen in a decade. Heaven only knew what things were like here now.

Everything changes, I told myself. Maybe if I got lucky, life at home would be different, too. Better, I hastily qualified.

Not that it was that bad growing up. How can I put it diplomatically? Life at 1431 Green Street had been just a bit too . . . *colorful* for my tastes.

I eased my car into the turn where Main Street became Green Street at the second dogleg, just past the most recent and ostentatious of the Breedlove mansions, now resurrected to its turn-of-the-century Italianate glory as a posh bed-and-breakfast. Miss Mamie had told me all about it, of course, but seeing the restored grounds and tastefully sandblasted sign, I felt an inexplicable sense of loss. The place seemed to wear its newfound prosperity uneasily, like a mechanic in a three-piece Brooks Brothers suit.

A bed-and-breakfast in a town that had always been a "meat and three" kind of place. Go figure.

Two more blocks of Green Street to home, railroad on the left now, houses on the right.

Bracing for a bump that didn't happen, I realized the city had finally done away with the abandoned sidetracks leading to the old mill. Farther down, the old Watkins place gleamed afresh with vinyl siding and dark green shutters. Law Office. Maybe they hadn't all gone away, just moved to larger quarters.

Beyond that, somebody was redoing Mrs. Duckett's fanciful Victorian from the studs out, complete with a copper cupola, scalloped shingles in the gables, suitably gaudy Chinese red paint on the gingerbread, and a real slate roof. Must have set them back at least a mil.

And across the next side street, 1431 Green Street loomed, the one thing in town besides Chief Parker's Drugs that still looked the same as it always had.

Home.

On its own, my foot eased back on the gas.

Bounded by shoulder-high camellia hedges that, like the rest of our home place, had seen better days, the sturdy old white Victorian sat firmly anchored by eighty feet of verandah—"Miss Mamie's Porch" to one and all in Mimosa Branch. Nothing fanciful about our house; it was massive, angular, and quintessentially functional. And as usual, it needed painting. Old Southern houses peel worse than Scandinavians at Miami Beach, so ownership conveys a constant cycle of scrape and paint, and I do mean constant. At least it gave my underemployed brother, Tommy, something useful to do.

As I neared the driveway, my car slowed to a crawl all by itself. I still could not accept that I was really doing this, so I distracted myself by focusing on the familiar landmarks. The same massive elm stumps rotted between the road and the cracked, uneven sidewalk. The same garden-club flower beds bloomed with marigolds and cockscomb by the railroad tracks across the street.

I reached the opening in our camellia hedge and squeezed my car past the historical marker onto the circular gravel driveway. My eyes scanned past the bronze letters: ALLEN BREEDLOVE MANSION, 1897. THE SECOND RESIDENCE OF ALLEN BREEDLOVE, FOUNDER OF MIMOSA BRANCH AND BREEDLOVE TEXTILES. . . . I used to take pride in reading my family's illustrious history, but ever since Granny Beth had spilled the beans about what a pompous son-of-a-bitch my great-grandfather had really been, the words rang false.

Up ahead, the house's wide, shallow steps and porch boards shone the same blue-gray against the white of the latticed foundation. The same sweet autumn clematis twined through the porch rails. And the same damned purple bathtub full of pink begonias reclined on its gilded ball-and-claw feet beside the front door, like a rich old socialite laid out on a swooning couch in her underwear. Miss Mamie had affixed 1431 to the side in big brass numbers, which only drew more attention to the embarrassing eyesore. Clearly, she'd given up even trying to find somebody to haul the thing away. How white-trash was *that*?

My foot hit the brake as if my body was telling me, "It's not too late! Get away! Run!"

The trouble was, I had no place else to run. The only people who would take me in lived inside those walls. And every last one of them was crazy to some degree.

Unlike me, of course. I was damaged, but normal. At least, that was the conviction I clung to.

I forced myself to drive the last few yards to the wide spot in the gravel where the porch steps came down to the edge of the driveway. There I stopped. Like it or not, I had arrived. A dull throb of pain bloomed in my right eye and deepened slightly with every heartbeat.

Oh, God. I was really doing this, moving back home at

fifty. The very thing I'd spent the past five years criticizing my brother for doing.

Judge not that ye be not judged, in spades.

But unlike Tommy, I had no intention of staying. I'd only be here until I got back on my feet. I'd be back out from under Miss Mamie's roof as soon as I made enough money to redo the garage apartment. Beyond that, who knew, but I had great hopes. I had to.

I'd escaped once; I could do it again. I'd be fine.

Right, the cynical new voice who lived inside me said. *You're fifty. No money. No degree. No technical skills. No real job experience. Knees too rotten to wait tables or work as a checkout clerk. Sure, you'll be fine.*

My spiral into self-pity was cut short when Uncle Bedford lurched out the front door in nothing but Depends, carrying a mahogany TV tray loaded with his shoes. (I recognized the white patent slip-ons.) His stocky, little hyperblond self had wasted away to almost nothing, but he descended the steps with surprising speed and agility.

I watched in morbid fascination. Hearing Miss Mamie's reports about his mental deterioration was one thing, but seeing him this way was quite another. Now I understood why Aunt Gloria had moved the two of them in with my parents six months ago. Who could cope with this alone?

"Don't try to deny it!" he hollered to nobody in particular.

Stupidly, I raised my hand and waved as he detoured around the front of my car, leaving a cordovan loafer on the hood. "Hey, Uncle Bedford." Since he'd been a well-respected podiatrist for more than forty years, the shoes seemed vaguely appropriate to me, which is pretty damned scary in retrospect, I can tell you.

Heedless of the gravel on his bare feet, Uncle Bedford stomped toward the late-blooming azaleas that separated the circular driveway from the front lawn.

Better stay out of Miss Mamie's pet azaleas, Uncle Bedford, or you'll really be in hot water. For reasons unknown to God or man, those gumpos had been flowering in mid-summer ever since my mother had planted them back in '73. They'd become her local claim to fame.

"That boy took my shoes, that gay guy," my uncle ranted. "He takes everything."

Miss Mamie's updates had informed me that Poor Aunt Gloria had become "that gay guy" to Uncle Bedford, just as she had become *Poor* Aunt Gloria to the rest of the family when Uncle Bedford had finally quit drinking three years ago and promptly gone into the permanent D.T.'s.

Poor Aunt Gloria, indeed. At least I was moving back to the bosom of my own family. She'd been forced to live at the sufferance of in-laws.

Speak of the devil, here Aunt Glory came out the front door, round, fierce, and firmly packed as ever, holding out one of the sheets Uncle Bedford used for keeping "the Japanese" off the furniture. Hobbling down the stairs on her arthritic knees, she said through her tiny teeth, "Don't you dare get out of that car, Lin. I'll take care of your uncle. He's my husband, so it's my shame to bear."

She caught up with him beside the Rose of Sharon that was in glorious fuchsia bloom. "Jackson Bedford Breedlove the Fourth." Owing to his deafness, she shouted loud enough to be heard a block away. "Cover up and come back to the house this instant before somebody from church sees you!"

Her husband hallucinated Japanese, thought she was a gay guy, and was running around in Depends with a TV tray full of shoes, and she was worried what *somebody from church* would think? Uncle Bedford wasn't the only crazy person in this scenario. Obviously, living with him had made Aunt Glory as loony as he was.

Never one to back down, Aunt Gloria held the sheet like a matador's cape and did her best to corral her husband. Uncle Bedford evaded her first few swoops, but he soon got enough of it and counterattacked with a powerful swing of the TV tray. Shoes went flying. Fortunately, Aunt Gloria managed to jump out of the way, because the tray made an ominous whooshing noise as it whizzed past her.

Damn, he was strong. I had read somewhere that when they were psychotic, even fragile old geezers like Uncle Bedford were strong as prizefighters on PCP, and now I believed it.

My conscience told me it was time to get out of the car and try to rescue my aunt from her husband, but not before I punched 911 into my cell phone and poised my finger over the send button. I opened the car door and stepped into humid, oppressive air that smelled of granite dust, fresh-cut grass, magnolia blooms, and honeysuckle.

My mother chose just that moment to emerge from the house in full dudgeon, broom in hand, still a force of nature despite her eighty years. "Good Lord, Bedford," she fumed, "if you weren't the General's baby brother and sole survivin' family, I'd shoot you dead on the spot. Now get back in the house. Poor Lin's gonna think this place is an insane asylum!"

"Poor Lin" knew it was an insane asylum and so did my mother, but my only thought was a desperate, *Dear God, please don't let me be* Poor Lin *from now on! I couldn't stand it. Anything but that.*

After a perfunctory, "Sorry, baby," to me, Miss Mamie bustled over and laid a firm hold onto Aunt Gloria's elbow. "Go back inside, Glory," she said with exaggerated diction, a manner of speaking reserved for embarrassing situations. The more embarrassing the situation, the more precise and gravid her speech. "You only make it worse when he's this way. Leave him to Lin and me."

I took another look at the heft of that TV tray and the brittle spark in Uncle Bedford's eyes and voted for 911, but I kept my mouth shut because I knew the mere mention of calling in strangers would send these women into a rage, or hysterics, or both.

Aunt Gloria, unwilling as ever to leave the field of dishonor without a clear victory, shot yet another anxious look up and down the empty pavement of Green Street. Then she deflated. "All right." She handed over the sheet, suddenly looking every bit of her worried, worn-out seventy-six years. "But at least try to keep him behind the azaleas where nobody can see him. I won't be able to lift my head in this town if anybody from church should drive by."

"They won't, sugar," my mother reassured her in her normal voice. "This time of day, they're all home napping or watching *All My Children*. You know that."

"Lord, I hope so." Aunt Glory glared at Uncle Bedford, which was all it took to set him off again.

He jabbed the TV tray in his beleaguered wife's direction. "That boy took my shoes! I want 'em back! These new ones hurt my feet!"

"Bedford," Aunt Gloria hollered, "look at your feet. You're not even wearing any shoes."

This was going to be my life: Aunt Gloria trying to use logic with Uncle Bedford in the midst of a psychotic break, and Miss Mamie thinking she can fix everything with confidence and a broom.

I'd married at nineteen to get away from crap like this!

The pain in my right eye bloomed to ice-pick intensity, stabbing through the back of my skull. I winced like Popeye.

Miss Mamie prodded Aunt Gloria toward the house. "He'll do better when you're out of sight, honey," she assured in her embarrassing-situation voice. "So hurry on outta here, before somebody from church really does come by."

Patting her sparse permanent wave, Aunt Gloria turned her silk-clad back on her husband with military precision, then marched her Talbot's flats toward the porte cochere. Uncle Bedford watched with a canny gleam of triumph. "Hah!"

Miss Mamie handed me the sheet. "Keep this ready, sugar. Let's just give him a little time to settle down."

Sure enough, the minute Aunt Gloria was out of sight,

Uncle Bedford lowered his weapon and cocked his head at me, his blue eyes clearing. "Hey, Lin. Where you been, little girl?" he muttered with the same sweet inflection he'd always used, but so softly I might have missed it if I hadn't been paying close attention.

Unexpected tears stung the backs of my eyes. I don't know if they were tears of sadness for what had been lost, or happiness for what, if only for a moment, had been resurrected. I wrapped the sheet around him and gave him a hug. "I came to see you, Uncle Bedford." He felt so small and frail, and his skin gave off an odd, sour odor that was completely out of character—Uncle Bedford, who'd always been so clean he smelled like disinfectant even when he played tennis in the summer.

"Let's go into the house so I can bake you a pumpkin pie," I suggested loudly, making sure he could see my mouth. He loved my pumpkin pies. Every Thanksgiving and Christmas, I always sent him home with one.

Uncle Bedford let out a chortle. "If those azaleas are right, it's nowhere near Thanksgiving," he mumbled with a spark of his old, dry wit. But the window of lucidity closed in the middle of his next sentence. "Still, I'll take one of your pumpkin tammis, and they never got it to the prookis." Just like that, the light extinguished, and he slumped, incoherent and unsteady, against me. I guided him toward the stairs.

"Gone again, bless his heart," Miss Mamie said. "Just like your dear, departed Uncle Garland toward the last." Her face hardened. "Alcohol. It steals your soul, every time."

Uh-oh. The Uncle Garland thing. I resisted the urge to roll my eyes. My mother's timeworn stories came with the lodgings. I might as well get used to it.

"I'll never forget the sight of Garland lying dead in all that blood in that filthy room," my mother repeated with the same words she'd been using since I was twelve. "That's what drinking does, Lin. True, Garland always had been a little *odd*"—a Southern euphemism that covers anything from the mildest peculiarities to full-blown schizophrenia—"but it was the drink that took him down. Steals your mind, your decency. I wish you'd stay away from it, honey. You never know when that wine at dinner will work its way into a fifth a night in the woodshop. Just look at Bedford."

I refrained from reminding her that Uncle Bedford had been pretty functional until he'd *stopped* drinking. Then it occurred to me that I had no idea what had gone on behind closed doors at my uncle's all these years. Maybe he hadn't been so functional after all.

Nothing else had turned out to be what I'd thought lately. Why should this be any different?

Miss Mamie took Uncle Bedford's other arm and helped me guide him toward the stairs. "It's the Breedlove curse, the oddness, the drink. I pray every day it's not hereditary. My Tommy. Your poor David."

Help. The poors were contagious. Now it was "my poor David." My strapping, world-beating, Emory graduate would *love* that.

"Thank goodness your David's sweet little girl wasn't afraid to marry him," Miss Mamie rattled on.

Not that again. My eye developed an annoyed tic, which I staunched with my index finger. "Her name is Barb."

"I know her name. David's my only grandson; of course I know his wife's name." My mother's features sharpened with interest. "Have they said anything to you about starting a family?" Miss Mamie was forever "takin' off down every conversational pig trail in north Georgia," as my daddy put it. I'd long since stopped wasting energy wishing she wouldn't. It was so much easier just to hop on and ride it out. "David's girl isn't getting any younger," she said for the hundredth time, "and neither am I. I'd like to be alive to see my great-grandchild."

"Tommy's oldest daughter has three kids," I reminded her. "Don't they count?"

"Frankly, no," my mother huffed. "*Tiffani-with-an-i* wasn't even married when she had the first one. My own granddaughter, an unwed mother."

"Judge not, Miss Mamie."

"Well, I'm hardly capable of bein' judged for *that*, Lin. I haven't had a uterus since 1958. And I haven't had . . . well, never mind about that."

I deliberately shifted the subject away from my mother's sex life, or lack of it, and my niece's past sins. "Anyway, where do you get off always making fun of Tiffani's name?" I countered. "You named me *Linwood*, for cryin' in a bucket. People who live in glass houses . . ."

My mother would not be diverted. "I haven't seen that Tiffani-with-an-i in fifteen years," she huffed. "Not since that first wife of Tommy's took her and Brandi-with-an-i to Detroit. Who in their right mind moves *to* Detroit, for God's sakes? I ask you."

Uncle Bedford managed another step along the gravel, but his knee didn't seem to work this time, so he sank toward the driveway like a penitent at the altar rail. "Whoa," Miss Mamie said as we pulled him back aright. Blessedly, it was enough of a diversion to send her down another conversational sidetrack. "I wish to goodness Glory would give Bedford his medicine like she's supposed to. This doesn't happen when she gives him his medicine like she's supposed to."

"What's he taking?"

"Ativan, I think."

Not the one I took every day. My magic pill was Prozac. Trying out several before I'd found one that worked, I'd learned that you can't just start and stop taking mood-altering drugs. The dosages have to be built up or decreased gradually. Otherwise, you might turn suicidal or attack people with a TV tray because "that gay guy" was stealing your shoes.

We finally got Uncle Bedford to the bottom of the stairs,

but at this rate of progress, the seven steps were going to take a while.

"Should we just hoist him up?"

"No," Miss Mamie said. "We might pull something, in him or us. It's best just to keep him steady until he hitches up his get-along. We'll get there eventually."

She bent her mouth to Uncle Bedford's ear. "Up we go," she hollered brightly. It took him three tries to make that first step, almost falling every time, but as she'd predicted, he managed.

Step one of seven.

"Why doesn't Aunt Glory give him his meds like she's supposed to?" I asked.

Miss Mamie rolled her eyes. "Says it makes him a zombie." She leaned behind Uncle Bedford to whisper, "I'd rather have him a zombie than a public menace running around good as nekkid in broad daylight."

I seconded that.

The women's shelter was beginning to look like a viable option.

We'd only reached step three when a man I'd never seen before emerged from the side yard, making straight for us with long, resolute strides. Tall, handsome, about my age, with sandy hair and a trim build, he held a most uncooperative little cat in his arms. A seething train of toms skulked through the bushes behind him.

Bold as you please, he strode right up to the bottom of the front stairs and stopped there. The tomcats swarmed into the azaleas, several of them making that guttural mating moan they do.

I could feel the man with the cat staring at us from behind, willing us to turn around.

Now I ask you, what kind of numbskull would intrude on people when they're clearly in the middle of a hideously embarrassing family crisis? And then stand there without even introducing himself? Had this guy been brought up in a barn?

I refused to look at him, figuring maybe if we didn't acknowledge him, he'd go back where he came from. As usual when it came to men, I figured wrong.

"Ah, hi. Excuse me for interrupting," the intruder said in a newscaster nonaccent, "but it took me over an hour to capture your cat, and I didn't want to risk losing her again. I have to go back to work. Could you take her? Please." He added the please begrudgingly. "She's come into season and needs to be spayed." He said it like a man who was used to having people do what he asked them to, even when he skipped the amenities, which he definitely had. The kitten hissed. "Ow! Quit that, cat."

So this was the California cat guy, Old Doc Owens's son, who had taken over Chief Parker's after his father died. Miss Mamie had told me all about him, of course. Despite the fact that he'd appropriated three of our pets this winter out of misdirected "kindness," my mother actually wanted me to meet him with dating in mind, "when you're ready."

If the annoyance I felt was any indication, I definitely wasn't ready—which came as no surprise. As far as I was concerned at that point in time, all men were peckerheads. The last thing I wanted was another one.

The most polite response I could manage was to continue ignoring him. But I did glare briefly at my mother. Miss Mamie winced, her matchmaking toes clearly trod upon, but blood being thicker than water, she tended Uncle Bedford as if the cat guy wasn't there.

I heard the kitten hiss and growl again. "As I said, she's in heat," the guy bit out in a strained cadence, "and she keeps sneaking into my father's—*my* house and eating Garfield's food."

A cat named Garfield. How original.

When we still refused to acknowledge his presence, his urbane accents took on a hint of belligerence. "I came home for lunch to find half the tomcats in town vying for your kitten's favors in my garage. The place stinks to high heaven now. Ow!" Score one for the wanton kitten. "I'm already half an hour late getting back to the store, so would you take this vicious little beast, or what?"

Since he obviously had no intention of leaving, I relented and said over my shoulder, "As you can plainly see, sir, we're a little busy here. Please leave."

"Not until you take this cat," he snapped.

Big mistake. Miss Mamie gave me a look that said, "Sic 'im, honey."

The only degree I have is a Ph.D. in Southern Bitch, so I shot back an answering "Oh goodie" look.

At last, we got Uncle Bedford securely onto the porch. Miss Mamie took over, waving me off. "Soon as I get Bedford settled and check on the General, Glory and I'll come help unload your car, sweetie."

"Where's Tommy?"

She steered Uncle Bedford toward the door. "Fishin'."

Typical. My brother was the only able-bodied male in the house, and the one time in thirty years I need him, he was out on his bass boat.

Fueled by that added insult, I turned to glare down on the tanned, middle-aged stranger holding my mother's six-month-old kitten at the bottom of the stairs. He was wearing expensive but decidedly non-Southern taupe silk trousers, European loafers, and a retro-chic cream-and-taupe Hawaiian print shirt. "I'm afraid we cannot deal with the kitten now," I said in my most condescending Garden Club voice. "As you can see, we've had a family emergency. My uncle is very ill. So please go back where you came from and take the kitten with you."

I granted him a frosty smile, gratified to see that the kitten was doing a nice job of shredding the hands that held her. I should have let it go at that, but being my mother's daughter, I couldn't resist adding, "That's the third of my family's pets you've seduced away with your canned cat food and open door and California ideas about animal cruelty. In the interest of neighborliness, my family has overlooked the other incidents, but enough is enough." Some shattered remnant of my old goodie-two-shoes self was just horrified enough to make this really fun, and the New Me gloated shamelessly. "My parents cannot afford shots and spaying for animals who don't live here, so I suggest if that one needs spaying, you pay for it, since you're the one who appropriated her."

"Appropriated?" The cat man tucked his chiseled chin, his sandy brows rising. "I don't want your cats. They're a nuisance. I can't keep the blasted animals out of my house."

"Only because you let them inside in the first place."

The toms circled closer like land sharks around his legs, and I treated myself to a vision of their climbing this pretentious tree-hugger's pricey pants.

"Our cats are used to being outside," I explained in what sounded frighteningly similar to my mother's embarrassing-situation voice. "We don't let them in because we're allergic. And we feed them kibble because it's better for their teeth and cheaper than canned cat food. If you persist in letting them into your house and giving them Fabulous Feline Gourmet, they'll never come home, and we'll be overrun with moles, voles, and snakes. That, sir, is not neighborly."

As he listened, the cat man's mouth flattened into an outraged line, his perfect nostrils flared, and his Malibu tan turned a satisfying shade of dusty rose. "Not neighborly?" he blustered. "The animals acted like they were starving. And it was cold outside when I let them in. I couldn't very well leave them out to freeze."

This guy was really getting on my nerves. "These are Georgia cats. They're used to cold weather, and we have plenty of warm nooks and crannies where they can get out of the elements. And in case you hadn't noticed, they come with fur coats supplied by the manufacturer."

He didn't back down. "Well, it's not cold anymore, but they keep sneaking into my house every time I open the blasted door." He scowled. "If you know of some way I can discourage them, you're welcome to 'em, fur coats, fleas, and all."

"I do know how to discourage them," I clipped out, ready for this to be over.

"Right." His eyes narrowed. "And just how do you suggest I do that? I tried throwing things at them and yelling, even spraying them with the hose, but that doesn't work."

"Of course not. They're cats, not idiot dogs. Here." I marched to the front door, opened it, then reached inside to the umbrella stand. That's where my mother keeps her BB gun for running off stray dogs, squirrels, and blue jays. I grabbed hold of the barrel and hoisted it out, then carried it past the damned bathtub full of begonias. "Use this."

You'd have thought I'd just slapped his mama and accused his daddy of working for the IRS. He bowed up in outrage. "Look, I don't know how you people—"

You people! A jolt of primal Southern Reconstruction adrenaline rattled the lid of my infamous temper, but I managed to keep my cool.

"—can talk about neighborly in one breath and come out with a gun in the next, but this is—"

"Oh, for criminy's sake, mister, it's just a dad-gum BB gun, not an Uzi." I stepped onto the driveway and cocked it twice to show him how. "As long as you don't pump it more than three times or shoot at close range, you couldn't hurt a flea with this thing." Aiming back toward a porch step, I pulled the trigger, and sure enough, the BB ricocheted harmlessly down the stairs. "See?" I proffered him the gun. "Keep your cat door locked and feed *Garfield* inside from now on. Then just pop the kitten in the butt the next few times she comes around, and she'll get the message. Same for the tomcats. It's the only thing that works."

He looked at me as if I were some serial pet molester. "No way."

"The object's not to hurt her," I felt compelled to explain, annoyed by my need to do so. "It's just to scare her off."

"Never mind," he said with a look that categorized me as just as loony as the rest of my family. "Just forget it. I'll take care of the kitten." He turned and strode back through the hedge, trailing his surreal feline entourage and leaving me with BB gun in hand amid a faint acrid whiff of male cat pee.

My ego had survived a lot tougher than that in the preceding eighteen months, so it shouldn't have bothered me that this complete stranger thought I was crazy or an irresponsible pet owner, or both, but it did bother me. It bothered me a lot. But then, I've always had this compulsion to be justified.

"Perfect." Stepping over Uncle Bedford's scattered shoes, I returned to my car and pulled out a couple of brimming shopping bags, my family's luggage of choice.

Then I pivoted to face 1431 Green Street, the house that held my past and my future. How long I could stay sane here, I didn't know, but I consoled myself that I was normal going in, at least.

Chapter 2

Being around my parents is like listening to Bartók: A little goes a long way.

But since Miss Mamie steadfastly demanded that the niceties be observed, I headed inside for what I hoped would be a brief opening visit.

I set my stuff on the bench beside the fireplace in the oak-paneled entry room. The air inside felt soggy and a little musty, and smelled faintly of furniture polish sharpened by a whiff of dank ashes, old paper, and even older dust. The odors throttled me instantly back to childhood, but my suburban self wondered how long it would take me to grow accustomed to the smell. Not to mention the heat.

May as well make up your mind to get used to it, my inner Puritan scolded. *Just like you'll have to get used to the heat.*

Not! my inner hedonist countered.

They were always bickering, not unlike my parents.

I scanned the empty parlor. Nothing had changed. Our once-elegant furniture sat in stately shabbiness exactly where it always had for my entire life. The same down cushion on the once-white camelback sofa was still turned zipper-forward, telling me the ink from my first real fountain pen still spattered the silk. Disconcerting, to be greeted by the lingering evidence of childhood sin.

Too Freudian.

Get the visit with the folks over with, I told myself, then you can unload your stuff, lock your door, and wallow in self-pity. Perhaps with chocolate. I'd packed a formidable supply.

"Miss Mamie?" I stepped to the bottom of the wide staircase and called up into the shady recesses of the upstairs hall. "Miss Mamie?" No response. She was probably in my old room holding Uncle Bedford in a headlock so Aunt Glory could get him into bed. I closed my eyes briefly, soaking in the quiet marred only by the muffled blaring of the General's TV from the far corner of the house. The rare, tranquil moment made home seem almost peaceful, but I knew better than to hope it would last.

The *Price Is Right* theme beckoned me, so I turned to enter the back hallway and walked past the closed door of my old suite, where the rumble of Miss Mamie's and Aunt Glory's admonitions escaped through the heavy oak panels. I tiptoed past, making a beeline toward the "Den of Iniquity," as Miss Mamie called my father's office.

I knocked, though I knew that even without the loud TV, my father was too deaf to hear me. Still, for form's sake, I knocked again before stepping into his private domain.

I found him lying stretched out on his old leather sofa, watching a pack of crocs have at a water buffalo. He'd set the volume so high it blared out into the yard to bounce off the closed windows of our neighbors' tiny air-conditioned bungalows and ranches.

I knew better than to try to turn it down, much less off. Not yet, anyway. I was moving into my parents' turf, after all. But I couldn't keep from commenting on the sorry state of his lair. It looked like the human equivalent of a beaver lodge with his dusty books, reactionary publications, and papers stacked haphazardly on every surface but where he was lying. I followed the narrow trail of open carpet to the sofa, waiting to speak until he could see me. "Good grief,

Daddy," I hollered good-naturedly. "How can you move with all this stuff in here?"

He popped upright with a flicker of confusion, but when he realized it was me, a broad smile transformed his features, making him look like his old self. You can say a lot of things about my father—and believe me, people do—but you have to give him credit where credit's due. He smiles just as easily as he flies off the handle, and the warmth in that big old grin never failed to warm me to my bones. "Hey there, little girl," he bellowed.

I sensed a subtle tentativeness about the way he held his large frame, and the skin on his arms and hands had gone almost transparent, mottled by bruises. Hard to think of the General as fragile, but that was the word that came to mind, prompting a sad tug inside my chest. But his grip was still strong when I sat down on a box of books beside him and took his work-scarred hand into my own.

To my surprise, he not only tolerated the contact, but his eyes lit with a rare glint of approval. "It's about time you came home. I been needin' somebody to protect me from your mother. Tommy's too scared of her to do me a lick of good." He covered my warm hand with his cool one.

"You're looking pretty good for an old geezer," I lied. "So, what's new?"

We exchanged awkward small talk. Making conversation with the General had been hard enough when he was his old charming but feisty self—anti-doctor, anti-government, anti-anything-but-reactionary-Caucasian-Southern-Methodist male. Now that he was losing his faculties, communication had become a subtle agony for us both. I could hardly stand to watch him struggle again and again to find the words he wanted, only to abandon the effort with a dry, self-conscious chuckle.

Then without warning, he grinned at me and cocked his head. "So. You're a free agent now. On your own. How long has it been? Eight months, now?"

"Nine." Nine months of dismal anti-climax since the decree—lonely, grieving months made almost unbearable by wrangling with the IRS and losing everything but the little I'd managed to hide with friends. And then the added sadness when I'd realized most of those same friends had recoiled into their couples' world as if the grim new realities of my life were somehow contagious. "Nine months."

Never in all my life had I felt so alone.

A devilish spark brightened the General's features. "Long time to be without a man. Are you gettin' any, now that you're a grass widow?"

I let out a strangled chortle as my mother burst into the room. Could this be the same straight-laced father who'd never even been able to bring himself to say the word "pregnant"?

"For God's sake, General! Remember yourself!" Miss Mamie navigated the narrow path to the sofa, full-bosomed with outrage, her ever-present needlepoint in hand. Another cover for the altar cushions at church. She glared at my father, her mouth flattened into a thin compression of indictment. "I swear, I don't know what to do with him," she fumed to me, then turned to scold him. "Have you lost all sense of decency? You're speaking to your *daughter*, for cryin' in a bucket!"

As usual, her indignation only energized my father. "Lin's past grown," he blared, "not some tight-assed debutante." He granted me another approving glance. "It's not her fault Phil went off the deep end. Now that she's free, why shouldn't she have a fling or two? She's still a fine-lookin' woman, has urges." At my mother's horrified gasp, he turned a canny expression on her. "Hell, she's only half your age, Mame, and *you* still have plenty of urges."

Rendered speechless for the first time in my recollection, Miss Mamie colored to the roots of her perfectly coiffed weekly "do." She pressed her needlepoint to her breast as if to shield it from my father's crassness.

Maybe coming home wouldn't turn out to be such an ordeal after all. This was getting good.

And my father had actually said I was a fine-looking woman. I tucked the compliment greedily into the sparse collection he had granted me over the years.

Miss Mamie came back to herself loaded for bear. "Thomas Dobson Breedlove, I forbid you to say another word about such private matters." She snatched one of Granny Faye's cutwork hankies from her pocket and patted dramatically at her neck. "Lin's hardly across the threshold, and you talking so crazy already. Behave yourself. Apologize immediately, then go back to your crocodile show on the TV."

Uh-oh. The dreaded "apologize immediately" sidetrack, guaranteed to escalate the simplest confrontation.

My father might be crazy, but he still knew when he'd hit a nerve with my mother. And he never backed down, much less apologized for anything. Fortunately, in this instance, he couldn't be diverted. "Do you expect her to become a nun? Ah, wake up and smell the coffee, Mame," he shot back with his old fire, energized by the confrontation.

My mother crossed her arms beneath her ample bosom and put her foot down, literally and figuratively. "This is not proper conversation between child and parent, and I will not have it," she declared. "Not in this house. Mama Beth must be spinnin' in her grave to hear you say such things."

"Leave my mother out of this," my father retorted. "Anyway, she's too busy smokin', sippin' bourbon, and playin' poker with all those other Baptist hypocrites in heaven to give a rat's ass what I say down here."

"Bite your tongue!" my mother parried. "How dare you speak ill of the dead! And your own mother!" Who, as we all well knew, was a whiz at poker and loved her daily sunset cigarette and bourbon-and-branch. The Mame responded with the old faithful counterattack from her own

Baptist origins. "Just because you took it into your head to join a drinkin' denomination forty years ago is no call to go maligning your own good Baptist, dear-departed mother."

It was the same old tango of blame, counterattack, justification, and diversion—a dance we all knew well. I had to keep reminding myself that my parents loved fighting. Why else would they have done it so often and for so long? Sixty-two years of mixing it up.

One thing about my marriage: Even though it had failed, we'd rarely fought. At that moment, though, I couldn't appreciate the irony in that.

"Lissen here." The General pointed menacingly at my mother. "I'm eighty-eight years old, and as long as I've got the mind left to speak, I'll say what I damn well please in my own house."

"Well, you *don't* have enough mind left to speak," my mother retorted. "Not in decent company, anyway."

I recoiled at the reference to his infirmity, but the General was undaunted. "Decent company?" He reared back, smug. "Hell, your bridge group makes Jerry Springer look like an amateur, the way those harpies drag out this town's dirty laundry and hang it up to dry. All that Gordon nonsense. Week after week—"

"Not another word about my friends," Miss Mamie charged back. "You're always doing that. Stick to the subject."

This could go on for hours. I started easing back toward the door. "Well, if you two will excuse me, I need to unload my things."

They both halted in midbicker to stare at me.

The General flashed a glimpse of consternation, then seemed to lose his steam. "Aw, can it, Mame," he said with a tentativeness that pinched my heart.

My mother spoke as if he weren't there. "I swear, Lin, he was bad enough before he got senile, but now he's not fit for polite company."

The truth was, he never had been. Only his financial generosity and flashes of sparkling charm had saved him from being banished to the outer darkness by Mimosa Branch society.

Abruptly, the General's eyes glazed and he sat down. "We were . . . what?"

Miss Mamie had preferred to think that Daddy's getting progressively more aphasic, disoriented, irrational, and paranoid was just the normal function of aging in a man of his difficult temperament. Then Uncle Bedford had moved in, providing a benchmark of insanity that convinced her Daddy was fine. I mean, compared to Uncle Bedford. . . . So now she simply turned a blind eye to Daddy's Alzheimer's.

"Don't go just yet, Lin." She shoved a stack of magazines off a chair and sat. "Let's visit just a little longer." She leaned over to hit the off button on the television. "Here. I'll even turn off the TV."

In the blessed silence that followed, she took up her needlepoint. "Tell Lin about Dr. Gordon," she instructed my father. "All that mess."

Oh, great. This was one of her favorite games.

She raised her voice another level. "You know. Dr. Gordon."

"Boardin'?" Daddy hollered back. "What the hell you talkin' about, Mamie, 'boardin' '? I outta knock you in the head, talkin' nonsense like that, tryin' to make me think I'm crazy."

I tensed at the specific, physical nature of his threat—that was something new—and at the ironic spark of truth in the last.

True to the game, my mother ignored him. "Dr. Gordon," she hollered. "About the divorce!"

We all knew she would end up telling the story, but this had been the way they'd played it even before Daddy's selective deafness had turned into the real thing.

I didn't want to do it, but old habits die hard, so I said

my part. "The Gordons are getting divorced?"

"Yes!" Miss Mamie glowed. I'd done it right. "Jury trial next month. Poor Reba. Everybody in town knows he's been foolin' around on her for years."

I wondered what had finally prompted timid, unstable Reba Gordon to challenge her Antichrist of a husband at last. "So she's taking him to court. Good for her. Hope she cleans his clock. It'll do me good to see *somebody* get what they deserve."

Tuning us out, the General slumped back onto his sofa and began to snore quietly.

Since this was definitely a women's topic, Miss Mamie took no offense at his inattention. "Geraldine and Frances have been keepin' us all informed. You know, Reba's been sayin' for years that he's been givin' her drugs, tryin' to ruin her mind." She leaned forward. "Now she's finally admitted that he only adopted those two children so he could molest them."

Pedophilia? (I used to think it meant foot fetish, so I never understood why people were so upset about it until somebody set me straight.) I found my mother's willingness to repeat the unsubstantiated accusation almost as disturbing as the possibility that Dr. Gordon might be guilty.

"Poor Reba," Miss Mamie went on. "We've been usin' the prayer chain so we'll know just how to pray for her. Such an ugly mess."

When Jesus said, "I am the vinekeeper, ye are the vine," I don't think he had the Methodist phone tree in mind, but my mother clearly saw nothing wrong with such a profaning of the spiritual grapevine.

She focused on her needlepoint, shaking her head. "Rich as Dr. Gordon is, do you think he'd do right by her? No. He bribed the two youngest with new cars to get them to turn on their mother. Expects her and her poor sick mama to live on almost nothin'. But a jury will see through that. I hope she sticks him good." She jabbed a stitch so hard she lost the needle on the other side.

"Drat." She flipped the piece. "And he's the sorriest excuse for a doctor this town has ever had. Nobody in their right mind would take their *dog* to that . . ." She reclaimed her needle and resumed her hostile stitches. ". . . white-trash, schemin' excuse for a human being."

Harsh words for the Mame.

"He's a sorry sonofabitch bastard!" The General launched upright in full dudgeon, scaring us both half out of our skins. "Where's my walkin' stick, Mame? That quack needs a lesson from Mr. Hickory about how to be a decent husband! Carryin' on with every floozie for fifty miles, then shamin' the mother of his children in public!"

My mother met the fire in his eyes with what I can only describe as affection tinged with wistful nostalgia. "And you're the man to do it, Tom." She rose and took his forearms to steady him. "But he's way over in Lawrenceville right now, so you'll have to wait till after supper. But you can show him then. You've done it before."

The spark of gratitude he sent her was so raw and intimate, I almost felt embarrassed to witness it. He gave her hand a brief pat, then pulled away to do a little more male posturing as he settled back down, then closed his eyes, as contented as a baby.

Miss Mamie eased gracefully back to her perch and resumed filling me in on the gory details.

"I never did trust that quack," my mother went on, "the way he dressed, with all that long hair and his flashy clothes and jewelry. Pierced ears. That should tell you right there. What sort of a man wears earrings?" she fumed. "Drivin' a Mercedes instead of a decent American car, and half of Mimosa Branch workin' at the GM Plant in Doraville once the mill closed. You can't expect people not to take it personally." She jabbed her needle my way again. "I always thought he looked more like some professional wrestler than a doctor."

The General dozed off immediately, the sound of my

mother's conversation being his second-most effective sop-
orific next to an Atlanta Braves game.

Miss Mamie poked emphatic stitches through her can-
vas. "Last month at UMW Ginna Patterson told me she'd
gone to Dr. Gordon for a cold, and he gave her a prescription for Percodan. For a *cold*. Not even an antibiotic. Percodan." She shook her head. "I told her that's what she got
for bein' too lazy to go to Gainesville for a *decent* doctor.
I mean, it wasn't like she had the flu. She could have driven
a few more minutes."

Percodan for a cold. Sounded real fine to me. I mean,
you'd still be sick; but you just wouldn't care. Like Nytime
cold medicine, only better.

My mother snipped a strand, then rethreaded her needle
with another color. "Sorry as he is, I never have understood
how Dr. Gordon stays in business. But his parking lot is
always full. Lots of tags from out of county, too."

I wondered if this was going anywhere. I needed to unload my car. Getting my mother to come to the point was
like trying to make an express out of a local, but I was an
optimist. "So. Is this all purely informational, or is there a
punch line?"

"Something's fishy there, you mark my words," she intoned. "And I'm not the only one who thinks so. That good-
lookin' Grant who just barged over here—the one from
next door who keeps stealin' our cats—he came over a few
months ago askin' if his dad had ever stored any records
in our car barn or attic from years past that might mention
Doc Gordon. I told him he was welcome to look, and lo
and behold, he turned up five or six boxes of records up in
the garage apartment. Said he was just tryin' to get the
drugstore's accounts put to rights so he can sell it, but there
was something"—she narrowed her eyes—"I don't know,
odd, about the way he mentioned Dr. Gordon's name and
none of the other doctors'." My mother had a better nose
for a story than the *National Enquirer*.

"Well, if it involves drugs and Dr. Gordon," I advised,

"you might want to lay low. You see what he did to poor Reba, and all she did was put up with him all those years." The cardinal sin, apparently.

"Bless his heart, Grant's daddy was as fine a druggist and as good a man as ever moved to this town," the Mame digressed, "but Grant's stepmother always kept the records. After she died, Ole Doc Owens never did get a handle on the business end of things. You never knew when you were goin' to get your bill. Sometimes three months, and that could knock a hole in your pocket, I can tell you." She shook her head, eyes on her work. "God knows what his prescription records looked like. No wonder Grant put in computers when he inherited the store."

Sidetracked again. My only consolation was that the train would eventually end up at the station. It always did.

"Geneva says he's had his nose in those old records every spare minute for weeks," she said dramatically.

"And?" Normally, I'd have been fascinated, but I *really* wanted to get unpacked. I tried not to let my irritation show, though, because that would trigger an all-too-familiar detour to the "no need to get all hurry" sidetrack.

She put down her needlepoint to underscore the gravity of her next statement. "Something is definitely up."

She was making me work for this. I'd hoped to unload my car before dark. "Like what?"

Her classic mouth flattened, her fine nostrils flaring. "I think Grant's gettin' the goods on Doctor Gordon." She returned to her stitching. "Leave it to the pharmacist to have to blow the whistle on him. Your daddy's right about doctors, you know. They're all in cahoots. None of *them* would turn him in."

Hearing my mother say Daddy was right about anything must have touched something deep inside him, because he sat up again, wide awake. "Got the jimjams, Mamie," he announced at full volume, standing with an ease that surprised me. "I'm gonna walk around a little out back, then work on my correspondence." Translate: shuffle his papers.

I rose, too. "I need to unload my car." That came first. Then finding a job, so I could earn enough money to fix up the garage apartment so I could move back out of the Big House.

My mother started to get up, too, but I put my hand on her shoulder. "Stay. I can do it."

"Don't be silly, Lin." She shrugged my hand away and stood. "You know you got the Breedlove bones. My Grainger knees are twice as good as yours, even if I am eighty. If you try to do all that by yourself, you'll end up in bed for three days, and you know it."

"I'd hoped Tommy could help," I couldn't resist saying. "Didn't he know I was coming?"

Miss Mamie sighed her usual, "Oh well, you know Tommy" sigh. "They're havin' that big pot tourney over on the lake, and he said he was hopin' to win some money."

That was Tommy. He couldn't find a job that suited him, so he went fishing with his "basshole" buddies on Lake Lanier to win some money. What was wrong with this picture?

I really didn't want to wait for him to get home. The sooner I was moved in, the sooner I could get my life put back together and move out again. "Okay, then. Let's unload my car."

My mother waited until we were outside to whisper, "Sorry I can't put you into your old room, but Bedford's so unsteady—"

"You were right to give him that room. He could never handle the stairs. I'll be just fine upstairs."

Ack! That sounded chillingly martyrish and motherish.

But I really didn't mind. At least my bad Breedlove knees were younger than Uncle Bedford's. And truthfully, my old main-floor suite was far too accessible to everyone and everything to suit my current state of mind. I popped the car trunk open and grabbed a suitcase and a carryall. "I'd rather take the east bedroom upstairs anyway, the one that used to be Zaida's."

"Phoo!" Miss Mamie hoisted out two crammed shopping bags as if they were only half-full. "That's the maid's room, Lin. Why on earth would you want to take that one?" She marched up the stairs beside me, her steps far surer than mine. "Either one of the guest rooms would be much nicer. My friends'll think I'm ashamed of you, crammin' you way back there in that little maid's room away from everybody else."

"It's not little. It's just not twenty-five by twenty-five like the others. But it has its own bath." Thanks to racism. I didn't bother even trying to explain that I wanted privacy. Privacy was anathema to Miss Mamie. She had no concept of boundaries and probably never would.

"Oh, yeah." Bathrooms, she understood, though. "I suppose it would be a bit awkward sharin' with Tommy."

"More than a bit." I followed her through the foyer and up the oak treads to the spacious landing that split the second story.

"We'll need to air it out," Miss Mamie fretted. "I went over both guest rooms with a fine-toothed comb, but I can't remember the last time I did that maid's room. I'll put these down and go get the cleaning things."

The phantom umbilicus snapped back with a vengeance. I was fifty years old, yet she didn't think I was capable of cleaning up my own room by myself. "I'll do it, Miss Mamie. I want to."

"But—"

"But, nothing." I kept my tone light. "Just because I don't have my own house anymore doesn't mean I can't clean my room by myself."

"Now, Lin. I know this is hard for you, honey, but that's no call to go and get all huffy."

Score one for the Mame. She got in her sidetrack after all.

I laughed out loud. "Come on, Mama," I said in a rare lapse that evoked a misty-eyed smile from her. "Let's check out Cinderella's quarters, where she shall be safely hidden away from all decently undivorced Baptist *and* United Methodist churchwomen."

"Sugar, nobody looks down on you for being divorced," she hastened to assure me as we entered the short rear hallway to the maid's room and attic stair. "Who's gonna throw stones? Almost everybody in the Garden Club has at least one child or grandchild who's gotten divorced. And half of both my church circles." She exhaled emphatically. "It's the men's fault. I think they've all gone crazy."

"Damned straight, they've all gone crazy."

Hiking up the shopping bags, Miss Mamie slid past me to open Zaida's door and push inside ahead of me. "Ugh. Musty, dusty." She dropped the bags and went to open the windows. "I'll have these up in a jiff."

I stepped inside, half expecting the room to smell faintly of Clorox the way Zaida always had. The air wasn't nearly as stuffy as I'd feared it would be, just toasty and a little musty, but everything looked immaculate.

Still, I felt a hot flash coming on.

Once you get used to air-conditioning, it's a bitch to do without it, which was one of the main reasons I hadn't been home since menopause had permanently ruined my thermostat. The other main reason was the fact that my parents seemed to behave themselves a lot better on my turf than on their own.

Since the only turf left was theirs, though, I steeled myself yet again to make the best of it, directing my attention to the room. The lath paneling was the same soft forties green I remembered from my childhood. Darker and bluer than celadon and probably loaded with lead. I resolved not to suck the windowsills or eat any errant chips.

A cream-and-celadon-braided rug covered most of the brown-painted floorboards. The iron double bed was spread with a vintage quilt softened by age to pale greens and gentle mauves. Irish lace hung behind the chintz floral drapes at the three tall, narrow windows that looked east over the porch roof and backyard.

I stepped to the lace and peered through. I could see Grant Owens's roof just past the camellias, framed by our huge magnolias.

Jerk.

"I don't know about this, Lin," Miss Mamie dithered on. "The drawers stick on that old dresser, and this mattress was one of Mama's."

"This will be fine, really. And anyway, it's only temporary. I meant what I said about moving out to the garage apartment. As soon as I can earn enough money, I'll have the plumbing replaced and move in there."

"I still don't see why you want to spend all that money, broke as you are, with room to spare here inside the house," she grumbled. All of us, back under the same roof. It was my mother's dream and my nightmare.

"Well," she deflected, seeing my annoyance. "We can cross that bridge when we come to it." Clearly, she hadn't accepted my wishes as yet. "I just want you to be comfortable."

Looking over my new quarters, I realized there was only one problem. "I forgot there wasn't a closet."

"I'll have Tommy move the chifferobe from the front room tomorrow," Miss Mamie volunteered.

"Good. We can hang everything on the foot of the bed till then." I peeked into the tiny bathroom and was gratified to find the worn octagonal tiles clean and mold-free despite their cracks and age. The ceiling looked new and improved. "Didn't it used to leak in here?"

"It did, but Tommy fixed it," Miss Mamie said. "Repaired the cricket drains on the roof, then replaced the old ceiling with Sheetrock. He's fixed a lot of things around here since he came home." She cocked an apologetic smile. "Whenever we can scrape up the money for the materials."

"It looks great. He did a nice job." Suddenly anxious to be moved in and have this latest difficult transition behind me, I urged her toward the door. "Come on. Let's get this over with. Then I'm going to crash and a take a long nap."

Maybe it was a stress defense, but sleep sounded really good to me.

I sensed an anxiety attack coming on, but warded it off by thinking myself past this the way I'd thought myself past the numerous orthopedic surgeries of my life. And my husband's midlife meltdown.

Just get through today. Do what has to be done today. And then the next day. And then the next, and pretty soon, it'll be four months from now, and you'll have a job and be in the garage apartment. Along with all my stuff that was now stashed in attics and basements from Collier Hills to Brookhaven back in Atlanta.

And a couple of window air conditioners humming away in the windows, I promised myself. Maybe then I would be able to breathe again, literally and figuratively.

But for now, it was musty furniture with drawers that played tug-o-war when it rained, a mattress older than I was, and no air-conditioning.

We emptied my car fairly quickly, but by then I was too fragile to handle a family dinner. I love my mother as fiercely as she loves me, but she still insisted on shoving me into an emotional high chair every time she got me to her table.

Not that night. Moving was all I could take.

So when suppertime rolled around, I pleaded a headache, closed my door, and unpacked in the tepid breeze of an oscillating fan. Then I snuck up into the oven-hot attic with a flashlight, hunting for some rabbit ears for my little TV. There were plenty up there, but I had to go through four before I found one equipped for UHF. Mission accomplished, I managed to get back to my room undetected. After a cold shower, I discovered in a cruel bit of divine irony that the only two stations I could get were wrestling and "The Big Hair Channel"—that's what I call that bizarre Pentecostal video marathon with the purple-coiffed Tammy-Faye-times-ten woman and all the gold and white

furniture. Both channels make my skin crawl, so I turned
the set off and tried to tune out the sound of my mother
and Aunt Glory hollering away in the kitchen downstairs.

"Bedford," Aunt Glory shouted. "You've got lasagna in
your pocket!" Pause. "Your pocket, Bedford! Lasagna!"
Pause. "Here, let me get that."

Miss Mamie was not as loud but every bit as beleaguered. "General, can I get you some more pintos?" Pause.
"Pintos. Do you want some more?"

"Stop yellin' at me, Mamie!" Daddy hollered. "I'm sittin' right here." Pause. "Can't you talk like a normal person
anymore? Mumblin' and yellin'. Always mumblin' and
yellin'."

It had that certain lethal rhythm.

I tuned my clock radio to the classical station and upped
the volume to drown them out, then crawled naked between
the clammy sheets. Even with the racket downstairs, I could
still catch snatches of the comforting nighttime sounds of
my childhood. Distant trucks shifted gears on the interstate
beyond town. July flies crescendoed in the oaks and magnolias underscored by a soothing chorus of crickets, and
tree frogs sang soprano from the branch below Doc
Owens's house.

I lay there, unable to kick off the sheet despite how hot
it was. I couldn't lie naked, uncovered, in my parents'
house, so I tried to think cool thoughts.

When I'd married, I'd been accustomed to falling asleep
in darkness with the windows open to the sweet lullaby of
nature. My husband, though, had liked to go to sleep and
wake up to light and sound. So as a compromise, we'd slept
with the TV on for thirty years. That was what I called "a
Scott Compromise." There had been a lot of them, a fact I
deeply resented but was still too clueless to see my part in.

I pulled my floppy little satin headache pillow over my
eyes and wished the radio was playing Debussy instead of
Dvořák.

No more *Win Ben Stein's Money* to make me smile and lull me to sleep.

How long would it be before I could afford cable?

Could you even *get* cable here?

Shit. Shit, shit, shit.

Chapter 3

I cried myself to sleep, then woke up gasping early the next morning, feeling as if I were trying to breathe underwater from the heat. Spurred by the coffee aroma from downstairs (Who could drink hot coffee in this weather?), I stumbled into the bathroom for a long, cold shower. That perked me up considerably.

Wrapped in a fresh, fluffy towel, I blew my hair dry, toweled off again from the resulting hot flash, put on my underwear, then set about choosing an outfit for my job application with all the gravity of a toreador preparing for the ring.

Something slimming. Professional. And slimming.

My clothes were all good quality, but of limited styles, having been selected for their ability to camouflage "The Ass That Ate Chicago," as Phil had dubbed my butt. I'd stopped paying attention to fashion altogether when the whole Twiggy-retro-Audrey-Hepburn phase had taken hold. Middle-aged bodies and Lycra should not exist in the same universe, if you ask me.

So I dug out my straight-cut, navy linen blazer, which fortunately appeared none the worse for hanging on the bedstead all night. I paired it with a demurely scooped-necked, white silk camisole. Debating between slacks and a skirt, I opted for the skirt, a straight, charcoal gray, faux linen (with elastic in the waist, of course) that ended just below the knee, showing off my relatively shapely calves. I tucked a long, colorful silk scarf under the blazer's lapels, then laid my selections on the bed.

Not the coolest outfit in the world in any sense of the word, but it would have to do.

By then, my underwear was damp through. I moved the fan into the bathroom, splashed my face with cold water, then made up. Professional—not too subtle, not too flashy. By the time I was done, though, I wondered if all my careful work would melt off before I even got there.

Pantyhose. After a brief war with the sticking drawer, I took out a fresh pair of summer-weight nude control-tops and held them up for inspection.

Ick. I had a hot flash just looking at them.

But vanity and breeding constrained me to put them on. Fashionably bare legs would mean letting the "Ass That Ate Chicago" run amok. Plus, I could still hear my Grainger grandmother's dire intonations that a real lady never went anywhere without her hose, hat, gloves, and hanky.

I'd managed to drop the hat and the gloves, but not the others. Like all Southern women of genteel poverty from my generation, I found myself compelled by voices of the dead.

A line from one of my favorite movies, *A New Leaf*, popped into my head. *Keeping alive traditions that were dead before you were born . . .*

So I dried off again, this time with a fresh towel, applied scads of talcum powder, and managed to squeeze myself into the pantyhose. Then I made a serious tactical error. I looked in the yet-to-be-tamed full-length mirror on the bathroom door.

The control-top compacted my hips and butt, but its pressure forced some of the fat up into my love handles, making me think of an old Phyllis Diller joke about a woman wearing a full-body girdle whose friends said behind her back, "Doesn't her figure look great these days? A shame about her neck, though."

I deflated, filled with self-loathing.

That's the trouble with once having been gorgeous. When you're not anymore, you're nothing but not gorgeous anymore. At least, that's how it was with me.

Fifty, fat, and flat broke.

Fuck.

I still took perverse pleasure in using that word—a word I hadn't been able to think, much less say, until Phil's moral meltdown. Now it was my mantra.

Closing my eyes, I allowed myself a sigh before sucking it up and getting on with what must be done in this one day.

Once I'd dressed and added my earrings and tasteful fake pearls, I put on all four of my real gold bracelets for courage. (After the dust had settled with the IRS, I'd gotten my bracelets out of hiding and tried to sell them, but the vultures know that when a woman's hard up enough to get rid of her play-pretties, she's really desperate. So when they'd offered me only a few hundred dollars for the lot, I'd resolved, like Scarlett in the radish patch, to keep them and wear every one until they were pried from my cold, dead wrist. The same went for my mink coat and jacket.)

Girded for battle in the big, bad, business world, I headed downstairs toward the kitchen, where I could hear the Mame bustling about. I pushed open the swinging door to the kitchen to find the air inside hot and redolent with the rich morning aromas of my childhood: country ham, bacon, coffee, and fresh biscuits.

Tommy sat reading the sports at his usual spot amid five empty places at the kitchen table.

As always, the meal was set with placemats, cloth napkins, napkin rings, and a hodgepodge of once-elegant china, glassware, and stainless. Some slightly wilted marigolds graced the center of the table, along with six jars of home-

made jam and a dish of glistening butter that hovered at
the point of liquefying.

My mother reserved her sterling flatware for dinner and
supper—as her mother had before her, when the utensils
for lesser meals were silver plate instead of stainless.

She greeted me brightly. "Mornin', sugar. Don't you
look pretty. Have a seat." She fetched two hot biscuits from
the oven, releasing more heat into the already warm room.
"Tommy, put down that paper," she scolded as she laid the
biscuits in front of me along with a cup of coffee. Coffee,
in this heat. "You haven't seen your sister since y'all went
down to her house last Christmas. Say hello to her, at least."

Ever obedient when it came to her direct orders, my
brother dropped *The Gwinnett Gazette* sports section only
to lurch toward me, grinning and trying to give me a noo-
gie. "Hey there, Sissy-ma-noo-noo."

Dodging him, I resolved to nip such juvenile behavior
in the bud. "Cut it out, Tommy," I snapped. "I've had
enough of grown men acting like twelve-year-olds. For
cryin' in a bucket, act your age." I knew it was futile to
ask; he never had so far.

The hurt in his hazel eyes might have made me feel
guilty had I not seen it so many times before when he'd
promised to be responsible, then failed to deliver.

"Ah, lighten up, Sis," he said with a defensive edge.
"Things are tense enough around here already, in case you
hadn't noticed." He retreated back behind the sports section.

I succumbed to a bite of the butter-drenched biscuit. Oh,
yum. Lord, it was a miracle everybody in this house didn't
weigh three hundred pounds, the way my mama cooked. I
resolved on the spot to breakfast on V-8 and a plain bagel
from now on—a resolution that probably had as much
chance of happening as Tommy's pledges of maturity.

Black iron skillet in hand, the Mame approached me.
"How you want your eggs, sugar?"

"No eggs. Biscuits are fine."

"Now, honey," she said in that same singsong she'd used when I was ten. "You know how you get when you don't have your protein with your carbohydrates. Eleven o'clock, and there goes the blood sugar, under the basement. I'll just scramble up a few, shiny, like you've always liked 'em."

I realized it would be a waste of effort to try to stop her. Worse still, we both knew she was right about my blood sugar, dammit.

I got up and went to the refrigerator, hoping to find the gallon containers of iced tea and lemonade still where I'd remembered them. Sure enough, there they were.

"Is the tea sweet?"

Miss Mamie nodded, intent on the eggs, "Um-hmm. But I made you some special with Sweet'N Low. It's in the blue pitcher."

How can you stay mad at somebody who remembers your personal policy that all calories have to be in chewable form?

Once we were all seated and I was eating my eggs with sliced homegrown tomatoes, the Mame took a sip of her coffee, then asked, "Well. Are you gonna tell us why you're all dressed up, or do we have to guess?"

I had no reason not to want to tell her, but some deep-seated streak of rebellion made it hard. "I'm going to sign up at that temp agency down by the Kroger. A lot of my friends who . . ."—I stopped short of saying "got dumped by their husbands"—"had to go back to work said it's a good way to earn some money while trying out a lot of different companies. They all ended up getting hired by one of the temp clients."

Miss Mamie leaned forward, her gracefully aged features furrowed with concern. "Are you sure you're up to it, sweetie? I don't want you to feel pressured."

"I'm fine," I cut in, recoiling from the "poor Lin" vibes she was putting out. "Really. It'll do me good to have something to keep me busy. And the sooner I get a pay-check, the sooner I can start fixing up the garage."

That got her started again. "Phht," she huffed. "That's just not sensible, honey. You need your money for other things. I don't see why—"

"I need to do it, Mama." I pinned her with a look of supplication, wishing that just this once she'd understand, but not daring to let her know how deeply I needed to be separate, just to myself, to see if I could do it. "I know it doesn't make any sense. Nothing in my life makes much sense anymore, but I want to fix up the apartment."

Only one thing in God's green earth can make my mother back down, and that's love. I saw it in her eyes before she spoke. "Well, then, sugar, you just do it," she said with brisk conviction. "And do it up brown. Heck." She pushed down Tommy's paper. "Tommy will help you, won't you, Tommy?"

"Oh sure." He raised it again, but I could almost hear him rolling his eyes behind it. "I'll help out."

"That's one promise, Thomas, that I mean to hold you to," I said with as much good humor as I could muster. Asking for help had never come easy to me, but I was realizing I had no choice.

Buoyed by my mother's understanding, I gave her a hug, then left to brush my teeth and take the next big step into my future.

A j-o-b job.

Damn. Damn, damn, damn.

I glided into the nondescript little storefront operation with a confidence I definitely did not feel. I had to say one thing for the place: it was cold as a meat locker, God bless 'em.

The young woman behind the desk had that currently popular "what do you get when you cross Twiggy and Morticia?" young professional look. I read her nametag. Kaitlyn.

Oh, please.

I had an overpowering urge to use one of her big paper

clips as a barrette on that raggedy "bed head" haircut so I could see both of her eyes, but I decided that wouldn't be politic. I'd only remind her even more of her mother, and it was obvious she hated her mother. No girl who loved her mother would wear black lipstick and quadruple-pierce her ears.

I couldn't help wondering if she would one day be as embarrassed to see her photos with black lips, Frankenstein shoes, and ill-fitting, shapeless knits, as I was of my snapshots with my friends in bouffants, bell-bottoms, hip-huggers, and halter tops.

But then again, all that's come back, hasn't it?

Now *that's* crazy.

Well, there I sat, butt, blazer, bracelets, and all. Suffice it to say, I was really nervous. No degree, no skills, no experience to speak of, no computer anything. Miss Mamie had assured me there were plenty of entry-level jobs in the area since the new mall had opened fifteen miles away at the interstate, but I hadn't been fortunate enough to inherit her cast-iron constitution. My bad Breedlove bones ruled out working on my feet, which included the only entry-level jobs I could think of. Even if I'd wanted to take them, which I certainly didn't. I might have taken up using the *F* word, but "Do you want fries with that?" shall not pass these lips.

I knew beggars can't be choosers, but I was hoping for a receptionist's job in a small company not too far from home. A company looking for dependable instead of flashy.

"We're so pleased you've decided to join our team at Worldtemp. I'm sure we can find something for you," Morticia/Kaitlyn condescended. "If you'll just go to computer number one and follow the tutorial, we'll get you registered."

Computer?

Shit, shit, shit.

My husband had had a computer at home, so I knew what some of the stuff was called, including the mouse, but

I had considered it a matter of personal pride that I'd never used the thing. Especially after seeing how furious Phil got when it screwed up or "ate" something.

To my mind, using a computer was like learning to type or sew. Once people found out you knew how, they expected you to do it, so I'd never learned.

I decided to tell the truth, since they'd find out anyway soon enough. "I'm afraid I've never used a computer. Don't you have some regular applications?"

She looked at me as if I'd just said I was HIV-positive. "I think there might be some in the back. I suppose you could use one, then I could enter the information for you. Just a minute. I'll see if I can find any."

She clomped away on her clunky sandals with two-inch platforms. After much rustling and opening and closing of file drawers, she returned with an application form on a clipboard.

One. Better get it right the first time.

She stuck in a pen, not a pencil that I could erase, then handed it to me. "Fill this out, please. You can use the desk in that cubicle there. Then we'll test your skills. Do you have a resumé?"

"Sorry." I took the form with as much grace as I could muster and retreated to the cubicle. *Break it down*, I told myself. *One thing at a time. One section of the application, then another. You can do this. You can face this.*

The computer monitor mocked me with its little blinking yellow thingie.

"Click your way to a new future," yourself, I silently railed back at it.

I'd never thought I'd come to this, not after more than thirty years as a corporate wife, twenty-five of them good ones.

Just fill out the application, my Puritan genes admonished. *What is, is.*

After putting down the pertinent name, address, etcetera, I got to the social security box. Had to fish my card out of my wallet for that one. Date of birth I knew.

Next section, Education. *Elementary school*. Year graduated?

We didn't *graduate* from elementary school. We just went to high school, and who the heck remembers when?

I did do some tortured mental math (I'm a words person, not a numbers one) and came up with the dates, not at all certain they were right.

High school: *Mimosa Branch, 1963–1968, Honors curriculum*. College: *Sandford College, Winter Park, Florida, 1968–1969. Academic scholarship and work grant*.

I'd chosen Sandford because, at the time I'd applied, it was a party school, only an hour from the beaches of Gulf or Atlantic, plus, the worst you could do was a D as long as you had perfect attendance. Unfortunately, between my applying and matriculating, they'd decided to get serious and instituted a brutal core curriculum, so I'd ended up doing fourteen papers my freshman year, getting mono, and burning out.

A genteel, small-town Southern girl had only two respectable options back then. She went to college and got a husband, or she went to college and got a teaching degree, then lived with several other genteel, young teacher friends until she got a husband.

Since I was sick of school and had no intention of becoming a teacher, a husband was my only recourse, and master's candidate Phillip Patrick Scott had more than filled the bill. It didn't hurt that he was the only Atlanta boy there and came from a good family (read, richer than mine).

The truth was, I'd taken one look at him and a magnificent obsession was born. I worked it so we were engaged by Christmas and married on Miss Mamie's porch as soon as he got his masters the following June.

I started to put *MRS.* in the undergraduate-degree column on the application, but Morticia/Kaitlyn didn't appear to have a sense of humor, so that wrapped up the education section.

Now, to the work record. Seeing the generous blanks, I realized my skimpy—mostly ancient—experience wouldn't fill but a few lines.

Just get it over with, I told myself.

Why hadn't I written all this stuff out ahead of time and come prepared? Kaitlyn was going to think I was borderline retarded taking so long over so little.

Oh, hell. You're here. Just do it.

First real job: *Teen Board, Baker's Department Store, Mimosa Branch.* Job description: *Retail sales, modeling.* (I was blonde then, "stacked," reasonably thin, and bore a passable resemblance to Kim Novak.)

That had lasted from sophomore to senior years. Reason for leaving? There wasn't room to put "The manager ambushed me in his office one night at closing." The slimy weasel had actually chased me around his desk like a Warner Brothers cartoon. We made two full circuits before I collected the wits to threaten to call his wife. End of chase.

When I'd gone home crying and told my parents, the General had wanted to kill the guy. It had taken some genuine hysterics by both me and the Mame to avert a homicide, but we'd finally convinced him to call the store owner and demand the man's job instead.

The rest of that summer before college, I'd worked as a receptionist for one of the General's surveyor friends. Job description: *Filing, phones, appointments secretary, light typing.* It was easy work, and safe, but because I couldn't touch-type, I got a quarter an hour less than the going rate. I'd asked for a raise after I started doing several letters a day, but my kindly boss had just looked at the trash can and chuckled. "Honey, you use up more'n that in stationery." I'd been mortified then, but now smiled at the memory, relishing it like a cherished photograph discovered forgotten in a drawer.

Then I forced myself back to the application. Reason for Leaving: *College.*

I moved to the next line of the application and filled in

Theater box office, Sandford College work grant. September 1969–May 1970.

Reason for leaving? *Marriage.*

It had seemed like a good idea at the time.

Next? First year of marriage. *Eastern Girls Temp Service, Hurt Building, Atlanta. September 1970–June 1972.* Position: *Receptionist.* Job description: *General office duties, processing applicants, filing, telephone work.*

Eastern Girls. I hadn't thought about that in *years.* What was my boss's name, the liberated Cosmo girl who'd "entertained" me with tales of her sordid sexual exploits? *Camille.* That was it.

Reason for leaving. I was sure they didn't want me to put, "Fired by Camille when the District Manager canned *her* after finding out she'd been sleeping with half our clients." He'd offered me her job, but I had run, not walked, away because I only wanted a nice, safe, nine-to-five job with no weekends.

Looking at my entries so far, I realized that all anybody else would see was a series of brief, menial positions held by a worker who couldn't seem to stay put. The truth was, I'd either organized myself out of a position, or worked my way too far up for my nine-to-five requirements. But as I said, I was certain they didn't want the truth, just the facts.

I listed my brief stint as a personal secretary for two civil engineers (they had a Dictaphone, and I got very good at correspondence because I could look at my hands while I typed.) They didn't really need a personal secretary, though, so it was a case of my organizing myself out of a job.

My final full-time job had been as a receptionist for a gym, but I'd quit when summer had arrived and I'd discovered the offices weren't air-conditioned.

After that, I'd decided to put an end to all the job nonsense and have myself a baby.

I did have that Christmas reserve job at Rich's Department Store after that, but decided not to put it on the application. Rich's still exists, so I thought better of mentioning anything on the off chance that they just might still have a record of that unfortunate incident where I pretended to have sore feet at the insistence of a "customer" with a movie camera who turned out to be a union agitator. Who knew I'd end up in their *Workers of the Mall, Unite!* movie?

Just as well I'd decided to quit before Christmas, anyway. I owed *them* every pay period, thanks to that seductive employee discount.

I filled in the next line with *October 1971–present: Full-time homemaker*.

The next section was skills, row on row of options with boxes to check. I'd never even heard of half the stuff. Quattro Pro? Peachtree Accounting? MS Word? WordPerfect? Lotus? Adobe? And on and on and on.

This was not good.

In the blank after Other, I wrote *I am a fast learner and willing to train on the job*.

The last section was References. Oh, good grief. Of course they'd want references. Had I brought addresses and phone numbers? No.

Yes. Pocket directory! I found it in my purse and located the info for my favorite priest, Jim Pritchett. Then I came up with Cooter Edwards, who'd been our state senator for years. And my old high-school pal Cissy Macklin, whose husband ran the bank over in Lawrenceville. I made a mental note to call them all as soon as I got home and ask their permission to list them as references.

Damn. That meant I'd have to tell them why.

Not that I minded telling total strangers what my rat husband had done—I'd told anyone and everyone at first, even the poor bag boy at the Publix. Of course, he *had* asked me how I was doing. But I'd finally realized that people don't really want to know how you are when they ask. They've got enough problems of their own, and it only scares them when you answer a polite inquiry by telling them that your husband of thirty years was engaged to a twenty-three-year-old stripper and had spent $200,000 we didn't have on her and the "champagne rooms" (where we are assured they do *not* have prostitution, wink, wink). Even *friends* run for cover when you drop a bombshell like that on them, almost as if they think it's catching.

Which had nothing to do with the job application. *Focus!* my inner Puritan scolded. I realized yet again how scatterbrained all this had left me, and despaired anew.

I signed and dated the application, then returned to Kaitlyn, appalled that I was about to be interviewed—and *tested*—by some anorexic twenty-something with a soap opera name.

She took one look at the almost blank application and raised a slender, penciled black brow. "Mmmm." Plastic smile. "Let me just get this entered." She tapped away busily on her keyboard, never once looking at her fingers, darn her. "There. Just a few more questions. Are you interested in any form of physical labor?"

Physical labor? "As in landscape maintenance?" This was a bad dream. "I'm afraid my arthritis would rule that out. Also working on my feet. I have bad knees. Not a scrap of cartilage left in 'em."

"Sorry, but I have to ask. We get a lot of calls for heavy work." She tapped away on her computer some more. "Tell me, do you have any life skills that might be useful in the business world?"

That was more like it. "Yes. I chaired numerous committees and successful fundraisers for Junior League, Read Atlanta, Second Harvest, The Speech School, and Symphony Guild. I've also chaired committees for the Friendship Force and hosted more than ten international exchanges. I speak rudimentary French with a good accent." What else? Criminy. Why hadn't I prepared? "I was an active member of Saint Phillip's Cathedral in Atlanta for thirty years and served on both the vestry and the Diocesan Council, as well as the Altar Guild."

"Excellent. So you have leadership skills and experience in coordinating, organizing, and completing projects."

"Yes." Saints preserve us, she sounded sincere. I forgave her for her black lipstick. Black cherry, on closer inspection.

Her next smile seemed sincere as well. "Let me take you back to the testing area. The computer's all set up, and I'll show you how to use the mouse. Then all you have to do is point and click and type. Trust me, you'll do fine."

"Sure."

I sat in the chair she pulled out, then turned to face the mocking monitor. It took several tries to get the hang of the mouse. The arrow kept disappearing off the edges of the screen, and I kept clicking the wrong button on the mouse itself, which caused these blasted boxes of writing to keep popping up where they weren't supposed to be. Three minutes in, I felt like a fool, but I refused to let it beat me, and eventually managed to complete the typing test at fifty words per minute.

"See?" Kaitlyn patronized. "That wasn't so hard, was it?"

"Nothing to it." I had sweated clean through my Clifford and Wills silk blouse.

Kaitlyn clomped back to her desk. "I'll enter your registration, but we have very few managerial opportunities. I think you might significantly improve your options if you signed up for some of our low-cost computer training sessions. Without better computer skills, I'm afraid we'll have a hard time placing you."

I'd come here to earn money, not spend it. "How much are the courses?"

"Only sixty dollars for four three-hour sessions. We try to keep the cost low for our workers."

I had exactly seventy-eight dollars left to my name, so that was out.

She handed me a brochure. "They're Tuesdays and Thursdays, seven to ten."

"Thank you." I rose. "You have my number." My mother's, I mentally corrected.

Knees or not, it looked like the Kroger was my best option. I was too young to be a greeter at MegaMart.

Shit. Shit, shit, shit.

Chapter 4

I came home just before lunchtime to find the furniture freshly covered against those pesky Japanese, but no sign of Aunt Glory, Uncle Bedford, or my parents. Feeling lower than the crumbs under a rug, I went upstairs and changed into my briefest sundress, then headed for the empty kitchen where I hastily slapped Blue Plate mayonnaise onto two slices of Pepperidge Farm white bread, then laid on a huge, beautiful slab of the General's Beefeater tomato, which I salted and peppered to within an inch of its life and topped with two strips of bacon before closing. After nabbing a cold Diet Coke from the fridge, I fled upstairs to solitude before the Mame could intercept me and start asking a lot of questions I didn't want to answer.

I ate, sulking, on the bed, but even something as celestial as a perfect tomato sandwich couldn't lift my mood. This called for stronger measures.

I rooted through my stuff until I found the extra-long phone cord I'd bought so I could bring the hall phone into my room for a private conversation. Cord in hand, I crossed the landing to the dresser and set about pulling it out when the front-door buzzer went off right over my head, scaring me half out of my wits.

Why was I so damned jumpy? I never used to be jumpy.

Heart pounding, I listened for Mame-sign and heard my

mother's footsteps tap briskly from her little sewing room downstairs, then stop as she opened the door to greet a very loud woman visitor.

Good. She was occupied, at least for a while. I finished hooking up the long cord to the ancient princess phone, then took it back to Zaida's room, where I closed the door and turned the bolt, just the way I had as a teenager. Ancient paranoia prompted me to stuff the keyhole with Kleenex, too. Only then did I feel safe to use my prepaid calling card—dear Lord, I didn't even have my own phone number anymore—to call my best friend, Tricia, in D.C. for a "Poor Baby" fix.

I dialed the phone-card access number, then punched in eighty-seven numbers on cue.

"You have three hundred fifty minutes of call time remaining for the number you have dialed," the automated voice informed me.

One ring.

Please be there.

Two.

You're off for the summer. She taught American Literature at George Washington. *Why can't you stay home once in a while?*

Halfway into the third ring, she picked up, thanks be to God. "Hello?"

"It's me," I moaned. "This is a fiver."

"Uh oh," she said with appropriate gravity, fivers being reserved for the most dreadful Poor Baby Club calamities. "Tell me what happened."

"This morning I went to a temp agency to apply for a job, and it was horrible. The girl looked like a middle-schooler. She had black lips and a dozen pierced earrings, and she only weighed eighty-seven pounds. And she wanted me to use the computer to fill out the application. A *computer*. I felt fat, stupid, old, and useless."

Tricia sighed. "That's bad, but it's not a fiver. Finding out your husband was engaged to a twenty-three-year-old stripper—*that* was a fiver. Finding out he'd wrecked your credit and run up two hundred thousand dollars in debts, not to mention the IRS—*that* was a fiver. This is only a three-er. Poor baby, poor baby, poor baby."

They were perfunctory, at best.

She was right, of course, about it only being a three-er, but I sulked anyway. "Hey, you know the rules. You're supposed to commiserate as extravagantly as possible, not correct me."

"Oops," she said without a shred of conviction.

Now in addition to feeling stupid, old, and unemployable, I felt childish and even more discontented with myself. "Damn. Now I don't even want to sit on the pity pot. Add 'spoiled brat' to my list of inadequacies."

She calmly shifted the subject. "Did you get moved in?"

"Yes. And it's sultry as hell. I'm melting. And my family is still bickering away bad as ever, only louder now that the General's going deaf. And Uncle Bedford's got the permanent D.T.'s."

"I thought you didn't want to sit on the pity pot," she said with her usual note of compassionate humor.

I exhaled heavily. The last thing I truly desired was to let my circumstances reduce me to a bitter, self-absorbed, ex-Buckhead matron. "Foul. No logic allowed."

Tricia let loose her infectious laugh. "Then I'll have to hang up. You got your Poor Babies. I wouldn't be much of a friend, though, if I encouraged you to wallow. So 'bye."

"Wait." I didn't want her to go, not yet. And painful as it was to hear, I valued her honesty. It had helped me stay sane this far. "I know I should be glad I had a place to go. My parents do love me in their own way. I should be grateful they've taken me in. It's just so blasted hot. And so awful to give up my independence. And my pride."

"Lin," she said gently, "you never were independent, never knew where you stopped and Phil began." Ouch! "Hard as it is, this is your chance to start from scratch. To

stand alone in spite of everything." I could almost hear her
gentle smile on the other end.

"I just don't know how I'm going to stay sane living
under the same roof with Miss Mamie. She's already driving me nuts, treating me like a child. Check your adult
status at the door, then come on in." Scary, scary, scary.
"You get along so well with your mother. How do you do
it?"

"I told you two years ago, after that trip Mom and I took
to England. A girlfriend passed on her favorite trick to me,
and it got me through three weeks sharing a room and a
rental car. Mom and I actually ended up better friends than
we'd ever been. Don't you remember?"

"You'll excuse me for forgetting," I grumped, "but I
don't remember much of anything from then except Phil's
atrocities. We were in major meltdown."

"Oh, yeah. Sorry."

"So what's this great trick that went in one ear and out
the other?"

"Every time she does something that makes me crazy, I
laugh."

"That's it?"

"I swear, it works," she vowed.

"When she makes me crazy, I just laugh?"

"Yep. Mama bowed up a little the first few times—I
think she was afraid I was laughing *at* her—but pretty soon,
she started to relax. By the end of the trip, she was telling
me stories from college that slayed me. I wouldn't take a
million dollars for that trip. And all it took to get past the
mother thing was a few chuckles. Plus, I felt better every
time I did it. I swear, it works like magic."

"I could use some magic. I'm really scared about all this.
I've barely gotten started, but already I feel like a failure."

"Stay strong. You can do this. Remember, it's only temporary. And as for feeling like a failure, talk to me in a
couple of months. You'll find a decent job. You're smart,

attractive, and honest. Trust me, any employer will be glad to get you."

Her confidence soothed my damaged ego but couldn't banish my fear. "Hmph. You're my best friend; you have to say stuff like that."

A big, wet raspberry blasted in my ear. "Call me back when you're done wallowing." The line went dead.

Smiling, I replaced the receiver and lay across the bed to stare at the ceiling, doing my best to fight down the growing sense of desperation that rose from low in my gut. The heat didn't help, or maybe I just noticed it more after being in that beautifully frigid office.

July in Georgia with nothing but a fan. Purgatory.

I was cranky about it and wanted to *stay* cranky about it.

I heard Miss Mamie talking animatedly from the back porch, joined by that strident woman's voice. Not one I recognized. Curious, perspiring, and suddenly anxious for a diversion, I abandoned the bedroom for the relative coolness of the shady porch.

Downstairs, as I crossed the kitchen, I saw that her visitor was a woman most kindly described as flamboyant—plump, over-made-up, over-coiffed, and over-jeweled in her tight, bright green silk pantsuit—definitely not my mother's type, which further piqued my interest. Both of them turned in mild expectation at the skreek of the screen door, and when they saw me, their faces brightened with a fiendish light.

Uh-oh.

My mother lifted a partially consumed quart glass of iced tea. (The Mame thinks a serving any smaller is less than hospitable and invites immediate dehydration.) "Lin," she exclaimed. "We were just talkin' about you."

Double uh-oh.

She motioned toward her grinning visitor. "You remember Julia Tankersly."

I blinked in astonishment. Plain Jane Julia Tankersly?

Under all that silk and makeup and blonde hair? I remembered her, all right, but not like this! Only the inflated Church of God French twist was familiar.

"Name's Puckett now," Julia corrected brightly. "Julia Tankersly Anderson Wilson Puckett, if you want to get technical." She waggled the fingers on her left hand to emphasize that the only one without a ring was the wedding finger. "But I'm blessedly single again, thank goodness."

Three husbands!

Rude as it was, I couldn't keep from staring. Two years ahead of me in school, she'd always been a staunch Holy Roller, eschewing such devil's snares as dancing, dating, cosmetics, "trousers," and rock 'n' roll. Clearly, *something* had gotten into her.

"Julia has just had the most wonderful idea," the Mame rattled on. "She thinks you'd be perfect selling real estate. We've just sat here and had the best old time figuring it all out."

Triple uh-oh.

"I've tucked away enough to cover the cost of the Barclay Williams Training Course," my mother declared.

Julia jumped right in. "They have it nights and weekends, so you could work during the day and still take the course. If you took it now, you could have your license before Christmas." Her gold bracelets jingled as she aimed a brilliant acrylic nail in my direction. "You know Mimosa Branch inside out, and you look so . . . *reliable*. Who wouldn't trust that face?" She and my mother exchanged smug nods.

"How about it?" Miss Mamie pressed. "The timing's perfect. They don't give the course up this way but once a year, and you're just in time to sign up."

"Divine intervention, if you ask me," Julia said. Then she sweetened the pot with, "I can promise you a place with my broker."

My mother leaned forward and confided in a stage whisper, "Julia makes more than a *hundred thousand dollars a year* selling real estate."

Julia preened. "Heck, business has been so good, I could use a 'junior' agent myself. It's a great way to learn the ropes. Whatcha say?"

"Why Julia," Miss Mamie oozed, "how generous!"

A daunting prospect, being lackey to aggressively transformed Julia. But the idea was not without merit. At least I wouldn't be stuck filing all day in some grubby office—or worse yet, struggling with a blasted computer.

But that didn't keep me from feeling railroaded. I took a small step backward and employed Tricia's suggestion. I laughed, but it didn't help. "Thanks. I'll think about it."

Their faces fell. Clearly, they'd expected me to be as enthusiastic about the idea as they were.

But *sales?* Especially real estate . . .

Despite my outgoing personality, I hated the idea of pushing myself onto people, especially people I knew. Unless it was for charity.

I still had a bad taste in my mouth from the real-estate agent "friends" who'd started calling "just to see how I was holding up" once the blood was in the water about me and Phil. Their concerned calls had stopped abruptly when word got out that the IRS was seizing the house and there would be no listing to snag.

Of course, *I* would never be so crass, I countered to myself. Anyway, the way things were these days in Mimosa Branch, my customers would probably all be transplants, not locals. Strangers.

I do fine with strangers. It was the people I loved who posed the problems.

"Really, I appreciate it," I said, "but that's a big step. I just need to mull it over."

"Well, don't mull for too long," Julia chided brightly. "Deadline for the training-course sign-up is day after tomorrow. Miss that, and you'll have to drive all the way to Atlanta."

No way I could handle that commute, especially at night. Especially with a job. A cold shard of panic bloomed inside me. Two days, to make such an important decision?

Don't get me wrong. I've always been one of those "fools rush in" kinds of people, but after a year of having my options stripped away along with my confidence, I was still feeling trapped and more than a little balky.

The "yeah-buts" set in with a vengeance, the loudest being, *What if I take the course and fail? Miss Mamie's hard-saved money* . . . I'd be even more beholden to her than I already was. "I . . . I'll let you know." It had cost me seven thousand pre-meltdown dollars' worth of therapy to learn to use that last phrase instead of continually making impulsive decisions on the spot.

I fled back to my room to retrieve the calling card. Tricia answered on the second ring.

"Here's the thing," I said without introduction. "The Mame said she'd pay for me to take a real-estate course, and Julia Tankersly offered me a job as her assistant selling houses if I get my license. The catch is, I have to decide by day after tomorrow about taking the training course, or I'd have to fight the traffic to take it later in Atlanta."

"Julia Tankersly?" Tricia diverted.

"Yep. Dyed, painted, dressed, and jeweled to within an inch of her thrice-married life," I confirmed.

Tricia hooted. "I'll be danged. So the devil got her after all, bless her heart."

You can say anything about anybody in the South and get away with it as long as you finish up with "bless her heart."

"I did not call you to talk about Julia," I groused. "She and the Mame have cooked up this scheme for me to sell real estate."

Her usual level-headed self, Tricia remained unruffled. "When did this happen? We just hung up."

"That's when it happened." Why was I so panicked? "I don't know why I'm so upset about it. I mean, I only have to decide about taking the course. But what if I fail?"

"You never failed a course in your life."

"Yes, I did: that short-quarter term paper in college. I got an *F*."

"You never even wrote the thing," Tricia huffed. "That was just Freshman rebellion. You drank, smoked, and played marathon bridge for four weeks. It doesn't count."

I was not comforted. "I haven't had to study for anything since 1970. There's the real-estate exam. Exam, at my age. Makes the backs of my knees sting just to think of it. And the Mame's hard-earned money—"

"You'll pass," she said. "But that's not what this is really about, is it? I mean, even if you should fail the course . . . heck, you'd gladly do for David what the Mame has offered to do for you. Why can't you accept it from your own mother?"

"You're being entirely too rational, here," I said, grateful despite the annoyance I felt.

"Does selling houses appeal to you at all?"

"Maybe," I had to admit. "Sure. I mean, the commissions are huge, aren't they? And I wouldn't be tied to some desk. Just the thought of being stuck in some nasty little office makes me cringe. I know I might have to do it, but I sure don't *want* to. If I did real estate, at least I'd be getting out, showing houses, meeting people."

"Meeting men," she chirped.

"*Married* men. Single men don't buy houses, at least not in Mimosa Branch."

"You never know." She paused. "Maybe you ought to give the course a try," she suggested. "Frankly, I can't see you in some boring little j-o-b, either. This might be a good opportunity."

"Julia's raking in more than a hundred thousand dollars a year," I mused aloud.

"There you go." She chuckled. "Anyway, it's not like you have to make up your mind about the rest of your life, for goodness' sake. Try it. If you don't like it, you can always do something else."

"Easy for you to say, Miss Ph.D."

She'd long ago stopped taking the bait in that topic. "I can see you as a real-estate agent."

I bristled, conjuring a flashy, pushy, obnoxious, deceptive stereotype that made even Julia seem tasteful. "Thanks a lot!"

Tricia bristled back. "Calm down. If you'll recall, John happens to be in real estate."

Her husband. Of course. Shit, shit, shit. "And he's adorable," I backpedaled. "The exception that proves the rule. Anyway, he's in commercial and renovations; that's different."

"I expect some serious sucking up for that one," she said loftily.

"And you'll get it."

"I'm hanging up now," she announced. "I'll call you back tomorrow on my dime."

Before I had a chance to dither, Miss Mamie's voice wafted up over the sound of the General's TV from the bottom of the back stair. "Lin? Lin, honey!"

I left the sanctuary of my room and leaned over the rail. "You rang?"

"Honey, would you mind running over to Chief Parker's to pick up your daddy's prescriptions?" Her voice dropped to a whisper. "I was just about to go when Julia dropped by."

I certainly didn't have anything else to do. "Might as well," I said in a broad cracker accent, quoting the punch line to an ancient bit of college humor.

I retrieved my purse, then went downstairs to my car. The interior was hot as a pizza oven, but after a few minutes the air-conditioning kicked in, bringing me alive. For a while I just sat there sucking in cold air from the top vents and letting it blow up my sundress from the bottom ones until at last I felt civilized again. Then I headed for Chief Parker's.

I had to park halfway up the block, so I was flushed and wilted when I entered the drugstore to the familiar tinkle of the bell over the door.

I was confronted by a prominent display of stuffed purple . . . whats? I picked up one of the long, floppy critters and discovered they were platypuses. Or was that platypi?

Looking around, I noted that the store was still as much a general emporium as it had been in Old Doc Owens's time. Kitchen implements, toys, spices, school supplies, and an odd assortment of canned goods and cleaning products competed with the cosmetics, over-the-counter remedies, and shampoo for space on the same vintage display shelves that had been there when I'd worked there after school. And the frankly fake ancient paneling was festooned with the same cream-colored scalloped border that matched the large letters that spelled out PHARMACY over the pass-through at the back.

My focus dropped from the letters to the familiar figure who was scribbling down a phone order behind the counter. Geneva Bates, God bless her. She'd been here since before I left. In a world where everything seemed to be unraveling, I took inordinate comfort from her presence. I waited quietly until she ended the call and saw me.

Instantly, her face lit up. "Lin! What a sight for sore eyes!"

"Hey, Geneva." I'd forgotten how good it was to run into somebody who was just plain glad to see me and didn't want to give me advice or pity me or fix me or cheat me or get a huge retainer.

"Well, it's about time. Miss Mamie said you were coming." Her blonde hair curly as ever, she hurried from behind the counter with her arms spread wide. "Come here and let me give you a hug, girl."

There was a good bit more of both of us than there had been the last time I'd seen her, but her smile was still as lively and her goodwill as infectious as ever. We shared a brief, well-cushioned embrace, then she drew back, her kind brown eyes level with mine. "I been prayin' for you a lot this past year."

If anyone else in town had said that, it might have rankled, knowing that Miss Mamie had kept the grapevine humming with lurid reports of my marriage's spectacular demise. But when Geneva said she'd prayed for me, I knew she meant it, and that God had been listening.

I fought to keep the huskiness from my voice. "Thanks. I needed it. Still do."

"Who's that?" Another familiar smiling face popped up over the pharmacy pass-through. "Well, Lin Breedlove!"

"Shelia!" We shared the same age and the bane of always having to spell our names to people. Hers was pronounced like plain *Sheila* but spelled otherwise, and everyone always assumed mine was spelled *Lynne*. I waved to her. "You haven't changed a bit."

"Neither have you," she gushed, patently ignoring the extra weight we'd both put on. "You always were the prettiest girl to come out of this town, and you still are."

Lord, but it felt good to be with real Southern women who knew all the rules and told bald-faced lies to make each other feel better. Atlanta might as well have been Cleveland for all the Southern I'd gotten there the past fifteen years.

Mimosa Branch had its drawbacks, but at least it still had roots and rules, and at that juncture in my life, both felt pretty good.

"How're the twins? Any grandbabies yet?" I asked, paying homage to the deeply held Southern conviction that being a grandmother was the culmination of womanhood.

"Not yet." Shelia bustled from the pharmacy holding a framed eight-by-ten of her and Ronnie flanked by their two tall, gorgeous, dark-haired sons, one tidy and one tousled. She handed it to me. "Brandon graduated from Georgia State last year and works for a big accounting firm down in Atlanta. Bobby made so much money doing landscaping over the summers that he dropped out of North Georgia and started his own business. Has seven crews, now, and is fixin' up Granny Wilson's old place across the street from us. He's marryin' Becka Mason, Tom and Sally's youngest, December twenty-eighth. You'll get an invitation."

I peered at the picture. "Wow. The last time I saw those two, they were snaggle-toothed six-year-olds in the Little League parade." Handing the photo back, I shook my head. "Get me my cane. They're *men*. Gorgeous ones."

"Speaking of gorgeous sons, how's David?" Geneva asked, really wanting to know, God bless her. "Has he finished workin' his way through Emory?"

"I'm surprised Miss Mamie hasn't bragged it all over town. He graduated two years ago. Eloped three weeks later with a great girl, Barb. I love her. She's from Oakwood, and she doesn't take any garbage off him. They're both in graduate school in Boston, still working their way through with fellowships and grants." I deliberately didn't mention Harvard. That would have been too shameless. "So no grandbabies for at least three more years, they tell me."

Both women clucked in sympathy. Geneva patted my arm. "It'll come."

I smiled. "Oh, I told Barb that I'd respect any decision they made about when and if they'd have children. But I also told her that honesty compelled me to let her know I'd be praying for their birth control to fail." Amid their laughter, I added, "She had the good grace to laugh, thank goodness. I swear, I don't know what I'd do with a daughter-in-law who didn't have a sense of humor."

"Did I hear somebody say something about birth control failing?" a serious male voice interjected from the bowels of the pharmacy. "Not one of our customers, I hope?"

I turned to find the California Cat Man approaching the pass-through. My good mood hit an air pocket.

"Lin," Geneva motioned from me to him. "Meet Grant.

Grant, this is Lin Breedlove, ah . . ." She faltered with that familiar post-divorce hesitation, clearly unsure if I'd kept my married name. Now I ask you, who in their right mind would go back to Breedlove after three decades of the simplicity of Scott?

"Scott. My last name's Scott," I said.

"Lin Breedlove Scott," Geneva trailed, picking up on the hostility that radiated between me and her boss.

Oblivious, Shelia forged ahead. "Lin's one of the best things to come out of this town. I just know you two are gonna like each other."

He briefly lifted his chin. "We've met."

"But we haven't been introduced," I said in perfect cultured Southern bitch. I looked back to Geneva. "I didn't catch his last name."

"It's Owens," he volunteered, pinning me with a haughty stare that dared me to look away.

I met the challenge. Out of the corner of my eye, I saw Geneva and Shelia exchange bewildered glances. "I came for my father's prescriptions. Are they ready?"

Ever the peacemaker, Shelia intervened. "Got 'em right here." She hurried to the *B* hook on the pegboard below the pass-through, and pulled off two bags instead of one. "Here're Doctor Bedford's, too. They're all charged."

Weary of staring down this Grant person, I looked at the receipt stapled to the General's prescriptions and gasped. "Good grief! That's a car payment."

"Idn't it awful?" Geneva commiserated. "And that's only half a month's worth. But our prices are cheaper than anybody else in town," she hastened, defensive. "We even beat the MegaMart over by the mall."

"I thought my parents had Medicare supplemental coverage for prescriptions and all. The General's always insisted—"

"They did." Geneva leaned closer and dropped her voice. "But when the General started to slip . . . well, I warned Miss Mamie as soon as the insurance company denied payment, told her she needed to look into it right away, but you know the General and Miss Mamie. She just fussed him out about it and told him to handle the matter. By the time I was able to convince her to do it herself, they'd run up a huge bill, and the insurance company wouldn't reinstate 'em. He hadn't paid the premiums in months." She sighed in frustration and shrugged.

Damn. God forbid they should have a real medical emergency.

I wondered how much they owed the drugstore, but wasn't up to finding out. The only consolation was that the rude, arrogant Grant was holding the bag instead of his kindly father.

What else had the General neglected to pay? I dearly hoped he'd remembered the homeowner's policy and Miss Mamie's auto coverage.

HUGE uh-oh.

Until that moment I had thought moving back to 1431 Green Street was as bad as things could be, but the notion of the lot of us burned or sued out of house and home sent my stomach plummeting. I resolved to investigate at the first opportunity.

I tucked the prescriptions under my arm and headed back out toward the July heat. "Good to see you, girls. Let's do lunch." The instant the words were out of my mouth, I realized how phony they sounded. "I'll make us some chicken salad," I added lamely, "and y'all can come over. If Grant can spare you."

"Great." Both women beamed.

Mortified, I escaped onto the sidewalk.

I hadn't taken three steps before a large-boned redhead in a purple batik caftan and a macramé brow-binder exited the gallery next door. She turned in my direction, tiny shells swinging on their cords as she moved her head. "Linnie!" Her strong, familiar features lit up.

"Cass!" Now, there was a sight for sore eyes. "I thought you moved away!"

"I did, but I'm back, with bells on." She all but tackled me, whacking my cheek with pendant shells. "Lin, Lin, Lin!"

Except for a few extra gray hairs, wrinkles, and pounds, she hadn't changed a whit from the sixties, right down to the strong odor of marijuana. I hadn't heard from her in decades. "You old hippie, you!" The deep lines in her face said life hadn't been smooth sailing, but she still radiated the same dogged optimism she always had.

"Boy," I told her, "I'll bet you just *love* all this New Age stuff around here these days." I gave her another hug, then pulled clear to bump right shoulders three times, the secret greeting of our high school sorority.

"Aaagh! Theta Alpha." Her distinctive laugh hadn't changed a bit, either. As always, it made me think of big bubbles erupting onto a strong spring breeze.

I glanced at the paper-covered display windows of the storefront she'd just left. COMING SOON: DAVIS SCULPTURE GALLERY. So she'd gone back to her maiden name. "What're you up to?"

"Just moved back. Bought the gallery for a song. I'm a sculptor now! How 'bout you?"

"Divorced after thirty years. Horrible, hurtful, humiliating, but that's behind me now." Why did I still feel such shame whenever I told someone who knew me? Strangers, I'd poured my heart out to with no regrets. But old friends . . . I still hated telling them, resented being reduced to just another midlife statistic. "I had to move back in with Mame and the General, just till I get back on my feet."

Back on my feet? Who was I kidding? Tricia was right: I'd never stood on my own two feet.

"Not you and Phil?" Cassie's eyes went huge. "Y'all were everybody's perfect sweethearts."

"That's what I thought, too, for a long time, but . . . Well, I'll tell you about it sometime, but it's too long a story for this heat."

Cassie motioned to the gallery. "It's cool inside. We can

talk in there. I've been setting up for my opening. Wanna see?"

I glanced at the prescriptions I was carrying and decided a few more minutes delay wouldn't do any harm. I was dying to see what kind of artist Cass had turned out to be, knowing it wouldn't be anything conventional.

She unlocked the door and pushed it open to an artistically stripped-down space with brick walls, scarred wooden floors, and a sparse forest of black pedestals bearing intricate, clear glass sculptures punctuated with frosty etchings and bold elements of blood red and yellow.

"Voila!" Her eyebrows shot up expectantly.

At first I thought they were all abstracts, but a second look brought down the truth like a sledgehammer: Cass's sculptures were hostile, aggressive renderings of genitalia! Vaginas with row on row of sharklike internal fangs. Huge, evil, cracked, misshapen, or spiked male members with jagged, rusting wire hairs. Breasts pulled to agonizing configurations by broken-nailed, scarred male hands. A classic female face made shocking by red irises with yellow slits and a red snakehead for an obscenely projecting tongue.

They were all brilliantly crafted, I had to give her that.

Cassie gestured broadly, clearly enjoying my discomfort. "So what do you think? The truth, now. One Theta Alpha to another."

Groping for words, I managed, "I think . . . it's pretty scary."

"Perfect!" She clapped, hopping on her toes the way she had when she was our high school mascot and we'd scored a basket. "That's just what I wanted to convey, the frightening power of feminine rage."

I studied her in a new light. "What's this all about, Cassie?"

She laughed again. "I can't believe the Mame didn't tell you. I've been the scandal du jour since yesterday. Even bumped the Gordons' divorce from top spot on the grapevine." She spread her arms in purple-batiked glory. "I'm gay. Found out six years ago, but it took the love of a good woman to give me the courage to move back home and come out at last." Another delighted laugh.

Cassie Davis, a *lesbian*? "Gay? Since when?" Flabbergasted, I tried to take it in, but my stubborn old brain never has been much good at switching course, especially about something as dire as this. "You were married. Three times! Had a child. How could you be gay?"

"Happens all the time," she explained with patience. "But Max is fine with it." Max—that was the son's name. "I didn't raise no uptight preppie," she said proudly.

Stunned, I peered at her as if there was some elusive mark of gayness I had missed. "You can't be gay. You were our high school mascot! Mascots aren't gay."

Her luminous expression did not fade. "Of course we are, Lin's-a-pin," she said using my old playground name. "All sorts of women are gay."

"I know that," I blustered. "I *know* that." Just not *my* childhood friends. Not *Cassie!*

Instead of getting defensive, Cassie laughed and began free-form dancing among her "Feminine Rage." Her strong alto rang out the tune of an old pep-rally fight song: "Mascots are gay. Home Ec teachers are gay. Nuns are gay. Police are gay. Mothers are gay." She wasn't taunting me, she was celebrating, freeing me to deal with my own tangled emotions. She danced to a stop beside me. "My loverly lover Sharon, a partner in a top-five CPA firm, is gay," she sang in a rush. "Even mistresses are gay." She stopped in front of me for the big finale. "And strippers. *Lots and lots* of strippers."

The last thing I wanted to hear about was strippers. "Not all of them," I said as she bowed dramatically.

She rose, a wide grin on her broad, homely face. "You want to know the best part? My last two exes are *mortified* that I've come out. Kashim"—her Iranian, more about that later—"would be too, if he knew. My latest ex, Fred, says he'll never live it down. He, the abusive alcoholic. Now *there's* a delicious little bit of irony for you." Another liberated grin. "Fact of bidness bein', I think he's most upset because it means I won't ever remarry and let him off the alimony hook."

I should have found that highly amusing, but I was still too shocked to appreciate it. Why was I, a firm believer in live and let live, so upset? Maybe because yet another thing I had believed for so long had turned out to be something totally, shockingly different. I had lost so many landmarks in my life.

But hey, what difference did one more make, really? So Cassie was gay. So what?

I gave myself a metaphysical slap upside the head, then faced the woman who had been one of my closest friends until I had turned gorgeous, and she had turned on and turned out. "So. You're gay. How the fuck about that?"

Cassie's mouth dropped open. "What? The *F* word? Did I just hear you say the *F* word?" She rolled her eyes toward heaven. "Sweet Jesus, the End Times are upon us for sure. Goody Two-shoes Lin's-a-pin has gone and said the *F* word."

I giggled. "I know. I know. For forty-nine years, I couldn't even make myself say it, no matter how hard I tried. Now I've entered the 'Fuck it' phase of my life." I shrugged. "Beats whining and crying."

Cassie let out a low whistle. "I bet the Mame's laid out with the vapors over that development."

"Not as bad as your mama's bound to be over yours," I countered.

"True," Cassie admitted. "Mama's still sedated with the shades drawn, but she'll come around. She really does love me. It'll just take some time to adjust to things. Good thing Daddy's dead, though."

Remembering her alcoholic, tobacco-chewin', huntin', cussin' redneck of a father, I concurred. He very well might have killed her.

"The Mame will crepe a brick that I found out you were

gay before she did," I said. "I can't believe I might have scooped her on something this big." I headed for the door, still trying to wrap myself around this newest surprise and the awkwardness it had spawned between us.

"It doesn't change anything between us, Lin," my old friend offered gently. "It's not contagious. We can still be plain old friends. I swear on a stack of Bibles, I won't hit on you. No offense, but you're not my type. Waaaay too uptight."

"Thank goodness for that."

She waggled her eyebrows. "I've got some great pot, though. The only safe cure for tightass. Be glad to bag you up a little welcome-home present."

I couldn't help laughing. Cassie had been trying to turn me on since her first effort had ended in disaster back in the sixties. Already drinking and smoking at seventeen, I'd shared the corncob pipe at her insistence, only to end up puking violently into a trashcan while she and a few of the more radical Theta Alphas scarfed chocolate chip cookie dough and grooved to "White Rabbit." I'd made up my mind, then and there, that I already had enough bad habits that were either fattening, lung destructive, or illegal. Since pot was all three, I'd sworn off without regret or reservation. But Cassie had never given up trying to convert me.

"Ask me again in a month or so," I quipped. "After living with my parents, I just might take you up on that."

Her face brightened with fiendish delight. "Oh, goodie. I just love bein' a bad influence."

"It's so great to see you, Cass." I gave her a parting hug that was stiffer than I intended. "I've always hoped you'd find yourself and settle down." I pushed open the door's cool metal bar, letting in waves of heat. "Let's have supper sometime. Give the gossips something to talk about for sure."

"I'll call you," she said, but we both knew she probably wouldn't.

I waved good-bye, then headed for my car in something

of a daze. Boy, was the Mame gonna be one-upped when I told her about Cassie. And shocked. I was just selfish enough to hope that this newest scandal would keep her distracted for a while.

And I loved the idea of getting the scoop on her.

But it turned out that I hadn't. She was waiting for me, irate, beside the bathtub begonias when I drove up. "Linwood Hansell Breedlove Scott," she ground out through a forced smile, "get in this house this minute."

One day. I'd been home one day, and she was already treating me like an errant ten-year-old. Over what?

The phone was ringing, yet she made no move to answer it. This *must* be serious. The ringing stopped, then started again almost immediately.

Deliberately casual, I took my time ascending the stairs to the front door. "Here you go." When I reached the porch, I handed her the prescriptions. "Geneva sent along Uncle Bedford's, too. Boy, those things are expensive."

The phone stopped ringing.

"How can you discuss the cost of prescriptions," she hissed through her drawn smile, "when you have just shamed me and your father like you have?" Her determinedly pleasant expression set in concrete, she gripped my arm and steered me emphatically past the purple bathtub and into the house.

"Miss Mamie, what's got into you?" As soon as she muscled me inside the foyer, I wrenched free of her. "All I did was what you asked me to."

The phone started ringing again. I heard the door to my old room open. "Mamie, are you sure you don't want me to answer that?" Aunt Glory hollered. "It's driving Bedford crazy."

"Let it ring," my mother roared, oblivious to the irony of what Aunt Glory had just said. After a glance up and down the empty street through the screen door, she turned on me, her bosom inflated to the max. "Hangin' all over that pervert right out in broad daylight on Main Street, in front of God and everybody!" she accused in a low voice that shook with righteous indignation. "What were you thinkin', Lin? Were you tryin' to embarrass us?" Her anger phased predictably into martyrdom. "Half the town saw you. I had to stop answerin' the phone. Three of the people who called me actually had the nerve to ask if you were a homo, too—if that was why you and Phil had gotten divorced, because you were a *lesbian*."

I didn't even know my mother even *knew* that word.

The old me would have been appalled, would have done anything to appease her and smooth things over, but the old me had disappeared long before the last item of our stuff had been auctioned on the front lawn.

The new me faced my mother head-on. "For cryin' out loud. You act like we stripped down and had sex on the sidewalk." I didn't give a flyin' flip what the old busybodies thought. "We simply hugged each other as old friends often do after a long separation. And lesbian or not, she's still my old friend."

The "Finger of Justice" jabbed in my direction. "Well, as long as you're living in this house, missy, I expect you to have another long separation when it comes to your old friend Cassie Davis. Steer clear, that's all I can say. Steer clear." She took three steps toward the back hall, then turned on me. " 'Give ye not the semblance of wrongdoing, lest ye cause your brother to stumble.' That's in the Bible, Lin, and you know it."

I wasn't convinced it was, but baiting my mother was not my idea of sport. She was eighty years old, after all, and I had no illusions of being able to raise her consciousness about anything, much less homosexuality.

I tried Tricia's trick again. I laughed.

My mother was not amused.

Giving up, I started for my room. I couldn't wait to tell Tricia about Cassie, and I still had 335 minutes left on my calling card.

Miss Mamie retreated, grumbling, down the back hall to

dose the General. "Right here in Mimosa Branch. One of our own. Why, poor Deanna Davis won't be able to lift her head in this town. Of all the places for Cassie to come to roost with that . . . that *woman*. The world's gone crazy. Pure-d crazy."

Two days later, I registered for the real-estate course.

A week after that, I'd signed up with three employment agencies in Gainesville and Gwinnett, gone on two dead-end temporary placements, and had four interviews, but still hadn't landed a permanent position. Overqualified, they kept on saying.

That was a joke.

When I wasn't trying to find a job, I distracted myself by cleaning out the garage apartment, a chore so big it felt like eating Stone Mountain with a teaspoon.

Then I went back to the drugstore, and things *really* got complicated.

Chapter 5

That Monday, July 16th, I saw my parents off to the doctor, took the last Prozac in the bottle, then headed to Chief Parker's Drugs for a refill, pronto. We do not face life without Prozac.

As I got out of my car, I noted that Cassie's studio windows were still papered over with COMING SOON. I'd thought she'd be open by now.

I stopped in front of her locked door, wondering why she hadn't.

Cold feet?

Surely not. Cassie had never been one to weigh the consequences about anything, including marrying that Iranian dropout from Tech who'd bowled her over in the early seventies. She'd been so convinced it was love that none of us had had the heart to set her straight. But she wasn't stupid, just naïve, so when her new husband lost interest after only a month and started acting like the Moslem male he was, she'd faced the fact that he'd only married her to keep from being deported. Brokenhearted, she'd promptly annulled him and sent his tight brown ass back to Teheran.

That had been a Poor Baby Club fiver, for sure. Followed by a long, heartbreaking line of romantic fivers brought on by her doggedly optimistic delusions about any man who even pretended to love her.

It occurred to me that Cassie probably hadn't been born a lesbian—she'd been driven to it by the succession of Mr. Wrongs in her life.

Shaking my head, I entered the drugstore to a tension so palpable you could almost see it hovering over the crowd of customers perched at the soda fountain or huddled back by the register.

The air hummed with brittle conversation. Taking up my place at the end of the line, I noted that, while Parker's may not have changed, the clientele certainly had. The gathering was the New South in microcosm. Two stout little Mexican mamas hefted infants on hips and chattered in Spanish to their toddlers. Three sullen, local teenaged girls slumped self-consciously in their multiple piercings, green lips, exposed middles, and Technicolor spiked hair. An oriental couple—Korean, Japanese, Vietnamese? I never could tell—hovered close to the register.

Two impatient, well-dressed suburbanites made it clear with their body language and pained expressions that they had more important places to be. A young black couple with a runny-nosed baby argued in some kind of indecipherable rap jargon while three gaunt, tobacco-ravaged, bleached-blonde biker moll types rummaged through the box of shopworn ten-cent greeting cards. The rest of the crowd was filled out by half a dozen just plain folks, most of them elderly, who stood waiting with the patience of people used to being overlooked.

When I'd worked there as a teenager, all the customers had fallen into one of three categories: blue-collar WASPS, white-collar WASPS, or quiet black folk who knew they could expect liberal credit, fair prices, and respect from old Doc Owens. Like most mill towns, the Mimosa Branch of my youth had no middle class, only management, labor, and "sorry, no 'count trash," as my Granny Beth used to call the town's layabouts, brawlers, and troublemakers, black or white.

Now I was hearing three languages in Chief Parker's on

a Thursday morning. Four, if you counted whatever it was those black kids were speaking.

Who'da thunk it?

I felt an irrational stab of nostalgia.

Granny Beth's strong, matter-of-fact voice resonated in my mind. *The only thing you can count on is change, Lin, so it's a big, fat waste of energy to fight it.* She'd always sighed after she'd said it, then stared into the middle distance, and added, *Everything changes, but everything stays the same.*

That last part had always seemed to contradict the first, but as for her initial advice, would that I had taken it more often. Instead, I'd spent my marriage trying to avoid change altogether, and you see where *that* had gotten me.

Geneva's phone rang, cutting into my reverie and bringing all conversation to an abrupt halt. Even the old men at the soda fountain poised on the inhale over their personalized coffee mugs.

What in the Sam Hill was going on? I hadn't seen folks acting like this since Desert Storm.

Anxious, Geneva snatched up the receiver. "Parker's. How may I help you?" After an expectant heartbeat, her features sagged with disappointment. "I'm sorry. The druggist has stepped out for a moment," she said with her usual aplomb. "This is Geneva. Can I help you?" (Only it sounded more like "Can I hep ya?") She picked up a pen and jotted down some prescription numbers.

The old men of the Coffee Club resumed their grave deliberations as the rest of the crowd went back to murmuring. The faint, acrid smell of burned coffee dregs drew my attention to the empty coffee pots behind the soda fountain.

"Next?" Geneva asked, her features strained.

A short, fat woman in a worn housedress stepped forward to hand over a prescription, then stood scowling at her.

"I'm sorry, Jennie Lou," Geneva explained, "but we

cain't fill this until the druggist gets back from taking Shelia to the emergency room. We'll get to it as soon as we can."

Taking Shelia to the emergency room? I opened my mouth to ask what had happened, but Jennie Lou's dogged reply cut me off.

"I cain't come back later," she said thickly. "Had to wait at the doctor's, now here. Clyde's been sittin' in the truck more'n twenty minutes already. Prob'ly smoked up all his Camels." Right on cue, a hoarse blast from an old, dull red Chevy pickup out front punctuated what she was saying. "See there. God forbid he should be a minute late for *People's Court*." Her scowl deepened. "You know how he is, Geneva. Once he's in his chair in front of that TV, there's no gittin' him up till supper, and I need my medicine before we eat."

Geneva shot her a beleaguered smile. "I'm so sorry. Please, just set down for a minute while I try to figure somethin' out." Geneva was an educated woman, but the more tired or pressed she got, the more country surfaced in her speech.

Jennie Lou headed for the chrome settee whose ancient, green vinyl upholstery was held together with the same plastic tape it had had when I was in high school.

Geneva scanned the waiting customers without even acknowledging my arrival, a sure sign she was stressed to the max. "Next?"

I knew I'd find out what had happened to Shelia in due time, but poor Geneva was so swamped, I decided against asking her now. Instead, I opted to make myself useful. My Prozac could wait until things calmed down a little.

I slipped behind the soda fountain to wash my hands and make more coffee. As I'd suspected, all the supplies were just where they'd been when I'd worked there three decades before.

The geezers perked up, to a man. "Hey there, good lookin'," a vaguely familiar old fellow said. "Where ya been all my life?"

Far from being complimented, I felt disgruntled that the first masculine attention I'd generated since my divorce had come from men my father's age.

The guy looked awfully familiar. I glanced down for a look at the name on his mug, but his hands covered all but a few fillips. I peered at his face. Of course. "Uncle" Delton, one of the many subcontractors who'd worked for the General. "Why, Delton Pirkle," I shot back. "Don't tell me you haven't come up with a new line in the thirty years I've been gone from here."

He tucked his chin in surprise amid a surge of chuckles and speculative whispers from his cronies. Then a grin of recognition rearranged the deep lines of his face. "Lin? Is that you, Little Linnie Breedlove?"

"One and the same." I hit the button to start the coffee brewing. "But nobody's called me *little* in a long, long time."

The geezers chuckled again, and as they offered me a wave or a wink, I began to connect a few of their faces with dusty names from the back of my brain.

"Just as pretty as ever," Delton gushed. "How come you're workin' here?"

"Well, I'm not exactly working here. Just helping Geneva out for the moment." I waited a few beats before asking the question they were all dying to answer. "So, what happened to Shelia?"

Delton leaned forward and dropped his voice. "Just fell out, right there next to the bathroom. Fainted dead away."

"Out cold. Flat as a flounder. White as paste," assorted geezers confirmed.

My chest contracted. "That sounds serious. Did they call an ambulance?"

"Naw." Delton shook his head. "Grant checked her over, then scooped her up and headed for his car. Said he didn't want to wait for an ambulance."

"Yeah," a round, balding geezer added. "Since they shut down the old hospital, takes at least thirty minutes to get a real ambulance"—as opposed to a fake one?—"and another thirty to get to Gwinnett Medical."

"She didn't come around at all?" I asked, truly worried. We were the same age, had gone from kindergarten to graduation together.

"Unh-unh." Freida Thompson's father shook his head. "We been waitin' to hear for more'n an hour now."

No wonder Geneva looked so drawn and worried. After working together in the drugstore for more than twenty years, she and Shelia were as close as sisters.

Hoping Shelia would be okay, I swapped out the now-full coffee pot for an empty one on the machine, got that one going, then started refilling the old men's cups.

Each time the phone rang, Geneva almost jumped out of her skin, but so far all the calls had been customers or doctors' offices.

Once everybody had coffee, I slipped behind the register with Geneva to help her with the rest of the backlog. "Hey. Thought you might need a hand. How about I help out?"

"God love ya." Relief eased her grim expression. "Thanks for takin' care of the Coffee Club. And thanks for steppin' in here. Every time I think I've got things under control, more people show up."

"Glad to be of assistance." I smiled. "It's like riding a bike. You never forget."

Clyde honked the horn again, prompting me to look over to Jennie Lou, who sat clutching her purse on the settee beside a frail old man who seemed to be enjoying the drama of the situation.

First things first. "As soon as the pharmacist gets back," I told Geneva, "I'll deliver the urgent prescriptions." I rummaged up a pen and pad from behind the counter, then crossed to the settee, and extended the tablet. "Jennie Lou, if you'll write down your name, address, and phone number, we'll see that you get your prescription before suppertime. I'll deliver it myself."

Jennie Lou's scowl flattened to a blank expression,

prompting me to wonder if that was as close as she ever got to a smile. I could hardly blame her if it was, what with Clyde honking for her in the truck or rooted like a house-plant in his recliner all day.

She took the pen and began writing in labored block print.

"Excuse me," I said to the rest of those gathered there. "If any of you have prescriptions that need to be filled today and you can't come back to pick them up later, please see me so we can get your addresses to deliver them."

The tension eased, replaced by a gentle rumble of approval.

Geneva and I both jumped when the phone rang again, but she beat me to it. Again, everybody went quiet. "Parker's Drugs. How can I hep ya?" she rattled out. I heard a decisive male voice from the receiver, then saw Geneva's face clear. "She is? Thank God." Her smile inverted to a frown. "Oh, no." She met my eyes with a look that communicated deep concern. "Were you able to get in touch with Ronnie?" Shelia's husband. "Oh, good. He's there." Biting the side of her lower lip, she listened on. "Already in surgery?" Pause. "I see. Well, let us know when she's"— more male voice elicited a surprised expression tinged with just a hint of disapproval—"All right then. See you within the hour."

She hung up the phone, then straightened to address the waiting audience. "Shelia is fine. They had to do emergency surgery, but she's going to be fine. The pharmacist will be back within the hour."

In the hubbub that followed, the scrawny old man beside Jennie Lou got up and tottered over to the counter. I remembered his name—Ottis Wilburne—just as he squawked out, "What kinda surgery? What's the matter with Shelia?"

The noise level dropped expectantly around us, but Geneva just smiled at him and repeated, "She's gonna be fine, but she can't come back to work for at least two months, maybe three."

By now the older women present had caught on to the fact that Shelia's problems were probably of a highly personal nature, but Ottis remained stubbornly curious. "I didn't ask ya when she was comin' back. I asked what was the matter with her!"

A plump grandma in a double-knit dress took Ottis's arm and hissed, "Female problems," sharply into his good ear.

He colored up immediately. "Ah-hah. Well, tell her we'll be prayin' for her." He beat a hasty retreat.

"Men," the woman huffed for the benefit of her prim compatriots. "Ya have to spell it out for 'em every blamed time."

Once things had settled back down, I whispered to Geneva, "What *is* the matter with Shelia?"

"She's been havin' female problems for more than a year," Geneva whispered back. "Hadn't been here ten minutes this mornin' before she rushed into the bathroom and hemorrhaged. I got her fixed up with pads and all, but as soon as she came out, she just fainted. Had this surprised look on her face, then just went down like a pulpwood pine." Tears welled in her kind brown eyes. "Grant checked her lower lids. She'd lost so much blood they were almost white, so he carried her out to the car and took Tricia O'Neal along to keep an eye on her." She straightened, her voice reverting to a normal conversational level. "Somebody had to stay, so I figured it'd best be me."

I gave her broad shoulders a reassuring squeeze. "Grant's sure lucky to have you."

"And I'm lucky to have *you*. Now let's take care of these people."

Satisfied that no more news was forthcoming, the Coffee Club moved on to the hardware store. With two of us working the remaining customers, Geneva and I had the store cleared out in fifteen minutes.

In the expectant silence that followed, she poured us both a diet soda, then flopped down onto the stool beside me at the counter. As I sipped the cold drink, a nagging question occurred to me. "What do we do if we get an urgent situation like a mother with a sick baby who needs antibiotics right away?"

Geneva's eyebrows lifted. "You could run the scrip up to Thrasher's"—the drugstore up the street—"I called Furman as soon as Grant left, and he said he'd be happy to help out."

"Oh. Good." Now, *that* was small-town: a back-alley competitor helping out in an emergency.

Geneva swiveled to face me. "God bless you for stepping in, you sweet thing. The Good Lord sent you here this morning, that's for sure."

"Glad to help." As always, I felt awkward with praise. "It's not like I had anything better to do. I've gone as far as I can with renovating the garage apartment, at least until I get some money. I've put my name in at a couple of employment agencies, but no luck so far, even from the temporary service." I scanned the store. "It feels good to be useful."

A spark of inspiration brightened Geneva's expression. "Do you think you might be able to fill in for Shelia until she comes back? Pay's eight-fifty an hour, four ten-hour days a week. Health insurance. I'd consider it a personal favor."

"*You* might consider it a favor," I demurred, "but I doubt your boss would."

"Pooh." She dismissed the argument with a flap of her hand. "Grant will be as grateful as I am. Trust me."

Remembering my first encounter with Grant Owens, I seriously doubted he'd want me around, but the prospect of a brief stint at the store certainly had its appeal. Close to home. Relaxed, friendly working environment—except for Grant, of course. And I sure could use the money.

Plus, the place was air-conditioned.

Looking around, I noted that a good bit of the inventory had been shifted from where it had always been during Old Doc Owens's tenure, but in a store this small, I was confident I could find things quickly enough. The only real drawback was Grant, the Cat Man, but for eighty-five dollars a day, he could be endured.

Living off my parents was taking its toll. I felt more guilty, trapped, and obligated by the week.

"No Sundays, as you know," Geneva nudged. "And we pay on Fridays for the week, no delays."

Eighty-five dollars a day. Three days off a week. And it wasn't like I was going to make a career of it or anything. Just a couple of months. I could handle most anything for a couple of months.

"I'll teach you how to run the computer," she offered.

"Computer?" My insides shivered. "Geneva, I don't even know how to turn one on, much less run it."

She dismissed my reservations with another wave of dark red nails. "Honey, if I can run that thing, anybody can, and you're ten times smarter than me. Trust me. Two weeks from now, you'll be usin' it like a pro."

Memories of Phil's computer-induced rages in his home office prompted me to ask, "What if I make it eat something?"

Geneva grinned. "Oh, all of us have done that at one time or another. That's why Grant has this fancy backup thingie. The worst you can do is lose a few hours' work and have to do it over."

I was unconvinced. But being the fools-rush-in kind of girl I was, I weighed Grant and the computer against the rest and decided to take the leap. I stuck out my hand. "Looks like I've got me a job," I said as we shook. "But there's just one condition. I might have to go on a job interview. And if a good opportunity comes up, I'll have to take it."

"Of course. No problem." Geneva's confident expression made me wonder if she wasn't praying even then that such eventualities would not come to pass. Then I chided myself for the unworthy suspicion. Geneva was too good a soul to think such a thing, much less pray it. "Grant said Shelia will be out at least three months."

I frowned. "I was hoping to have something permanent before then. I don't know how much longer I can go without health insurance, and there's always a waiting period after you start with a company."

Her expression clouded. "Oh, yeah. Come to think of it, I think it's three months for ours." She cocked her head, apologetic. "Not meanin' to be nosey," she said, "but what sort of shape did that husband of yours leave you in? I have a reason for askin'."

I sighed. We both knew Miss Mamie had long since broadcast the lurid details of my financial downfall. At least Geneva was granting me the dignity of telling her myself, and I knew she asked out of genuine concern. "I got zip," I confessed. "No support. No settlement. No house. No nothing." It was all a matter of public record, anyway. "All I ended up with was my clothes, plus some furniture and things I managed to squirrel away so the taxman wouldn't get them." I made a feeble attempt at humor. "Heck, if it wasn't for the 'Innocent Spouse' policy, I'd have ended up with half the remaining forty thousand dollars Phil still owes the IRS."

"That's what I was afraid of." She gave my arm a consoling pat. "Don't you worry, honey. My cousin runs DE-FACS in this county. We'll get you some help, pronto. Food stamps, for sure, maybe even assistance. You are a displaced housewife—"

"Welfare!" I bristled with indignation. "Geneva Taylor, no Breedlove has ever—"

"Calm down," she chided, matching my outrage with a pragmatic expression. "Think of all that money you just got through paying, all those penalties and interest. Those weren't your fault. It only seems fair to me that you get some of it back."

I'd never thought of it that way.

"And nobody has to know, not even your parents," she added. "Just you and me and my cousin. Trust me, she'll keep her mouth shut."

I let out an embarrassed chuckle. "How can you be so sure of that?"

It was Geneva's turn to bristle. " 'Cause if she doesn't, I'd be forced to tell where she really was and what she was doing that summer back in '83, and believe me, she wouldn't want *that* to get out."

Just because Geneva didn't engage in idle gossip didn't mean she wasn't privy to plenty. I'd always suspected her soft heart had a core of steel, and now I knew it. "I'll think about it." I offered her a lopsided smile. "One major decision per day is about all I can handle lately. I took the job. I'll have to let you know about the other."

Welfare! Food stamps!

"Okay." She went to the register to pick up the phone receiver. "Here."

"Here, what?" I asked as I took it. "You want me to call them now?"

"No, silly. Not DEFACS." She began dialing. "You'd better tell Miss Mamie I hired you. She'll never forgive you if somebody scoops her on that one."

Sadly, she was right. We were alone, but such local tidbits had a way of leaking out under the door, and the Mame would be mortally offended if I wasn't the one to tell her. I put the receiver to my ear just in time to hear Uncle Bedford's voice chirp, "H'lo?"

Odd, that he would answer the phone. "Uncle Bedford?" I hollered. "This is Lin. Is Miss Mamie home?"

"Naw," he huffed. "Ain't back yet."

"Let me speak to Aunt Glory, then."

"She's gone. Got mad and left. Good riddance, I say."

A shard of alarm shot through me. Aunt Glory would never leave Uncle Bedford alone.

Had he gotten fed up and killed "that gay guy"?

"Uncle Bedford, you know Aunt Glory would never leave you alone."

"Who said I was alone?" he railed. "The Klan's here, and you know how your Aunt Glory feels about the Klan. Stomped right outta here the minute they came in."

I fought down growing panic. "Uncle Bedford," I said in my mother's dire-situation voice, "You know the Ku Klux Klan isn't there with you—"

"Are too!" he said like a petulant child. "Grand Dragon's standin' right here! Wanna talk to him?"

"The Grand Dragon?" If I hadn't been so frightened, I might have recognized the insanity of what I was doing, but as it was, I jumped in, hook, line, and sinker. "Yeah. Let me speak to him."

I heard a rustle, then Aunt Glory's beleaguered voice came through the receiver. "Well, it seems I'm the Grand Dragon of the Ku Klux Klan today."

I was too relieved to appreciate the humor. "Thank God. Aunt Glory, I was afraid Uncle Bedford had—"

Determined not to acknowledge the danger her husband might be, she cut me off with a brisk, "Miss Mamie and the General decided to have lunch and go shoppin' on the way home from the doctor's. Want me to give them a message, sugar?" I couldn't help wondering if Aunt Glory might actually prefer being murdered to facing the truth of her predicament.

"No." My heart still pounding in my chest, I took a leveling breath. "Just ask her to call me at the drugstore as soon as she gets in."

"Okay. 'Bye."

I hung up. Heaven help us all, the madness was contagious. I'd actually tried to reason my uncle out of his delusions!

Geneva, usually the soul of discretion, was eaten up with curiosity. "I know it's not a bit of my business," she said, "but if you'll tell me what that was all about before anybody comes in, I'll buy you a drink next door after work. Two."

"Deal." I told her. We were still laughing when the bell announced the next incoming wave.

Forty minutes later, we were knee-deep in customers again when Grant Owens strode toward the back of the store. Even grim-faced, he was better looking than I remembered.

Geneva waved to him over the heads of the waiting customers. "Thank goodness. Not a minute too soon." She shushed everybody as he approached. "How's Shelia?"

"Fine." He looked straight through me as he passed. "Ronnie just called me on my car phone. She's in recovery, doing well."

A portly retiree lifted his nose from the *Farmer's Almanac* and asked, "What kinda surgery?" but his wife shushed him up with a none-too-gentle whack of her purse and a whispered, "Female problems, old man, if it's any of your business, which it isn't."

He frowned, tucked his chin, and blushed as he dived back into the almanac.

I remembered overhearing scandalous snatches of murmured conversations in my childhood about "Aint Minnie's hysterectum" and "Uncle Cletus's prostrate trouble" and found the remnant of such small-town sensibilities endearing in this shameless age of condom and diarrhea ads.

Everything changes, but everything stays the same.

"Thanks for your concern, Mr. Beard," Grant said smoothly. "I know Shelia would appreciate it." It surprised me to see that Grant Owens did, in fact, possess at least some tact and discretion. "Now if you folks will excuse me, I'll head back to the pharmacy and try to get caught up." He scanned the crowd. "Anybody here with sickness or an emergency?"

A thin woman in a sleeveless dress waved a prescription. "My boy's sick as a cat with the stomach bug. I'd 'preciate it if you could fill this right away."

"Sure." Grant looked over the remaining customers again, still not registering my presence. "Anybody else?"

For some reason I could not fathom, it bothered me that he was ignoring my help. Determined not to pay him any mind, I did my best to keep occupied.

"Grant," Geneva called without looking up from the charge receipt she was writing. "I hired a replacement for Shelia."

"Good."

Not, "Who?" Just, "Good."

Geneva straightened to glare at her employer—*our* employer. "Don't you want to know who it is?"

Grant deigned only a brief glance before going back to his prescriptions. "Seems pretty obvious, since she's standing right there."

"How do you know it's Lin?" she challenged. "Maybe she just pitched in for the afternoon. It could be somebody else."

"Is it?" His smug little smile said he knew it wasn't.

"Well, no." Flatmouthed, Geneva sighed in my direction. "Men. I have yet to meet one who can carry on a simple, logical conversation." She wadded up a sheet of notebook paper and fired a direct hit on the top of Grant's bent, tawny head.

To his credit, he recovered with a grin, waiting until her back was turned to send the crumpled missile whizzing into Geneva's backside.

"Children, children," I heard myself saying.

Children, children? How dumb was that? What was I, a schoolmarm?

And why did I care what Grant Owens heard me say? I retreated to the soda fountain to wash mugs until the heat in my neck and cheeks faded.

Of all the times and places for me to become aware of a man. And of all the men. But I was. He intruded on my consciousness like the sound of distant thunder in a drought.

Oh, lord . . . I busied myself cleaning the tiny kitchen, a surefire way to take my mind off troubling thoughts.

Eighty-five dollars a day, I kept reminding myself. *Eighty-five dollars a day.*

By the time the customers slacked off at last, evening sun was slanting through the aisles. I looked to the clock and was surprised to see it was already quarter to seven. "Fifteen more minutes," I reminded Geneva, "and I'm gonna take you up on that drink."

My stomach promptly let out a huge growl.

"My goodness," she commented. "We didn't even have lunch, did we? Much less a break." She plopped onto the settee. "What a day." Stretching, she yawned hugely, then closed her eyes. "Did Miss Mamie ever call back?"

"Yep. While you were in the stockroom looking for that vaporizer. She approves."

Geneva looked at me with calm compassion. "It only matters that *you* approve."

I let out a long breath. "I know that."

She shifted the subject. "You did a great job running the register. Tomorrow I'll show you how to work the money-order machine and the fax. Once you've got those down, we'll tackle the computer."

My lungs tingled with dread. "You're gonna have to be very basic with me," I confessed. "Machines hate me."

"You can do it." She got up, her eyes merry. "Like I said, *I* can do it, and I didn't make National Honor Society. You're tons smarter than I am."

"Not about men," I blurted out from nowhere.

"Well, I'll give you that," she conceded with a grin, "but in everything else, you ran rings around me. Just you wait. By the end of next week, you'll be laughin' at how easy it is. Mark my words."

The bell tinkled, and we looked up to see an old black man of majestic bearing glide into the store. "Franklin Harris," I exclaimed, warmed by the very sight of him. Hands extended, I met him in the aisle. "How are you? You probably don't remember me but—"

He took my hands into his large, warm ones. "How could I forget little Miss Lin Breedlove who loved my marching men?"

The reference triggered happy memories of sunny afternoons spent in Franklin's marvelous wildflower garden, where we'd carefully placed tiny orange butterfly-weed blooms on their points atop a gently sloping cookie sheet, then tapped the metal so the "marching men" promenaded to the bottom of the sheet. "Do you still have your garden?"

Sadness pinched the depths of his compelling dark eyes. "Yes. But how much longer, I couldn't say, what with this drought and all."

Our third summer of drought. "Can't you water it?" I asked him, ever the fixer.

He shot Geneva a knowing glance and shook his head. "Not enough to help much. We hardly got any pressure in our neighborhood"—read, poor and black—"and next to none up on my little hill. But you know how things go." The pained resignation in his face brought back some of the reasons I'd shaken the dust of this town from my shoes thirty years before. The prejudice and injustice.

"Oh, Franklin. Your garden is a treasure. We can't let it die. Surely there must be some way to save it."

Geneva nodded. "She's right, Franklin." But, in the way of small-town people faced with entrenched unfairness, she changed the subject, motioning to the prescription peeking out of Franklin's pocket. "Here, let me get that filled for you."

Uninvited, Grant chimed in from the pharmacy. "The city's responsible for providing water. They ought to put in new lines."

Geneva and Franklin exchanged knowing looks. "Been tryin' to get 'em to for five years," Franklin said. "And they say they will. But there never seems to be equipment available to do it. All tied up with the new developments in town. Our neighborhood never has been able to get a fair shake when it comes to services."

"Sounds like somebody needs to kick some municipal ass," Grant grumbled as he retreated into the pharmacy.

The rest of us shook our heads.

Geneva seemed to feel it her duty as an employee to cover for her boss's ignorance. "He's new. Has no idea how things are."

"Well," Franklin said judiciously, "I just hope he doesn't take it into his head to go helpin' me on this one. Lord knows what kind of hornets' nest that could stir up."

Mimosa Branch's three-man city council had once been an equitable form of government, but over the past twenty years, the worst kind of political cronyism had cemented a corrupt alliance between one of the two councilmen and Mayor Hamilton Stubbs, leaving the town at the mayor's mercy. Without Ham Stubbs's endorsement, nothing in Mimosa Branch got done. And rumor had it, his endorsement didn't come cheap. Little wonder he had no inclination to help the poor sections of the city now that developers with deep pockets beckoned.

Unfair! Deep inside, an all-too-familiar aching chord of anger and frustration rose from its thirty-year slumber. We were in a new century, a new millennium. Things like these shouldn't still be happening here.

"The Fixer" in me stepped up onto her soap box. Somebody ought to do something! The rest of the thought was in my Granny Beth's voice: *Somebody who knows that the way you do things ain't the way you do things in this town. And you know who that is.*

She'd always said that whenever you think "somebody ought to do something," God's letting you know you've been appointed. Maybe I could help make things better. At least for Franklin.

"Don't you worry, Franklin," I assured him. "I'll think of something. Something that won't put you on a hit list."

His dark eyes sparked with energy from the broad grin

that spread across his face. "Why, I believe you will, Miss Lin."

My strong sense of justice recoiled. "Not *Miss* Lin. Unless you want me to call you *Mr.* Harris after all these years."

He studied me before nodding in approval. "Thank you, Lin. I'll try to remember, but old habits die hard."

"A lot of things die hard, Franklin," I responded. "But that doesn't mean they deserve to live."

He studied me again. "Sounds like you've grown mighty wise since those days in my garden."

I quoted his own words back to him. "You live, you learn, and God willin', you don't make the same mistake twice."

We shared a comforting chuckle that was interrupted by the entrance of a frowning sixtyish matron in expensive clothes. I recognized her instantly as Gertrude Booth, the mill superintendent's widow and reigning bitch of Mimosa Branch's Old Guard. Even Miss Mamie was afraid of her. I never could stand that woman.

Franklin stepped back from the counter, yielding the space to this small-town tyrant, and my heightened sensibilities recoiled even more.

The strong odor of liquor overrode even the heavy perfume the old bat was wearing. "Grant," she coaxed, leaning over the counter to waggle several prescriptions at him. "I'm running late. I need this right away." She completely ignored me and Geneva. "I know you can squeeze me in next, can't you?"

Grant looked down on her in mild reproach. "I'll get to it before we close, Mrs. Booth, but Mr. Harris was ahead of you. First come, first served. I'm sure you understand." Ignoring the looks of warning that Geneva, Franklin, and I shot him, Grant turned to Franklin with exaggerated deference. "Yours will be ready in just a few minutes, sir."

Mrs. Booth's thick neck reddened and puffed like a toad's. "See here, Mr. Owens," she spat out, "I am not accustomed to being kept waiting by the likes of Franklin

Harris, if you get my drift. I need these prescriptions immediately. If you value my business, you'll take care of me first."

In an effort to avoid a pointless confrontation, Franklin said quietly, "Go ahead and do hers next, Grant. I'm in no hurry."

Now it was Grant's turn to flush. Apparently, he didn't subscribe to the "pick your battles" school of coexistence when it came to racists.

Before he could open his mouth and escalate things further, Geneva snatched the prescriptions, handed them to me, then took Mrs. Booth's arm and dragged her toward the platypus display. "How's that precious granddaughter Katie of yours? I swear, she is the prettiest child I ever saw in my life. How old is she now, anyway?"

Still flushed, Mrs. Booth shot a brief glare back at Grant, but the call to grandmotherhood worked its spell. "Katie's five now. Already reads at second-grade level."

"Everybody in town was just thrilled to hear she won the Preschool Miss Gwinnett Dynamite pageant," Geneva gushed. "I know you must be so proud." Her grip firm on Mrs. Booth's elbow, she steered the irate woman's attention to the stuffed animals. "She's bound to love one of these. Just got 'em in. Every little girl who's anybody in Mimosa Branch will be dyin' to have one on her bed by the end of the week. Why don't you just pick one out for her while we wait, and I'll wrap it up, no charge?"

Grant colored, obviously appalled by Geneva's effort to appease the obnoxious Mrs. Booth, but a sharp glance and shake of the head from Franklin kept him from responding.

"Fill her prescriptions first, please," Franklin murmured with quiet authority.

"If that's what you really want," Grant clipped out.

Franklin nodded.

By the time Geneva finished wrapping the platypus and tying the bows, Grant smacked the offending prescriptions onto the pass-through. "There you are."

Bagging them, I saw they were all tranquilizers or narcotics, prescribed by Dr. Gordon. Mrs. Booth tucked the platypus under her arm with a smug sneer. "I'm glad to see you came to your senses, Mr. Owens." She snatched the bag from me and sailed out.

Nobody breathed until she backed her Mercedes out into Main Street and gunned away.

His brows lowered in disapproval, Grant turned on Geneva. "Geneva, I know you keep telling me that 'the way you do things ain't the way you do things' in this town, but I cannot condone what just happened. Giving in to prejudice like that just makes it worse."

Geneva and Franklin exchanged a glance that communicated just how clueless they thought Grant was, but it was Franklin who spoke. "I appreciate what you tried to do for me, Grant, truly I do, but Geneva's right. Sometimes the way you do things ain't the way you do things. Miz Booth thinks pushin' ahead of me makes her more important." He shook his head. "I think that's pretty sad. But it don't take nothin' away from me unless I let it." He smiled, his features calm with wisdom and self-assurance. "I don't have to go first to feel like somebody."

Grant shifted to Geneva. "Well, you didn't have to *reward* her," he fumed. "Giving her that stuffed animal, free . . ."

Geneva laughed. "I didn't give it to her free. I said I'd *wrap* it free, and I did." Her eyes sharpened with mischief. "We wrap anything for free. But I've already charged her double for the platypus."

I couldn't help it. I burst out laughing. "Perfect." I looked up to find annoyance warring with amusement in Grant's expression. "Now *that's* the way you do things," I couldn't resist telling him.

Grant smacked Franklin's medicine onto the passthrough. "Here you go, Franklin. Sorry about the delay."

Franklin just smiled.

I bagged the prescriptions and handed them to him. "I

meant what I said about helping with the garden. Soon as I figure something out, I'll come by." I had an idea, one that involved calling everybody in the Garden Club. Everybody except Gertrude Booth.

"You do that." His smile enveloped me like a warm hug, then he turned and glided with great dignity toward the door.

"I'll see what I can do, too," Grant called after him. "Kick some butt with that two-bit Boss Hogg in Town Hall," he muttered under his breath.

Geneva and I just rolled our eyes. Clearly, today's lesson hadn't sunk in.

"How many times do I haveta tell you, Grant?" she chided gently. "The way you do things *ain't* the way you do things in this town."

He waved off her advice without comment.

Geneva sighed. "Some people just hafta learn the hard way." She handed me my purse, then grabbed hers, and called back to Grant, "Quittin' time. You close up, Boss. I'll open at eight." Beckoning me after her, she made a bee line toward the bistro. "C'mon, woman. I owe you a drink. Two. You've more than earned 'em."

"Yeah." Smiling, I followed her toward the quaint little restaurant next door.

A nice glass of wine, right here on Main Street.

Yep. Change had come to Mimosa Branch, all right.

And if I had anything to say about it, there'd be some more—in Franklin's garden. For that matter, maybe even in city hall.

Chapter 6

Chief Parker's Drugs might not have changed, but the old Western Auto next door certainly had. Stepping through the antique etched doors, I marveled at the building's urbane transformation into the Café Luna. The old dropped ceiling had been stripped to reveal hand-hewn beams and braces fifteen feet overhead. Sprayed chocolate brown along with the exposed ductwork, the arrangement was both artistic and functional. Exposed brick walls had been partially stuccoed and illustrated with crude facsimiles of European wine labels. New Age "unmusic" wafted quietly through potted palms and ficus trees.

Very trendy. Very chic.

I leaned in to Geneva. "This looks like half the bars in Buckhead."

"The owners had one," she reported, "before they sold it and retired to their lake place over on Chattahoochee Bay." She scanned the white-clothed tables. "Then they got bored and decided to open this place up. It's been real popular. Cain't get in on the weekends." She lowered her voice to a whisper. "But it's high as a cat's back."

"I liked it better when it was a Western Auto," I murmured.

"Yeah, but the booze is a whole lot better here," Geneva

said. "That 'shine they sold out the back of the hardware store always tasted like turpentine to me."

We shared a highly unsophisticated giggle.

"Two for dinner?" The black-clad maitre d'—*a maitre d' in Mimosa Branch*—glided up from the back to ask in condescending tones.

"Just drinks," Geneva corrected brightly. "But I'd rather sit at a table than the bar." Oblivious to the self-conscious assortment of predatory women and clearly married men at the bar, she pointed to the sculptured brushed-chrome stools they sat on. "Those stools gave me a backache last time."

You could smell the hormones and desperation all the way across the room.

Just like being back in Buckhead. Not that the see-and-be-seen spots had been my style. My tastes had run to quiet, reasonable little places with good food. Phil, however . . .

I bent to whisper to Geneva, "I don't want to sit at the bar, either. We might catch herpes."

She hooted, drawing the attention of several dining couples and the derision of the trendy barflies.

The host managed a pained smile.

Undaunted, Geneva grabbed his arm and indicated a candlelit table in a quiet corner near the back hall. "How 'bout that one right there?"

I reveled in the pretentious guy's almost undetectable shudder. "I think we can arrange that," he said as if it were dinner with the governor instead of a simple seating in a half-empty restaurant.

He led us to the table, clearly hoping we would settle down and conduct ourselves accordingly. As we sat, I resolved to act up, just on general principle.

"I'll have an iced-cold white zinfandel with cranberry juice cocktail," I ordered, eliciting a chortle from the yuppies sipping on their dry merlots at the next table. "Phil used to call it my Kool-Aid cocktail. How 'bout you, Geneva?"

"Hot weather like this . . ." She thought a minute, then

nodded to the host. "I've got me a taste for a Bud Lite."

"I believe we might have some in the back," he deigned.

"I didn't know you drank beer, Geneva," I said as he left to fill our blue-collar order.

"Haven't had one in years." She settled back with an impish smile. "Don't know what made me want one now, but there you are."

God, but it was good to be with somebody *real* after all the lies I'd lived without even knowing it. "I swan, woman, you are a tonic."

"You sound just like Miss Beth," she said, correctly identifying one of my paternal grandmother's favorite sayings.

The connection to my past felt good, prompting me to hope that there would be other compensations to moving back home. We chatted about Shelia until a studly young waiter arrived with our drinks. I glanced up to see Geneva's longneck, discreetly swaddled in a napkin, but my attention immediately shifted to the tanned, muscular young man who held the tray. Short, but gorgeous.

"Good evening, ladies," he said with a dazzling down-home smile.

Never mind that I probably weighed as much as he did and was old enough to be his mama; I reacted to his male-ness, nonetheless. It was progress of a sort—hopeless, but a sign that the woman in me was still alive down in there somewhere.

"How about some peanuts or pretzels to go with these?" he asked in a sexy, cultured voice.

"No thanks." The knee-jerk denial came more from my awkward awareness than from the snacks he'd offered. If I'd had a lick of sense, I'd have remembered I hadn't eaten since breakfast.

He granted us another smile. "You ladies need anything, just wave. I am at your command."

BIG tip for this one, I decided as I watched him retreat toward the kitchen.

When I looked back to Geneva, I found her grinning at me like a mule eating briars, her bottle raised in a toast. "Here's to wakin' up, kiddo. It's never too late."

Mortified that she had seen through me so easily, I hid behind a bravado I did not feel. "To waking up."

I took a few sips of my Kool-Aid cocktail. The tart cranberry juice balanced the sweetness of the wine, and the cold concoction went straight through my empty stomach lining into my bloodstream. On a surge of glucose and alcohol, I felt the day's tension begin to unravel almost immediately.

We settled back to our drinks and conversation.

"Oh, in all the excitement, I completely forgot to tell you." Geneva dropped her voice to a confidential level. "You'll never believe what happened at the city council meeting last night. You remember Fred Waller—"

The only honest soul on the three-man council. Not the brightest bulb in the pack, but decent as the day was long. "Let me guess." This was July. And Mimosa Branch, judging from Franklin Harris's problems, was still a backward, corrupt little town despite its suburban veneer. "It's time to name the chairman of the school board, and it was Fred's turn again, and they voted two-to-one to skip him. Again."

Geneva flapped her hand in dismissal. "So what else is new? That's only part of it." She looked left and right, but we were the only natives in the place. "You'd think Fred would be used to it after all these years, but I guess even he has his limits. This time when they took the vote, the mayor had the nerve to laugh. Well, Fred just snapped, right there in front of the rezoning applicants and four preachers from the Interfaith Council, includin' his own. Just snapped. Started cussin' the air blue. Stood up and told the mayor and that slimy toady Gary Mayfield exactly what he thought of their crooked ways and how they'd abused him and fleeced the taxpayers all these years."

"Fred Waller?" As long as I could remember, the meek little man had been the backbone of the Church of God of

Mimosa Branch, and had never so much as raised an eyebrow even at his own domineering wife.

"It gets better," she continued, her eyes alight. "Still cussin' away, he resigned on the spot, said hell would freeze over before he'd run again, then stormed out in the middle of the meeting. Slammed the door so hard behind him, it shattered the glass, even with that chicken wire in it.

"Preacher Biffle went after him, bein' his pastor and all. Followed him home and right into the house, but Fred ignored him completely. Still wild as a jackrabbit, he went straight to his den and started grabbin' up all his city papers."

She took a deep swig of beer to wet her whistle.

Fascinated, I sipped away at my wine cooler.

"Well, you can imagine what Maryann thought," she went on. "Preacher Biffle said she was runnin' around tellin' Fred to quit it, but he just started heavin' all those papers down the basement stairs. When she tried to lay hold of him—I swear, I wouldn't have believed this myself if Vollie Biffle hadn't told me over the phone first thing this morning"—so much for pastoral privilege—"Fred stuck his finger in Maryann's face and ordered her to freeze. Then he said if she so much as touched him or any of those papers, she'd live to regret it, but not for long."

"Ohmygod. He stood up to Maryann?" The worm had turned, indeed. Taking on political corruption was one thing, but standing up to a Pentecostal battleaxe like Maryann Waller . . . now, *that* took courage. Nobody in Mimosa Branch had ever dared to do it. "Even the mayor is scared of Maryann."

"Honey, the *devil's* scared of Maryann Waller."

"Boy, would I have loved to be a fly on the wall for that. What did she do?"

"She asked the preacher if he was going to sit there and let her husband talk to her that way." Geneva's brown eyes sparkled. "And do you know what Preacher Biffle told her? I've never had much use for that man, God love him, but

I do now, 'cause he told Maryann Waller it was about time Fred took control of his household."

"Holy crow. Did she hit him?"

"Nah. She was so shocked, she didn't say a word. The preacher just congratulated Fred, then took him to Shoney's for a hot fudge cake. Then the two of them went bowling all night at that black-light place way down in Chamblee. Didn't tell anybody where they were."

Geneva looked as smug as a Democrat legislator who'd just gotten out of a DUI. "Maryann had called the police and all the hospitals by the time they got home, but Fred just told her to shut her trap and fix his breakfast. Then he went to work."

I took another sip of my wine cooler in a pleasant buzz enhanced by the delicious image of Fred Waller standing down first the city council, then his wife. "He's up for reelection this fall, isn't he?"

"Not anymore."

"He was serious about resigning?"

"Yep. Told Preacher Biffle he was good and through."

"Oh, lord. What's gonna happen if the mayor puts one of his people in that spot? We're doomed for sure." My words came out far too thick and more than a little fuzzy. Too late, I realized I should have taken that cute waiter up on the pretzels. "Somebody decent oughta run."

"Dern tootin', " Geneva seconded. "Better still, somebody decent ought to run against the mayor. He's up for reelection, too."

Maybe it was the alcohol, but I surprised myself by caring very much what happened to my old home town. I'd moved back planning to stay out of all things local and leave as soon as I could. But first Franklin's troubles, and now this, stirred the moral outrage of my youth.

Across the room, the door opened and I, along with every other woman in the place besides Geneva—who was sitting with her back to him—looked up to see Grant

Owens enter. He moved smoothly to an empty spot at the far end of the bar.

Immediately, I lost my train of thought, which annoyed me. Why did it bother me so much that he was one of those men who couldn't go unnoticed, even by me?

The bar queens preened as the disgruntled men beside them sucked in their guts and turned their backs to the competition.

For one irrational moment, I wondered if Grant had followed us in there. Then I pounded myself for being so narcissistic.

Why shouldn't he go next door for a drink after work? We had. And after what he'd been through with Shelia, nobody could blame him.

The last thing I needed was for eagle-eyed Geneva to pick up on my reaction to Grant Owens, so I kept my gaze glued to her and my expression pleasant as she discussed the mayor's certain reelection and the pitfalls of finding a decent replacement for Fred Waller.

Yet hard as I tried to ignore my new boss, I couldn't help watching at the edge of my vision as he ordered a drink, then unfolded the paper he was carrying and started to read it, oblivious to the looks of open invitation he generated in the women beside him at the bar.

After disappointed lash-flicks and shifting of long legs, the cats on the stools turned back to their more cooperative prey.

Take a leaf out of Grant Owens's book, I told myself, and ignore him the way he was ignoring everybody else. Then I totally blew my aloof self-image by swallowing the last sip of my drink down the wrong way and exploding into a paroxysm of coughing.

"You okay, honey?" Geneva grabbed my arm and held it up to pound me on the back, drawing even more attention to me. I hung there, coughing, wanting to slither under the table and disappear.

The cute young waiter rushed over with a glass of water,

and concerned diners craned their necks. Only Grant, absorbed in his paper, acted as if nothing was going on.

Napkin in hand, the yuppie from the next table leapt to my side. "Do you need the Heimlich?" he demanded earnestly. "Nod if you want the Heimlich."

"No," I managed to croak out through my napkin. "Thank you, but I just swallowed the wrong way." Gasp, cough. "I'm fine." Hack, hack, hack. I wriggled free of Geneva and sat down with a thump. Summoning up every ounce of self-control, I quashed the subsiding spasms until, at last, all was quiet.

I was left, wheezing slightly, with the irrational conviction that the whole thing had somehow been Grant Owens's fault.

How crazy was *that*?

"So, Geneva," a rough baritone voice said through my lips. "Who would you pick to run for Fred's seat?"

Bless her heart, she understood my desperate wish to get past the embarrassing incident and cheerfully obliged. "I know this sounds crazy, but I think Grant would be a good choice."

"Grant?" The word came out far louder than I intended. I hunkered lower, praying he hadn't heard me.

My lips began to lose sensation, which happens when I drink on an empty stomach. Unless I ate something, pronto, an unmentionable portion of my anatomy would go numb next, then I'd fall asleep where I sat. I shot a longing glance toward the bowls of party mix on the bar and ended up looking straight into Grant Owens's amused face.

Damn! I was looking at the pretzels, you jerk, not you!

A red-hot jolt of embarrassed adrenaline made my ears throb.

Geneva stopped in midsentence and studied me in concern. "Honey, what's wrong?"

"I should have had some peanut butter crackers before we came over here," I rasped. "I'm afraid my drink has gone to my head."

No sooner had I spoken than the waiter appeared with another round and an elegant appetizer of baked Brie surrounded by gourmet crackers and seedless grapes.

Eyebrows raised, Geneva pointed to the cheese. "Sugar, you got somethin' confused here. We didn't order this. I'll have to wash dishes if y'all expect me to—"

The waiter grinned. "Compliments of the gentleman at the far end of the bar. With his thanks for service 'above and beyond the call of duty' this morning."

Geneva swiveled in her chair. "Grant!" Before I could stop her, she rose and flagged him with her napkin. "Come on over here and help us eat this," she called with an adorable lack of pretense that kept me from being annoyed with her.

After a brief flash of uncomfortable indecision, Grant did as she asked. We both knew Geneva wouldn't take no for an answer.

He sat down beside her, bringing the faint odor of Mercurochrome with the drink in his hand.

Scotch. I hated Scotch drinkers. Pretentious bastards cultivated a taste for Mercurochrome just because it was supposed to be cool.

Phil had taken up Scotch the year it had all started to go downhill.

Grant nodded at me with only a hint of a stiff little smile. "We meet again."

Now I was saddled with my new boss, who clearly hadn't planned to join us. But Geneva was delighted. It hadn't occurred to her that Grant might not have been angling for an invitation, or that I might not want him there.

But if he was so happy alone at the bar, my new self argued, why had he sent the stuff over?

"Good grief," Geneva chided. "You two act like a couple of strange huntin' dogs stuffed in the same sack. Relax. Nobody here bites."

I told myself that only a woman with Geneva's good heart and secure status could afford to be so dead-bone honest, but there was no denying the thawing effect her words had on Grant Owens. He melted into a genuine grin.

"Good God, Geneva—"

She leveled a mock scowl at him, having no truck with those who took the Lord's name in vain.

"I mean . . . man, Geneva," he corrected. "Do you always say exactly what you think?"

"Unless it'll do more harm than good. Then I keep my mouth shut." She lifted her beer, undaunted. "After workin' with me for a year, you should know that. I swear, Grant," she said good-naturedly, "sometimes I think you just don't pay attention to anything but business."

"Can you blame me, considering the shape things were in when I got there?" he asked with a careful neutrality contradicted by a hard glint of judgment in his eyes. "My father left a real mess behind."

"Your father," Geneva said gently, "might not have been the best businessman in the world, but he was one of the best men I've ever had the privilege to know. You can be proud of him."

Clearly, Grant wasn't. "He was kind, I'll give him that. And good. A good man."

"Precious few of those," I heard myself say with a nasty edge. Uck. What inner harpy had lobbed that lovely little dart?

Grant's good humor congealed. "I just love judgmental women. It's so appealing."

"Truce, you two," Geneva intervened. She handed me a cracker smeared with warm cheese. "Eat this before you take another sip." She shot a warning look at Grant. "I think this nonsense has gone far enough. You are both good people who just got off on the wrong foot. But we're going to be working together every day." She lifted her beer. "So I propose a toast." Her bright eyes commanded us to join her. "To a fresh start. Right here. Right now."

She turned to me. "No more hard feelings about those blessed cats and Grant's horrendous timing."

"Horrendous timing?" he protested.

She aimed her longneck at him. "Barging in on Miss Mamie and Lin when poor Dr. B. was loose half-nekkid in the yard. What in dear heaven were you thinkin', man? Weren't they embarrassed enough without you traipsin' up with some blamed cat?"

Grant froze, clearly astounded that his actions might have been considered rude.

Hah! Chew on that, you jerk!

But before I could hitch up my smug britches too high, she turned to me. "And you, my precious girl." Her tone softened only slightly. "Just because Grant's a man, doesn't automatically make him the enemy. True, he's as clueless as most males about noticin' other people's problems. But he's not your sorry, thievin', philanderin' ex-husband." I could have sworn he squirmed when she said that. "Cut him some slack. I'll vouch for him. He's not half-bad for a foreigner."

If anybody but Geneva Bates had taken me to school that way, I'd have gotten up and left—especially since she'd hit upon the painful truth so squarely. Stung, I was still considering leaving when Grant Owens did the one thing guaranteed to make me rethink my opinion of him: He laughed, without artifice or restraint—not at me, but at himself.

It started in surprise, then grew into a cleansing, unself-conscious swell of amusement. Then he exhaled heavily, looking ten years younger and twice as appealing. "Well, when you put it that way, Geneva, I'm surprised Lin didn't use her BB gun on *me* when I barged in on her, as you so aptly put it." He raised his Scotch to me. "Clearly, I owe you an apology," he said with convincing sincerity. "I humbly beg your pardon, ma'am. For intruding. And for cat-rustling."

No excuses. No bluster.

Just that killer smile and a genuine apology.

Dammit. Why couldn't he have just stayed a jerk? A

halfway jerk was the most dangerous kind. I might end up liking the good half, a surefire formula for disaster. Damn, damn, damn.

"Apology accepted," I said, wishing I could sound as convincing as he had. Wishing even more that I could mean it.

I had enough grudges in my life. Why did I insist on collecting more?

"So. We start over." Grant rose, proffering his perfect man's hand. I've always been a sucker for gorgeous Greco-Roman hands, and he had them. His shake was warm and strong and certain.

Threatened by just how good it felt, I pulled away before manners allowed.

He didn't seem to notice. "If you ladies will excuse me, it's back to the store for a bowl of Beanie Weenies and a couple of hours of catch-up."

For the first time since he'd walked into the store that afternoon, I noticed the fatigue lines in his face. Here I'd condemned him for being insensitive, and I hadn't once really considered how gruesome this day must have been for him.

My old self immediately felt sorry for him and guilty for me. My new self reminded me to take the lesson and move on. And not enable.

"Thanks for the drinks. And the Brie," I blurted out lamely. "And the apology."

Nodding, he suppressed a yawn, and I got a fleeting impression of what he must have looked like when he'd stayed up past his bedtime when he was a little boy. "See you two tomorrow."

"I'm openin'," Geneva reminded him, "so take your time comin' in."

He nodded again and waved his hand without looking back. His leaving attracted just as much attention as his arrival.

Damn. He did look good.

I had enough trouble without feeling sorry for a half-jerk like Grant Owens. "Geneva, I'm going to drink the rest of this Kool-Aid cocktail, then I want you to drive me home."

"Okay. Hand over your keys. We'll get your car back there someway."

I didn't argue. It was nice to have somebody else take care of the details for a change.

She dropped my keys into her purse. "Now, get good and tipsy," she said without a trace of reproach. "Grant rubs a lot of people the wrong way at first, but just until they get to know him." She popped a grape into her mouth, then couldn't suppress another of those Cheshire-cat looks. "I gotta tell you, though, it sure has been fun watchin' you try not to look at him since he came in."

"You knew!" I should have suspected; nothing got past Geneva. "Why didn't you say anything?"

"Heck, it was lots more fun to play along. But I gotta tell you, honey. With that short hair and those ears that go red at the drop of a hat, you should never play poker for money."

Or have anything to do with a handsome semi-jerk like Grant Owens.

I could work for him. Fine. But that was as far as it would ever go, regardless of Geneva and the Mame's matchmaking efforts. My ears and I had no more use for a man like him than he so clearly had for me.

I just love judgmental women. It's so appealing.

I lifted my glass. "Here's to celibacy." Then I did as Geneva suggested and got good and snockered—on only two drinks.

Chapter 7

That night I woke sitting up at three o'clock in the morning, gasping for breath, thirsty and crying, inexplicably aroused despite the lingering fear that left me shaking. Again. I'd had a dream—frantic and shattering—but the specifics held themselves just beyond retrieval. Whatever demons had pursued me in my sleep, I stubbornly kept them secret from myself.

The first time it had happened, I'd dismissed it as the heat. But after the third episode, I knew something else was going on. Some cruel, dark part of me seemed determined to keep punishing me.

After slugging down two tumblers of water that tasted faintly of iron, I lurched to the shower, turned on the cold, and stepped under the spray—nightgown and all—wishing the tepid baptism could rinse away the secret sins that tormented my dreams. Propping my forehead against the tile wall, I angled there until my blood cooled. Then I peeled the slip of satin off my body and turned slowly in the water, arching my back as the spray hit my breasts.

It didn't help. My skin craved the stroke of a hand besides my own, the pressure of a man's weight against me. Not sex, necessarily.

Well, yes, sex. I felt achingly empty, no denying that.

But what I missed most was the solid presence, the scent

of a man. The taste of him. The feel of his arms around me. I'd tried to imagine a phantom lover but failed dismally. Phil was the only man I'd ever wanted. In all our years together, I'd never fantasized about anyone else—not even Paul McCartney or Michael Rennie. Now I didn't even want Phil—hadn't since I'd found out about the champagne rooms.

I'd always loved sex, and Phil had been Ready Freddie until the past few years. He'd often told me I made love like a man. It took little foreplay to bring me to the brink, and I liked it quick and hard. I'd never failed to have at least one orgasm—usually several—whenever we'd made love. But it occurred to me, standing under that shower, that I may never really have been made love to.

Quick, hard, and dirty was all I'd ever known. It was the old "which came first" dilemma. Did I really prefer it quick and hard, or had I liked quick and hard with little foreplay and no denouement because that was the only sex I'd ever had?

Maybe Phil wasn't the great lover I'd always thought him to be. Maybe he wasn't a lover at all. Maybe there was something else out there, something better.

Which only made me feel worse as I stood there, horny, with only the shower to touch me.

Perhaps the time had come to go to one of those adult toy stores down in Atlanta, after all. I'd often considered it. Only the expense, not conscience, had stopped me.

How much could a dildo cost, anyway?

I turned off the water and had just begun to dry myself when my mind conjured up a shocking flash of Grant Owens lying naked and aroused in my bed.

Zap! A bolt of desire shot to where it mattered and exploded, searing the fantasy into my consciousness.

Lord, not him!

Great. How in blazes was I supposed to face him now? All I would see was . . .

Determined not to go there, I toweled my hair into damp

ringlets, slipped on a lightweight, shapeless summer shift, then grabbed my pillow and car keys.

The gravel on the driveway was brutal underneath my bare feet, but I managed to lock myself in my car without waking anybody. I turned on the ignition and the CD. *The Best of the Four Tops* filled the car along with blessedly cool air.

I crawled into the back seat with my pillow and settled down for exorcism by beach music and cold air. I must have dozed, because a thumping on the window brought me bolt aright, heart pounding, with the taste of sleep in my mouth. I looked out to find Aunt Glory in her robe, waving at me through the glass as if I were a toddler in a school play.

"Hey, sweetie. Can I come in?"

Dear Lord, I couldn't even get away from them in my car at three o'clock in the morning. But I couldn't very well tell her to go away. *Miz Scott is not receiving at the moment. Please call again later.*

Damn. I didn't have on any underpants.

"Just a minute." I reached between the driver's seat and door to hit the unlock button.

Aunt Glory hopped into the passenger seat and whipped the door shut behind her in record time. She took a deep breath of cool. "Aahhh. That feels *so* good." She leaned around, way too perky for this hour of the night. "You okay, sweetie?"

"Yeah," I lied. "Just hot. How 'bout you?" What was she *doing* there?

"Same." She inspected the interior. "Boy, you've got a lot of room in this thing. It's real comfortable, too."

"Mostly, it's paid for. I pray daily that it'll last another one hundred thousand miles."

"I hear you," she said with uncharacteristic informality. Careful of "the do," she eased back against the headrest and closed her eyes.

My Southern rearing kept me from asking her outright

why she'd come. Then it occurred to me that there was really nothing stopping me.

My family had never shared their true reasons for anything, and it had hurt us all. So I finally dared to ask the unaskable question. "What brings you out here, Aunt Glory?"

The world kept right on spinning. Aunt Glory wasn't even taken aback. She looked around, her eyes so much younger than the rest of her. "I don't want you tellin' Miss Mamie, now," she confided, " 'cause I'd rather die than seem ungrateful, but I was about to roast alive in there. Sometimes it seems like the walls are closin' in on me. I was sittin' out on the back porch when I heard you come down. At first, I didn't want to intrude. But I got so hot. . . ."

Why hadn't it occurred to me before that Aunt Glory had been just as accustomed to air-conditioning as I was? More, as a matter of fact; in summer, she'd kept their little house in Peachtree Hills frigid as a meat locker. "This weather must have been brutal for y'all."

"Not for Bedford. His blood's gotten so thin, his hands and feet are cold as a carp all the time. It's that Breedlove blood." She leaned her face into the stream of cool air from the dash vents. "But I don't mind tellin' you, I've had my problems adjustin' to things. You can't imagine how awful it feels to lose your home and your things and . . ." She gasped. "Oh, Lin. Of course you know how that feels. I'm so sorry, runnin' my mouth like that without even thinkin' how you—"

"Aunt Glory, do not waste one atom of energy feeling bad about what you said," I ordered sternly. "We're in the same boat when it comes to *stuff*, but I cannot conceive how you have survived this awful mess with Uncle Bedford. At least Phil is bothering some other woman now. You're stuck with a crazy man who isn't even your husband most of the time."

"No, he's not," she said emphatically, grateful that I understood. "I just wish my girls could understand that the way you do. Still . . . Just when I decide he's completely gone, there's a flicker"—*Hey, there, Little Girl. Where you been?*—"and I can't let go, because I see there's some of the old Bedford, no matter how little, trapped inside."

I wished I could wrap her in a great big hug, but all I could manage was a consoling squeeze of her upper arm. She placed her hand over mine and left it there for a long time.

I wondered if she had been as long without a man's comforting touch as I had, and if she missed it as much. Would it be worse to sleep beside the tormented shell of a man you'd once loved, or do without one entirely?

She sighed. "Change is hard at my age. I often wonder if I'll ever get used to things the way they are." Her voice quivered on the last, but she didn't give in to self-pity. "Just wait'll you're seventy-six like me," she said with forced levity. "You'll see."

"Aunt Glory, you look better than most of the sixty-year-olds I know, and you've got twice the ginger."

She waved off the compliment. "I feel like a hundred."

Little wonder. In her place, I'd probably have taken a bottle of pills long before this. "What have the doctors said about Uncle Bedford's prognosis?"

Head back, she closed her eyes again. "Hard to say with Alzheimer's. People in his condition can plateau and go on for years. Or they can nosedive and be gone in months. Nobody knows. They give you averages—three years—but we're already past that, and he's still strong as an ox."

No end in sight. No game plan. No hope.

How did she manage?

I plumped my pillow and used it to prop myself where I could see her better. "It must be so hard for you to look after Uncle Bedford day in and day out. Isn't there some way you could get some help?"

She shook her head. "Our Medicare supplemental insurance provided for in-home care, but he let it lapse just like the General did with his. By the time I realized he hadn't paid it, it was too late. That left VA. They couldn't keep him for more than a month, so they referred him to that nursing home. Moved him in the night when I wasn't even there." Anger and frustration seeped into her voice. "When I went to see him the next morning, I found him bare from the waist down, strapped into a chair in his own waste, wild as a snakebit cat."

She shuddered. "I had to take him out of there. I couldn't live with the image of him like that. You know his claustrophobia. It was hell for him. Hell. No matter what he'd done to us, nobody deserves that. I had to take him home."

"Oh, Aunt Glory. I'm so sorry." Our front-seat, backseat arrangement took on the feel of a confessional.

"The girls said we could come live with them," she went on, "but I couldn't do that, either. Buck was so wild from what they'd done to him in that place. Who knows what he might have done to those precious grandbabies? He's so strong. . . ." She rubbed her ribs, and I wondered what injury she'd been hiding. "Thank God Mamie asked us here. She said the General and Bedford might be good for each other. Bless her heart; your mother is a saint. A saint."

Right up there on her own cross beside you.

Not me. Not anymore. "How have you stood it for so long? Nine months, with no relief—I'd be crazier than he is by now."

She drew in a slow breath, then exhaled in a rush. "I can't tell you how many times I've wanted to get in my car and just keep on driving. Anywhere. Just call the girls, tell them he's theirs for a few weeks, and get away."

"Why haven't you?"

She curled around to face me. "Would you do that to David? Especially if he had children?" She shook her head. "No. I couldn't inflict him on them, even for a little while." She rolled back to stare unseeing into the night. "He's my burden to bear."

The CD shifted from the Four Tops to Otis Redding.

I've been loving yoooou . . . too looong, to stop now.

"It's not too late to do something, Aunt Glory." Lin, the Fixer, to the rescue, as usual. "Holly and Lucy Wright love you. I'm sure they could work something out so you could get away. Keep each other's kids while they took turns with Uncle Bedford." I leaned forward. "I have a friend with a condo in Destin she never uses. Sea breezes, white beaches, air-conditioning. I know she'd be delighted to let you stay there."

"That's so sweet, but no." She winced, venturing only a brief glance my way. "I'm not like you, Lin, all brave and self-sufficient. I've never been alone in my life. Goin' off by myself . . ."

Why wouldn't she at least consider it? As always when I met resistance, I pushed harder. "You'd be in good company. Trust me."

"It's a little late in the game to find out," she said with just a touch of wistfulness. "Even if I could get away, I wouldn't want to do it alone."

Stupidly, I continued to address her objections as if they were the real reasons she refused to allow herself to be helped. "Okay, then. So get somebody to go with you. One of your mah-jongg group."

I could sense her growing annoyance with my well-intentioned efforts. "No. No." A tense pause. "Better I just stay here. We've caused enough trouble."

"Aunt Glory, you haven't caused a lick of trouble to anybody in your life."

"Oh, yes, I did. I used to give Bedford the very devil. We had fights that make your parents' seem tame." That, I doubted. "Maybe this is my penance for bein' so hateful."

Another unaskable question came to me: What guilt kept her hanging on that martyr's cross?

My subconscious responded with its own snide query: What guilt had kept me married to Phil so long after I'd known the truth, deep down, but refused to face it?

People who live in glass houses . . .

I didn't confront Aunt Glory. Anyway, she was the last person on earth I would want to hurt, even with the truth.

She grasped the door handle. "This sure has felt good, sweetie, but I guess I'd better go back. God knows what Bedford might do if he wakes up wild, and I'm not there to calm him down."

I decided to risk bringing up the medication. "Has he waked up wild lately?"

She paused. "Come to think of it, no. Not for a week or so."

"You know why, don't you?"

She paused, weighing her response. Another sigh, then, "I think so."

"How long have you known?"

"Since that first day, when I couldn't find the pills." She fiddled with the sash of her robe. "I knew Buck hadn't gotten hold of them. They were too high for him to reach, and nothing else was disturbed. And Mamie said she hadn't seen them. Then you came home from work and asked to take him down to the Tote-A-Poke for a Nehi. It wasn't hard to figure out what you were up to, especially when you kept on taking him every evenin'."

"Did you mind? My giving him the pills . . ."

"No. I'm grateful," she confessed, her voice weary. "I don't know why I couldn't bring myself to do it. Maybe because he was so . . . *flat* when he took the medicine. I was afraid there would be no more of those precious glimpses." So she did love him. "I knew I should give him what the doctor prescribed, but he was a zombie. When I didn't give them to him, though, he got so wild. . . ."

Little wonder, with her randomly dosing and withholding. But now that I had had a glimpse of her side of things, I could no longer judge her. So little to ask, those tiny remnants of the man she had once loved. "Would you like to take over, now?"

"No." No hesitation there. "Please. It's better this way. And truth be told, he's not as zoned out as he was at first."

She turned to me with a soft smile. "You don't have to keep takin' him to the Tote-A-Poke, though."

I chuckled. "Well, maybe not every night, but I don't want to quit entirely. He seems to enjoy it, and so do I."

"I'm glad you came home, sweetie." She opened the door. "Sad for you, but awful glad for us."

"You come back any night I'm out here. *Mi frio es su frio.*"

"I have no idea what you just said, but I'm sure you mean it, precious." Granting me a tiny-toothed grin, she closed the car door and headed for the house.

Inmates though we might be, I felt a new closeness to my aunt. And my time in the Chrysler confessional had proven constructive. I hadn't thought about that pesky Grant Owens since Aunt Glory had waked me up.

My thermostat restored, I decided to go back into the house to try for a few hours' sleep.

Not having a man in my bed wasn't nearly so bad if the man I didn't have was anything like Phil—or what my mother and Aunt Glory had to put up with. Yawning, I resolved that the adult toy store would be, by far, my safest option.

The next morning my only penance was slightly gritty eyeballs when I got up early—six-thirty: alert the media—hoping to sneak downstairs before everyone else so I could have my bagel in peace. But by the time I got out of the shower, the smell of coffee had wafted up to my room along with the sounds of scraping chairs and muffled conversations from the kitchen below me.

I couldn't help wondering if I'd roused the household simply by stirring around. If so, there would be no solitary bagels until I moved into the garage apartment.

Funny, the things that get to you when your life blows up. I'd survived so much, yet after starting my weekdays alone at nine with my bagel for the past ten years, I suddenly grieved the loss of that simple, solitary ritual.

Move on, my new self exhorted. It's only temporary. You'll be in the garage apartment before too long.

I was in no mood to analyze either the changes or the jarring new necessities of my life. Doggedly, I focused only on getting ready for work.

Doing, I understood. Feeling, questioning, examining: all those things were far too dangerous for my fragile condition.

Don't think, do: that was what had gotten me through the past thirty years. It was also, I realized with a troubling tug of self-awareness, what had allowed me to slide deep, deep into trouble without ever knowing it.

Threatened by that insight, I reverted to form and concentrated on makeup. Then I donned black knit slacks, a cotton camisole, and a starched overshirt—my "decent" summer uniform. To my surprise, the pants were looser than I could remember their being in a long time. On that happy note, I braved the bosom of my family.

I walked into the kitchen to the bright glare of eastern sun reflected off the porch floor. The General and Tommy mumbled greetings from behind their sections of the paper at the table. As usual, my father had "Today's Business" and Tommy, the "Sports." Aunt Glory stopped scraping eggs off Uncle Bedford's terrycloth "apron" (bib) for a cheerful, "Hey, honey."

Uncle Bedford looked at me like I'd just popped naked out of a cake. "Where'd you come from, little girl?"

"A nice, cold shower," I replied, feeling crowded and more than a little resentful of their presence, which made no sense, since *I* was the one who had invaded their turf, not the other way around.

But having people around all the time was almost as frustrating as celibacy. BIG adjustment needed. My inner child wanted to sulk and rebel, but since I had not one drop of emotional energy to spare, I told myself I'd get used to it in time, just like I'd gotten used to hormonal blotchiness and vaginal dryness.

Miss Mamie got up from her funnies and headed for the stove. "I'll fix your eggs in a jiffy, sugar."

"Sit. Sit." I was fat enough. I made a mental note to pick up some V-8 at the store and start a diet tomorrow. If I ate the way they did every morning, my pants would be too tight in no time. "I'll just grab a blueberry bagel and a Diet Coke."

"That's no breakfast." My mother lit the burner, then slid Granny Beth's cast-iron skillet onto the blue flame. "Remember your protein. You're starting a new job. Nobody can do a decent day's work without protein in the morning. You need your strength, even though the job is only temporary and far beneath you."

"It's not beneath her," my father declared. "Honest work is not beneath anybody. At least she'll be contributin' to the household." He cast a baleful eye at my brother. "Which is more'n I can say for some people."

I cringed for Tommy. *Everything changes, but everything stays the same.*

"There's more than money in this world, old man," Miss Mamie shot back in defense of her only begotten son. "Tommy has helped us out since the day he came here—"

"I appreciate it, Mama, but I don't need you taking up for me," Tommy said from behind the Sports. "I'm a grown man. I can take care of myself."

The General flapped the business section for emphasis. "Not the way I see it."

"Your eggs, Lin?" my mother deflected. "Scrambled soft, like you like them?"

I considered laughing, but thought better of it. "No eggs. Please."

"Let her eat what she wants, Mamie," Daddy bellowed through the newsprint. "She's not in any danger of starvin'."

The blunt reference to my weight stung. I'd forgotten

how thick-skinned a person had to be to live with the General. Smarting, I tried to ignore the sympathetic look Aunt Glory shot me.

My mother had never spoken up for herself at his constant criticism of her weight, but when he went for me, the lioness took over. "General!" she snapped, "No gentleman ever makes reference to a lady's age or her weight. Apologize immediately."

Oh, no. Not the "apologize immediately" counterattack. This could end up escalating to stony silence between them for a month.

This time, I did laugh, but it was too late. Neither of them paid any attention.

Tommy slapped down his paper abruptly and stood, eyes averted, wearing the same grim expression he'd had as a teenager when the General had started in on him. "I'm outta here." He headed for the door. "Johnny Mac needs some help with that remodel he's doin'." He snagged his green John Deere cap from the pegs by the door. "Don't wait supper for me." The screen slammed in his wake.

"Make sure he pays you!" the General hollered after him.

Part of me was grateful my brother had shifted the focus off of me, but the rest of me judged my father for picking on Tommy, and Tommy because, even after all these years, he still let the General get away with such bad behavior unchallenged.

The brief, awkward lull that followed was sharp with all the poisonous truths nobody ever talked about inside these walls.

As usual, it was my mother who felt compelled to smooth the moment over with bright denial. "So," she said, regarding me with an expectant smile. "What'll it be? Over easy or scrambled?"

"Neither." If I was going to survive here until I could escape to the apartment, boundaries must be drawn. "All I want is a bagel and a drink. Really." I opened the refrigerator in search of a Diet Coke.

Damn. Not so much as a single soda, not even the wretched store-brand the Mame insisted on buying. I got a go-cup from the cabinet, popped a plastic tray of ice into it, then filled it with artificially sweetened tea.

"Awk!" Uncle Bedford abruptly scooted his chair away from the table. "Get the Windex, boy! He's back."

"He?" I whispered to Miss Mamie.

She turned her head so Uncle Bedford couldn't see her lips. "A two-foot tall little black man with no arms who hides under tables so he can bite your uncle's kneecaps."

As with the phantom Japanese, I couldn't help finding Uncle Bedford's hallucinations morbidly entertaining. They certainly were creative. And deliciously ironic, considering his racism.

Aunt Glory let out a benighted sigh as she reached over to the counter for the Windex sitting at the ready—for just this purpose, I supposed. Then she lifted the plastic tablecloth and bent low to fire off a few ammonia-laden puffs underneath. "There," she announced as she straightened aright. "Now finish your breakfast, Bedford. He's gone."

Uncle Bedford bristled, pointing under the table. "Don't try to trick me! He's still there, hiding behind the post. You never spray behind the post."

She exhaled sharply, then half-shouted to my father. "Watch your feet, General. The cannibal's on the loose again."

Still poring over his paper, the General swung his feet aside without comment, the same way he had for sixty years of my mother's sweep-ups.

Aunt Glory dutifully squirted away behind the post, muttering, "Why does it have to be Windex? If he'd let me use deodorizer, at least it would make the room smell better." She flipped back up, catching a curl of her sacred "do" on the edge of the tablecloth and sending it awry. "Now," she snapped at Uncle Bedford, "Are you satisfied?"

"Tryin' to trick me," he grumbled as he warily skooched his chair back toward the table. He glared in my direction. "That boy is always stealin' my things and tryin' to trick me."

Guided by that inexplicable ESP old women have about their "do's," Aunt Glory patted her hair back into place. "So, Mamie," she said, her tone brisk. "You still want me to make that giant éclair for WMU, or should we do Mrs. Orr's dump cake?"

Miss Mamie shook her head. "Dump cake's too heavy for this weather. They always love the éclair, anyway. Do we have enough graham crackers?"

Watching them, I realized that there were times when denial made sense.

And running away.

While things were relatively quiet, I decided to try Tommy's methods and escape for a stroll. I grabbed my tea, bagel, and purse, then headed for the door myself. "I'm off for a walk before work. See y'all tonight."

"Good idea," the General declared from behind his paper. "You could use some exercise. Might work off a few of those extra pounds you're carryin'."

Apparently I had already started getting my emotional armor out of mothballs, because this attack didn't hurt nearly as much as the first. Not that I relished the prospect of my father's fixating on my weight.

"Good lord, Thomas," Miss Mamie shot back, "give it a rest. Lin's got enough on her plate without you harpin' about a few extra pounds. She's just"—I winced, knowing what she was going to say before the words that had been the bane of my childhood were out of her mouth—"pleasingly plump."

Aaaargh! I laughed, but it came out rather spooky.

Oblivious, my mother turned to me with an expectant smile. "Aren't you coming home for lunch?"

The dreaded mommy-net tightened.

"No," I answered, a tad too emphatic. "See you tonight

at sevenish." Only when I was walking out, purse in hand, did I realize I'd probably just cut off my nose to spite my face. I had no lunch money, and only a bagel between me and seven o'clock.

Dumb, dumb, dumb. But I was too proud to retract. And as the General had pointed out, I could afford to skip a few meals.

Don't beat yourself up, my new self counseled. Take the lesson and move on.

So I moved on—down the driveway to the sidewalk. Halfway down, I remembered the Garden Club. Drat.

I considered going back for the directory, but decided that Franklin Harris's wildflowers could probably survive another day without water better than I could survive the risk of searching for that directory and encountering my mother.

Maybe I could still do some calling from the store. Geneva would have the numbers. I continued on my pleasantly solitary way toward the square.

When I reached the end of the driveway, though, I discovered to my chagrin that I wasn't alone. Grant Owens— looking all golden, godlike, and resolute—strode in my direction from the cul-de-sac.

Perfect. Just what I needed.

I felt my heartbeat in my ears and actually considered returning to the house so he would get ahead of me. By now the old me would have been halfway back up the driveway, behind a bush, to avoid facing him. But the new me had no intention of giving ground, regardless of my lingering embarrassment about last night. The sidewalk was as much mine as it was his, and I refused to be intimidated.

What was he doing out so early, anyway? Geneva had said he didn't come in until nine on the days she opened.

Head high, I set out at a brisk pace toward the park on the square, where I planned to eat my bagel and drink my tea. Alone.

Grant's footsteps approached from behind, swift and

solid. Obviously, he meant to catch up with me. Another unwelcome intrusion.

I supposed I'd have to be polite; he was my boss.

I prepared myself for a pleasant, noncommittal greeting. He was close now, moving up fast. Then he breezed right past with a curt, "hi," and a wave.

Irrationally, his brush-off annoyed me twice as much as his presence had.

He moved beyond me with the long, decisive strides of a power walker.

Great. The man was simply taking his exercise. But there I'd been, thinking his presence had something to do with me.

That was the worst part of what the past two years had done. They had left me incapable of relating to the world beyond my own skin.

Totally self-absorbed. Disgusting.

I'd never wanted to be that kind of person. Couldn't remember exactly why and when I had become so. I did know, though, that I was soul-sick of only being about what Phil had done to me. But how could I change it? There had to be a way.

Whenever you think somebody ought to do something, Granny Bess prodded, *God's lettin' you know you've just been appointed.*

I'd said somebody ought to do something twice the day before when I'd found out about Franklin's dying wild-flower garden, and when Geneva had told me about Fred Waller and the mayor.

If I *had* been appointed, I could begin by helping Franklin with an immediate solution, then working to clean up city hall without getting anybody killed.

I knew when the idea hit me that it was right and solid. It felt good. Really good.

Like it or not, I cared what happened, not just for my own sake, but for Franklin's and my parents' and all the other people who still got the short end of the stick in

Mimosa Branch. Getting involved was as good a start as any toward escaping the prison of my self-obsession.

For now, my practical self nudged, *just go to the park and eat your bagel and drink your tea. Then work. Then call the Garden Club and talk Tommy into helping you help Franklin Harris.*

Very good, indeed.

Chapter 8

Forty minutes later, I stood under the drugstore's aluminum awning with the first wave of the Coffee Club while Geneva unlocked the door. Once inside, the men headed straight for the same stools they'd claimed since joining their morning get-together. Death might leave a seat empty for a time, but retirement soon filled it.

"Why don't you make the coffee, Lin?" Geneva suggested. "Only one pot of decaf, the rest high-test." She reached out to me. "Here. Hand me your purse. I'll put it with mine." She stowed them under the counter in the pharmacy, safely beyond reach of the Dutch door.

Making the coffee would be a cinch, but the row of personalized mugs gave me pause. "How do I know whose cup is whose?" I whispered after her.

"Boys," she called over the closed bottom half of the pharmacy door, "y'all help Lin out. Tell her your names so she can begin to learn 'em all."

"Geneva," I wheezed, "*I* could have done that, but I didn't want to start off hurting their feelings."

She let loose her infectious chuckle. "Any you boys offended that Lin cain't keep your names straight after thirty years?"

"Shoot, no," an old man in a battered rainhat said, his broad smile counteracting the crooked yellow teeth it exposed. "On a good day, half of us cain't even remember our own names, much less ever'body else's."

Good-natured laughter followed, and I relaxed a bit, reminding myself that I didn't have to master everything in a day. There was time—to get my bearings, and to find my place in the town I'd been so anxious to leave three decades ago.

Home. I'd actually been forced to move back home. This was *real,* and way too familiar for comfort. And here I was in the same job I'd had at sixteen—talk about starting over.

I stuffed down yet another a shard of panic. I mean, what good was it to panic about my circumstances? I couldn't change them. Not yet, anyway.

Just do the next right thing, I told myself, and then the next.

I poured the last pot of water into the coffeemakers, then picked up the ticket book to take orders for toast—our only food offering besides yesterday's self-serve Dunkin' Donuts under their glass dome.

"So," I said with a brightness I did not feel, pen poised. As I recalled, the Coffee Club had a strict policy of first-come-first-served. Who had sat down first? I decided asking would be safest. "Anybody want toast?"

Four hands went up.

No help. "Okay, then. Tell me who gets to order first?"

Three of the hands curled to point at the man in the rainhat, who dutifully kept his aloft until I stood before him. "Walter Lott, here," he said, then without pause or segue, launched into, "So, how's your real-estate course goin'?" The question was clearly rhetorical; he didn't wait for a response. "My niece Betty is in your class. She said you took lots of notes all the time. Asked lots of questions."

A stab of annoyance hit home as if the past thirty years had never happened. All of a sudden, I was nineteen again and resentful that my personal affairs somehow qualified as other people's entertainment. But I managed to keep my cool—outwardly, at least. "Betty? I'll have to look her up."

"Maybe y'all could study together for the exam," he said cheerfully. "You takin' all them notes and all. Betty said you seemed real smart."

It's only temporary. As soon as you're on your feet financially, you're out of here. "You want that toast light or dark, wet or dry?" I managed, acutely aware that my ears were burning, which meant they were bright red by now.

"Medium, with lots of butter."

By the time I got everyone coffeed up and well toasted, it was almost nine o'clock. The bell tinkled at the front of the store, and all eyes turned to see none other than the Church of God minister cruise in with the flamboyant assurance of a brand-new rock star. What had Geneva called him? Something odd.

"Now we'll get the lowdown on Fred," Ottis Wilburne said with relish.

"Hey, Vollie," another of the regulars called. "Seen Fred lately?"

Everyone but the minister laughed. He shook his head gravely. "This is nothin' to joke about, Rex. There's barely a week left to qualify for the race. The Good Lord knows we need somebody decent in that seat, a man of conscience. Who're we gonna get to sign up on such short notice?" He scanned the crowd. "Any of you willin' to take on Tommy and the mayor?"

"Nobody in his right mind," another of the regulars piped up. "What good would it do, anyway? They'd be outvoted two-to-one, just like Fred."

The solution seemed simple to me. "Why doesn't somebody run against the mayor, then?" I suggested. "Break the deadlock?"

Geneva rolled her eyes and retreated into the apothecary. "Oh, Lord. Here we go."

The front bell tinkled again, but nobody paid any notice. They were all too busy looking at me with expressions that ranged from pity to scorn. You'd have thought I'd just suggested somebody climb the water tower butt naked and jump off.

Being a minister, Vollie Biffle took it upon himself to set me straight. He hitched up the belt that clung tenuously beneath his substantial gut, reminding me of all those big-bellied men on *America's Funniest Home Videos* who lose their britches if they so much as take a deep breath. "The last feller who ran against the mayor was without water, then electricity, then gas, off and on, for a year," he explained in his best preacher voice. "The city dug up his street and blocked his driveway for more than six months. Had to park way down at the bottom of the hill and walk up, rain or shine. Big, nasty ditch. Mud everywhere.

"Then they reassessed his property taxes and doubled his bill. When he tried to fight it, they gave him such a runaround, his blood pressure went through the ceiling. He finally gave up and moved to Oakwood."

A murmur of confirmation rumbled through the men.

After a dramatic pause, Preacher Biffle leaned closer to me, intent. "You bein' just moved back here, you cain't run for mayor"—a few ill-concealed whispers of "not no woman, anyhow" reached my ears—"but say you could. . . . What do you think would happen to your parents, them tryin' to keep up that big ole house and look after Dr. B?" He plunked himself down onto an empty stool. "When was the last time that place was reassessed?" More murmurs. "I'm guessin' the forties. How'd you like to see their tax bill if it was figured off a *real* fair market value? And their utilities . . . would you want to risk leavin' them with no heat or water?"

Since I'm constitutionally incapable of backing down, I argued, "Well, surely there's *somebody* in this town brave enough to take on the mayor."

"Yep. There is," a strong male voice asserted from the aisle. I, along with all the others, looked back to see a short, homely man whose plain white golf shirt showed off his bodybuilder's torso while exposing muscular arms bright with Harley tattoos and cruder prison efforts. But there was a light in his expression that overrode the deep creases and pits on his face.

"Hey, there, Donnie," the preacher exclaimed with a smile contradicted by his eyes.

Everyone stilled. I had the distinct sense that a new dog had just entered Preacher Biffle's backyard.

"I was just askin' myself," Preacher Biffle said in a patronizing tone, "what's ole Donnie up to these days?"

"Same as you, Vollie," the newcomer responded with a genuine twinkle in his eye and a hearty handshake. "Bringin' the Good News and feedin' His sheep."

Preacher Biffle let out a deprecating chuckle. "Well, now, I cain't say as we do it the same, Donnie, but each must serve as he is called."

"Amen, brother preacher," Donnie replied without offense.

This guy, a minister? I had to admit, he had the charisma for it, but he looked more like a Hell's Angel. His hands and forearms were scarred like those of a serious scrapper yet, with the notable exception of his fellow minister, the men responded to him with warmth and respect.

"What was that, Donnie," Ottis Wilburne asked, "about somebody takin' on the mayor?"

Before he could reply, Geneva's voice interrupted from the pharmacy. "Yike! It's past nine o'clock. Turn the radio up, Lin. Quick."

I leapt to the ancient plastic radio on the shelf over the microwave and dutifully turned the volume up until the local 500-watt station dissolved into fuzzy incoherence. Then I backed the volume down just enough to understand the final lines of the ad for Duncan's Superette.

Everyone fell silent, poised, as smarmy organ music filed the store. After a lengthy organ interlude, a somber *basso profundo* intoned, "Welcome to *In Memoriam*, sponsored by Trapp's Funeral Home, the funeral home with a heart. We care for your loved ones as if they were our very own. Plenty of lighted parking for the ladies. Drop by our blue parlor for a look at the new curio cabinet and our display of priceless porcelain mourning doves."

In Memoriam! I couldn't believe they were still doing it. Or that they were advertising their new curio cabinet.

More music, then the deep male voice announced, "There have been no deaths in the Mimosa Branch area in the past twenty-four hours."

Conversations resumed with a vengeance over the regular announcer's lead-in for "The Birthday Break."

Uncle Delton tried to shush everybody. "Hush up, y'all. Today's me and Montine's forty-sixth, and Cathy's gonna call it in. I don't want to miss it."

But Ottis overrode him. "Hey, Donnie," he shouted over the din, "what was that about somebody runnin' against the mayor? Who'd be fool enough to do a thing like that?"

Donnie quirked a rueful little half-smile. "I would."

To a man, every soul at that soda fountain went silent on a shocked inhale.

"This is Cathy Davis," the radio interjected. "I just want to wish a happy forty-sixth anniversary to my mama and daddy, Montine and Delton Pirkle, from their four children, eleven grandchildren, and six great-grands. We love y'all. And everybody out there is invited to help us celebrate this Sunday afternoon at two o'clock in the West Mimosa Branch Baptist Fellowship Hall. No gifts, please."

After a heartbeat's pause, the delayed reaction to Donnie's announcement exploded.

I watched with interest as Donnie calmed the furor following his announcement, reminded of Edward James Olmos in that movie about helping troubled kids. Donnie had charisma in abundance, but he didn't seem like a manipulator. The impression I got was of a straight-shooter. From the looks of him, if anybody had the guts to take on the mayor, he probably did. I eased over to the Dutch door. "Geneva," I whispered askance. "You know anything about this guy?"

"Lots." She leaned in close. "He's the best, even if he is Holiness"—a necessary disclaimer, considering her conservative Methodist convictions—"Mind you, I don't hold with their fallin' from grace nonsense—bouncin' in and out of salvation like it was some kinda trampoline, but aside from that, I have nothin' but the highest praise for the man."

She nodded toward him in approval, her tone confidential. "He's from here, probably ten years behind you in school. Always in trouble, dropped out at sixteen. Used to be hell on a Harley, literally—drugs, booze, theft, brawls, jail—but fifteen years ago he came home for his mother's birthday and ended up in a Holiness tent revival. Says the fire of heaven fell on him, purged him of his addictions, and called him to bring others out of darkness. And he's been doin' just that ever since, straight and honest. Tough as nails when he needs to be, but gentle with kids and old people. These past ten years he's done wonders with that little church near the trailer park over past the mill village, reachin' out to people everybody else would rather ignore or lock away. His congregation just loves him. Even Ardell Watson, and you how hard *she* is to please."

This looked promising, but my sourpuss Puritan had to ask, "Could the mayor use his past against him?"

Geneva dismissed the question with a wave. "Couldn't come up with anything Donnie hasn't already told on himself. He makes no secret of what he came from; it's one of his most powerful persuaders."

Very promising. For the first time in recent memory, I felt the inklings of wholesome excitement. "What about the rest of the town? How do they feel about him?"

"Almost everybody respects him," Geneva responded without hesitation. "The only people who don't like him don't like anybody. Even the mayor's been outwardly supportive, though there's no love lost between 'em. Donnie's always been too outspoken. Still, that little church has gone a long way toward cleaning up drugs and abuse in the trailer park—in the mill village, too. Word is, even the drug pushers leave Donnie alone. I've got a suspicion that some of his converts wouldn't be above some get-to-glory righteous retribution if anybody tried to hurt Donnie or his family, which is just as well. We're talking about some rough folks."

"Fascinating." I watched the animation with which Donnie circulated among the Coffee Club, making each man feel special and important. Preacher Biffle, determined not to be outshone, raised the decibel level of his forced jollity, but even so, Donnie's quiet charisma dominated the room. "Kind of like our own little Father Teresa."

"Well, I wouldn't say that, exactly," Geneva countered. "Come to think of it, though, Donnie's probably the only man in Mimosa Branch who *could* beat the mayor and get away with it."

Elegant. Elegant, elegant, elegant.

An ex-hoodlum with God in his corner and a goon squad already in place to protect his family. Not only was he tough enough to take on the mayor, but he'd already told all his own sordid secrets from the pulpit.

"You know what, Geneva? I think this could work. Then all we'd need would be somebody decent to win Fred Waller's seat, and we'd be set. No more dirty politics in Mimosa Branch."

I really was getting excited, and it felt great.

"I'd love to see it." She patted my arm in dismissal. "But right this second, I've gotta finish the mornin' orders on the computer."

I sat on the swivel chair behind the register, with one eye on the storefront and the other on the Coffee Club.

"Donnie West," Fred Martin piped up over the others, "Have you lost your mind? Don't you remember what they did to Joe Ellis for runnin' against Gary Mayfield?"

Donnie laughed. "I'm not poor old Joe Ellis. I'm a take-no-prisoners, full-gospel preacher who's been to hell and back, saved by Jesus Christ and anointed with fire by the

Holy Ghost!" He spoke it with the cadence of his preaching. "I'm not scared of the devil, so I'm sure as Sunday not scared of old Ham Stubbs! But I *am* sick of the corruption in this town." He prowled the linoleum behind the stools, drawing everyone's eyes with him. "I kept thinkin' somebody ought to do something about it. Then I remembered one of my sermons where I said that if you think God oughta tell somebody to do something, maybe He already has!" Bingo! "So I prayed about it, and sure enough, looks like He wants me to do this thing."

His manner would have turned me off completely on the Big Hair channel, but in person, his unvarnished intensity was mesmerizing.

"He didn't promise me I was gonna win, though, so I figured I'll have to put my back to it, then trust Him for the outcome. Win or lose, it's what I'm called to do."

"You're not worried what'll happen if you lose?" Ottis Wilburne asked in awe.

Donnie sobered. "God doesn't punish his children for being obedient, so I fear no man as long as I am doin' the Lord's will. And anyway, my kids are grown and gone, so nobody can get at me by threatenin' them."

The reference to how Gary Mayfield had become the mayor's toady sent a crackle of tension through the gathering. Ten years before, Gary had been elected on a "Clean Up City Hall" platform. Right off the bat, he'd cost the mayor and incumbent councilman over thirty thousand apiece by exposing expense-account irregularities. Miss Mamie had sent me all the clippings. But before Gary could accomplish any more reforms, his family started receiving threatening notes and phone calls. Then one morning he went to wake his four-year-old daughter and found a note pinned to her nightgown that read, "This time, just a warning." Miss Mamie had reported that, too, in ominous whispers on the phone, since it never made the papers.

After that, the reform candidate had climbed in bed with the mayor and prospered with ill-gotten gains ever since.

Now Donnie, a man with a mission, pushed up the sleeves of his white golf shirt to expose the worldly markings on his skin. "Anyway, it's about time we had a candidate who's got a little color to him."

General laughter broke the tension.

Donnie raised his hands to quiet them. "But to ease your mind, I doubt the city will mess with my utilities if I lose. It's one thing to harass a private citizen like Joe Ellis, but it's another to abuse a pastorium owned by 347 decent, votin' Holiness citizens."

Applause erupted along with more laughter.

Geneva came up beside me, a gleam in her eye. "By golly, I think he just might have a chance." She ducked back into the pharmacy, then returned with a twenty-dollar bill and an empty basket. Waving both in the air, she announced, "Okay, Donnie! Let me be the first to contribute to your campaign!" She dropped the bill into the basket, then handed it to Uncle Delton with a pointed, "The first of many."

Now, getting so much as an extra quarter out of the Coffee Club constituted a Red Sea miracle, but lo and behold, the old men actually dredged up some folding money as the basket made its way down the stools. I even saw a five go in! But before it reached Vollie Biffle, he beat a hasty retreat to the sun-baked sidewalk.

"Who you gonna get to be your campaign manager?" Geneva asked Donnie.

"Campaign manager?" He shook his head, smiling. "Nothin' that fancy for me. I was just figurin' Lacey and I would make a few posters. Some of my congregation have offered to help put 'em up."

"You need real posters, Donnie," Geneva argued. "Plastic ones people can stick in their yards, rain or shine."

"I doubt many folks would want to risk that."

"I'd take one," Fred Martin volunteered.

"Me, too," Uncle Delton braved.

"Not me," Geneva said, effectively bringing conversation to a halt. "I live in the county, so it'd be a waste of a good sign." Chuckles broke out. "But I will volunteer to be your campaign manager. Unless you think of somebody else you'd rather have."

"Geneva," Donnie responded with a smile, "I cain't think of anybody I'd rather have runnin' my campaign, even if you are a Methodist."

"Well, you know what they say," she shot back, sassy. "Politics makes strange bedfellows. I reckon I might be able to drum up a few Baptists and Presbyterians, even."

"I'd be glad to help with whatever I can," I volunteered, wondering how I could convince my mother to let Donnie speak to both her Baptist and Methodist circles.

By the time *The Swap Shop* came over the airwaves at nine-thirty, Geneva was already making up a list of people to call, and Donnie was deep in conversation with the men about their civic concerns.

The bell over the door announced Grant's arrival. "Sorry I'm late, Geneva." Mail in hand, he strode toward us, sorting as he went. "I don't believe it," he mumbled, ripping open a small envelope. "We actually got a check from the Carters." Only then did he look up and notice the charged atmosphere at the soda fountain. Tucking the mail under his arm, he turned to me. "What's up?"

"Donnie's going to run for mayor." I didn't realize I was smiling until he smiled back.

"Well, I'll be damned. It's about time somebody did something about that crooked snake-oil salesman who runs this town." He glowered. "I went to talk to that sleazebag this morning about the water problems in Harris's neighborhood, and I felt like I'd been slimed. The unctuous bastard kept agreeing with me, but wouldn't promise anything. How do people around here stand it?"

"I'm told you can get used to anything. Maybe they're just used to him. The devil you know . . ."

"Well, Donnie's no devil." Grant glanced over with admiration. "His ministry has helped more people than you know kick their addictions. Quite a few of them prescription junkies. He's got my vote."

"I'm glad to hear you say that," Geneva interjected. "Because we need donations and volunteers."

"We?" Grant asked.

"Geneva's Donnie's campaign manager," I, for some reason, felt compelled to explain. "And I'm a volunteer."

"So fork over some green, mister," Geneva demanded of her employer. "And I'll be expecting you next Tuesday night at the first campaign meeting. Eight-thirty, sharp."

"And where will that be?"

"Here," she said without turning a hair. The large storeroom downstairs opened onto a wide service alley where people could park. "We'll have plenty of room downstairs once Lin and I get the place sorted out and cleaned up." Eyebrows lifted, she shot Grant a hopeful smile. "You've been wantin' the place cleared out. How 'bout it?"

Grant regarded her with the same wry resignation Adam must have felt when Eve said, "Here, you gotta try this."

After only a moment's consideration, he relented. "Sure. Why not?" He pulled out his wallet and extracted a fifty. "For the cause."

What was it with men and big bills?

But he'd ponied up without a flinch. Despite my resolution to the contrary, I couldn't help thinking that maybe my boss was a pretty good egg, after all.

Fatal mistake. Fatal, fatal, fatal.

The store was busy all day, so I never got time to call anybody in the Garden Club about my idea for helping Franklin. As soon as I got home, though, I asked the Mame for her directory and got a pleasant surprise when I explained that I wanted to round up as many hoses as we could and string them together to get water to Franklin's garden right away. Mame not only endorsed the idea, she also commandeered the phone and did the calling for me.

By eight-thirty, there were nineteen garden hoses waiting for us at Eva Beard's garden spigot on the next hill over from Franklin's. A longtime admirer of Franklin's achievement, Eva was thrilled to supply the water.

It wasn't a lasting solution to the problem, but at least the flowers would survive. Miss Mamie informed me proudly that every one of those she'd enlisted to help us had urged me to join the Garden Club as soon as an opening was available.

God forbid. I managed a glazed smile and noncommittal noises, then escaped to my mission.

A quarter mile of steep, wooded ravine separated Eva's from Franklin's, the haves from the have-nots, so Tommy and I set out together, weighted down with hoses. It was the first time in decades we'd been alone together, but we didn't talk, not about anything that mattered. So many disappointments and judgments hung between us, I wondered if we'd ever be able to bridge them. Still, it felt good to be working together toward a common cause. Just as twilight faded to darkness, we emerged—bug-bitten, hot, and worn out, but with plenty of hose to spare—to Franklin's hearty welcome.

A call to Eva produced what seemed like an eternity of popping and gurgling before several explosive bursts were followed by a strong, steady stream from Franklin's sprinkler.

We celebrated together, and I felt closer to Tommy than I had since our childhood. Buoyed by our accomplishment, Franklin drove us back to Tommy's truck.

On the way home, I ventured, "Thanks for helping out, Brud-o. Couldn't have managed without you."

Tommy glanced over with a brief, cynical smile. "I know you think I'm a failure, Sissie-ma-noo-noo, but I do know my way around a woods."

"I never said you were a failure!" I defended, my chest all peppery from the impact of his blunt statement.

"You didn't have to." His tone was even. "But you made

it clear." He tightened his grip on the wheel, his eyes on the road. "I've often wondered what it was that turned you against me instead of for me. I was kind of hoping that by this time in our lives, we could accept each other as we are."

Me? It was Tommy who'd screwed up his life like some trash on *The Jerry Springer Show*! I was the one who'd overlooked it all, kept the bridges open in spite of his short-comings. Wounded, I opened my mouth to launch into a full-scale justification, but I snapped it shut when I realized I was too upset to come across as anything but a self-righteous martyr. It never occurred to me at the time that I might actually *be* a self-righteous martyr. And a judgmental one, at that.

I had wanted us to talk about things that mattered, not be attacked!

Can we say *controlling* and *denial*?

I took several leveling breaths before uttering a snide, "Gee, thanks, Tommy. And just when I was feeling so great about us helping Franklin."

He frowned in consternation, then retreated into sullen silence.

It was contagious.

Miss Mamie and Aunt Glory were waiting for us when we got home, primed to hear all the details, but Tommy weaseled around back to the kitchen, leaving me to deflect their enthusiastic questions with pleas of grime and fatigue. "Tomorrow. I promise, I'll fill you in at breakfast. Right now, I'm worn slap out, and I need a bath."

I sulked in a cold tub for an hour before going to bed. And "God bless Tommy" was *not* included in my prayers.

Chapter 9

The next Tuesday night, forty-seven people showed up for the first meeting of the "Elect Donnie West" committee. Watching people come in from the back alley gave me a subtle speakeasy kind of thrill. Geneva and I had only set out seats for twenty, but as the bright blue plastic chairs filled and people continued to come in, we'd deputized a few able-bodied members of Donnie's congregation to put out more.

"Grant's been complainin' about those chairs bein' in the way ever since he took over the store," she confided. "His daddy bought a hundred of 'em back in '88 when the missionary Baptist church finally got up enough money to put in real pews." She surveyed the impressive crowd. There must have been forty people there. "Next time, we'll need every one of those chairs. Mark my words." I could see the wheels turning in her head. "I *told* Grant they'd come in handy one day."

"Speaking of Grant," I said, "did he ever say anything about coming tonight?"

The corners of Geneva's mouth tightened down. "I asked him three times." She exhaled sharply. "But he just smiled and never did answer me. He does it all the time, just to torture me."

Men.

I would have said, "If he can't take a joke, fuck 'im," but out of respect for her gentle sensibilities, I confined myself to, "Oh well. At least he let us have it here. And I must say, the place cleaned up better than I ever thought it would."

The two of us had taken turns coming down during lulls to sweep, dust, and sort through the piles of old inventory to make room for the meeting. Now the beamed ceiling, brick walls, and scarred oak floors were without dirt and cobwebs for the first time in a long time, giving the dusky semi-basement a trendy sort of subterranean loft look.

I glanced at my watch. Eight-thirty on the nose. "It's time. Shouldn't we start?"

Geneva waved me off. "Not just yet. You always need to allow at least ten minutes leeway for things like this."

In my book, you started meetings when you were supposed to, especially volunteer functions. If you said eight-thirty, you started at eight-thirty. Otherwise, everybody would get the message that it was okay to be late, and there would never be any real discipline. But this was Geneva's show, so I kept my opinions to myself.

As a few stragglers entered from the door beside the loading dock, Donnie approached Geneva with a smile. He nodded to the last two who had come in. "Countin' them, that makes forty-seven by my count. Forty-seven. The Good Lord has blessed, indeed."

"Amen." Geneva beamed. "Why don't you go on up to your place at the front? I'll be there in a minute, and we'll get this show on the road."

Basement though it might be, the atmosphere in that old place was anything but stale. It vibrated with the hopeful vigor of people long harassed and willing to work for change, sharpened by a palpable tension between the gathered factions.

An odd mix of people they were. Most of the Coffee Club had arrived early so they could nab front-row seats. Behind them on one end sat a cheerful bank of young teachers who'd loaned us a portable microphone from their county school. Franklin Harris, my old school friend Jacey, and several black people I recognized from the drugstore completed the second row. The center section had quickly filled with the arrival of a large blue-collar contingent from Donnie's church, who now whispered among themselves, maybe about Franklin and his friends.

Along the left side sat a smattering of men in jeans and workboots, with about twice as many scrawny, hard-looking women who were old before their time—probably from the mobile-home park that was Donnie's mission field. Opposite them along the right side, a dozen bluehairs from the Garden Club and both Miss Mamie's church circles claimed a substantial block of seats.

Top and bottom of Mimosa Branch's social strata eyed each other with equal suspicion across the gang of Holiness in the middle.

At the rear, a vocal collection of tattooed biker types joked with some morbid-looking teenagers sporting weird hair and piercings that made me wince. Rounding out the crowd was a cluster of bearded, mountain-man-looking artists in overalls, accompanied by their female counterparts decked out in clogs and flamboyant New Age jewelry to complement their artistically baggy summer dresses.

In a rare flash of insight, I realized I was looking at a microcosm of Mimosa Branch society who had unconsciously sorted themselves according to stereotype: left, right, staunch blue-collar middle, and fringe. Except for the Coffee Club, of course, whose deafness, not their social status, had forced them front and center.

Geneva looked past me and her face lit up. "Well, look who's here! Why didn't you tell me your parents were coming?" She waved enthusiastically. "Idn't this great? Just like old times."

Sure enough, there they came, struggling up the stairs by the loading dock. A jolt of adrenaline sizzled through me, like when you look up and realize you've gone into the men's room instead of the ladies', and you're paralyzed with shock just long enough for the men at the urinals to glance over their shoulders in amusement at your horrified self.

The Mame alone, I could have handled. But my father . . . he'd embarrassed her in public bad enough when he was *sane*. Why in blue blazes would she risk bringing him here in his condition?

"She said she wasn't coming," I hissed out, grabbing Geneva's arm harder than I intended. "What in pluperfect perdition possessed her to bring *him*?"

Geneva pried loose my fingers, then gave my hand a consoling pat. "Don't worry, sugar. Donnie's handled worse'n your feisty ole daddy without battin' an eyelash. And if he cain't, there's always those biker boys of his. I don't think even the General could scare them."

"Great. Just what we need to get off on the right foot, here. A rumble at our first meeting with my father in the middle of it."

"Oooh." Her face glowed with mischief. "Wouldn't that be *exciting*?"

My parents advanced, giving every appearance of being their old selves as the Mame spotted her friends on the right and headed that way.

My first instinct was to make some excuse and leave, but duty and good manners compelled me to go over and greet them. I said a desperate prayer that my father would behave himself. Yet I had to concede that he had a right to be there. He hadn't been certified—yet—so he was still a voter.

"Hey, there, daughter," he bellowed as I approached. "Mamie tells me we've got somebody willin' to run against that skunk of a mayor." He shot my mother a brief, poisonous look. "She tried to make me stay home, but I'd have none of that. I want to meet this fella, take his measure. Hear what he has to say."

"So you will," I said with a forced smile. "Let me get y'all a seat up close, so you can hear."

Donnie was already adding two more chairs to the front row on the Garden Club side.

"Get us a seat up front," the General thundered, "so I can hear."

Donnie met us halfway, his hand extended to my father. "I'm honored to see you here tonight, sir." He nodded to my mother. "Miz Breedlove." When the General took his hand, I noted with approval that Donnie's grip was firm, but careful of my father's aged bones. It was the General who clamped down like a vise, one of his favorite tricks with "snot-nosed kids" (anybody under sixty).

Donnie's half-coughed, half-laughed. "That's some grip you got there, General." He looked up to my father with what appeared to be genuine admiration. "You're a legend in this town, sir. I hope you'll like what you see and hear tonight." Only then did the General release him, and when Donnie wagged his reddened hand, Daddy preened like he'd just won his bid on a new strip mall. "We'll see about that."

Then a dreaded cast of confusion flickered in his eyes. "Do I know this boy?"

"The name's Donnie," Donnie said clearly over the relative silence that had fallen around us. He smiled the gentlest smile at my mother, then took her arm. "Here, Miz Breedlove. Let me show you to your seats."

As soon as they were safely situated, I retreated to the back of the gathering. No guessing at the body language in that.

Geneva stepped up to the folding table and thumped the microphone to bring the room to order. She leaned close, practically eating the mike. "Helloo. Can we all get started?" It came out so loud that half the old folks' index fingers shot to the volume controls on their hearing aids.

She backed off in alarm. "Oops. Sorry." She eyed the mike as if it were a snake, then resumed, too far away and too softly this time. "First, I'd like to thank all you good folks for comin' out tonight." The old folks' fingers turned their volume back up until several soft squeals broke the uneasy quiet. The offenders were oblivious, of course.

It never fails to amaze me how anybody can ignore that kind of feedback in his own ear, but that seems to be the case more often than not.

"Can't hear you," a biker called from the back.

One of the teachers jumped up and reset the volume, then gave Geneva a quick lesson in where to stand. "Is this okay?" Geneva asked at a bearably elevated volume.

Polite applause confirmed that it was. She visibly relaxed. "Thanks to all you good folks for comin' out tonight. Let's give everybody a big hand."

Enthusiastic applause, with ear-splitting whistles from the back.

"Before I outline a few plans for how we can help Donnie win his race for mayor, I'd like to turn the dais over to him for a few brief words from our candidate, Donnie West." Clapping as she stepped back, she ceded the mike to the man of the hour.

"Hey, y'all," Donnie said with a smile, clearly at home in front of a microphone.

The crowd responded with an assortment of "Yo, Donnie," "Hi," and "Hey."

He scanned the gathering with compelling intensity. "First off, I'd like to thank my congregation, who is behind me one hundred percent in this. I wouldn't be here tonight unless they were, because my ministry is, and always will be, my first priority."

The center section erupted with amens and "We're behind you, Brother Donnie!"

"God bless you." Those piercing eyes swept to the others. "Anybody who has a problem with me bein' a minister first and a mayor second can get up and leave now. I won't hold it against them." He remained serious in the dramatic pause that followed, then broke into that infectious grin.

"All right, then. We're all rowin' in the same direction."

The crowd responded with brief applause, amens, and boot stomping, but I could still sense a definite undercurrent of social tension.

Donnie motioned them to silence. "I want to take just a minute to tell you what I stand for and what kind of campaign I intend to run." He stepped out from behind the mike and circled to the front of the table so no barrier separated him from his supporters. "Can you hear me without that thing?" he asked in a ringing baritone that carried to the very back where I was standing. Even the General nodded. "Okay, then. My platform is simple: truth, honesty, and full accountability to the people of this town."

Instant applause. Several of the Garden Club ladies even raised their hands as they clapped, a gesture that amounted to frenzy in their set. I saw the General nodding gravely.

"Y'all know me," Donnie continued. "I'm a man who trusts God to meet my needs. That's *needs*, not *wants*. If I'm elected mayor, I can promise y'all that I will do nothing to line my own pockets at the expense of Mimosa Branch's taxpayers."

More cheers and applause.

He paced before them, accepting the energy of their support and transmitting it back with charismatic intensity. "I pledge to have open city council meetings, with all records available to the public. Your city council works for *you*!" Applause. "There will be honest bids for contracts, everything on the record. And I also promise to make sure all our city services are working properly for *all* our people before we lay any more new utilities for the subdivisions."

Franklin's section shot to their feet with cheers, raised hands, and amens. "Word!" "Tell it, brother! Tell it!"

"But my first act as mayor," Donnie went on when they settled back down, "will be to call for a full, independent audit of both the city budget and the board of education. I know it'll cost us, but it's the only way we can see where all our tax dollars have been going."

Half the audience rose amid enthusiastic shouts and whistles that almost drowned out the sound of a heavy truck rumbling up the alley behind me. But it was a low whistle close beside me that snatched my attention with a start.

"Uh-oh. Now he's gone to meddlin'," Grant said quietly in a convincing imitation of small-town Southern. "That last plank in the platform just might get him killed."

Only the chilling truth in what he said kept me from chewing him out for sneaking up on me. "Don't say that. You're speaking destruction on him."

Grant eyed me with cynicism. "From what I know of Donnie, he'd be the first to defend me for telling the truth." He cocked a condescending half-smile. "And anyway, where's your faith? Don't you believe that God has raised up Donnie to be David to Mayor Stubbs's Goliath? *He* does, and so does his congregation."

"Oh, shut up." The time when I would endure being patronized by a man—any man—was long past. "What I believe is none of your business." I wanted to say "fucking business," but for some reason, it wouldn't come out.

Instead of being offended, Grant invoked the ultimate curse of Southern womanhood. "Ah-ah-ah," he chided. "Be sweet, now."

"Fuck sweet, and fuck you," I said with elegant precision. So much for my previous inhibition. I kept my eyes on Donnie who was now explaining that he would not tolerate a negative campaign.

Grant laughed, drawing several glances from the biker fringe.

I turned on him, energized for a confrontation. "Look," I whispered. "You may be my boss, but with the exception of Donnie, your entire gender is at the bottom of my list these days. So let's get the ground rules straight, here. I will not tolerate being patronized, harassed, discounted, teased, or lied to. I *hate* lying men." He met my hostile stare with mild amusement, unflinching, which only made me madder. "I do not want to date you, or anybody else for that matter. And I react very unpleasantly to being snuck up on. So watch your step, mister." He'd gotten me so het up, I'd completely forgotten to worry about the General, who was behaving beautifully.

"You're safe from me," Grant said smoothly. "Ball-busting man-haters never were my type."

Our low exchange was interrupted by big applause as Donnie turned the audience back over to Geneva.

"Okay, everybody," she announced over the PA. "Now let's get down to the game plan. I want to throw out a few ideas, then I want to hear from you. And feel free to ask questions anytime."

Abruptly, we were plunged into darkness, distracting me completely from my set-to with Grant. Gasps gave way to thick silence, but within seconds, more than a dozen lighters broke the gloom.

"All right!" Donnie clapped his hands in appreciation. "Let's hear it for the smokers!"

Laughter and mild applause dispelled the tension, but without the fans, the air hung heavy in the darkened room. The closed-in space seemed to soak up even the little remaining twilight that filtered into the open alley door.

"I'll go check the breakers." Grant borrowed a lighter from a biker. "Donnie, you got us so excited we blew a fuse," he quipped as he loped up the stairs, giving rise to a few chuckles.

"What's goin' on?" my father bellowed, prompting two of the Coffee Club to come over and reassure him.

Uh-oh.

I tensed. Fortunately, the fresh attention seemed to mollify him.

True to form, my mother's friends remained in their seats, confident that the ever-present Someone would take care of things.

A hum of conversation filled the next few minutes as overheated lighters flicked off, then on again after they'd cooled. Spurred by the power of suggestion, several of the bikers and teens lit up without bothering to go outside, much to my annoyance.

It's true, there's nobody less tolerant of cigarettes than an ex-smoker.

The smoke and growing closeness drove me nearer to the open alley door, but it was hotter outside than in the relative cool of the basement. My errant thermostat cranked up for a hot flash, forcing me to fend it off by flapping the bodice of my sleeveless dress in a most unladylike fashion.

Grant seemed to be taking a long time upstairs. I considered opening the loading-dock door, but thought better of it when I saw how dark it was getting outside. Then a flashlight beam preceded Grant as he brought down a box of something. "Half this side of the street is out," he informed us. Once down, he handed me a flashlight and a pack of batteries, then began distributing more to the others. "Here. These are all we have in stock, but they should help a little."

It took several tries in the dim light, but I finally got the batteries into mine right-way up. No sooner had I snapped on the switch, than one of the smokers strolled out onto the landing, stopped, and pointed up.

"Hey! Look!"

Grant was close behind me as I went outside to find a City of Mimosa Branch power truck blocking the alley just beyond us, its cherry-picker extended to the transformer behind the Café Luna next door. When the beams of our flashlights hit him, the technician said without surprise, "Oh, hey. Where did y'all come from?"

"We were having a meeting," Grant said coldly. "As well you knew."

The man went back to his wiring. "Nobody told us nothin' 'bout any meeting," he said in a cocky tone that exposed his bald-faced lie.

As I've already said, I hate lying men.

"What are you doing up there?" the head of the Modern

Artist's Guild demanded as more people came out into the sultry twilight.

"Routine maintenance. Gotta replace this transformer." The technician loosed a wire. "After-hours, like we agreed with the merchants' association."

"It's not after-hours for the café," I shot back.

"It is tonight," he said, unfazed. "They closed down to cater a big party." He shot us an insolent grin. "Now, *they* notified us."

Donnie eased through the crowd to stand beside me. "Evenin', brother," he called up to the electrician.

"Evenin'." The man didn't bother to look away from his work.

"Who'm I talkin' to up there?" Donnie asked him in a friendly tone.

The guy flicked his ID badge. "Roger Carlin."

"Glad to meet you, Roger." Donnie kept his cool, but his politeness was power under control. "Clearly, we have a misunderstanding here. I know you're just doing your job, Roger, and I wouldn't want to interfere in that. But how 'bout cuttin' us a break, please? We got more'n forty people down here. We only need about another hour. Can you give us some juice and finish this some other time? Later tonight, even."

"Sorry." The man took a big wrench from his belt and started loosening the bolts that held the transformer. "Almost got this baby loose, and the new one in the basket. It'd take almost as long to hook this'n back up as to install the new one. So, sorry. I might was well go on and finish."

Mutinous rumblings broke out among the various factions who had spilled into the alley, now thoroughly homogenized in their anger and frustration.

"Are we done talkin', now?" the technician asked Donnie in annoyance. " 'Cause I really need to get back to my work."

My ferocious new self wanted to climb up into that truck and give the jerk a ride he wouldn't soon forget, but Donnie took my arm and drew me away. "Okay, everybody. Back inside so we can figure out what we want to do next."

"We *want* to administer a little kick-ass," one of the bikers growled, setting off a wave of grumbled threats among the men—including the Holiness.

Donnie laughed. "That's just the old Keith talkin'. Back inside y'all. Shepherd's orders. Move it." He managed to get everyone out of the alley without incident. Once inside, bikers helped WMUs, once-sullen teenagers chatted up unadorned Holiness ladies, and work-shirted Holiness elders escorted the more daring Garden Club dowagers back to their timid sisters.

"That's good. Back to your seats," I heard Donnie call after the last retreating constituents. "Careful, there." He lingered outside to turn and look up for a last word with the technician. Over the grumbling and clatter of chairs inside, I heard him say, "God loves you, Roger, even in your sin. And He can use even the unrighteous to work His will." I heard no malice in his voice. "Truth is, till you came along and cut the power, I was pretty worried about how to get all those diverse folks inside to feel comfortable with one another." His big grin reflected the feeble light. "Praise God, there's nothing like a blackout to bring people together. You have been used of God this night, Roger, and I want to thank you." That said, he walked past me toward the makeshift dais.

"Well, I'll be damned," Grant breathed close beside me.

"You most probably will," I retorted despite the swell of awe I felt for Donnie. "And stop sneakin' up on me. I hate that."

"You hate a lot of things, don't you?" he asked archly.

"C'mon, you two," Donnie summoned. "Let's take advantage of this blackout."

Grant touched my arm, serious. "When you guys were cleaning down here, did you run across those oil lamps we had left over from Christmas?"

Of course! "In those boxes next to the popcorn wagon."

Flashlight in hand, I followed him over to the now-orderly stack of boxes. "The oil's in the one on top. Lamps in the next one down."

While we began unpacking, several flashlight beams trained on Donnie at the front. Wincing, he turned his face to the side with upraised hands. "Not right in my eyes, please." The beams shot away, leaving his face so dark that everyone laughed. After some shifting, they reached a happy medium. "Great. Okay." He faced them comfortably. "Since the lights are out, does anybody want to go home and try again later?"

"No!" the crowd said in vigorous unison.

"The mayor'll have to do more than cut the lights to run us off!" somebody piped up.

"Isaiah sixty and twenty," another man called from the center section. " 'The Lord shall be your everlasting light, and your days of sorrow shall end'! "

Easy laughter and applause, even from the teens.

"Hang on, you guys," Grant called to them. "I've got some lights even the mayor can't put out."

In minutes, the room was bathed in the old-fashioned mellow glow of a dozen oil lamps.

"Eye God," the General exclaimed. "Just like camp meetin' down in Lawrenceville back in the twenties. Remember, Mamie?" Nodding, my mother actually hooked her arm in his and leaned against him. It was the most intimate gesture of affection I had ever seen between them.

Hooray for blackouts.

There we all were in the same place with the same people who had sized each other up in uneasy suspicion under electric lights and cooling fans. Now we'd been bonded by two powerful forces: a common emergency and a common enemy. Donnie was right.

Even as I said a quick prayer of thanks for the mayor's machinations, I couldn't help wondering if there might not be another way of looking at my own setbacks, too. But before I waxed too philosophical, Geneva stepped forward to resume her battle plan.

"Okay!" She spoke up fine without assistance. "Let's get down to business."

Forty-five minutes later, we'd put together the beginnings of what might well be an effective campaign. Volunteers had stepped forward or been drafted for a phone committee (chaired by Miss Mamie, of course), signs and poster production (me), slogans (Donnie's organist, whose suggestion of "West Is Best" met with immediate approval), bake sale (Judge Christianson's gracious widow, Velma), sign distribution (the biker boys), poster distribution (the teens and several of Donnie's congregation), mailings (the Garden Club, led by their corresponding secretary), and last but by no means least, Grant as treasurer. (He was the only one who would take it.)

And everyone had agreed to beat the bushes for a good candidate for Fred Waller's seat on the council.

Best of all, we collected more than $700 in small bills and bigger checks, which Grant took up to the safe until he could open an account and deposit it.

Then Velma Christianson offered her mansion just beyond town for campaign central.

Velma's late husband, the judge, had long been in bed with Mayor Stubbs, much to Velma's dismay. And his political bedfellow, the mayor, had long covered for the judge's extramarital adventures with a succession of sleazy women, a fact Velma had to have known but steadfastly refused to face. But her late husband's parting insult had been one even Velma couldn't ignore, thanks to *The Atlanta Journal*. The judge had stroked out riding a fifteen-year-old black prostitute in a downtown hotel, pinning the hapless whore so securely with his bulk she could barely manage to dial 911. Talk about *coitus interruptus*. And just in time to make the front page.

Maybe Velma saw putting Ham Stubbs out of commission (pun intended) as a bit of postmortem revenge for the mayor's complicity.

Her public reasons for volunteering the mansion for Donnie's campaign brought down the house: "Because I have plenty of room, air-conditioning, a well, and a *generator*!" On a roll, she added, "And a pool! Bring your suits." The teens high-fived while the Holiness twittered in alarm about "mixed bathing."

"Tuesday and Thursday nights, and all day Saturdays, unless you hear otherwise," Geneva said. "Come whenever you can. Every hour of help makes a difference, so don't stay home just because you think we can do without you. We can't!"

As the meeting adjourned in a happy hubbub, I heard ninety-year-old Eula Spears say to her maiden sister in a thready soprano as they tottered out with the rest of the Garden Club, "Just think, Lillian. Won't it be exciting if Donnie wins? It's worth livin' another three months just to see the look on that crooked asshole of a mayor's face when we beat him."

"Damn straight!" Lillian confirmed.

It was all I could do to keep from laughing out loud. All this time, I'd thought those two paragons of Mimosa Branch society peed perfume—if they peed at all.

"There she is," my father said when he saw me. He jabbed a finger in Donnie's direction. "That's a fine feller you got there. He has my vote, even if he cain't pay his light bill."

I knew better than to try to correct him. "Thanks, Daddy," I responded with a warmth I hadn't felt for him in a long time.

Only then did I realize that my prayer had been answered. He hadn't acted up at all. And he and my mother looked as happy as I'd ever seen them.

I turned to Miss Mamie. "I'm glad you came. Glad you brought him."

"*He* brought *me*," she said dryly, shaking her head. "I

never dreamed he was payin' any attention when I told him where you were and why. I should have realized it might set him off. You know how he hates the mayor. Wouldn't hear anything but comin' down here. I had to take him, or he'd still be wanderin' the neighborhood tryin' to find y'all."

"Come on, daughter," the General said with growing impatience. "Let's go home. It's way past my bedtime."

"Y'all go on," I urged him. "I need to stay and help Geneva clean up."

"Go home." Yet again, Grant spoke up beside me without my having been aware he was there. "I'll close up here. You and Geneva have done enough for today."

I *was* tired. And I couldn't wait to drag the princess phone into my room so I could call Tricia and tell her all about tonight.

"Okay." Without another word to Grant, I took my daddy's arm and headed for the door. "Let's go, General. I'll walk you to the car."

It was Saturday night before I had time for another call to Tricia. I tracked her down at her beach house.

She picked up on the second ring. "Hello?"

"Help," I said. "I have just gotten home from a full day of real-estate school—the operative word being *school*—and I am terrified."

"Mmm." As usual, she was not properly impressed. "Terrified. As in, 'I've found a lump' terrified?"

"Logic? Do I hear logic?" I protested. "If I'd wanted logic, I'd have called David."

"Okay. So you're terrified. Of what?"

"Tricia, I have no brain anymore. I cannot memorize things. I try, but my mind is about as focused as a roomful of roaches."

"And why do you think that is?"

"'Cause when you're a mom, you have to keep six or

eight things on the bubble all the time. You have to spread yourself thin mentally. I've been doing that for thirty years, taking care of everything and everybody."

A pregnant pause, then, "Do you want Poor Babies, or the truth?"

"The truth, I guess," I said reluctantly. "You're a teacher. Why is this so hard for me?"

"You've been through a lot, are still going through a lot." Her tone was firm, but gentle. "Your life's unsettled, and it's going to take some time for you to adjust and recover." This was sounding like a lecture. "Even without the stresses you're under, the crazy way we live in this country fragments people, especially people as bright and compulsive as you are."

"Ouch. You used that *C* word."

"Compulsive?"

"Ooh. Ugly word."

"But apropos, and we both know it. I only mention it because I love every compulsive molecule of you, my friend."

"Watch your step. I'm not as resilient as I seem." But we both knew I was.

"I see this same problem a lot with older students who come back after a long absence from study. Retraining your thought processes takes time. It won't happen overnight, but it will happen. Those old pathways aren't gone, they're just overgrown from disuse. Don't be so hard on yourself. It'll come."

"I flunked the practice test on terms in my real-estate class today. Flunked the fucking thing!"

Tricia laughed. "I still cannot get used to hearing you say that word. Coming from you, it sounds like roses."

"Great. I can't even cuss right."

"Oh, stop it."

"You're no fun."

"You asked for truth. What you haven't asked, for a long time, is how *I* am."

Ouch, ouch, ouch. "Oh, God. You're right." I gave myself a mental shake. "So, how are you? And John? And the boys?"

"John's still working on that huge renovation over at Justice." The FBI, mind you. "It's driving him nuts—late hours, weekends, major stresses, yadda, yadda." Late hours? Weekends? My hard-earned husband-suspector alarm went off, but I held my peace as she went on. "Pepper's acting the big sophomore on campus at GW. Living in a dorm, studying too little, and partying too much, but at least he's passing. Thank God we get the family rate, is all I can say. He's off working this summer at a camp in Colorado. It pays pretty well, so that helps."

"And Peyton?"

"Tennis, soccer, swimming, and getting ready for all the usual high school senior stuff. He's fine."

"Senior. Get me my cane."

"Yep. Another year, and I'll have an empty nest."

There was an odd, awkward silence between us. Concerned, I asked, "And how is Tricia? Really?"

Another weighted pause. "Tricia is . . . choosing not to rock the boat. My eyes are wide open, Lin, but life is just a lot simpler when I take things at face value. For now, anyway. I may change my mind after Peyton leaves home. Maybe then I'll dare to look under rocks. Not now." She brightened, as if to console me. "There's much good in my life, Lin's-a-pin. I don't think I ever lost myself the way you did with Phil."

"Ouch, ouch, ouch." If anyone else had said that to me, I'd have retreated into injured silence at the blunt offhandedness of her statement. As it was, I gave her truth for truth. "Why is it always we women who pay the cost of having men in our lives?"

"Ah, 'why,' the scientist's key and the philosopher's trap." Tricia sighed. "Gee, it's been great talkin' to ya, kid. I think I'll go have a little hemlock."

I jumped in with an extravagant, "Poor baby, poor baby, poor baby, poor baby!"

She chuckled. "See, there you go. Just when I start to get ticked off at you, you make me laugh." She took a cleansing breath. "I'm so proud of you. Do you know that?"

I knew she meant it, and my eyes welled with gratitude, a sudden longing in my chest. "God, I wish you could come see me. We could sneak out to the garage for a cold one after everybody else has gone to bed, just like we used to when we were twelve."

"Sorry. No offense, but I'm not stayin' in that loony bin. I love you, but not enough to deal with your parents—especially without air-conditioning." Tricia had been dead-set against my coming home, predicting that I would be sucked into the raging vortex of dysfunction and never be seen again. "You come to me here," she countered. "The beach is great. The pool is great. And I hardly ever see Peyton. He's either lifeguarding, sleeping, or out with his pals."

"You know perfectly well I can't come up there. I have this *job* and these *classes*, not to mention the campaign. And getting the apartment into shape."

"The apartment. Now, there're some memories."

"Mmmm." How many hours up there we'd smoked, talked, and experimented with boys and liquor as teenagers.

"How's the place coming along?" she asked.

"It's coming. Tommy helped me get it cleaned out. Under duress, but we're making progress with everything but the pool table. Tommy and the Mame decided to donate that to the VFW." Which was good, because it took up the whole living room. "We pulled off that cheap paneling, and guess what?"

"You found Mavis Jenkins!"

"No." Mavis had disappeared on her way home from a bar in 1958, and her name had been invoked ever since. "No Mavis. And no insulation. Not a scrap."

"No wonder that little gas furnace never did much good."

"Tommy said he could get it all insulated and Sheet-rocked for less than my first full paycheck. I can't wait to see the difference."

"Are you serious? He's actually going to *work* on the apartment?"

The criticism in her voice stung, because I knew I was responsible for it. It was one thing for me to be critical of him, but anybody outside the family, even Tricia . . .

I know you think I'm a failure, Lin, but I do *know my way around a woods.* And he knew his way around the garage apartment. Despite the fact that I'd had to ask often and remind him, he hadn't once complained.

I leapt to defend him. "Tommy's been great, really help-ful. He's . . .well, we're not what you call close, but at least he's helped me."

"Now, that's news," Tricia said without sarcasm. "Good for him. Maybe the old home place isn't as lethal as I thought."

"Am I allowed an I-told-you-so?"

"No. Not for another six months. I'll issue an official ruling then."

My heart smiled along with my face.

"Have you tried the mother-trick?" she asked me.

"Yep. Several times."

"And?"

"And it doesn't seem to work," I confessed.

"Keep trying. It will."

"If you say so."

"I'm hanging up now," she announced. "It's my turn to call next time. When?"

"Friday. Ten?" After class.

"Ten it is."

I hung up and went downstairs for a cold one, for old times' sake. The house was quiet. Tommy hadn't come home from hanging out with his buddies, and everyone else was in bed.

Out on the back porch, I took the key from its nail high on the siding, then opened the padlock that sealed the rusting spare refrigerator. The padlock was obviously to keep Uncle Bedford out of the sauce. As I reached for the ever-present carton of long-necks beside the cache of liquor bottles and my mother's wretched store-brand sodas, I realized I hadn't seen Tommy drinking since I'd come home. Probably just doing it out of sight to keep my parents off his back, I decided.

I looked at the kitchen clock. Almost ten. Tommy never came home till at least eleven on Saturdays, so I figured I had plenty of time to finish my beer without setting a bad example. I opened the bottle, stuck it into a caddy, then headed for the front porch to watch for the ten-thirty freight out of Atlanta. The sight and sound of trains had always comforted me.

In the faint, familiar light of the little Tiffany lamp Miss Mamie always left burning in the living room, I passed the damned bathtub full of pink begonias and settled into a rocker on the front porch with my beer.

I closed my eyes to the sounds of midsummer, breathing in the scents of red dirt and musky magnolias and new-mown fescue and Sweet Autumn clematis. The hot days would last into October, but the growing proportion of crickets in the night chorus promised that the very worst would eventually be over.

Heat lightning flickered through my lids as I heard the measured beat of someone jogging toward the sidewalk in front of our house. I opened my eyes to see Grant running past our first driveway on his way home.

He waved.

Drat. He'd seen me.

"Don't know what you're drinking," he panted out, his head bobbing along beyond the shoulder-high camellias, "but it looks awful good."

In a total brain fart, I heard myself saying, "It is. Want one?"

Shit! Where had *that* come from?

To my dismay, he swung into the far entrance of the driveway and ran his soaking-wet self right up to stand jogging in place as he greeted me over the Gumpos. "Hi. I sure could use something cool right about now."

"Tea, lemonade, Kamikaze cola, or Sam Adams?"

"Sam Adams. Please."

I set my bottle down and went inside, kicking myself for inviting him. True, we'd gotten along fine ever since I'd laid down the ground rules Tuesday night, especially when we'd all been working to set up campaign central at the Widow Christianson's. But what had possessed me to ask if he wanted a drink?

By the time I got back with his beer, he had thoughtfully removed the cushions on the rocker beside mine and collapsed. "Great." He pulled the bottle from its caddy and rolled the wet glass against his flushed face before replacing it and taking a grateful gulp. "Man, that tastes good. Thanks." His head dropped to the chair back, eyes closed, his long legs crossed at the ankle.

Soaked though he was, he didn't repulse me. I was all too conscious of his smell. It wasn't bad, mind you. He emitted the compelling tang of a healthy man after honest exertion.

I picked up my beer to distract myself. After checking it for bugs by the light from the living room, I reclaimed the chair beside him.

Then a diabolical notion occurred to me.

Maybe it wouldn't be so bad having him there. Come to think of it, this just might be a unique opportunity. I might enjoy having a completely honest conversation with a man. After all, I had nothing to lose.

Except my job.

Ahh, Grant wouldn't fire me, not till Shelia came back, anyway. In only a week, I had gotten a decent grasp of the billing program and mastered ordering supplies on the computer. Compared to the ditzy collection of teenagers who worked after school and on Saturdays, I was a whiz.

I scanned my boss's long, relaxed body, considering what to ask him first. This could be fun. No games. No lies. Nothing held back.

To ask the unaskable question . . . yep, I had to do it.

But I had no intention of being the first one to speak. The first one to speak loses; I'd learned that in contract-negotiation class.

He sat forward to take another swig. "For some reason, a beer always seems to taste better when you're not alone."

It was an oblique confession, but one that gave me pause. "Yeah." Grant had seemed so composed, so self-sufficient, that I hadn't considered he might be lonely sometimes, too.

Probably lonelier than I was. He had no old friends or family here. No friends at all, as far as I could tell, unless you counted Geneva.

"I didn't expect you to ask me up here," he admitted. "After what happened that first time, I figured I'd never get an invitation to the famous Miss Mamie's porch."

I pretended to have forgotten all about it. "After *what* happened?" Then I chided myself for being the one to play games.

He chuckled.

The night sounds stretched between us. This was really alien to me, but I resisted the compulsion to fill the word-less space.

Again, it was he who spoke up. "So. How's your uncle? I haven't seen him out lately."

"Meaning," I shot back, "he hasn't escaped to run wild through the yard lately?"

"Meaning," he said evenly, "I haven't seen him out lately, wild or otherwise."

Chastened for being so hostile by the ghost of my proper Nana Grainger, I backed down a bit. Truth, I reminded myself. "I started giving him his Ativan myself. Aunt Glory wasn't doing it, so I swiped the pills out of their medicine cabinet and made sure he got the prescribed dosage on schedule. He's much calmer now."

"Does your aunt know you're doing that?" he asked without accusation.

"That's none of your goddamn business," I said sweetly.

Again, he chuckled. We rocked along for several more minutes without speaking until my old self got the best of me. "As long as we're asking personal questions, how come you refused to come help your father with the drugstore after your stepmother died?" Equally appalled and delighted with myself, I realized this had promise, asking what I really wanted to ask. It felt dangerous and very empowering.

"That's none of your goddamn business," he parroted evenly with a sly smile.

So he'd wiggled out of that one, and not without wit. That didn't mean I had to give up and retreat into civilized territory. "Okay, then. Here's a question: what is it about middle age that makes a perfectly sane man turn his back on everything good and real in his life—family, career, faith—and jump headfirst into a sexual cesspool?"

Grant's eyes widened, then narrowed. "Why the hell do you ask *me* that particular question? Who have you been talking to?"

"Nobody." I totally missed the cue, so no alarm bells went off. "You're a man. Geneva said you were married before." I leaned forward, rolling the beer caddy between my hands. "Look, there's no axe to grind between us. What say we be honest with each other? No games. Just honest." I glanced over to find him mirroring my position. "Maybe that's why I asked you up here. I don't know."

"I swear, Lin, you are an odd bird."

"We can discuss my idiosyncrasies some other time. I want to talk about men. Not you, specifically. I just want an honest, no-holds-barred man's perspective so I can try to make some sense of things."

"Geeze." He shifted uneasily in his chair. "All I wanted was a beer."

"There!" I raised my bottle in salute to him. "Now that's informative. I'm looking for meaning, and the man just wants a beer. Go on. This is educational. Does that characteristic extend into other areas?"

"I don't know what the hell you're talking about," he said, visibly uncomfortable with the turn of conversation.

"Let's try it this way, like a game. Fill in the blank. *She* wants him to hold her hand, but the man just wants . . ."

"A beer," he quipped with a smile.

I couldn't help smiling back. "Now, if we're going to do this, you're going to have to cooperate."

"I never volunteered to 'do this' in the first place," he declared, propping his other ankle on the opposite knee.

"Hmm. You have a point." An inspiration hit me. "Okay. How about this? You answer my questions about men, and I'll answer yours about women. Anything you want to ask."

"Anything?" He relaxed into his chair to take another swig, considering. The gesture told me it was only a matter of time until he agreed.

"Anything. But only here on Miss Mamie's porch. And only when everybody else in safely tucked in." I couldn't very well risk having my mother overhear us.

"Maybe." He eyed me with interest. "How about a test question?"

"Fire away."

"When I was a teenager at the lake, my girlfriend stayed out on the boat all day most of the time. But some weekends she insisted I take her back to the bathroom every hour. What's with that?"

"Easy." Thank goodness, he'd started with something simple. Relief erased whatever embarrassment I should have felt. "Tampons. She had her period," I explained.

"When you're heavy, you can't go more than an hour or so in a bathing suit without risking a disaster."

"Tampons," he repeated. The light bulb did not go on. Or was he only pretending ignorance?

"You're a druggist. Surely you know what tampons are. We carry them at the store."

At last, his impenetrable confidence foundered. "Of course. I mean, generally. But I still don't get the hour part."

I decided the specifics were entirely too gross for our limited level of acquaintance. Let him do his own homework. "Check out one of the boxes at the store. It has diagrams and everything inside. You'll figure it out."

I could not believe the tangent this whole thing had taken.

"Hmm." He took another swig. "Okay, here's another one. The first time I—"

"Whoa, there." I raised a staying hand. "You've had your mulligan. And anyway, we're supposed to take turns."

"You never said anything about taking turns. Are you going to keep making up rules as we go along? If so, no way."

"The take turns is the last rule." I raised a finger for each stipulation. "One, complete honesty. Two, nowhere but here on the porch in private. Three, take turns." Then another necessity occurred to me. "Oh, no, there's got to be one more." I raised a fourth finger.

Standing, he waved me off. "Forget it."

"No. This really, truly last rule is for your sake as much as mine." I motioned him to sit back down. "Neither one of us can tell anybody else about this. Nobody." Excluding Tricia, of course, but she didn't count because she lived in D.C. and would never meet Grant, much less talk about him with anybody but me. "Mutual, complete confidentiality."

"That sounds fine to me," he conceded as he sat with a middle-aged wince. "But how do I know I can trust you to keep your mouth shut? Most of the women I know blab everything."

"I'll give you a truth," I bartered. "Women talk to other women about their men because the men in their lives won't talk to them about things that matter." Let him chew on that one.

"And I'll give you a truth," he shot back. "Men don't talk to women about things that matter, because the man just wants . . ." He extended his hands as a cue for me to finish. "Fill in the blank."

"The man just wants . . . ?" The light went on. "A beer!" we both said together, then laughed.

"Do we have a deal or not?" I persisted.

"Geeze, you are relentless." He eyed me, skeptical. "No fragile feelings, no feminine tears. No deflections."

"And no lies." I stuck out my hand to shake. "You lie, you die."

"That sounds like a threat."

"It is." I smiled when I said it. "Lie to me, and I'll give Uncle Bedford a butcher knife, tell him the little cannibal works for you, and let him into your house while you're sleeping."

"The little cannibal?" As I'd hoped, my dark sense of humor deflected his reservations. He looked at my hand. "Something tells me I'm going to live to regret this, but okay. We have a deal." We shook. "Now ask your next question, then I'm going to have to hit the road. I'm beat."

"Why do men run in the heat?" I asked off the top of my head. "Only idiots run in this heat."

He imitated a buzzer. "Aanh! That is not a legitimate man-question. It's an insult."

"It is too a legitimate man-question. Couched in an in-sult, maybe, but a legitimate man-question."

"Nope. Men are not the only ones who run in the heat. There are fifty-five thousand runners in the Peachtree Road Race, and a huge number of them are women. So that is not a legitimate man-question." He killed his beer with a self-satisfied swig. "You lose your turn, and I'm going home."

"Hey, wait a minute. Who says I lose my turn?" I stood along with him. "Who's making up rules now?"

"It's only fair. You got to do all the other rules."

"Okay," I conceded.

He stretched, then made a great effort to appear casual as he went down the stairs, but he couldn't hide the stiffness that had set in.

Face it, you man you. Jog all you want. You're still over fifty, no matter how good those legs might look. And they did look good. Not that I cared, mind you.

And, of course, he'd left his empty beer bottle sitting on the railing. I called after him as I collected it. "Why do men always leave their empties lying around for somebody else to pick up?"

He pivoted, a dark silhouette in the light of the authentic reproduction Victorian gas lamp on the corner. "Because beer bottles cease to exist when they're empty," he said quietly enough to keep from waking the household. "Cans, too. Glasses. Cups. Poof. Gone." Then he turned toward home and disappeared behind our huge magnolia.

"They cease to exist when they're empty?" I carried the bottles inside and locked the door behind me. Tommy always came in through the back. "They cease to exist when they're empty," I repeated as I rinsed the long-necks and left them in the kitchen sink. The road to opposite-sex enlightenment was going to be steeper than I thought.

At the bottom of the stairs I paused, sensing something amiss. My eyes were drawn to the clock and I realized what it was.

The ten-thirty freight was late.

I hadn't been home long, but it was long enough for me to notice when the train *didn't* come.

Scary.

Chapter 10

The next night I woke up thirsty after midnight and crept downstairs for a cold decaf diet drink, then took it to the front porch and turned on the ceiling fan to blow away the mosquitoes. I sipped for twenty minutes or so before tiptoeing back inside. I didn't hear anyone up when I locked the door, but a thunk, then the sound of furniture bumping around in the darkened kitchen set the hairs on the back of my neck upright. Scared half out of my wits, I eased cautiously through the dining room and into the big butler's pantry that connected through to the kitchen. There, in the darkness, I saw what looked like two substantial men struggling in the kitchen.

I poised for action, my heart hammering in alarm. Armed with only an empty glass, I don't know what I expected to be able to do about anything. I should have run screaming for help, but thank goodness I didn't, because the next noise was one that silenced me to an awful stillness.

It was the sound of my father crying. "I can't do it," he said in a desperate whisper thickened by his sobs. "I used to be able to. Nobody knew. But now I can't. She can't see this, Tommy. She can't."

The stench of feces caused me to stifle a gag.

"Don't worry, Pop," Tommy soothed as he helped my

father up. He snatched a dishtowel and draped it across a chair, then lowered my father to sit. The General was holding an armful of soiled clothes. "You just stay right there," Tommy murmured as he used another towel to wipe the worst of the mess off my father's feet and legs without a flinch. "Us guys will take care of this." That done, he gave my father a fierce hug, then got the cleaning bucket and some rags out from under the sink. Careful adjustment kept the faucet from making too much noise as he filled the bucket. Then I smelled my mother's favorite pine cleaner. "We'll do okay, old man," Tommy said softly as he wrung out the rag and started mopping up the trail of filth my father had left across the linoleum.

Pop sat watching and crying, his soiled clothes clutched in his lap.

The strong odor of waste and pine almost did me in, but I managed to stay still and quiet. I knew I should have left them, but I couldn't. Something in me needed to see my father's vulnerability and the unexpected bond of tenderness my brother had for him.

Once the floor was done, Tommy gave the General another hug. "There. All clean. See? Just like last time. No big deal." He took the waste water to the tiny maid's toilet and poured it away, then washed out the pail and replaced it under the sink, tidy as you please.

He returned to my father, who had finally stopped crying and sat there staring blankly into the darkness. "Okay, Pop," Tommy coaxed. "Let's have those clothes so I can get 'em all washed up before the Mame sees 'em."

The General handed them over. "She can't see them." Despite his stony manner, there was nothing dead in his murmured statement. "Tommy, I'd have to eat my daddy's shotgun if she ever saw these."

My heart broke for him. For both my parents. For what they'd come to.

Thank God for Tommy.

"I told you, Pop, I don't wanta hear any of that kinda

talk. I'll take care of you. Didn't I promise you that? No more gun talk, Pop. That's the coward's way out, and Thomas Breedlove is not a coward."

"Not a coward," my father repeated without conviction.

"Okay." Tommy squeezed his shoulders. "Now just wait here while I start these clothes, then we'll go get you cleaned up."

I eased back into the dining room so he wouldn't see me as he passed on his way to the laundry that had once been a silver closet. To my amazement, Tommy reached straight for the enzyme pretreat Aunt Glory used on Uncle Bedford's accidents, then poured it into the wash, added the clothes, set the dials, and topped the load off with a proper measurement of detergent.

My brother, who had never shown even a nodding interest in a washing machine since I'd known him!

I'd always figured that was why he'd married so many times—he'd run out of clothes.

He went back to the kitchen and helped my father up. "Okay, Pop. Up we go for a nice warm bath and some clean clothes. Then I'll get you back into bed like last time." Tommy steered him toward the back stairs. "The Mame will never know you were gone."

I wasn't so sure about that. Usually not so much as a pin dropped, night or day, in this house without my mother's knowing it. I suspected she might be aware of all this, too, but had simply chosen not to humiliate my father, despite the lifetime of indignities he had heaped on her.

I had often wondered if my parents had ever really loved each other. Now I began to see that theirs might be a deeper kind of caring that had nothing soft or sentimental about it. Perhaps what they shared was made of stronger stuff, forged in the very conflicts I had always hated.

And Tommy. Who would have guessed him capable of such unqualified tenderness for the man who had put him down ever since he could walk?

I wouldn't, and it made me ashamed.

So many things I had misjudged about my life and the people in it. So much I hadn't seen.

Waiting for my brother to get my father upstairs into the tub, I sat at the banquet table in our dining room and wept silent tears—for myself and for my family. But they were grateful tears, too, because I was beginning to see the saving graces that had always been there and were there still.

I was waking up. It wasn't easy, but I was doing it, and I was glad.

After real-estate class Monday night, I came home late to find Tommy rocking, drinking iced tea on the front porch by the night-light in the parlor. Haunted by what I'd seen in the darkened kitchen, I wanted to reach out but knew he wouldn't take kindly to my having spied on him.

"Hey." I settled in the rocker beside him, hoping the awkward silence between us would dissipate. When it didn't, I made an overture. "It's been an awful long time since I asked you how your life was going, Tommy, and I'm sorry for that. I'm sorry for a lot of things." I stared above the darkened houses across the tracks. "I've always been so mad at the General for never giving you a chance, but lately I've realized I never did, either." Eating crow wasn't as hard as I'd feared it would be. "I'd like to start over. Is that okay with you?"

"We haven't talked in a long, long time," he said, guarded.

"We've talked." The old defensiveness sprang up of its own accord. "I called you."

"To ask about my job and my kids. Or when you needed my truck."

Ouch. "We've been together every Thanksgiving and Christmas for the past decade."

"Yep. Great food. Beautiful decorations. And you running around frantically in the kitchen until it was time to say good-bye. That doesn't count."

Ouch again. Had I really insulated myself that much from my own family? Looking back, I had to admit Tommy and I really hadn't had what I could call a relationship for a long, long time. Maybe never. "Okay. I get an *F* in sister. But I want to change that."

"Why?"

I couldn't blame him for being suspicious, not after all those years of judgment and surreptitious criticism I'd dished out. "Like you said, by this time in our lives, we ought to be able to accept each other. Be there for each other. It took me fifty years to come to my senses, but I want to be your sister. Okay? Please?"

He remained silent for what seemed like a long time, staring into the same safe, noncommittal space beyond the boundaries of 1431 Green Street. When he finally spoke, his voice was husky. "Yeah. That's real okay with me."

"So." I lightened my tone. "What's it like being Tommy these days?" For the first time, I really wanted to know.

He took a swig of his tea, then risked a glance my way. "Pretty good, actually."

"Yeah?" That was a surprise. "And why is that?"

"AA," he said as calm as you please. Only then did he really look at me.

"Tommy!" I wheezed out in a loud stage whisper, then dropped my voice so no one upstairs could overhear. "You're in AA? When did this happen? Why didn't you tell me?"

His spoke with quiet conviction. "I've been sober fourteen months—fourteen of the hardest, best months of my life, working the steps with my sponsor, working my program. Going to meetings." All those nights I'd thought he was out drinking with his buddies. "And I didn't tell you because you had enough on your mind with Phil."

He stilled, a dark silhouette in the shadows. "No. That's a lie. I didn't tell you because I didn't want you to know about one more failure if I couldn't stay sober."

The last knifed through me like a white-oak stake to the

heart. All this had been happening with my only brother, and I had been so wrapped up in my own cares, I hadn't even noticed.

It occurred to me that if I'd still had my life in Buckhead, I probably never would have. I'd have charged along in my golden bubble, spending all my energies—and my love—on maintaining my illusion of a marriage while my own brother was quietly facing his own demons as resolutely as my parents were denying theirs.

But he'd told me now. I wanted to cry, to hug him, to beg his forgiveness for not paying attention. Instead, I took his hand, awkward with the physical contact. "I'm so proud of you, Tommy," was all I could give him.

He looked my way with that same quiet assurance in his face. "Thanks. That means a lot to me." He put his callused hand over mine and gave it a squeeze, then both of us released, unused to such intimate connection.

"Mame and the General must be proud, too."

He glanced up sharply, his features drawn. "They don't know, Lin, and I don't want them to. Not yet. I still have a lot of work to do with them. A lot of amends."

"Amends?" Like what he'd done for the General?

"You'll see." He peered at me in the darkness, his posture tense. "Anonymity is the foundation of AA. It's a safe place because we guard each other's identities and the failures we all have on our way to recovery. My sobriety is mine to tell, and I'm not ready yet. I want my actions to speak for me with the folks. Can I trust you not to say anything?"

Trust. Tommy had trusted me with the truth, and even though I had no trust of my own left to give, I resolved to merit his. "It'll be our secret. Cross my heart and hope to die."

His broad smile seemed unnaturally white in the faint light from the parlor. "Thanks. I know I can count on you, Lin. That's one of your best qualities. You keep your promises."

Except *till death do us part*. Talk about a failure. The weight of it fell, thick and sour, onto my soul, as heavy as it had ever been. Tears welled in my eyes, but I didn't let Tommy see them.

"Thanks for telling me." I rose. "I love you Brud-o." It had taken me half a century, but I was beginning to understand what that was supposed to mean.

"Love you, too, Sis."

I left him sitting there, the fragile bond between us glowing like a thread of light.

The next morning everything seemed brighter, not just because I'd made peace with my brother, but also because the jet stream had decided to take a rare plunge south, bringing with it clear skies and highs in the low eighties, unheard of for the thirtieth of July. For the first time since I'd started walking to work, I'd actually been able to enjoy the trip. And everybody at the store seemed energized, including the Coffee Club. Grant, too. Ever since we'd talked on the porch, things had definitely been lighter between us.

As soon as he made sure all the prescriptions were caught up, he started gathering the nursing-home order in a box. "Okay, you guys"—we'd tried to train him in the proper use of *y'all*, but he still insisted on calling Geneva and me *you guys*—"I'm off to the nursing home."

Geneva looked up from the old-fashioned payroll ledger she insisted on using. "Don't you want me to take those for you?" I could see she was torn, clearly upset about being late with payroll for the first time ever. "I mean, I still have a little to go on our checks, but I'd be glad to take those if—"

"That's okay." If Grant minded about the checks' being late, he certainly hadn't shown it. "You stay put and get caught up."

"I'm really sorry, Grant," she apologized for the twentieth time. "With everything with the campaign and all, I just ended up so far behind. I swear, though, no more pol-itickin' at work."

"I told you, one late payroll in twenty-six years is not a major catastrophe." He picked up the box of meds. "Just as long as you don't make a habit of it." He raised an eyebrow. "I'm telling you, though, you could do that pay-roll a lot faster and easier on the computer. The software's all set up and ready to go."

Geneva's abashed smile hardened just a hair. "So you've told me for the last year."

It was a minor war of wills, a game they played every week, according to Geneva. Grant always prodded, and she always resisted tackling the payroll software.

Head shaking, he chuckled and made for the door.

With Grant gone, I was left to tend the Coffee Club while Geneva worked at the desk in the pharmacy. I felt so good from my cool morning walk that even Preacher Bif-fle's entrance couldn't dampen my good mood.

Until the bell tinkled and Ham Stubbs strolled in with Gary Mayfield close behind, both of them wearing Bill Clinton grins and conservative suits. I had seen them briefly in passing around town, never paying much attention one way or the other, but a dark energy invaded along with them. Both tall and fit—the mayor distinguished, Gary ath-letic and boyish in his middle age—they were opposites of the usual Boss Hogg image of small-town Southern dem-agogues. Halfway down the aisle, they split up and started to work the room like pros.

Geneva promptly went MIA, leaving me stuck with the register. With all the money orders "those Mexicans" sent, we sometimes had several thousand dollars in the till, so I dared not abandon it.

The mayor clapped Vollie on the back, taking his hand. "Hey there, Vollie!"

"Good to see ya, Ham." Biffle pumped his hand enthu-siastically. "Good to see ya."

While Gary worked the other end of the row, Stubbs

progressed down the stools. "Walter. You still got your own gas tank out by the barn? Bet that comes in handy." Unless the city decided to make a fuss about it and call in the EPA.

"Rex, how's your granddaughter likin' that apartment we got her into?" The mayor didn't have to say it was public housing, or that she'd had an illegitimate child at thirteen by her black boyfriend. Everybody present knew, just as they knew she'd gotten housing thanks to the mayor's intervention, and what might happen if Rex backed the wrong candidate. Rex colored darkly, but said nothing.

Stubbs zeroed in with accuracy and precision on the others. What might have been ordinary politickin' by anybody else took on a sinister edge coming from him. "Delton, you're lookin' fit as a bear in a blackberry patch. Enjoyin' that barn you put up with the variance we gave you?" Uncle Delton's mouth clamped into a tight line, and he snatched his hand away after the mayor claimed it.

Stubbs clapped Ottis on the shoulder. "Ottis, how's that sweet, little, deaf grandbaby Carla? She doin' okay in our preschool program for the hearing impaired? We gotta help 'em young. Those precious little grandbabies are so vulnerable in this big, bad world."

He made no direct threats, just sly, unctuous references to every man's point of vulnerability. Nothing had changed since the mayor had put Gary Mayfield in his hip pocket by having some lowlife threaten Gary's little girl. I looked to Gary for some reaction as the mayor snaked his way through the gathering, dispensing fear under the smiling guise of concern, but you'd never know that he had once been the victim of the same tactics. Jacket off, sleeves rolled, tie loosened, he was doing his best to jolly everybody up.

His efforts didn't work. The men maintained their guarded silence, with the notable exception of Preacher Biffle, who administered as loud, insincere, and obnoxious a bootlicking as I have ever witnessed.

I bowed up in righteous indignation, wishing somebody would put a stop to it but afraid that if I opened my big mouth, I would blow my cool completely. So I decided to abandon my post and seek refuge in the stockroom. The register would be safe with the Coffee Club, I decided. But I had scarcely turned around when the mayor's voice stopped me.

"Well, would you look who we have here. Little Miss Linwood Breedlove, pretty as ever." He strolled closer. Above his smile, his eyes held a cold, malicious glint, doubtless meant to intimidate.

All it did was make me madder, but I refused to give him the satisfaction of seeing my anger. "Why, Mayor, I'm surprised you remember me at all."

"Prettiest girl in town." He invaded my space, his features congealed. "How's that fine brother of yours? Still keepin' his wagon in the road?"

Tommy! He knew; I could see it in his smug expression. Not about the drinking—everybody knew about the drinking—but about Tommy's sobriety. His hard-fought, fragile sobriety.

How? Tommy said AAs protected each others' anonymity.

"And the General?" the mayor went on with unctuous concern. "I hear he's been under the weather lately. I know it must be really hard for your family, bein' on a fixed income with that great old place to keep up. What you imagine that place is worth, these days, anyway?" Reassessment, reassessment, reassessment.

Bile rose in my throat. That dirty, lowdown snake! Like most Southerners, I could hold my own with most anybody, but let somebody go after my family, and Katie bar the door!

I wanted to grab his coiffed gray hair, jerk his head back, and yell, "Fuck you and your sleazy innuendoes, scumbag," but instead I summoned up my best Buckhead Princess and brushed him off with a smooth, "Oh, you know Daddy.

Still rarin' to give it to any lowlife who needs a lesson from Mr. Hickory." The Coffee Club chortled. "As for Tommy, he's doing great. He has so many loyal supportive friends now, registered voters all. Nice of you to ask after him, though, *Ham*. I'll be sure to tell him exactly what you said." I batted my eyelashes, but Stubbs didn't respond directly.

He just grinned and flipped three quarters onto the counter. "Great. Now how 'bout a cup of coffee, sugar?" I sensed, more than heard, a collective intake of breath from the Coffee Club.

Hell would freeze over before I served that man a cup of coffee. Two could play his game. "Sure," I lied, giving him my best, "hold for the photo" smile as I left his money untouched. "Just as soon as I find a few urgent items in the back." I turned the dazzle toward Uncle Delton. "Keep an eye on the register for me, please, Uncle Delton. We can't be too careful now, can we? You never know what kind of thievin' crooks might come waltzin' in here." I turned and glided toward the back, composed on the outside but underneath, boiling hotter'n a roadside kettle of peanuts.

In the stockroom, I found Geneva pounding her fists on her knees.

I shut the door behind me, whispering, "Geneva, what's wrong?"

"I should be out there," she said in an angry whisper, "facin' those two weasels. But no. What do I do? Turn tail and run, leavin' you manage all by yourself." Her eyes welled with tears. "Lin, I'm so sorry. I don't know why I'm so afraid. I mean, he knows I'm Donnie's campaign manager. Why hide? But I just couldn't make myself go out there."

"Aw heck, Geneva, forget it." I gave her a hug, my own anger cooled in the face of her anxiety. "He's just a two-bit tyrant. The people of this town deserve better, and we're gonna help 'em get it. Come on. It's no big deal." I continued to console her for several minutes, concluding with,

"You have nothing to prove by confronting him."

"You're right. Nothing to prove." She drew in a shuddering breath. "I swear, Lin, you are a tonic to me."

I opened the door, letting in cool air. "Now let's both get out there and back to work." I stuck out my hand for a shake. "Betcha ten dollars they'll be gone."

Geneva chuckled as she rose. "I've got too much sense to bet against you."

Sure enough, the mayor, Gary, and Vollie Biffle were nowhere to be seen when we emerged into the store. Geneva made straight for her payroll in the pharmacy.

"Don't worry," Fred Martin piped up as I returned to the register. "We made sure they didn't get their paws in the till."

In the laughter that followed, Ottis Wilburne added, "That was right rare, the way you took the mayor down."

"I'm sure I don't know what you mean," I said with my most innocent Southern bitch insincerity.

Silent Rex spoke up. "Soon as Stubbs realized you weren't comin' back, he picked up his money and left with Vollie Biffle trailin' behind like a puppy."

"Well, this has been interesting, but somebody had better turn up the radio, because *In Memoriam* is about to come on."

I'd had enough of the mayor for one day. If the Coffee Club got to rehashing things, I wasn't sure I could put the incident behind me. So I prayed we'd have lots of customers, and sure enough, we got them. By the time things slowed down again, *The Swap Shop* was ending, reminding us it was eleven o'clock.

After a few more minutes at her ledgers, Geneva franked the last check, signed it, picked up the books, and came my way. "Here you go, at long last." She presented my folded check. "Sorry for the delay."

I paused, my feather duster hovering over the douches. "That's the thirty-leventh time you've apologized," I told her with mock severity. "It's getting on my nerves. If you don't stop it, I'll be forced to ask Vollie Biffle to cast out your demon of self-condemnation."

"Oh, please! Deliver me." It was the closest she ever came to saying she didn't like somebody—the mayor and Gary excepted, of course.

Glancing over to make certain the Coffee Club hadn't overheard, Geneva motioned me to keep my voice down, but she couldn't suppress a smile.

I opened my paycheck and gasped in delight. Four hundred eighty-two fifty, after taxes! (Which I immediately rounded up to five hundred—it sounded so much better.) "Holy crow. Is this right?"

"Right as rain." She tapped the ledger. "Eleven hours overtime at double pay."

That many! I'd left it to her to keep up with my time-sheet. As long as I got to class or campaign headquarters on time, I'd gratefully accepted all the work she could give me, regardless of my achy Breedlove knees.

"That's enough to pay for the plumbing and start the Sheetrock," I realized aloud.

How far I had fallen from Buckhead, where I'd spent more than that a month on club dues, lawn service, and maids. But Buckhead was my old life, a dream that had been blown irrevocably into the million lies that made it up. I did not wish for it back.

How could I? It was never real.

So at that moment, I rejoiced instead in far more concrete things. Real things, appropriate to the new life I was trying to make. "A few more weeks like this one, and I'll be in the apartment."

First, the garage's ancient pipes. And after the plumbing would come insulation, walls, paint, and paper. And varnish for the pine floors. And after that . . . *air conditioners*!

"Geneva, do you know a good plumber?"

"Frank the Plumber," she said as she carried the ledger back to its shelf in the pharmacy. "I've got his number at home. He's not the cheapest, but he's the only one left who knows about old houses—what you should mess with and what you should leave alone." She popped up on the other side of the pass-through. "And that'll be well worth the difference with that old place of yours, believe me."

Since the apartment had been built for Granny Beth's cook back in the twenties, I agreed. "Great. What's this Frank's last name?" I wanted to call him right away.

She tucked her chin, her eyebrows lowered. "Last name?" Her mouth pursed askew. "All I've ever heard was Frank the Plumber." She went to the half-open Dutch door and addressed the Coffee Club stragglers. "Any y'all know Frank the Plumber's last name?"

After murmured consultation, they came up dry. "Frank the Plumber's all we know, either," Walter Lott announced in his unofficial capacity as spokesperson.

"Wait a minute." Geneva smacked her forehead. "Where is my brain?" She pointed toward the dog-eared Rolodex by the register. "It's right there on his card."

I frowned. "But how can I look it up if I don't know his last name?"

She cocked an indulgent smile. "Under *F*, of course. If *I* don't know his last name, I couldn't very well file him under anything but *F* now, could I?" Which pretty much summed up her haphazard filing methods—her only fault as an employee.

I found the card near the back of the *F*'s. Frank the Plumber. 197 New Street, Mimosa Branch 30899, followed by the phone number.

Maybe he didn't *have* a last name.

"This is Frank the Plumber," he growled on his message. "Leave a number. And a name." He sounded like a real curmudgeon, but I did as instructed, asking him to call me at the store until seven, or at home between seven-thirty and eight. Then I went back to shelving and dusting the inventory.

"Have you heard anything new from Shelia?" I asked Geneva.

"Oh, she's doin' real good," she told me from behind the register. "She's still weak. Cain't stand on her feet for long, but she's feelin' a hundred percent better." She leaned closer and dropped her voice so the Coffee Club couldn't overhear. "I been tellin' her for five years she needed to have that thing out, but her mother had read all those articles back in the eighties about unnecessary hysterectomies, so she raised Cain every time Shelia brought it up."

"What *is* it about mothers," I asked, "that renders perfectly capable grown daughters unable to make a simple decision about their own health?"

"Would *you* want to take on *your* mother about something like that?" Geneva challenged.

"Touché," I conceded. "But I wouldn't let her stop me, either. I just wouldn't tell her until afterwards."

"Well, Shelia didn't have that luxury," Geneva explained. "Miz Ledbetter moved in after Mr. Ledbetter died of that stroke back in '91, and Shelia hasn't had a lick of privacy since. Miz Ledbetter even listens in on her phone calls."

"Poor Shelia." We were both trapped.

I banished the unhappy thought with another look at my check. My mind started placing my furniture in the apartment, and I felt a happy tug of anticipation. Then it dawned on me: I felt good—really good. Between the store and my classes and the campaign, I hadn't even had time to sit on the pity pot lately. And I hadn't thought about Phil since . . .

Since right that moment. But the mere thought of him no longer triggered the rage or anguish it always used to.

This was good. Very good.

If I could think about Phil without getting ill or angry, maybe I might even be able to get used to being celibate. Maybe.

Chapter 11

Wednesday night I came in from my real-estate class to find Tommy drinking iced tea on the porch again. I sat beside him and told him exactly what had transpired that morning with the mayor.

He frowned, took a long draught of tea, then leaned back in the rocker, staring into the sky. "He's got spies everywhere in this town. It stands to reason he'd have 'em in the program. It's disgusting, but there you are."

"That's it?" I didn't understand; he seemed so calm.

He sighed, smiling. "What is, is, Lin's-a-pin. We all know Stubbs is slime. As for what he insinuated, I have a choice. I can live my life with gratitude, regardless, or I can hand my hard-won serenity over to him on a silver platter and get all bent out of shape." He placed a finger beside his mouth. "Now which choice should I make? Mmmm. Very hard. Anger that won't change anything, or serenity?" His eyes twinkled. "Worrying about what somebody says about me, or serenity?" He shot me an impish grin. "I think I pick serenity."

Was this Tommy, the guy who always flew off the handle at the first sign of trouble, then sulked away to drink himself into oblivion?

No, it wasn't. This was a calm, considered adult, not nearly as fragile as I had thought.

"But what if he tells?" I challenged. "You were so adamant. You said your sobriety was yours to tell."

"So he tells," he said evenly. "At least it would be something good for a change." He leveled a serious look on me. "Get one thing straight: Nobody else can take my sobriety from me. I can throw it away—which I have no intention of doing—but nobody can steal it from me. So you don't need to worry about me, Sissie-ma-noo-noo." He rose. "And on that note, I'm gonna hit the hay."

"Tommy." I looked up at him, proud, proud, proud. "You're amazing."

"Not me, my program. Don't worry about me, Sis. I can take care of myself. You've got enough in your own little red wagon, anyway." He grinned. "Not that I mind your runnin' it over Ham Stubbs's toes the way you did this morning."

"I'm glad you said that." I rose to head for bed myself. "I was beginning to think you'd gotten a little too perfect."

The next day at noon on my way to the corner cleaners for my shirts, I bumped into Cassie on the sidewalk. She was wearing an emerald green outfit with bold patterns of shiny gold that my experience with charity receptions told me was Nigerian. I couldn't help smiling. All through the Civil Rights movement, Cassie had secretly wished she'd been born black, so her dressing like a true African princess made perfect sense.

Still guilty for my negative reaction to her coming out, I made a point of speaking first. "Hey, there," I said a little too brightly, pulling her into a brief, awkward hug. "So what's with the paper still over the windows? I thought you'd be open by now."

"Sharon and I have been arguing over how I can express my First Amendment rights without getting raided and shut down at the opening. I want to display my work openly. She wants to cover the windows with blowups of my good reviews and pictures of my awards so as not to offend the locals." She relaxed a bit, but not fully. "We'll work something out eventually. There's no great rush. Most of my sales come from the Internet, anyway." A brief pause. "How 'bout you? Whazzuh?"

"I'm booked tighter'n a dad-gummed airline," I informed myself as well as her. "Working at the drugstore all week. Then real-estate classes every Monday, Wednesday, and Friday night, and all day Saturdays. On Sundays, Tommy's been helping me get the garage apartment cleared out so I can fix it up to live in. Oh yeah, and I've been going to campaign meetings on Tuesdays and Thursdays out at Velma Christianson's. We're trying to get Donnie West elected mayor."

"When you don't have anything *else* to do." Cassie shook her head. "I swear Lin, still chasin' your tail at our age. Don't you get tired?"

"Sure. But it's all a means to an end, so I don't mind too much. I'm in transition."

She looked at me with sympathy. "Toward what?"

That one was easy, now. "Only tomorrow." I smiled. "That simple. Just tomorrow. And one of those tomorrows not too far off, I'll move into the garage apartment. It's enough to look forward to for now."

Uncomfortable with the brief silence that followed, I shifted the subject. "I really think Donnie West has a shot at unseating the mayor."

"Donnie's good people," Cass said. "He treats everybody with respect, even gays. The other preachers in this town could take a leaf from his book."

"You ought to come work for him, then. You and Sharon, both."

"Ah, Lin. Get real." Cassie shook her head with a rueful smile. "This is still Mimosa Branch we're talking about. With friends like me, Donnie wouldn't need enemies."

She had a point, and it would be stupid for me to deny it. "Oh. Yeah." In an effort to lighten the moment, I said the first thing that popped into my head. "Y'all could always go to work for the mayor, then. Spread it on thick. High profile. He wouldn't dare reject you publicly—too politically incorrect, even in Mimosa Branch."

Cassie let loose her infectious giggle. "That's an idea. Maybe we will."

She sobered, studying me in that intense way she had. There was nothing sexual about it; she'd done it since we were kids—looked at things so hard you'd swear she could see down to the bones. "One of those tomorrows before too long," she said, "I'd like to do a sculpture of you, a bust."

"Me?" Caught off-guard, I hesitated. "We're not talking horns or slitty irises or snake tongues or anything, are we?"

"Nope." I could almost see the image forming in her eyes. "Just plain ole Lin's-a-pin, at rest." She grinned and burbled that laugh of hers. "It's the only way anybody will ever get to see you sitting still."

A statue of me?

I would have said yes and quite possibly regretted it later, but $7000 worth of therapy kicked in, so instead I told her, "I'll think about it and let you know." A lot of money for those eight little words. Make that eleven little words—I'd also learned to say, "I don't know." So the investment had definitely been a good one.

"You won't have to do sittings," she coaxed. "All I need is a few hours to cast your face."

"Cast?"

"Yep. A life-cast. Vaseline, straws. Latex. I use that to make a clay positive, and from that, a permanent mold for the bronze or glass sculpture."

"Sounds pretty complicated."

An impish spark of the Cass I knew erupted. "It's what I do."

"A life-cast." Sounded awfully claustrophobic to me. Still, the idea of me as a sculpture did have its appeal. "I'll get back to you. Really."

"The session goes a lot easier if you have a joint before

we start," she propositioned, tongue-in-cheek. "You really ought to try it."

"Not yet," I deferred.

"Aha!" Cassie glowed with satisfaction. "Progress. She said 'not yet.' "

I turned. "I'm going to the cleaners now," I called back over my shoulder. The troubling thing was, I could actually imagine my giving weed another chance. Was I loosening up, or starting down sin's slippery slope?

Where the mind goes, the body follows, Granny Beth chided sternly from her throne deep in my conscience. *Beware!* But the moral alarms that usually conjured guilt and visions of divine retribution seemed muffled and far away.

You just never know what's going to happen when you get up in the morning, do you?

That night I drove under the huge "West Is Best" banner stretched between the massive stone pillars leading into Velma Christianson's rolling acreage—acreage the late judge was rumored to have acquired under questionable circumstances in an estate matter he'd overseen. Up ahead, the elaborate Euro-pseudo-sorta-something stucco mansion stood stark and graceless in the middle of pastures dotted with grazing sheep and llamas. ("Because they look so picturesque," Velma had explained, ingenuous as ever.)

The large graveled area next to her detached garage was already crowded with cars, pickups, and motorcycles presided over by a blissfully officious Walter Lott. Despite the fact that it was still daylight, he directed me into place with one of Grant's blackout flashlights, his emblem of authority.

I went inside the garage and marveled at the transformation that had been accomplished since we'd started setting up only a week before. The immaculate space was filled with long tables on loan from Donnie's church, and volunteers were already busily working away, seated in Ole Doc Owens's blue Baptist chairs.

The Coffee Club welcomed me from their spot in the corner (next to the coffee urn, of course). I waved back to them, surprised by the affection I'd developed for Mimosa Branch's own little Greek chorus. Several other volunteers greeted me just as warmly, some of them people I'd only met the week before. Across the room, a raw-boned redhead shot to her feet and waved. "Lin! Get yourself over here right this minute!"

I recognized her immediately as Gladys Soseby, High Holy Keeper of Miss Mamie's Sacred "Do" and taproot of the local grapevine. The last time I'd seen her, she'd been a brunette, but that had been more than ten years ago.

I went right over. One did not dare offend the biggest gossip in three counties. "Hey, there, Gladys."

She crushed me in a bear hug. "Oh, you poor sweet thing, you. How in the world are you holdin' up?"

Oh no, here we go, I thought.

I must have stiffened, because she thrust me to arm's length to look me over with laser-eyed assessment. "Goodness, child. You definitely need a facial," she announced for anyone to hear. "Maybe even a fruit peel. Not that it's any surprise considering what you're going through. Your skin's breakin' out like an eighth grader's."

The women around her suppressed chuckles.

Just what I needed—a serving of public humiliation. But since I knew better than to square off with her, I decided this was one of those times to try lightening up. "Ain't it a bitch? Zits and arthritis. A teenaged disease and an old-age disease at the same time."

The eavesdroppers laughed with me, which shifted the balance of power in the conversation to my side. Visibly miffed, Gladys eyed my short, tousled hair. "Who cuts your hair these days? It's gettin' a little shaggy in the back, there."

Oh, Lord! She was fishing for business. How was I go-

ing to get out of this one? I did *not* want Gladys within a
mile of my hair. I changed the subject. "So, Gladys . . .
what brings you here? I thought you lived in the county?"

"I do." She straightened. "But there's more to me than
scrubbin' heads. Donnie's a good man, the real thing. So
when Ginna Patterson told me he was going to run against
that crook Ham Stubbs, I vowed to help."

I backed away. "Well, we sure are glad to have you here.
Now if you'll excuse me, I have to see about some things
upstairs." I fled to the apartment above us, where I found
Grant surrounded by several computer types who were
helping him get the financial software up and running on
one of the judge's old computers.

As always when he was busy, Grant didn't even register
my being there, which was ironic since I couldn't shake an
unsettling awareness of his presence. Somehow at the drugstore, it was different, safer, but anywhere else. . . .

Determined to distract myself, I turned to Velma who
was in the kitchen presiding over an inviting array of sodas,
tomato juice for me, sweet tea, real lemonade, doughnuts
of every imaginable kind, sandwich makings, and crudités
for the more health-minded, which I was trying desperately
to be. Thanks to my busy schedule and lots of tomato juice,
I'd already lost eleven pounds. Since I wanted to keep them
off, I avoided the doughnuts and sandwiches.

Frail and elegant, Velma hovered over the food with a
lively enthusiasm that was a far cry from her initial reserve
of only a week ago. "I have a standing order with the
doughnut shop and the supermarket for every Tuesday,
Thursday, and Saturday," she announced proudly as I
nabbed a can of tomato juice and a plateful of veggies.
"They even deliver."

She shot a happy glance at Grant and his helpers. "Isn't
this *fun?* I haven't been this excited since . . . gosh, since I
had my last grandbaby, and she's eleven."

Fun?

Come to think of it, it was. Grown-up fun, the first I'd

had in a long, long time. Unless I counted that conversation with Grant the other night. That had been pretty fun, too, in its own bizarre way.

"We can't begin to thank you enough, Velma," I told her. "All these refreshments, though. You've already been so generous. We don't want to put a financial burden on you."

"Piffle!" she dismissed the idea with a genteel flap of her hand. "Besides my precious children, the only thing the judge ever gave me was heartache and ill-gotten gains. I can't undo what he did to get that money, but it gives me great joy to spend it on worthwhile things." She met my eyes with happy resolution. "I only wish I could do more, but Grant and Donnie have cautioned me to stick to the legal limits. So I called up a few old friends who've agreed to sponsor the refreshments from now until the election."

"That's fabulous."

"It gets better," she said. "I called a few more friends and raised fifteen thousand dollars. They've promised the checks within a week. And if they don't arrive on time, I'll call 'em again."

"Fifteen thousand dollars!"

Grant and his helpers looked up, grinning. Obviously, they already knew. Why hadn't Grant said something at work?

I let out a low whistle. "I didn't know there were that many people in Mimosa Branch who could give that kind of money."

"Oh, most of 'em aren't from Mimosa Branch," she explained. "They're from all over the county. I've done a lot of volunteering over the years. It's about time I called in a few chips."

A few more miracles like this one, and we just might have a big miracle at the polls.

A couple of biker types entered from the stairway lugging a two-drawer file cabinet that, judging from the effort in their faces, was fully loaded. "Where you want this, Miz Christianson?" one of them ground out, visibly strained.

Only then did I notice the gray in his long ponytail.

Velma rushed right over. "Oh, my goodness. I meant to empty out those files before you brought that down, but in all the excitement . . ." She looked around for a place to put it. "Just set it over there for now, out of the way. And don't worry about those other ones in the judge's study. I promise to have them emptied before Saturday. We'll bring them down then."

She returned to the kitchen area, shaking her head. "I should have cleared all that legal stuff out of the judge's study ages ago. I meant to, but since it wasn't anything urgent, I just never got around to it. I can hardly believe it's been three years."

"What do you do with files like that?" I asked, unaware then of the potent seeds my question sowed. "Can you just throw them away? Or should they be kept somewhere, just in case?"

"When I sold the practice, I did go through and round up all the case files for the new owner. The rest . . ." She tugged absently at her soft blonde bob. "I don't know. I'll call one of the boys and ask." All four of her sons were successful lawyers with their own practices. "I'd planned to go through them again anyway, just in case we'd missed something when we settled the estate. Like I said, time just got away from me."

"Happens to all of us." I headed out with my food and drink. "I'm off to crack the whip over the voter-registration team."

Grant glanced up as I passed, and I could have sworn I saw a flicker of worry in his eyes before he went back to his work.

What was eating him? I wondered. *And why did I care?*

Minding my own business was another resolution I was working to keep, but it didn't come easy.

Back downstairs, the tables had filled with volunteer teams, and the sound of animated voices competed with hammering from outside, where signs were being assembled. Exhilarated by the positive energy in the noisy room, I plunged into cross-referencing the registered-voter print-out against the phone listings from our zip code to find people we could call, interview, and encourage to register if they were sympathetic. The process was labor intensive, but labor was the one thing we seemed to have in abundance. Every meeting, there were more and more volunteers. Geneva's speech had worked. Even if they only had an hour to give, our people came.

Beside my team, ten of our best callers were busy contacting people in their own neighborhoods to encourage them to register and vote for Donnie. Each section of the city had its own issues with the current administration, so our callers had plenty of incentive to work with.

At least thirty more volunteers were writing personal letters of recommendation to their friends and relatives inside the city limits. Another two dozen (mostly transplants) were addressing preprinted postcards to everyone who had bought property in Mimosa Branch in the past five years.

The methods were crude, the slogans were simple, but the fire of conviction burned bright.

I'd been working about thirty minutes when Geneva approached and bent down to murmur discreetly into my ear. "As soon as Donnie gets here, Grant wants us to get together in private."

The last word set off alarm bells. "I thought everything here was going to be open and aboveboard," I said quietly.

"Me, too." Her eyes crinkled in that "I'm worried" way of hers.

"Upstairs?"

She shook her head. "Outside."

This definitely smelled. The cynical part of my old self immediately began spewing dire suspicions. "Okay. Just let me know."

Fifteen minutes later, Grant came down from upstairs and motioned both of us to follow him out.

I left the volunteers, praying my newfound confidence

in grassroots politics wasn't about to be shattered.

We met Donnie halfway to his motorcycle, and as usual, his welcoming wave was confirmed by a broad smile that made his eyes dance. "Hey, y'all. Idn't that banner somethin'? I had to fight the sin of pride when I saw that thing, fight it with the Holy Ghost and fire."

Grant intercepted him. "Hi, guy." They shook hands, and as they did, Grant took Donnie's elbow. Donnie shot a warning look at the point of contact. "Before you go inside," Grant said evenly, steering Donnie toward the pasture gate, "can we have a little powwow?"

Donnie halted, giving us a glimpse of the savvy streetfighter he'd once been. His eyes went hard, his body tense. "That depends. Why?"

Grant looked past him to the grazing sheep. "I've found out some information that has a direct effect on the campaign, but I don't think it's safe to discuss it inside."

"Why not?" Donnie clipped out.

"One of my customers told me Stubbs has sent in several 'moles.' And Velma said she caught a city meter-reader inside the garage with one of the phones in his hands. She said he jumped a mile when she opened the door. He claimed he was just calling in a page, but he wasn't wearing a pager. She thinks he was tampering with the phone."

"They use radios, not pagers, anyway," Donnie confirmed.

"Holy crow," Geneva breathed. "Spies? Are you for real?"

My old self spewed out more dire cynicisms. "Would they really tap our phones?"

"I don't think we can afford to dismiss the possibility," Grant answered. "And there are the computers to consider. Velma's loaning us several from the judge's old office and study. We're vulnerable there, too."

"Fleas, already," I breathed out. You lie down with dogs . . . "Damn, that was quick."

"So what else is new?" Donnie grinned, relaxing. "I've

been sparrin' with the devil for fifteen years. I'm used to dirtier tricks than this. I don't shock. And as long as I'm doing what the Big Guy tells me to, I don't scare, either." He shrugged. "So. What comes next?"

"Let me make some calls—from a pay phone," Grant qualified wryly. "I've got a couple of poker partners back in California who work in corporate security for the Silicon Valley. I'll get them to recommend somebody local who can sweep us for bugs and check out the computers. Thanks to Velma's war chest, we can afford it. Until then, I think it would be best to keep this under our hats and play it straight, 'cause anything we say can be used against us."

"Son, straight is the only way I ever play it," Donnie declared, undaunted. He took Grant's elbow and steered him toward the garage, just the way Grant had tried to steer him toward the pasture. "Now let's get in there and make a difference."

When Geneva lagged back, visibly disturbed, I did, too.

"Up to now, I never really considered how ugly this could get," she said quietly. "I mean, I knew what everybody said about how the mayor corrupted Gary Mayfield, but this and all that mess this morning . . ." She looked up into the cloudless evening sky. "This is too real. It makes me realize he might do worse. Lots worse."

I put my hand on her arm. "You've got kids in town. Grandchildren." I could see from the way she looked at me that I'd hit on what she was thinking. "We all knew Ham Stubbs plays dirty." She had good reason to worry about her own family. "I just hadn't expected it so soon."

Since I was in my "fuck it" phase, I wasn't frightened. But Geneva . . . "If you want out, Geneva, nobody will hold it against you. I'd be glad to take over. I'm not vulnerable the way you are."

"Will you let a person worry a little?" she grumbled, giving me a half-hearted poke. "It doesn't mean I'm chicken. Of course I don't want out. This kind of stuff makes me more *in* than ever." She pinned me with an assessing look. "How 'bout you? Having second thoughts?"

"And thirds and fourths," I admitted. "But all of them involve kicking Ham Stubbs's crooked ass at the polls."

"All of them?" She waggled her eyebrows, the sparkle returning to her eyes. "Not even one little thought about Grant?"

"Shut your mouth, Geneva Bates," I whispered, giving her a playful poke back. "Grant and I are friends. Not even that." My confidentiality clause kept me from telling her he was merely my man-source.

"That's not what Kenneth Ledford told me," she leaned close to say. "He said he saw you two sittin' out on Miss Mamie's porch big as life after ten o'clock at night, and Grant was nekkid to the waist."

I cursed the flush that betrayed my embarrassment. I should have known better than to think anything in Mimosa Branch could be a secret. "Big deal. He only took off his shirt because it was soaked. He'd been running and said the beer I was drinking looked good. I had no choice but to offer him one."

"No choice," she repeated, grinning. "None at all."

"Sarcasm doesn't become you, Geneva," I said with a stab at dignity that didn't even convince me.

"You're not the only one who can turn over a new leaf, missy." She resumed her progress toward the garage. "Now that I'm a real, live, campaign manager, I could probably use some sarcasm."

"You'll have to do better than that," I challenged. "Maybe Gertrude Booth could give you some lessons."

We were both laughing when we walked inside.

Chapter 12

The following Sunday after church, Tommy and I were sanding Sheetrock joints in the apartment when we heard a knock at the door. My skin and hair coated in Sheetrock dust, a painter's mask over my nose and mouth, and a pair of my father's old work gloves on my hands, I looked over my granny glasses to find an amused Grant waiting in the doorway.

Even in cutoffs and a T-shirt, he looked crisp and collected and way too gorgeous. Those long, hard, tanned runner's legs . . .

"Hi. I heard you guys working and wondered if you could use a little help."

Suddenly conscious of my appearance, I brushed vigorously at my hair, which succeeded only in raising a Pigpen-esque cloud around my head that set Grant coughing.

"Nice to see you." Tommy stepped over and shook his hand. "We can use all the help we can get." He pulled a mask from the box and handed it to Grant. "Here. Better start with this." He waved his sanding sponge at the newly sealed, insulated, and Sheetrocked walls. "We were just about to finish up these joints. Then I was going to start laying the new tile in the bathroom while Lin cleans up so we can paint."

As Grant put on the mask, Tommy paused. "No offense meant, but have you ever done anything like this before?"

Grant blinked at him, deadpan. "I put myself through college working residential construction."

Tommy chuckled. "Great. You can be the foreman." He handed Grant his sponge, then headed for the bathroom with the sledgehammer.

I just stood there like an idiot, wishing I hadn't worn the old T-shirt with a hole in the side that exposed what was left of my love handles. And my baggy cutoffs made me look wide as a recliner.

The sudden self-assessment—and resulting insecurity— felt all too adolescent.

What was I doing? I was a fifty-year-old woman, not some kid on the prowl. *Remember your motto,* I exhorted myself. *If he doesn't like the way you look, fuck him.*

The trouble was, I really wanted a roll in the hay with him, which was insane because I knew virtually nothing about him. At least, he was my only fantasy, so I must have wanted to go to bed with him, right? But only if I could give him an amnesiac so he wouldn't remember anything.

Or maybe I only wanted to *want* to go to bed with him. After all, he was from California. He probably had a whole smorgasbord of venereal diseases. Why couldn't he just remain my fantasy lover, leave it at that?

It was all quite exhausting.

What makes you think a good-looking man like him would even consider going to bed with a woman like you? my old self sneered. *He could have any of the barflirts at Café Luna. Maybe he does.*

If he did, it wasn't at home. I'd never seen another car there besides his or heard a whiff of gossip connecting him to anybody in town.

He had, though, been getting mysterious calls at work lately from a sultry female voice. Whenever he took the call, his body language had instantly betrayed that something big was going on *there*. Geneva was all stirred up about it, but I had dismissed her wild conjectures, trying to convince myself that it didn't matter because I wasn't really interested in him. I just had this sexual aberration.

He was, after all, a dangerous half-jerk. Well, maybe one-third jerk.

"Okay," Grant said, clearly oblivious to what I was thinking, thank God. "Where did you leave off with the sanding?"

Finally, I found my voice. "Right there." I pointed to the final section.

"Nice job. Who did your mud work?"

"One of my father's retired subcontractors, Delton Pirkle. You know him, from the Coffee Club. But he can't sand anymore. Bad lungs."

"Mmm." Clearly, Grant didn't put a face to the name. He approached the wall, smoothing his shapely Roman hand over the joint to feel for flaws. My treacherous mind imagined that same hand stroking up my torso with similar studied pressure.

Zap from the hot button.

Humiliated, I commenced sanding as far away from him as I could. "So you worked your way through college. Where was that?"

"L.A." He stroked the sanding block with perfect pressure over the joint. "My mother and I moved there when my parents divorced. I was thirteen." The bitterness in his voice was cloaked by time, but I could hear it.

The worst time possible for a boy to lose his father.

I did some quick math. Doc Owens had taken over the drugstore in 1962. I remembered the year because I'd had my eleventh birthday party at the soda fountain just after he'd come here with his wife. Grant was fifty-three now (I'd seen his birth date on our insurance records) so that meant Mrs. Owens had most probably been the other woman.

Plain, plump Mrs. Owens! Backbone of the tiny Presbyterian church.

Little wonder Grant had never wanted to come back east to visit. "So I take it the divorce wasn't amicable."

He stopped sanding to peer at me over the mask, his eyes guarded. "No matter what anybody says, divorces never are."

"I hear you, there."

He resumed sanding. "I know everybody in this town thinks my father was some kind of saint, but he wasn't. He left my mother and me for another woman."

"It's the American way," I said without trying to hide my own resentment.

"Is that what happened to you?"

You'd think, after a year of crisis and nine months single, that I'd have been sick of talking about it, but I blurted out, "My husband managed to carry midlife madness to creative new heights. I found out he was engaged to a twenty-three-year-old stripper who looked all of twelve, and he'd spent two hundred thousand dollars we didn't have on her and strip clubs." I scrubbed a little too hard over a rough patch, leaving faint gouges. "God only knows how much he spent of what we *did* have. By the time I found out, we had nothing left but huge debts. He'd mortgaged our house to one hundred ten percent and hadn't even filed his taxes in three years, much less paid them. This, from a CPA." So much for being mysterious.

A low whistle escaped from behind Grant's mask. "That's pretty spectacular, all right. No wonder you're bitter."

It rubbed me the wrong way for him to say that. "And you're not?"

"That's different. I was a kid. My father abandoned us. I had a right to be bitter."

The dull thunk of Tommy sledgehammering the old bathroom floor set the fine Sheetrock dust in the air to pulsing. Suddenly the atmosphere seemed close and sour.

"My Granny Beth used to tell me that being bitter about

somebody was like drinking strychnine and expecting it to poison the other person."

"I hate platitudes," he bit out. "Especially when it's the pot calling the kettle black."

I refused to take the bait. "Your father didn't support y'all?"

"Oh, he sent a little, but it wasn't ever enough. My mother worked herself into an early grave as a live-in housekeeper in Brentwood. I spent my teenaged years in servants' quarters trying to stay invisible so I wouldn't jeopardize her job. They expected me to do yard work for free. And other things." The last was thick with vitriol, conjuring images of rich matrons and pool boys.

Bitter, bitter, bitter, but who could blame him? my less-judgmental new self observed. At least he'd spoken openly about his past. Actually talked to me.

I don't think Phil ever talked to me about himself that way in the thirty years we were married. We'd talked about things: his work, David, our social lives, stuff about the house, my charity work. Never anything about his feelings. All "whats," no "whys." I never did know what was going on inside his head.

The next unaskable question was obvious. "How about you?" I ventured. "Were you ever married?"

Grant's whole body tensed.

Aha. I'd hit a nerve there.

"Yes."

Ah. Phil-talk. One-word answer, no elaboration. Here we go again. . . .

"Once, twice?" I asked sweetly.

"None of your goddamn business," he answered just as sweetly.

Oh, great. He probably thought I was feeling him out with dating in mind.

My sly old self dropped in an ominous thought, which I promptly blurted out. "You don't have a wife back in

L.A., do you?" Perfect. Now he'd be convinced I had dating in mind, but fuck it.

He actually chuckled. "No. No wife. Just exes."

Exes, plural. This man was not a good risk.

And I was neither vulnerable nor stupid enough to get involved, I told myself, despite my inappropriate fantasies about him.

I gave the wall a final swipe. "We're done in here. The bedroom's all that's left."

Grant unplugged the oscillating fan and followed me into the twelve-foot-square room. "Do the outlets in here work?"

"I don't know." Seven thousand dollars of therapy at work. "Try one." I pointed to the outlet, but suddenly all I saw was my bed in this room with Grant Owens in it, naked and ready to roll.

This was ridiculous. I wouldn't be able to look the man in the face unless I could get a grip on myself. My ears commenced to throbbing with every heartbeat.

I came out of my lapse to find him peering at me, his brows drawn together above his mask. "Are you okay? You just went all red and your pupils dilated." He glanced around, then back at me. "I'd suggest you sit down, but there's no chair."

Mortified, I felt a blast of adrenaline erupt that left my hands and legs tingling and my head full of fuzz.

"Wup!" Grant grabbed my elbow. "Tommy, I'm taking your sister through the hedge for some cool air and lemonade. We'll be back in a minute."

Tommy stuck his head out the bathroom door. "You okay, Sissie-ma-noo-noo?"

Perfect. Now Grant had heard that ridiculous nickname. "I'm fine. Just a little overheated." A burp of semi-hysterical laughter escaped me at the double entendre. If only he knew.

Both men peered at me in concern.

"Good idea," Tommy said. "Get her cooled down."

"Ha!" Oh, Lord. I'd done it again, but my salacious mind seemed determined to give everything a double meaning. Biting my lips, I took a deep breath to stave off a Mary-Tyler-Moore-at-Chuckles-the-Clown's-Funeral outburst.

Grant pulled the leather work gloves off my hands as if I were a feeble child. "Here. Let's get you out of these things."

Another double entendre, but I managed to stave off hysterics. I removed my mask myself.

His hand firmly on my elbow, he guided me to the tiny stoop at the top of the garage stairs. Even in the shade of our giant oaks, the brilliant light from the early August sky made me wince until my eyes adjusted. Fortunately, it was enough of a distraction to calm the giggles.

"You first," Grant said politely.

"No, really, you." I hated going down before people because my bad knees made me so slow.

His sandy brows knit again, but then his face cleared, and he did as I asked. "Okay. Whatever the lady wants."

Still a little rocky in the self-control department, I followed him down as gracefully as I could manage. We walked alongside each other to the hedge, where he held back the camellia branches in the thin spot that had always been the pathway between our houses. When we came out on the other side, I was pleasantly surprised at the transformation of the brick bungalow that had been his father's.

The grass was thick and green, and petunias and impatiens flourished in the beds around the house. Fresh paint brightened the white trimwork and dark green shutters. Even the graveled driveway looked neat. Gone was the clutter that had been piled up for as long as I could remember behind the "car house" as my Granny Beth had called it.

"Wow. This looks great."

"You should have seen it when I came here," he said easily. "It was a mess. I don't think my father had done

anything to the place in twenty years." He motioned me
onto the tidy patio. "Here. Let me get that door." He
climbed the concrete stoop to unlock the door. When he
opened it, I was pleased to see that the cat door had been
sealed with a strip of lath inside. Waiting in the kitchen,
my mother's kitten sat fat and happy beside an enormous
orange tiger cat. Neither of them made any effort to escape
into the heat.

I stepped into the cool and gratefully inhaled. "Oh, that
does feel good."

The place was immaculate. "Where are all the invisible
empties?" I couldn't resist asking.

His answering grin was boyish and open. "That man-
rule doesn't apply at my place. Only everywhere else." He
motioned to the vintage fifties chrome-and-formica breakfast set. "Have a seat. Velma sent me home with two gallons of fresh lemonade, so I'll have some for us in no time."

The plastic seat was cold on the backs of my legs, which
sent a delicious shiver through me. While Grant got out
two mismatched glasses (he was a bachelor, after all) and
filled them with ice, I scanned the tidy interior of the house.
"I haven't been in here since I was a kid selling Girl Scout
cookies." What were the owners' names then? They'd lived
next door to us until Grant's daddy had bought the place.
Why couldn't I remember?

"Are these your things or your father's?" I asked as I
took in the hodgepodge of furniture.

Grant set my lemonade on a napkin in front of me before
joining me with his own. He had good manners, at least.
Then I remembered what he'd said about his adolescence.
He'd probably picked them up from the outside looking in,
in Brentwood.

If they even *had* manners in California.

But he was neat, I gave him that. Phil wouldn't pick up
so much as a sock. His bachelor apartment had looked like
a street person had been camping there.

I caught myself in the comparison and went sour. I

didn't want to think of Phil, period, and here I was comparing him to the first eligible man I'd met.

Damn.

Not that I was actually considering any kind of real relationship with Grant Owens. Strictly fantasy. That was it.

"What's the matter?" Grant asked, regarding me with that same baffled concern he'd shown up in the apartment.

What would he do if I told him the truth? *Oh, I was just comparing you favorably to my ex-husband. And fantasizing about you naked with a ten-inch hard-on. And wondering what in pluperfect perdition is the* matter *with me.*

I had to laugh. "Nothing. Nothing." I stood up and walked into the modest living-dining area. "You sure are tidy for a man."

He rose, too, and followed. Quite the gentleman. "You don't think much of my gender, do you?" he retorted. "Not every man is a slob."

"All the men I know are messy."

"And all the women I know are nosey," he shot back. "So what?"

This was going nowhere. "Truce." I lifted my lemonade. "Thank you, Grant, for helping out in the apartment. And for bringing me over for lemonade and air conditioning. I truly appreciate it."

There was that killer smile. "See. Now that wasn't so hard, was it?"

"Yes," I teased. "It was excruciating."

"I have a woman-question for you," he posed.

I prayed he hadn't sensed what I'd been thinking about him. Could he smell the hormones? "We're not on Miss Mamie's porch."

"No, but we are alone," he reasoned. "Couldn't we add an amendment to the agreement? Make it okay if we're not on Miss Mamie's porch as long as we're alone and both parties are willing?"

"I suppose so." I had to admit, he'd piqued my curiosity.

"Okay," he said. "Why do women always ask so many personal questions?"

"Is this a dig masquerading as a woman-question? Because if it is, you lose your turn."

Humor brightened his hazel eyes. "This is not a dig. It's a legitimate question. True, you did ask personal questions back there. What I want to know is why."

"Usually it's the women who are big on whys," I observed.

"There you go, deflecting with another wry observation. Will you answer the question?" he challenged.

"Sure. Would you accept 'I don't know' for an answer? It took seven thousand dollars' worth of therapy for me to be able to admit that, you know. Of course, that was back when we still *had* seven thousand dollars."

He looked at me as if I'd gone green. "The more you talk, the more confused I get. Is that how this thing is supposed to work?"

"No. No, it's not. Although I'm still chewing on that 'drinks don't exist when they're empty' answer of yours. Especially with the 'except in my own house' codicil."

"That's pretty clear to me. Unless I'm at home, if it's empty, I don't see it."

"But it's *there*," I argued. "How could you not see it? And why can you see it at home?"

"Will you accept 'I don't know' for an answer, even though it didn't cost me a thing to learn how to say it?"

I had to give it to this guy. He was sharp. And I liked the repartee. It made me feel adult and human. "Okay."

"But I do not accept your 'I don't know.' Come on. Enlighten me." A slow smile lifted one side of his mouth. "Why the personal questions?"

Could I answer that question? "I suppose I can come up with something, but it has no warranties."

"Fire away." He pulled out one of the four padded dining room chairs for me to sit. After I did, he took the seat to my right. "I'm all ears."

By the seat of my pants, I said, "Context, relationship, is primary with women. Maybe it's cultural. Maybe it's anthropological, but we define ourselves and everyone else by relationships and context. Like men define themselves by what they do."

"So?"

"So we relate to men by establishing a context. 'Is he married?' comes first. For most women, that's a major barrier. For some"—like Phil's strippers—"it's a turn-on. Beyond that, we want to know what makes you tick. Your past tells us a lot about that."

"So my past told you . . . what?"

Oh, hell. I might as well be honest, at least about this. "That you had good reason for not wanting to come see your father, much less go into business with him. Up to then, I'd thought you must have been pretty selfish and hard-hearted to turn you back on a sweet man like Doc Owens. Now I know your father had another side."

Grant drew back, his jaw set. "So, knowing nothing about me, you had decided I was selfish and hard-hearted?"

"It was judgmental, I admit. I'm cursed with a 'black-and-white' mentality. But our first meeting hardly did anything to counteract that opinion."

He eased somewhat. "Well, I suppose I wasn't very thoughtful there. But I'd been chasing that damned cat for almost an hour, and she was shredding my hands, and those toms were circling the house, pissing all over everything."

"I see we share a compulsion to be justified, as well as a cat."

"Do you talk to all men this way?" he asked, frowning.

"I don't know. You're my first, really."

"What do you mean, I'm your first?" he demanded. "Geneva said you were married for thirty years."

"Yes, I was. But you see, we never talked. Not really. Not about things that mattered." Why was I saying all this to *him?* Where was it coming from? "Phil might as well have been my accountant for all he ever gave me of himself. Of course, he was—a CPA, that is. The strange thing was, I never realized we hadn't really talked until it was all over."

"Spare me." Grant's eyes narrowed. "Why is it that what we *are* is never enough for women?"

Taking the question to be rhetorical, I decided to employ my "lighten up" resolution and started humming "Feelings." (Humming is the extent of my musical talents.)

"If you burst into song," he said, annoyed, "I'm liable to throw up."

For some reason, that struck me as funny. "Oh, you might throw up, but only because of my voice. I was the only person in Mimosa Branch Methodist who was ever forbidden to sing. The choir director put me on consonant patrol, told me to lip-synch until we came to the word *Lord*, whereupon I was to say the *d* on the end 'crisply and clearly' as she'd instructed."

Unable to suppress a smile, Grant shook his head. "You just said 'whereupon' in casual conversation. I know Ph.D.'s who wouldn't use that word in casual conversation."

My hormones had almost made me forget that I was dealing with a half-jerk, but that brilliant observation reminded me in spades. "See, now there's a perfect example of the difference between men and women," I shot back. "I just revealed a weakness of mine, exposed an imperfection. And instead of processing what I told you, you criticize the way I said it. So in exchange for a confession, I get a put-down. This is not a good thing."

He actually colored. "I only—I mean, it wasn't a putdown. I was just—"

I rose, cutting him off. "Look, I answered your question. And I do appreciate the break, really. But now I need to go back to the apartment. I have to finish the sanding, then try to get the place vacuumed out so Tommy can start painting as soon as he's done with the tile." Why was I explaining? I always explained too much. This was not good.

The next thing I knew, I wanted to cry. Why? Just because some jerk had criticized the way I talk?

Grow up, I told myself. *Toughen up!*

"Geeze, Lin, you look like a little kid who just found out there's no Santa Claus." Grant's concern seemed genuine. "I'm sorry I said that. It was never intended to make you feel bad."

"Intent has no bearing on the quality of your communication," I quoted from my sales training. "The quality of your communication is determined by the response it evokes."

He tried not to smile, but didn't succeed. "There you go again. I have no idea what that means."

"It means," I minced out in my primmest lady voice, "fuck you, Grant Owens. And thank you for the lemonade. It was delightful. I can't say the same for the conversation."

Head high, I left him leaning against the table.

As I stomped past our kitten, I bent down to hiss "traitor," whereupon she scrambled under the dinette set.

From that day on, *whereupon* became my favorite word.

Chapter 13

The next Tuesday night at campaign headquarters, Velma was waiting when Geneva and I drove up. I could see from the drawn look on her face that something was wrong.

Something besides the mayor's messing with our phones?

She trailed us to our regular parking place. Once we were out, she motioned us to the pasture fence, out of earshot from the others who were arriving.

"Lin. Geneva." She bit her lip, a sure giveaway that what she was about to tell us was a thing that, once said, she might regret. That let out the business with the phones.

But old habits die hard, so I jumped in with conjecture. "Is it the phones, Velma?"

"No." She glanced nervously toward the arriving workers. "The security man came this morning. He didn't find a tap on the lines inside, but there was one out at the pole. He fixed it and notified the phone company, then spent most of the day straightening out the computers. That's what I need to talk to y'all about." Another pregnant hesitation. "I know you trust Grant, and he seems a fine man, but he's not from here, and this is such a volatile thing. . . ."

Geneva grasped Velma's upper arms and looked her in the eye. "Just tell us. We won't say a word to anybody, including Grant, if you don't want us to."

Reassured, Velma nodded. "It's about the judge's files. You know I promised to clean out those cabinets in his office. Well, I spent all day Saturday sorting them into boxes. Then I started reading through them. That's when I started finding things."

"What sort of things?" I prodded gently.

She glanced aside again, then turned troubled eyes to us. "Cryptic notes to and from the mayor involving those subdivisions he and the judge were doing together. You know, the two out on Mason's Mill Road, and that new one they had annexed into the city."

"And?"

"It has something to do with the city crews. I couldn't figure out exactly what, but it was obviously something they didn't want anybody else finding out." She exhaled heavily. "So when that security man started working on the judge's old computer and asked me if I wanted to try to recover any of the data that had been erased, I said yes." Her eyes welled. "I don't know why I said it. I didn't really think anything would come of it. But I couldn't help wondering if there might be some answers there."

"And there were?" Geneva asked, though the answer was obvious to all of us.

Velma nodded. "The best I can tell, they were using city equipment and crews to put in the utilities to their subdivisions, then billing it to the taxpayers as regular maintenance."

Geneva and I both whistled. Velma had just handed us the race on a silver platter. That is, *if* she would let us use this.

Geneva asked the question before I could. "Is this something we can bring out against the mayor, Velma? Or do you want it kept under wraps? The judge was your husband. We can certainly understand if you don't want to stain his memory—"

"I don't give a possum's dribble for the judge's reputation. He ruined that all by himself, dyin' the way he did"—riding a cheap prostitute—"and endin' up on the front page of the papers and all the TV news," Velma said with cold, hard composure. There was nothing timid or naïve in her response. "After the way he cheated the people of this county—and me—and shamed my children, why should I care? The kids won't care either. I asked them. They know what he was." She looked from me to Geneva with deadly resolution. "But if we use this, somebody really might get hurt. We have to be careful. I don't know how low the mayor would go to preserve his power."

After all those years of thinking of Velma as the sheltered, long-suffering, martyred wife of a local-boy-made-good-gone-bad, it was a surprise to see the grit and stony pragmatism she now revealed.

"Where is the information?" Geneva asked.

"I didn't trust the safe at the house," Velma said, "so I had my daughter-in-law Mary rent us a large safe-deposit box up at the branch she manages in Gainesville. We put the files and one set of the diskettes in there this morning." She fished a key from her pocket and slipped it to Geneva. "You're on the card. Here's your key." She drew out three diskettes neatly labeled FILES AUGUST 14. "Here. Put these where nobody can get them."

Geneva glanced at them as if they were radioactive, then slipped them into the pocket of her jacket. "What now?" she asked Velma. "You tell us. It's your call."

"No, it isn't," she corrected gently. "It's Donnie's. He said he didn't want a negative campaign."

"But Velma," I protested, "this is criminal. The taxpayers have a right to know."

"I agree," she said, contradicting her words with a shake of her head. "Still, I want Donnie to make the decision."

"So why tell us?" I challenged.

Velma's grin chased the anxiety from her face. "You always were a sharp one." She relaxed a bit. "I figured y'all could be more persuasive than I could. Nothing wrong with giving him a little wise counsel, is there?"

It was my turn to shake my head and grin. "Whoo, Velma. Maybe we should have run you for mayor."

"Not mayor," she said firmly. "But I just might consider gettin' this place annexed into the city so that the next time that skunk Gary Mayfield's up for reelection to the council, I could run against him."

"Now *that* would be a horse race!" Geneva seemed as delighted as I was at the prospect.

"I'll leave you two out here to talk to Donnie. I think I hear his motorcycle roarin' down Bradburn Avenue." She headed for the garage, cool as you please.

Sure enough, Donnie arrived in a cloud of granite dust and rolling thunder. We flanked him as he parked, then herded him over to "the conference room," as Geneva had dubbed the patch of sweet clover by the pasture gate.

Geneva explained things with her usual brief clarity.

As we'd anticipated, he said he'd have to pray about the matter.

"Just remember when you do," Geneva advised him, "that the Lord loves the truth and hates a lie. People have a right to know this, Donnie."

"The ways of God are not the ways of a man," our candidate said with a smile.

"And He is a God of justice as well as mercy," I reminded him, "who does not wink at sin."

"Trust in the Lord, and lean not to thine own understanding," he countered. "I just love swappin' scriptures with y'all, but I'm gonna have to get a clear leadin' from the Holy Ghost on this one. It's too important—and too dangerous—not to."

"Consider the timing, Donnie," I added. "Seems to me that the Lord has handed you a sword."

"Or the enemy has," he amended. "It's a sword, all right. I just gotta be sure where it came from, and what I'm supposed to do with it."

"We trust your faith," Geneva affirmed, "and your leading."

I watched him walk toward the garage with his usual easy confidence. "And now?" I asked Geneva.

"And now," she answered, "we trust the Lord's leadin', but work like it's all up to us."

"My Granny Beth used to say that," I told her as we headed back inside.

"I know. She said it to me, too, when she was my teacher in combined Vacation Bible School."

After the work session and a cool shower, I told myself I was thirsty and wired when I took my iced decaffeinated tea out front to Miss Mamie's porch at ten o'clock to rock and sip. Maybe I was just lonely and hoped Grant would come jogging along. Either way, I was rocking beside the swing, protected from mosquitoes by the strong downdraft of the ceiling fan, when he jogged into our driveway, then slowed to a loose walk, hands on hips, and climbed the stairs to join me without an invitation.

Unnerving, how he'd just materialized when I'd been thinking about him—and thinking most inappropriately.

"Hey," he panted out, collapsing into the swing with a whiff of that same toasty, tangy, hot-man smell that was so incongruously erotic.

"Hey, yourself." I raised my glass. "Want some tea?"

"No, thanks. But water would be great."

"Water, it is."

By the time I got back, he was gliding slowly to the measured creak of the swing's chains. He sat forward and lifted his sodden T-shirt. "Do you mind?"

Seeing him half-naked? Heck, no. "Sure. Go ahead."

He peeled off the shirt and heaved it onto the lawn near the driveway, to protect my delicate sensibilities, I guessed.

All too aware of his muscular shoulders, I handed him the heavy quart glass of iced water. "Here."

He poured some of the cold liquid into his palm, wiped his face with it, then sat back for a long quaff. After a satisfied sigh, he said, "So. What was going on with Geneva and you tonight?"

So he *had* noticed. Taken aback, I responded, "Foul. That is not a woman-question."

"No. It's a Lin and Geneva question," he said evenly. "Are you saying normal questions aren't allowed on Miss Mamie's porch?"

"Maybe. But if we're asking regular questions, I have one for you." As usual when somebody asks me a question I didn't want to answer, I countered with one just as invasive. "What was it like when you were a little boy? Before your parents divorced?"

"Ah. More context," he said with only mild exasperation. After an assessing pause, he obliged. "Okay, I'll tell you. But not until you tell me what it was like growing up in this house."

Drat. He'd turned my own tactics against me. "Mmm. My childhood." A safer subject than his well-founded suspicions about me and Geneva. "That's a hard one." I stared across the tracks to the darkened houses on Bradburn Avenue. "Before I moved back home, I didn't recall much about my childhood. What little I remembered was mostly bad—not seriously bad, just minor disappointments, embarrassments. But being here has made me start remembering some of the good things. And every new memory triggers others, until now I'm realizing that there was more good than bad. It was just my own little black-cloud perspective that made things seem so negative."

"Like what things?"

"Like resentments about my parents. I hated the fact that my father was so loud and coarse and autocratic and critical—and racist. And that my mother was so strict and nosey and controlling. And Tommy, he drove me nuts. The Cleavers, we were not."

"Hell, even the Cleavers weren't perfect," Grant observed. "Look at the Beaver. He turned out gay."

I laughed. Then an introspective mood settled over me.

"I never knew how lucky I was. I had my Granny Beth and Nana Grainger right here with me. Two doting grandmothers at my beck and call. And the whole of Mimosa Branch for my playground—it was safe back then. I had parents who loved me, regardless of the way they fought with each other. And I never lacked for anything material. A pretty idyllic childhood, really."

A distant train whistle sounded. The ten-thirty freight.

"Listen," I told him. "Zaida used to be able to tell if it was going to rain from the sound of the train whistle."

"Who's Zaida?"

"Our maid. She raised Miss Mamie, and then she raised me."

"Good Lord," he hooted way too loud. "You had a mammy. I might have known."

"Shhh! I did *not* have a mammy," I hissed. "Were you brought up in a pool hall, or did you come to this height of rudeness all by yourself?"

"It's not rudeness," he whipped out like a true self-righteous transplant. "I simply refuse to wrap the evils of the racist past in sugar-coated nostalgia." I felt him staring at me. "Admit it. You had a mammy."

"I had nothing of the sort." My Delta-is-ready-when-you-are juices boiled. "Lord, I get sick of people who move here, then start criticizing things they don't understand." I shifted in my seat to face him. He was leaning forward intently in the swing, his arms propped on his thighs, water in hand. "Zaida was a second mother to me, a decent, strong, fierce, hard-working, God-fearing woman who taught me the meaning of true dignity and pride. A woman so gracious, she understood bigotry for what it really is: the refuge of frightened, insecure people."

"Dangerous people," Grant qualified. "Evil people."

"Some dangerous, sure. But most of them are just insecure, angry, and afraid. Take my father—all thunder and no rain. I can't count the times his obnoxious racist remarks have embarrassed me, but those are just words. I've never seen him treat anybody, black or white, unfairly." Oops. Well . . . "Except waiters; he would insult the waiters if he thought they weren't paying him enough attention. But at least I finally convinced him to cool it with the racial epithets, at least until *after* we'd gotten our food."

"How'd you manage that?"

"I told him they were probably in the kitchen spitting in his food because of what he'd said. Heck, for all I know, they were. Who would blame them? But the tactic worked; it played right into his paranoia, so he finally kept his racism to himself. In restaurants, anyway."

"Lord." Grant shook his head.

"At least he's evenhanded in his prejudices. He's always been paranoid about anybody who isn't a Southern, white male, chauvinist reactionary. Particularly women, which includes me. An equal-opportunity bigot."

"And you condone that?"

"Of course not." How had he come up with that non sequitur? "God knows, I've judged him. But I've realized lately that there's a difference between condoning and accepting. My parents are who they are. They're deeply flawed, but the noises they make don't erase the good they've done." The insight hit home even as I said it. "Racism doesn't erase a person's humanity."

"Just everybody else's," Grant clipped out.

"Oh, spare me. There are bigots everywhere." I glared at him. "How many Chicanos did you pal around with back in Brentwood?"

"There aren't any Chicanos in Brentwood."

"A bigoted statement if ever there was one." I eyed him askance over the internal nagging of my mother: *Hush up, Lin, for glory's sake. You'll scare him off, talkin' like that.* But I'd had my fill of hushin' up. At that point in my life, what came up came out. "Of course there were Chicanos in Brentwood. They just did the lawns and cleaned the houses and bused the tables and washed the dishes at the restaurants, then went back to their barrios at night."

I saw him tense, felt him withdraw, but I didn't care. I was in no mood to play games. "Yep. The South has a lock on prejudice, all right. South Philly, South Central L.A., South Boston, South Bronx, Southern Iraq, South Africa, South Bosnia. Shall I go on?"

"This has ceased to be a conversation and has become a lecture," he said, terse.

"Okay," I obliged. "Your turn to talk, then. Tell me about your last marriage. What happened?"

"Shit, Lin," he responded, appalled. "You use that mouth like a machete."

"No, I don't. I'm just too old and too angry not to ask the questions I want to ask," the new me informed him, enjoying this immensely. "Feel free to tell me to fuck off," I added with a genuine smile. "But if you tell me the truth, we both might just learn something important."

"Like what?" he asked, suspicious.

"Who can say?" I stared out into the night. "Like what really happened, maybe."

"I know what happened," he said. "I was there."

I shook my head in denial. "Noooo. You think you know what happened. Phil thought he knew what happened to us, too, but he didn't. And neither do I, not really."

"You'll pardon me, but the manure is getting a bit deep here," Grant said.

"Do you want to hear my story or not," I asked.

After a few heartbeats' pause, he admitted, "Sure. Let's hear your version. 'Cause that's what it is, you know," he chided, "your version."

"Okay. Subjectively speaking, then." I did not look at him. It felt safer just to gaze out onto the familiar setting of my childhood. "Phil had always been around, but the first time I really noticed him was at a youth musical at church when I was fourteen. I fell in instant obsession with him that night and never changed my mind. Until he betrayed me."

"Ah. The standard description: betrayal," Grant injected.

"That's what it was. But I'm jumping ahead." I rocked as I revisited the grand illusion of my life. "I thought he was perfect. I thought our lives were perfect. I was the perfect corporate wife. I kept his house, entertained his business associates and clients. Bore him a perfect son. Helped him move up the ladder. Did all the right things."

"So where's the flaw?" Grant challenged.

"It wasn't real." I dared a glance at him. "It was all an illusion, one I had constructed and spent a lifetime maintaining, but it wasn't real. I never bothered to find out who he really was. All I know is that the pedestal I put him on must have gotten awfully small. He'd never raised hell as a kid; I was there to make sure he didn't. But when he hit fifty, he took a swan dive into the demon's maw."

"Picturesque, but what specifically does that mean?" Grant prodded.

"It means he grew a stupid Van Dyke beard that made him look like the devil, lost twenty pounds, then started working out and quit coming home."

Looking back, I was forced yet again to acknowledge that I'd known the truth long before I could let myself accept it. "And things went wrong with the money. Suddenly, there was never enough. Checks bounced.

"Senior partners in his firm do *not* bounce checks, but we did. When I tried to find out what was going on, he started keeping the bills at work. Suddenly he was traveling more and playing an awful lot of tennis with his buddies. Only he wasn't away on business, and he wasn't playing tennis."

A deep sigh escaped me as the weight of that hard-fought realization settled heavy across my shoulders. "All the usual symptoms were there, but I kept telling myself this was Phil—Phil the straight arrow, the church treasurer, the model husband, the devoted dad, the pillar of his firm. Then one day poking around his briefcase for bills, I found some internet porn, images of naked oriental women who barely looked pubescent." The memory still had the power to slam me in the chest.

I could see that Grant was very, very uncomfortable with the turn of conversation. Tough. I abandoned any hope of being aloof and mysterious. But like I said, I was too old and too angry to play games, even if I'd known how, which I didn't.

"I started to search in earnest then," I continued. "He told me he'd 'lost' the records of our joint account. Him, the CPA. Even *I* wasn't that gullible. So I borrowed money from a friend to get copies of all the checks from microfilm, then had an audit done. I also used his social security number to get a copy of his credit report.

"That was an eye-opener. We were ruined, and he was carrying enough plastic debt to fund a South American junta—more than two hundred thousand. And all the while, I'd been home clipping coupons."

The gall of it still rankled.

"In the end," I summarized, "I found out he'd spent more than eighty thousand in hotels, entertainment, appliances, women's clothes, and strip clubs in less than a year. And those were just charges or checks I could trace. Over the course of four years, he'd drained our IRA, sold all our stocks, and refinanced the house to one hundred ten percent— all without my knowledge or consent." I eyed Grant. "Of course, that's just my side of the story." Would the bitterness always be there? I wondered as I heard it in my voice.

"Damn. This guy makes Bill Clinton look like Billy Graham."

"The kicker, though, was finding the receipt for the engagement ring he'd given his blonde waif of a stripper."

"You knew what she looked like?" Finally, I'd surprised him.

"Oh, yes. He carried her professional photo composites in his briefcase along with some very damaging financial records. I used to go through his papers while he was sleep-

ing and sneak them down to the basement office to pho-
tocopy them."

I leaned my head back and closed my eyes. "Who would
have thought I'd ever have to sit across the breakfast table
from my husband and tell him you can't be engaged and
married at the same time?" I could see the humor in it now,
but I certainly hadn't then.

How naïve I had been. "I had great evidence against
him, but in the end, it did me no good, because once the
IRS was through with us, there was nothing left. Except
some furniture and things I hid with friends." Part of me
still couldn't believe it. "For a CPA he did a crappy job of
covering his tracks. It's almost as if there was no connection between his actions and any possible consequences.
When I confronted him with the proof, he never even bothered to deny anything. Just said he was crazy and he was
sorry."

"So then you filed."

"Oh, no. Stupid me, I believed him and thought we still
might have a chance. So we went into therapy." How stupid
I had been. "Correction, I went into therapy; he went *to*
therapy. Phil just never quite grasped the concept that saving our marriage required his participation." There was that
bitterness again, creeping back up like kudzu. "I filed for
divorce a year later, after he and his stripper walked into a
restaurant where my son happened to be having a business
lunch. Talk about busted. God nailed him, big time. My
son knocked over a table going after them, but Phil managed to get away. After dumping off his bimbo, he tried to
beat David back to the house to tell me first. They both
ended up there at the same time. Lord, I thought David was
going to kill his father."

"What did you do?" Grant asked with keen interest.

"I collapsed, I'm ashamed to say. Just shattered into
smithereens on the floor. Sobbed until I was sick. He had
thrown us away with both hands." Just thinking about it
made my stomach roil. "My son ordered him out of the

house, then called my therapist and took me to a friend's for the night. The sedatives my therapist prescribed drugged me so heavily, I almost drowned in the bathtub."

"Geeze, Lin. Was that on purpose?"

"No." A brittle chuckle escaped me. "It's pretty hard for a grown-up to drown sitting in an American bathtub. A British bathtub, definitely, but not in an American." I crossed my leg and stifled a yawn. It was way past my bedtime. "I was just cold, chilled to the bone, so I ran a hot tub. It felt so good when I got in that I fell asleep before I turned it off. Woke up chin-deep in freezing water. Ruined my friend's kitchen ceiling downstairs."

"Why does that make me think of Rhett telling Scarlett she's never had a proper handkerchief in all the crises of her life."

What? "Lord, that sounds like something my feeble, fragmented brain would conjure up." I leaned up and frowned at him askance. "Are you accusing me of being like my favorite melodramatic, alcoholic, self-absorbed, fictional bitch?"

"I was thinking more of her survival skills. You had a helluva curve ball thrown at you, but seem to have taken control of your life and survived."

"Ah, yes. Control." The ultimate illusion. Somewhat mollified, I relaxed into my chair. "Did you know that in most marriages where there's a controlling partner and a passive partner, it's the passive partner who invariably does the marriage-breaking thing?"

Grant groaned. "Save me. Pop psychology."

"Well, it's true," I justified. "After I read that, I didn't feel quite such a failure."

"But you weren't the one who failed. He did."

"We both did. I lived on a bubble with a man I never really knew."

"Did it ever occur to you that he never knew who he was either, Lin?" Grant asked a little too sharply. "What's the point of introspection, anyway? Most men only have enough moxie to do what they have to do. God forbid we should spend the energy finding fault with ourselves." He glanced my way. "Anyway, we have you women to do that for us."

"Only because you won't."

He redirected the conversation to Phil. "Sounds like he was a pretty good husband for a long time."

"He was," I freely acknowledged. "I loved him deeply for a long time, and I think he loved me as best he knew how. Illusion or not, we were happy. We gave David a wonderful childhood." Only recently had I been able to acknowledge that, so it still didn't come easy. "I wouldn't do it over differently, I don't think. Just the last part." I faltered then. This was bringing things too close to the surface, stirring up all the old poisons I'd fought so hard to purge from my heart. "I just can't help wondering who he really was."

Grant took the offensive. "Why is it women always want to strip us down to our smallest components? Do you have any idea how threatening that is to a man? What if you see what's there, and it doesn't measure up? Why isn't what we *are* ever enough?"

One of his wives must have tried to make him look at himself, too. "I told you, women want context. We're emotionally greedy. We want your thoughts—and each others'. That's why female friendships are so difficult; we demand so much of each other. But men—"

Grant grinned. "The man just wants . . ."

"A *beer*," we finished in unison, defusing the situation. But I had no intention of letting him get off so easily "Okay. I've told you my story. Your turn now."

A small gust of wind brought with it a faint, tantalizing whiff of coolness. I could see the fan was drying his tanned skin.

"The whole thing?" I could tell he didn't want to.

"Yep. Don't leave out anything important, either. If you

do, you have to answer one excruciatingly personal question for each significant omission."

"More made-up rules. Would it do me any good to argue?"

"Not a whit. Let's have it. Life story."

"The truth is, I've been trying hard to *forget* the last twenty years, not remember them."

"Aaah." I mimicked his earlier dismissive tone. "The old 'I vant to forget' routine. Even worse than pop psychology."

His smile escaped in spite of himself. "Okay. Born in Cleveland. Moved to L.A. when I was thirteen and my parents divorced, as you already know. Worked my way through UCLA undergrad and Pharmacy School, as you already know." The same profession as his "hated" father. "Met and married wife number one in graduate school. Had two daughters a year apart, right off the bat."

"Aaah," I interrupted sagely in my Charlie Chan persona. "Refers to women in his life by numbers, not names."

"I seem to recall someone telling me recently," he retorted, "that it's bad manners to criticize a person's form when he's exposing a vulnerability."

Oooh. Score one for the California Cat Man. "Point taken. Go on."

"Went to work for a major drug chain in Fresno in '75. Long hours. Marriage didn't work out. Wife moved east to her parents' with the kids."

How typically peckerheaded: Long hours; marriage didn't work out.

Done. Gone. Forgotten. No whys. No insights. No mention of who his wife was or why he had once loved her enough to marry her. No affectionate stories of his kids. Hell, no *names,* even.

"Paid alimony until my ex remarried eleven years later," he went on, "and child support until my kids finished Stanford and Pepperdine."

Seriously peckerheaded. Nothing about his daughters, just that he'd made his payments.

My new self warned me away from this guy, but my old self was absolutely fascinated, which figured, because he was perfect poison for a woman like me.

If I'd known then what I know now. But we don't, do we?

"I moved to another chain to manage a district in Fullerton," Grant continued. "That was '83. Remarried in '86 for two years. Well out of that one. Thank God the judge only made me pay for as long as we'd been married. After that I swore off marriage altogether. I was recruited by a major pharmaceutical company as liaison to all the research facilities in the Southwest region, so I lived out of a suitcase until '91 when I met a gal in Vegas—"

Oh, God. Did he really just say, "met a gal in Vegas"? My feminist sensibilities curdled.

"I married her in a major lapse in judgment abetted by alcohol. Fortunately we both knew within a week that it was a big mistake, so we got annulled. No payments, thank God."

So that was what marriage boiled down to? Mistakes whose severity was determined by the size of the bill?

I'd wanted to know more about him, and this was what I'd gotten.

That was the deal, my new self reminded me. *You asked for honesty, and you got it. This is who he is—not who you want him to be.*

That last little zinger stung. But it also left me wondering if the entire gender was made up of dumb dickheads, as Cassie professed.

"So. That pretty much says it," he summed up. "Then my father died and left me the store and the house, so I moved here to get things into shape to sell them. Which, as you know, has taken a lot longer than I thought it would."

I should hate this man, despise his Neanderthal mindset

and his dry, statistical rendition of three failed marriages and two abandoned daughters.

You don't know the whole story, my new self chided. *Remember our resolution. We're not going to jump to conclusions and judge people.*

Facts are facts, my inner Puritan argued emphatically. *He didn't even call his daughters by name! The guy's a hopeless jerk when it comes to women. And he is not your lawfully wedded husband. Run away! Run away!*

So why was all my sexual apparatus humming away at full-throttle?

Help! I've fallen in lust and I can't get up!

Despite the turmoil within me, I managed to sound calm when I said, "How come you never said a word about two grown daughters?"

"They don't have much to do with me, thanks to their mother." He finished off his water and set the glass on the floor beside the swing. "I messed up big time with Cathy, their mom, and she couldn't forgive me."

Finally, a name. And some accountability. "Messed up how?"

"There was a pharmacist at work." He avoided my eyes. "Straight out of school, fresh and seriously female. She looked up to me like I was God. Hung on my every word. Made me remember what it felt like to be a world-beater. I'd almost forgotten, thanks to the kids and the bills and the yard work and the in-laws."

Oh, please. "Spare me. The American script, episode six-hundred-and-fifty-two-million." Cassie was right. Dumb dickheads, all of them.

"I don't defend what happened," he said, bristling, "but as soon as Cathy found out, I stopped the affair and wanted to work on things. Cathy didn't. She took the kids east and filed for divorce."

"And your daughters?"

"I called them a lot at first, but they always ended up crying, begging to come home to California. After a while,

I felt guilty for stirring them up. Cathy moved in with an old flame right away, so my babies were already calling another man Daddy."

Neither my old self nor my new felt sorry for him. My Puritan had the pitchfork heating in the forge for an old-fashioned man-sticking.

"What is *wrong* with men?" I blurted out. "Why isn't reality enough for you? Is it so much to ask that you simply be faithful and kind and true to your family? Why do you have to have dewy-eyed child-women? Don't you know infidelity destroys us?"

Grant stiffened. "I'm assuming those questions are rhetorical."

"No." I felt the old anger boiling up. "They're as honest-to-God questions as I've ever asked. Does it not occur to y'all that even Miss Chickie-Boom is gonna want you to put the top on the toothpaste one day?" Screw the Miss Mamie's porch rules of engagement. "Why do you chase the myth when there's a real-live woman in your bed and children who look up to you as a father? Was it worth it?"

I could tell he was smoldering; I'd attacked him and his gender. But he didn't do the usual man thing, which was clam up or leave in a huff. "No, it wasn't worth it. But you don't think about the cost. I didn't think, period. Most men don't under those circumstances. We just give in to the fantasy. And by the time we realize how deep we're in, it's too late."

All the old resentments rose up, yellow-slitted eyes blazing. "You'll pardon me for noticing that there's no personal responsibility in your explanation."

"I said I messed up." He glared at me. "It's never enough that we admit we're wrong. You women want to grind our faces in it forever. Nothing is ever about just one thing. Geeze, living with a woman is like living in a mine field. Every single thing gets blown up into a major ordeal."

My new self had to admit he had a point—he'd exaggerated, but hit a nerve. But instead of lashing out as I

wanted to, I changed course, which felt novel and dangerous, but good. "You're right. Why is that? We do make a
major case out of everything. Even the little stuff." I felt
the tension lower. "*Especially* the little stuff—it's like the
Chinese water torture. Every time Phil left his shoes in the
middle of the floor, I took it personally." I looked at Grant.
"Maybe that's it. We always take it personally. Maybe
we're hardwired that way."

"And men are hardwired to react negatively to constant
criticism." His anger faded. "How would *you* like to carry
around some great big Santa Claus bag of sins that gets
added to every time you're not perfect?"

Another good point. "I did the opposite to Phil," I confessed. "I saw no imperfections, because I couldn't let myself." Philip, we never knew ye. "I wonder now how he
managed to live as long as he did without shattering that
particular tyranny."

"He was lucky," Grant said flatly.

"Oh, right. So lucky, he destroyed himself."

"You didn't do it, Lin. Just because you can see things
for the way they really were doesn't make you responsible
for his insanity." He stilled. "As I see it, the man was a
fool. How many people are blessed with that kind of love?"

"Obsession is probably a more accurate word."

"I'd call it love. You gave; he took. You accepted him
as you thought he was. Most men would kill for that."

"Oh, sure. You see how many men have gotten in line
since my divorce."

He chuckled. "Not with those spikes of disillusionment
you're still wearing. They still stick out a mile." He stood
and stretched, stirring his male scent into the downwash of
the fan with a ripple of fairly taut torso. "Not to mention
the fact that you're too good-looking and way too smart.
It's gonna take some kinda man to be brave enough for a
woman like you, Lin, believe me." He grinned. "But he'll
be the lucky one."

Why did I feel like I'd just been given the brush-off

instead of being complimented? I stood, grumpy. "Pick up that invisible glass."

He tried to conceal a wince of pain as he scooped it up. Then he stepped over to hand it to me. "You never answered my question," he breathed, closer than he had to be.

I inhaled the scent of bare skin. How long had it been? "And what question was that?" I dared not look up into his eyes.

"What's going on with you and Geneva?"

Damn.

Flustered, I looked up after all, and when I did, the wry masculinity of his face sent me beyond rational thought, beyond discretion, beyond anything but the overwhelming sense of wanting.

My hand hooked the back of his neck and pulled him forward, hard, until his mouth was crushed against mine.

The distant sound of the empty glass bouncing onto the porch boards reached my ears as I realized I was kissing Grant Owens. My boss, the half-jerk.

He tasted strange, exotic. Not like Phil.

And he didn't kiss me back.

Horrified, I pulled away from him, adrenaline pumping humiliation to my throbbing lips, ears, and extremities. "Judas, Herod, and Jezebel," I quoted Geneva from behind the fingers that covered my mouth. "I do not know where that came from. Oh, God. Please, forget that ever happened."

Shit, shit, shit! Tricia was never going to believe this. *I* didn't believe this!

Grant stared at me as if I had just morphed into a giant white rabbit. Then something shifted in his expression. He scowled down at me with daunting intensity for what seemed like eons. Then he pulled me hard against him for a kiss that was both fierce and hungry.

Tongues!

Eek. Phil had never done tongues, at least not with me. I had a sudden flash of a basketball player in tenth grade who'd looked like he meant to swallow my head when he'd tried to kiss me goodnight.

But the taste and feel of Grant snatched me back to the present, and I opened to the invasion, praying I wouldn't make snorking noises in my sinuses.

This was nothing like my fantasies. I was totally self-conscious, hopelessly analytical of every taste, every move, every sensation. But there was chemistry. Definite chemistry, which probably accounted for my freezing up.

Gradually, the tongue thing became less awkward than at first, and I felt myself relax a little. Grant's body full against mine felt both shockingly alien and seductively familiar, and there was no guessing at the effect this was having on him. It took all my self-control not to wiggle against the evidence.

But after the first explosive awareness, fear mixed with the surge of pure physical response, making me want to laugh and bawl at the same time. How could something feel so right and so horribly, hopelessly wrong all at once?

Like a tree struck by lightning, I split into two people bound by the same skin. One wanted to throw up and run shrieking to the confessional, even though I'm not Catholic. The other wanted to throw down and get wild on the porch floor, self-respect, gossips, and STDs be damned.

An involuntary groan of protest escaped past the tongue thing, which I was definitely getting the hang of. I felt myself push Grant away. I lurched free of him, speechless, torn by a battle of sensation, emotion, and feeble reason that had no hope of a winner.

Grant scowled down at me again, this time in consternation. Both of us were breathing hard. "What's going on here, Lin?" His hands gripped my upper arms.

Tears sprang to my eyes even as a semi-hysterical laugh escaped me. "Damn if I know." I couldn't very well tell him I felt like I'd just committed adultery, but I wanted to rip off the rest of his clothes and go down on him.

He released me, then stepped aside to rub the heels of

his hands into his eyes with a monumental sigh. "You're not ready for this, are you?" It was a statement, not a question. Arms akimbo, he turned to face the tracks. "Damn. I never should have done that. I knew you weren't ready."

Some perverse part of me was jumping up and down, hand in the air, yelling, *Yes I am! I'm ready for this! Here! Kiss me again! Do that tongue thing! I liked it!*

My old self had sentenced us to bread and water for a month and was rooting around in my psychological baggage for the hair shirt.

I collapsed into the rocker. "God, Grant, I'm sorry. Will this ruin things between us?"

He sat down on the swing. "No. But it definitely complicates matters. Don't get me wrong; I liked it, a lot. But you work for me. And you're obviously not ready." He shot me a comforting smile. "It's not adultery, you know. Not even fornication." He waggled his eyebrows suggestively. "Yet."

"Do you have any diseases?" I was horrified to hear myself ask. "Herpes? Genital warts? HIV?"

"Geeze, Lin. Does everything that goes through that big brain of yours come out?"

"Apparently so," I answered, appalled. "It's beyond my control." *Dangerous Liaisons.* I horrified myself even further by pressing the point. "Well, do you have any diseases, or not?" Might as well settle that much, at least. Assuming he'd tell the truth.

"No," he said with convincing surety. "I've been both selective and lucky in my love life. But we're a long way from needing to know about that."

"Of course. But we're also on Miss Mamie's porch. I'm allowed to ask what I want to ask."

"I admit, dating has changed a lot in the past thirty years," he said, not without humor, "but I don't think it was proper form even then to ask a guy if he had any social diseases just because he kissed you." He raised his eyebrows. "Trust me, you'll scare all the good ones off."

"Did I scare you off?" Some idiot had taken over my vocal cords and kidnapped my inhibitions!

"I don't count. I like you. I'm not trying to get into your pants."

And why not? my perverse self demanded.

This was getting totally out of control.

"A lot of women in your position are vulnerable, and a lot of guys are more than ready to take advantage of that," he explained gently. "But I don't see you as the revenge-fuck type. Or as someone so wounded she has to make love with just anybody to prove she's still a woman."

I put my head in my hands. "Oh, really. So what kind of woman do you think I am, then?"

"Complicated. Confused. Fascinating. And very, very risky."

I could live with that.

He stilled. "Now it's my turn to ask a question. Do you want to go to bed with me? That's not an invitation," he hastened to qualify, "just a clarification."

I could have lied, but what would be the point? I'd had enough of lies. "Yes. Desperately. And no. Desperately."

"An honest answer." He took my hand and gave it a squeeze, then let it go as if the contact was too dangerous.

"What about you?" I challenged.

"The same." He headed for the stairs. "On that note, I'm going home to bed. Alone, with nothing but my hand to keep me company."

I laughed. Phil had never so much as acknowledged the existence of masturbation, much less doing it.

Grant tried to hide his stiff muscles as he descended to the driveway. When he was even with where I was sitting, he peered over the porch rail at me, his runner's silhouette looking like a man in his prime. "Night, Lin. See you at work in the morning." He scooped up his shirt.

"What's going to happen with us now, Grant?" I couldn't help asking. I am a woman; we must ask these things.

"To quote a schizophrenic Goody Two-shoes of a wild woman I happen to have had the privilege to kiss, 'Damn if I know.' "

It was enough, I supposed. For then.

Chapter 14

Why is Grant actin' so odd?" Geneva asked me after the Birthday Break the next morning at the drugstore. "Is he mad at me about somethin'?"

I glanced back to make sure he was occupied before answering in a whisper, "He asked me what you and I were up to last night at the meeting."

"Rats." Geneva shot him a worried look. "You didn't tell him, did you?"

My ears went neon. "Of course not." She would die if she knew what I *had* done. And said. "I avoided his question. Several times. But I doubt he'll let it drop."

"No." She rubbed a finger across her upper lip. "No. He never lets anything drop. But we cain't tell him. And we cain't lie. So that's just what we'll hafta say: We cain't tell him."

"Okay."

Both of us did our best to ignore the subtle strain that radiated between us and Grant, but the day was turning out to be a long one until Geraldine Poole and Frances Cain burst in from the sidewalk all atwitter.

"Oh, my goodness, Geneva," Frances said breathlessly, her hand on her ample bosom for emphasis. "You will not believe it. You just will not believe it."

"It's gonna be on the evenin' news!" Geraldine bemoaned. "Poor Reba Gordon. You know it was a setup." Her usually sunny face clamped down into a demon-Methodist-gargoyle expression that made me think of Cassie's snake-tongued woman. "That sorry scum of a devil husband framed her. That's all there is to it."

"Just because the jury had begun to believe Reba and was going to give her a decent settlement," Frances asserted.

"Framed her? For what?" Geneva waved her hands. "Back up, Geraldine. Start from the beginning."

"Well," Geraldine obliged, "as you know, the divorce trial started Monday morning, and—"

"Y'all already told us all about that. And Tuesday. What happened *today*?"

You could hear a pin drop at the soda fountain. Somebody had turned the radio off! Even Grant was leaning into the pass-through as he worked.

"Well," Geraldine started again. "You know all those awful lies Dr. Gordon told about Reba on the stand yesterday. Claimed she ran nekkid through the yard and didn't feed the children." She jerked her blouse tab straight. "Bold-faced lies, and him sittin' up there with his hair cut decent for the first time in ten years and finally wearin' a respectable suit instead of those silk shirts with no collars and Eye-talian shoes." The two women exchanged critical frowns.

Margaret hijacked the narrative. "Well, today was Reba's turn to testify. She took the stand and calm as you please told them what he'd done to her all those years. Left her to raise those children without any help from him and precious little money. And him drivin' those fancy cars that cost more'n my house."

"Forr'n cars!" Ottis Wilburne piped up from the soda fountain. "And most of this town workin' for the GM Plant down in Doraville after the mill closed. Is that any way to act? I say no!"

"Not to mention all that flashy jewelry he always wears,"

Frances added, shaking the "Finger of Justice." "My daddy always said, you can't trust a man who wears diamonds. Not a one."

Geraldine nodded. "So anyway, Reba's lawyer started askin' her about all those drugs her husband had given her. She had the bottles with her from six different drugstores where Doc Gordon had got 'em from, with her name just a little different at each store. Then the lawyer gave the judge a list of all the prescriptions Dr. Gordon had ordered for Reba over the past ten years." She nodded in approval to Grant. "Thank you, sir, for your part in that. I know it helped, because the judge had all the information admitted into evidence.

"Then Reba's lawyer asked her if she had ever wanted any of those medications, and she said no, she didn't want to take 'em, but Dr. Gordon had insisted. He said she had to calm her nerves for the children's sake, so she went along with it."

"But," Frances interrupted dramatically, "the lawyer called another doctor, a psychiatrist, to the stand, who had studied the list, and he said the drugs were given in wrong doses and mixed up with others that would make anybody confused."

"So he *was* druggin' her!" Geneva slapped her thigh. "I knew it."

"So did the jury." This, from Geraldine. "You could see they were all upset. Even Doc Gordon's lawyer couldn't shake Reba when he cross-examined her. She stayed cool as you please and sane as you or me. She said she'd gradually stopped taking those pills after she'd finally gotten a lawyer, and now she feels a hundred percent better."

"Some of the women in the jury were actually cryin'," Frances said dramatically. "And I thought one of the men was gonna climb out of that box and sock Doc Gordon right in his bleached, bonded teeth."

I couldn't stand it any longer. I had to cut to the chase. "You said she was framed? For what?"

"Murder," Frances announced, clutching her purse at the clasp with both hands.

"Well, not murder exactly," Geraldine corrected. "Solicitation of murder."

That stood everybody in the place on his ear!

"When did *that* happen?" Geneva demanded.

"Out in the hall during lunch break." Frances.

"You see," Geraldine explained, "after they adjourned for lunch, Dr. Gordon waited until Reba's lawyer went to make some phone calls, then he cornered Reba in the hall and said he'd see her dead before he let her extort his hard-earned money out of him. He said she was a crazy woman, and he could prove it, and she'd end up with nothing."

"Did you see this?" Grant asked.

"No. He was too smart for that. He got her where nobody else could see. But I saw her when she came out. She was sobbing. Frances and I did our best to comfort her, but she didn't want anybody around her, so we went to get her a Coke."

"And?" My blood pressure was rising by the second.

"That's when they sat the crooked narc down beside her," Geraldine said.

"It was all fixed," Frances announced. "He had them do it. Set the whole thing up."

"Who?" Geneva asked.

"Dr. Gordon," Geraldine and Frances and I answered in unison.

"If you don't tell me what happened, and quick," I pleaded, "I swear I'm going to stroke out right here on the spot."

"Well, the guy was in cuffs and looked like the worst kind of criminal, but Reba was too upset to move. And the next thing you know, he's askin' Reba what's wrong, and she's tellin' him about what Doc Gordon just said, and he starts tellin' her she shouldn't have to put up with that, and the next thing you know, she's promised him two thousand dollars to kill the bastard."

"Entrapment, pure and simple," Geraldine said.

"Two thousand dollars." Frances shook her head. "Every cent that poor woman had left in the world."

I truly didn't know whether to laugh or cry. Regardless of Reba's mental instability, another faithful wife had just gotten screwed. I couldn't blame her for what she'd done. Too bad she'd just testified that she'd stopped taking all those drugs. "What happened then?"

"The narc went straight to the DA. They came and arrested Reba while we were sittin' in the snack bar. Since Reba couldn't come back to court, the judge ordered a continuance, but Reba's lawyer says this will go really bad for her side in the divorce."

A masterpiece of understatement.

"Did they post bail?" I wondered aloud.

"Yes, but it's five hundred thousand dollars." Geraldine told us sadly. "Reba will never make it. The rotten judge who did it is in the same Mason Lodge as Doc Gordon."

I looked up into the pass-through to see Grant's head down on the counter. When he looked up, there was such open fury in his face that I was afraid of what he might do next.

He stormed out of the pharmacy. "Cover for me. I'll be back in an hour." It struck me as ironic that he was so angry after having been so anxious to get out of his own divorce payments. Why should he care so much what happened to Reba Gordon? Then I remembered Miss Mamie's conjecture that Grant might be getting the goods on Dr. Gordon. Clearly, this was getting personal.

Grant jerked open the door to the basement stairs with such force I thought it would come off its ancient hinges.

"Grant." I couldn't help myself; I followed after him. "Where are you going?"

"To the gym," he called back as he reached the bottom of the stairs. "To hit something, hard, for long enough so I won't finish off Mack Gordon myself." The heavy steel outer door rang like a vault when he slammed it behind him.

The next week Grant was more distant and subdued than ever. At work, he was all business. Never rude, but never relaxed. Afterward, he came to the campaign meetings and continued to work with the computers, but was barely civil, even to Velma.

And at work he had more and more of those phone calls from his mysterious female friend.

Thursday night, Donnie pulled Geneva and me off the phone committee and led us outside to "the conference room."

The air hung hot and dusty over the pastures in this, our fourth consecutive year of drought. "You may be wondering why I've asked you out here," Donnie quipped when we reached the now-matted patch of clover.

I saw no sense in beating around the bush. But then, I never have. "Have you reached a decision about the files?"

"That's my Lin." He clapped a work-worn hand on my shoulder. "Always a straight-shooter."

Geneva, as usual, was more diplomatic, willing to wait for Donnie to tell us in his own way.

"Yep," he told us. "After two days of prayer and fasting, the Lord has showed me that I need to commit this to Him and let it go."

"So you don't want us to use it," Geneva said.

"What I want doesn't matter. I just cain't be the one to decide this. That much is clear."

"Is it all right if we kick it back to Velma?"

"Do as the Lord leads. I'm outta the loop." He said it with perfect peace.

"And if Velma decides to go with it?" I asked him.

"If she does—and I want you two not to pressure her about this—I know an investigative reporter she can trust."

"Who?"

"Sally Hester. She just signed on with that new cable news channel in Atlanta. I've known her for a long time. She's a straight-shooter just like you, Lin. And a true believer. So she won't publish anything she can't prove."

"I've heard that name," Geneva mused.

Me, too. "Didn't she win a Peabody or something?"

"Yep. Four of 'em." Donnie's big-toothed grin radiated into the twilight. "And a Pulitzer."

"I swear," Geneva said as we followed him back inside. "For a man who never really left Mimosa Branch, you are without a doubt the most *connected* fella I ever met."

"The drug scene, rehab, and the foot of the Cross, darlin'," Donnie crowed. "You meet just about everybody at one of 'em, and I've been to all three."

I don't know exactly when or how things changed at 1431 Green Street. Maybe it was only me who changed. But in the coming weeks, I felt closer to my parents and Tommy than I ever had.

When school started back, I rejoiced, as I had every fall since I'd quit college, that I wasn't a student or a teacher. Business fell off at the drugstore, so I worked fewer hours, but still managed to get some overtime.

I settled into a comfortable routine, not looking too far ahead and never looking back if I could help it. Except, maybe, to that kiss on the porch.

I still took Uncle Bedford to the store for ice cream, and often, the whole family sat out on the porch of an evening listening to the growing tide of cricket song that promised cooler days ahead.

My parents still bickered and hollered, but it no longer threatened me the way it once had. I came to see it as two whales sounding for each other in the treacherous deep that surrounded them.

The General and Tommy seemed to have reached a lasting truce, which made Miss Mamie happy, too. Even Uncle

Bedford appeared almost content now that he was getting his anti-psychotics on schedule. Aunt Glory had dared to start up a local mah-jongg group and acted more like her usual feisty self.

There had been a falling into place that I found both comforting and disturbing. I did not want this to be my life, but it was life enough for now. I stayed busy, but it wasn't the kind of desperate, denying busy from my past. For the first time, I was taking the days as they came.

If I could just purge myself of those damned Grant fantasies, I could honestly say I was happy.

Then one Sunday in early September, my real-estate course had just ended with a marathon weekend of review and practice tests. As soon as I got home from the impromptu after-party we'd thrown at the steakhouse over by the mall, I dragged the phone into my room to call Tricia.

I no longer locked the door or stuffed the keyhole, I am proud to say.

After the usual jillion numbers dialed, the voice announced, "You have forty-seven minutes of call time left for the number you have dialed."

Eeyew. And this was my second five-hundred-minute card.

Two rings. Three.

"Oh, please be there. I'm so proud of myself. I want to tell you!"

"You know better than to call me this late on a school night," Tricia said, her voice thick with sleep.

"Late? It's only . . ." I looked at the clock. "Uh-oh. Eleven."

"Yes, eleven, on a Sunday night," she grumbled. "And I have class at nine."

"Humble apologies," I said, unable to keep the disappointment out of my voice. "Go back to sleep. Call me tomorrow night, any time. I don't have night classes anymore."

I heard mouth breathing, then a more alert, "I'm sitting

up now." Covers rustled. "Okay." I could just imagine her lurching aright in one of those satin sleep shirts she always wore with her black satin eye mask. "What's up? You didn't call me at this hour for nothing." Brief pause ending in alarm. "Don't tell me you kissed the Filthy Beast again!"

Tricia had taken to referring to Grant as the Filthy Beast, one of our favorite Cary Grant characters, from the movie *Father·Goose*. She found it appropriate, I suppose, because Leslie Caron played Goody Two-shoes opposite him.

"No. I did not kiss the Filthy Beast again. But he continues to torment my dreams."

"This is not good. The man is a disaster waiting to happen, Lin. You must resist him."

"I don't have to resist him," I shot back, annoyed. "He's doing plenty of resisting for both of us. I might as well be Grandma Moses for all the attention he pays to me anymore. And he never comes to the porch now. I've lost my man-source. Probably scared him away with that whole STD thing."

"Good. I hope you did." She yawned hugely.

"That is not why I called," I grumped.

"Okay, then." Sound of scratching. "Why did you call?"

"I called to tell you you were right. I took two practice exams this weekend and made above ninety on both of them."

"Fabulous! I knew you could do it." The pride in her voice made up for the scolding she'd given me about Grant. "So when's the real thing?"

"Next Saturday, September 18th. At the Junior College." I only hoped I could retain it all till then. "I wish it was tomorrow, while everything's still fresh."

"Just brush up the night before, then go to bed early. You'll ace it."

"Your mouth to God's ear."

"Have you told that gorgeous son of yours?"

"Lord, no." Perish the thought. "I haven't said a word about the course. I won't, unless I pass."

"You'll pass. And you should have told him. I know he'd be proud of you."

"He has his own life. David and Barb exist in another world. They don't need me butting in. And I don't want him worrying about me, either."

"Pffft. Call him. He loves you dearly, knucklehead."

"I know it." It sure felt good to have somebody to talk to who understood me better than I understood myself.

"So how's the apartment coming?" Tricia asked.

"Almost ready, and it looks great. We pickled the floors and painted the walls a color between peach and terra-cotta. Desert Sunrise. Kinda salmon, but not so pink. With white cabinets and trim. I call it my perfect girly apartment. And I found a great little white refrigerator at a garage sale."

"So when are you moving in? Or out? Or whatever." She was fading.

"Next Sunday, the day after the exam. I'm renting a big truck, and Tommy and I are collecting all my stuff from town. I can hardly wait. Neither can my friends who've been harboring my furniture." I lay back against the pillows. "The funny thing is, I'm not nearly as rabid to move out as I was at first. It feels more like a logical progression than an escape, now."

"Sounds like Tombo's really been there for you lately."

"It's nice having a brother. And I've discovered that there was always a lot of good in him that I never bothered to see."

"Ohmigod. Is this more sanity I hear emanating from the heart of the loony bin? Insight? Maturity? Dare I say it . . . *acceptance*?"

She'd hit the nail right on the head, I realized with a shock. "Maybe so."

"On that note, I'm hanging up, completely overwhelmed."

"Trish . . ." There was so much to say. Why didn't I have the words? "Thanks. For being there, even at eleven o'clock on a school night." Unexpected tears leaked out of me, but thank goodness, you couldn't hear them in my voice. "For loving me anyway."

"There is no anyway, Lin's-a-pin," she said gently. "Haven't you figured out how great you are?"

I hadn't. At that moment, I felt like Tricia was the only person in the whole huge world who truly loved me or ever would. Except maybe Tommy, but he was my brother, so he didn't really count. And he didn't know me, not really. "Just thanks." The tears came harder, but they were bittersweet—healing, somehow.

I swiped them from my cheeks. "I wish you were here. I wish we could watch old movies and get drunk and sing songs."

Her small, pregnant pause was resonant with emotion. "We will, honey. You just hang in there, and some day soon there'll be a knock on the garage apartment door, and it'll be me. I promise."

"Soon." It was a plea. I hung up and bawled my eyes out.

But you never know what life will bring you, and mine still had a few curve balls in store, the operative word being *balls*.

Chapter 15

Geneva and I did as Donnie asked; we didn't try to influence Velma about the files. But it didn't take her long to make up her mind. The very next day she called the investigative reporter, Sally Hester, who promptly copied the diskettes and every scrap of paper in the files, returned the originals to the safe deposit box, and said she'd let Velma know when she should hand it all over to the district attorney.

When Velma told us about it in "the conference room" that night at the regular Tuesday night work session, she said her only regret was putting Donnie on the spot by asking him to decide what she should have in the first place. So we consigned the matter to God and Sally Hester, and resolved to work hard and pray harder.

The next morning, Wednesday, September 15th, Geneva and I were rearranging and restocking when Grant arrived with a spring in his step for the first time in weeks. I couldn't say he looked happy. More . . . resolute. Like a knight primed for battle against the forces of darkness.

A prophetic image, as it turned out.

It made me wonder if he knew about the files, after all.

On his way past us, he announced, "Clear the aisles, ladies. We're having company."

"Company?" Geneva stood up, her hands filled with tubes of hemorrhoid remedy.

"Yep. And I want everything shipshape before they get here."

They?

The Coffee Club perked up immediately.

"You, too, guys," Grant said to them. "Let's keep everything over there picked up, please. I want to make a good impression."

He disappeared into the stockroom, where he'd piled box after dusty box of records in the past few weeks, leaving almost no room for the fresh stock. Geneva and I had been forced to unload the wholesaler's containers in the aisles.

We exchanged glances as the geezers murmured among themselves.

"The girlfriend?" I whispered to Geneva with more than a hint of concealed jealousy.

She shook her head. "He said 'they.' More likely, buyers."

"For the store?" I'd known from the beginning that he meant to sell it, but the idea of that actually happening was far more upsetting than it should have been.

"Yeah." Geneva scanned the place, wistful. "I guess that's what the records are all about. Grant must have finally finished getting the books in order."

We stood there, strangely deflated, maybe because we both sensed that Main Street's last remnant from our past might very well be on its way out.

"C'mon, ladies." Progress. He hadn't called us *you guys*. "Step lively. They're bringing cameras."

"Cameras?" It made sense that the buyers would want to take photos. Geneva and I looked at each other. "Photo alert," I announced.

"Lipstick," she told me, even as I said, "Hair."

After a quick personal freshen up, we did one for the store.

Then we sat behind the register and waited while Grant rummaged around in the pharmacy fiddling with the tape backup and the computer.

As if some cosmic vibration had warned away the customers, our usual morning traffic failed to materialize. But the Coffee Club remained firmly planted, eschewing the hardware store in anticipation of "their" arrival.

You could definitely feel it; something was about to happen.

Something bigger than a girlfriend? I hoped.

But a buyer?

Just after eleven, four dark cars with government plates pulled up in front of the store. Out popped a stunning black woman dressed in navy blue slacks and a matching T-shirt blazoned with a bright yellow DEA. Hot on her heels, six men in the same attire exploded the other doors and followed her in.

Adrenaline planted me, tingling with shock, where I stood beside Geneva.

She grabbed my hand and held on to it for dear life, huddled close as the storm troopers rumbled past us through the center aisle. "Oh, dear Lord. What is happening here?" she breathed out.

Then up screeched a remote van from CTNC, the same cable news channel that Donnie's investigative reporter worked for. And out popped a film crew, led by none other than Sally Hester, herself.

The minute I recognized her, my obsessive little mind started trying to figure out what connection this had to Donnie and the judge's files. But Velma hadn't breathed a word about any drugs! And as far as I was aware, Grant didn't even know about the judge's files. All very confusing.

Sally Hester, her sound man, and the cameraman piled into the store, lights blazing, and took the far aisle back to the SWAT Team gathered at the register. In person, the diminutive reporter looked even more like somebody's grandmother instead of a top investigative reporter, but there was nothing grandmotherly about the way she went after a story.

Clearly, these were the cameras Grant had told us about. He'd been expecting them and seemed anything but disturbed by what was happening.

Geneva and I eased past the greeting cards and shampoo for a better look at the unfolding drama. The Coffee Club had fallen mute, agog.

A burly DEA agent stood blocking the front entrance, and another stood guard at the door to the basement stairs.

Grant emerged from the pharmacy to shake the gorgeous black woman's hand. "Hi, Carmen." Despite his serious expression, the glory of the righteous shone in his eyes. "Everything's ready for you. I put it all back in the stockroom. Finally got the last of the records sorted and entered onto my spreadsheet program."

"Great." All business, the gorgeous DEA agent handed him what I assumed was a warrant. She glanced around, wary. "How about the computers? Are we okay there?"

Grant's mysterious lady caller! I'd know that voice anywhere.

"All ready. I've backed everything up and made copies."

"We'll get your equipment back to you as soon as we can," she told him as the rest of her men looked on, grim and intimidating. "Sorry for the inconvenience, especially after all the work you've done for us."

"I have a spare CPU down in my car," Grant said. "Shouldn't be too hard to get everything functional with the tape backup."

Sally Hester stuck out her hand to the gorgeous agent. "Hi. Sally Hester with CTNC."

"Glad y'all could make it." The DEA agent shook firmly.

Grant offered his hand to the reporter. "I really appreciate this. The wider the coverage we can get, the better."

Sally Hester looked up at him with raised brows. "I'll do my best to give this as much exposure as we can without jeopardizing the prosecution." When Grant frowned, she reassured him. "Don't worry. I wouldn't have gotten very far in this business if I went around screwing up cases. Trust me, I've done this before."

"We know," Carmen from the DEA said. "That's why Grant called you."

Grant had called *her*. This was too Byzantine for me. I was getting a headache trying to connect everything.

"Okay. Where are the records?" Sally Hester asked. "We'll want to get a shot of your men carrying them out. And also seizing the computers. Grant, I'd like you in that shot with Carmen. These shelves of drugs make a good backdrop."

"Set it up," Carmen told her, clearly not adverse to some face time on camera. "Okay, guys," she instructed her men. "Let's make the six-o'clock news. Ms. Hester will tell you what she needs, but remember to follow proper procedure. To the letter, guys. We want this one to stick and stick hard." She reached out for a graying white man. "Jim, keep an eye on everything back there."

"Aye-aye, cap'n." Agent Jim pushed past the cameraman into the narrow corridor.

I liked this Carmen woman. She was a DEA goddess, firmly in charge.

"So," Grant asked her. "When does the next phase go down?"

"As soon as we finish here. He's under surveillance. Two of our undercover people posing as patients saw him this morning. He bit big. Now he's backed up with appointments."

Him? Patients?

A doctor.

Oh, please let it be the doctor I hoped it was! It would go a long way toward restoring my faith in humanity.

Grant looked worried. "Wouldn't it have been safer to nab him before you came here?"

She shook her head. "Strengthens our case to have

plenty of probable cause in hand before we arrest him."
She met his doubt with unrelenting confidence. "Trust me.
I've been doing this for twenty years. It'll stick. The·guy's
a sleaze, but he's not very smart. We've got him."

"And he'll be out on bail by supper," a passing agent
complained.

More agents started moving past the camera carrying the
boxes of old records. They took them to the trunk of one
of the cars, where the guy from the front door now stood
guard.

"Oh, and by the way." The DEA goddess turned so we
couldn't see her mouth, but I still managed to make out
what she said despite the surrounding ruckus. "We facili-
tated that meeting you asked for between the local DA and
your friend's psychiatrist. Charges have been dropped, on
the condition that she keeps a low profile from now on. No
Jerry Springer appearances, or all bets are off."

"I think after today," Grant assured her, "my friend will
be happy to lie low."

"Agent Johnson," one of the men called to the DEA
goddess. "Could I have a word with you?"

She excused herself, leaving Grant free. I wasted no time
in getting to him. "Okay, let's have it. What's this all
about? And who's this friend?"

"This is all about a drug bust."

"And?" I squeezed his forearms in exasperation. "Why
do men make you pull everything out of them? Explain."

He actually smiled. "Six months ago, Reba Gordon's
attorney asked me to gather her drug records for the divorce
case, and I agreed. It was disgusting, what he'd done to her
with drugs. The poor woman, no wonder she's unstable."
He scowled. "I was already on alert because of some serious irregularities in Mack Gordon's prescription patterns,
but it took a lot of rooting around in the old records and
putting things into my computer to prove how deep he was
into this, and how blatant. As soon as I had some proof, I

took what I'd found to the authorities. They started an investigation and a sting operation."

"And who called Sally Hester?" I asked. "Surely not the DEA."

He reddened and gave me a man-answer. "Me."

He looked askance to make sure nobody was watching us or listening in. The Coffee Club had lined the far aisle to watch the boxes go out. Besides Geneva, we were alone on that side of the store. Apparently she didn't count, because Grant went right on as if she weren't standing attentively three feet away. "I only wish I'd been able to pull everything together sooner." He shot a tormented glance at me, then averted his eyes. "Maybe if I had, Reba Gordon would never have gone to jail."

So the friend *was* Reba! At least she was off the hook. And her evil, sorry-ass husband was about to get his.

There was a God, after all.

"But the DEA goddess said the charges were dropped," I said, relieved.

"Who?" Grant scowled in confusion.

"Carmen, the DEA goddess." Speak of the devil, here she came with camera crew, reporter, and all.

"Okay," Sally Hester motioned Grant back into the pharmacy. "We'll set up the shot this way, with the two of you standing behind the crouching agent as he disconnects the computer and raises it to stand beside you."

"But it's already disconnected on the counter," Grant told them as he escorted the DEA goddess to their positions.

"So, we'll put it on the floor and pretend to disconnect it," Sally Hester decreed.

Geneva and I peered over the bottom half of the Dutch door to watch the complexities of setting up a shot. Just when it looked like things were ready, Sally Hester pointed an accusing microphone at us. "Who are they?"

Grant pushed her microphone aside. "They're my employees, Geneva Bates and Lin Breedlove. You're on their turf, not the other way around."

Sally Hester looked up at him with mild amusement and more than a little admiration. "Good man. I like a boss who takes up for his employees." Then she was back to business. "If you two ladies will please step out of the shot, we can get this rolling. Please."

We circled reluctantly to the register to watch as best we could over the pass-through.

"Okay," Sally ordered from off-camera. "You, pick up the computer and exit as far to the left of the camera as you can, but don't look at the lens. You're just going about your business, putting another bad guy away. Meanwhile, you, Agent Johnson, reach over and shake Grant's hand, but stay serious, you two. I guarantee we'll use that shot."

Everyone did as he or she was told, while Sally spoke into the mike off-camera. "Here we see Chief Agent Carmen Johnson of the Drug Enforcement Agency supervising the seizure of vital computer records thanks to pharmacist Grant Owens's alert detection and cooperation." The agent with the computer moved past the cameraman as instructed. "And, cut."

She leaned close to the cameraman for a look at his viewer. "How was it?" They watched the replay together and agreed. "Good one."

"Thank you, Chief Agent Johnson, for taking time to do the interview. I really appreciate your allowing us to film with you today." It was a thank you, but one that clearly dismissed the agent. Sally took the arm of Grant's white lab coat. "Interview next." She positioned him in front of one of the drug racks, then shifted several bottles around him.

"Those were where they were for a reason," he told her, visibly annoyed.

"Well, you must put them right back where they belong as soon as we're done, then." She peered at him critically through narrowed eyes, then reached up to finger-comb an errant lock of sandy hair.

Grant recoiled. "Geeze. Quit that."

Sally stood him down, all five feet of her. "We cannot have you looking like you have horns, now, can we? You're supposed to be the good guy in this piece."

Grudgingly, he smoothed over where she had touched.

"Great. Here we go, then." The light blared back on, and instantly Sally Hester went sharp as the crack of a hickory switch. "Three, two, one. This is Sally Hester for CTNC Investigative Reports. I am here at Chief Parker's Drugs in Mimosa Branch, Georgia, with owner Grant Owens, the courageous pharmacist who uncovered a three-state network of prescription-drug abuse that has implicated a prominent local doctor." She turned to Grant. "Tell me, Grant. What tipped you off that there was trouble right here in Mimosa Branch?"

"My father had been ill for some time before he died and left me the drugstore, so the records were pretty disorganized. When I—"

The mike flipped back to Sally. "Your father was a pharmacist, too?"

Back to Grant. "Yes, he owned this store for thirty-six years. When he died, he left it to me. As I said, the records were disorganized. My first priority was to get them onto computer so I could sell the store and return to California."

"So the drugstore is currently for sale?"

The mike flipped back to Grant. "Yes, but that has nothing to do with what's happening here today." He looked adorably grave. "Most people think drug deals involve the mob or gangs or pushers. Unfortunately, that's not always the case. Sometimes members of the medical community betray the trust of those they serve and get into illegal trafficking. When my computer program red-flagged some pretty disturbing prescription patterns, I discovered that a doctor may have done just that. So I went to the authorities. The DEA took it from there."

Sally nodded gravely. "And today, they have come to collect that evidence. Were you ever concerned for your own safety? Or for your father's reputation?"

Grant went deadly still. "My father took care of the people of this town for more than thirty years. Ask anybody who knew him, and you'll find that he was a well-respected, generous, and profoundly honest man. No, I was not worried about danger to my father's reputation."

Good for Grant! He'd finally taken up for his dad.

Applause and whistles erupted from the locals, including me. Did I mention I could whistle through my teeth without using my fingers?

Sally beamed at Grant's response, then sobered. "And your own safety, Mr. Owens? Weren't you worried about that? These things can get pretty ugly."

"No." He colored, looking convincingly humble and entirely too handsome. "I never even considered it."

Back to Sally. "So there you have it." The cameraman zoomed in on her. "Pharmacist Grant Owens, a concerned citizen who, with no thought of his own safety, uncovered an interstate drug conspiracy and helped expose at least one crooked doctor to the harsh light of justice. And I'm Sally Hester, your voice of truth from CTNC's Investigative Reports." Serious expression, eyes trained into the camera.

"And off." The cameraman killed the lights.

Sally shook Grant's hand. "You were perfect. Your phone's gonna ring off the hook with buyers for this place."

"We're done here, Grant," the DEA goddess said. She left the store with the last of the agents after checking to make sure they hadn't missed anything. "I'll call you tonight at home to report on phase two."

"Okay." Grant turned to Sally. "Thanks for the plug about the store being on the market," he said, visibly rattled now that everything was all over. His motives hadn't been a hundred percent altruistic, after all. The news story had ended up being a sales tool.

"Hope you sell it." Sally gathered the mike cord into a

tidy loop. "If I need any more quotes for the print story, I'll call you before three. I want it on the wires well before prime time."

The DEA agents had gathered out by their cars, the trunks now closed and locked with all the evidence safely inside.

Sally stopped by to shake Geneva's and my hands on her way out. "Sorry I had to shove you ladies aside."

"I was sort of surprised to see you here," I couldn't resist saying. "Geneva and I are friends of Velma Christianson and Donnie West. Close friends." I studied her face to gauge her reaction.

Only her pupils betrayed her. "Where have I heard that name before?" She looked past us toward the soda fountain. "Donnie West. Oh yes. He's running for mayor, isn't he?"

She was playing it cool. Understandable. I nodded sagely. "You knew."

She laughed. "Hard not to, honey. At least in this place." She waved her mike toward the three-foot high "Donnie West for Mayor" poster over the soda fountain. And the two in the front windows. "Nice talkin' to you, but I've gotta run. Don't want to miss the arrest. That's the money shot."

Geneva waited until the van pulled away to bend over and whack her thigh. "Eee-heee-hee!" Clearly, my stab at brilliant deductive reasoning had amused her greatly. Of *course* Sally knew about Donnie's candidacy. Geneva came up laughing so hard she was crying. When she finally found her voice, she pointed to me and repeated my dramatic, "You knew, nudge, nudge, wink, wink." Another brief spate of hysterics intervened before she could get a grip on herself to say, "Oh, honey, I'm sorry. I don't mean to laugh at you, but that was so darn funny." Off she went again.

Ears throbbing, I started to defend myself for trying to play Natasha to Grant's Boris, then realized I didn't have a leg to stand on. Grudgingly, I let myself chuckle. Geneva was so contagious when she really cut loose that soon I was hanging on to her and hoo-hawing, too.

Maybe it was a reaction to the shock of the "raid," or relief from discovering that poor Reba Gordon was off the hook, or the realization that Grant had had bigger things than "The Kiss" on his mind for the past few weeks, but suddenly I found the world a very funny place.

Grant approached us, hands on the hips of his white coat. "Pretty great, isn't it? Tonight, Mack Gordon will see how it feels to be thrown into a jail cell."

"Huh?" Geneva wiped her eyes, doing her best to regain her control.

"Mack Gordon. They're arresting him right now. That was what you guys were laughing about, wasn't it?"

Geneva's face all but imploded. "Mmmm."

I didn't trust myself to words, either. I just nodded vigorously, grateful that he would never know what a really bad spy I'd make.

"Okay." He eyed us with suspicion, but didn't make an issue of it. "I'm going down to my car for the spare computer. Need to get it up and running right away."

Still not trusting ourselves, we both nodded again.

I couldn't wait to get Geneva alone in a safe place to figure out what the Sam Hill was going on. But at that moment, laughing at myself had left my soul feeling like it had just been washed and fluffed.

Chapter 16

That night Geneva's husband dropped her off after choir practice so we could put our heads together on Miss Mamie's porch. Over wine and cheese and crackers, we did our best to figure out if Grant's connection to Sally Hester had anything to do with Donnie. In the end, the only thing we came up with was a slight buzz and the fact that we'd have to ask Grant or Donnie to find out. Since we couldn't ask Grant without raising his suspicions, we decided to ask Donnie the next night at campaign headquarters.

Not a fruitful session, but a good time was had by all. Geneva called her husband to come pick her up, and when she got into the car, he got a whiff of her breath and glared up at me as the bad influence I was.

Geneva and I just giggled.

The next night at Velma's we dragged Donnie out to "the conference room." It was cool and dark and peaceful under the cobalt blue autumn sky.

"Donnie," Geneva began. "Lin and I are really confused about something, and we decided the best way to clear it up was to ask you outright."

"Go for it," Donnie told us, completely at ease.

"Well, when Sally Hester showed up with the DEA at the store, we were really confused."

"I bet you were." He smiled, clearly enjoying this.

"I mean, we couldn't help wondering if it had anything to do with the judge's files, since she's workin' on that."

"Sally's being there at the seizure had nothin' to do with the judge's files," he said calmly. "Nothin' at all."

We both stared at him. We'd wanted a full explanation, but what we'd gotten was a typical man-answer. Absolutely unsatisfying.

"Are you saying," I pressed, "it's just a coincidence that Grant called in Sally Hester about Doc Gordon?"

Geneva's penciled brows squinched into confused points.

"Nope." He was loving this big time.

"Listen, Donnie." This from impatient me. "Could you just explain why she was there?"

"Grant said I could tell y'all if you asked. About Sally, anyway."

At last.

"He came to me months ago about the stuff he'd un-covered. It's no secret I've had plenty of experience with the drug scene, and I guess he knew he could trust me not to spill the beans. I suggested he call the DEA and Sally Hester. That way he'd get action, and with Sally on the case, Mack Gordon wouldn't be able to sweep everything under the rug."

"So it was just a coincidence that Sally Hester was cov-ering the seizure."

"No." He faced me squarely, but with compassion. "I told Grant to call her. That's not a coincidence."

Semantics. Big deal. "But Mack Gordon doesn't have anything to do with the judge's files."

I sensed him take a mental step back, but he remained pleasant. "Do you do that a lot, Lin?"

"What?"

"Ask somebody a question, then argue with them about the answer they give."

"No. My mother does, but I—" I halted abruptly when I saw Geneva's lips fold inward, her eyes rolling. "Oh God. I guess I do."

Mame-sign. The horror, the horror.

Fortunately, Donnie didn't take umbrage at my use of the Lord's name in vain. He just beamed at me without a shred of condemnation. "It's okay. The Good Lord made you the way you are for a reason."

"So this whole thing with Grant and Doc Gordon had nothing to do with the judge's files," Geneva said.

"Well, I couldn't say that." He sobered, the harsh intensity in his face a testimony to the darkness he had since escaped. "As it turns out, there is a connection, but I cain't discuss it."

"Perfect." I raised my hands in frustration. "Now you've got my curiosity up even worse than when we started."

"Lin," he said, dead serious. "This is no matter for idle curiosity. There's serious stuff goin' down here. A lot more than the campaign. We're talkin' about people's lives, their reputations, even their freedom. No matter what Doc Gordon did, or the mayor, they are still human beings, worthy of compassion as well as justice. Trust me, we'll all be better off leavin' the judgin' to the Lord." He softened slightly. "And count yourselves lucky that you don't know all the gory details. I wish I didn't."

I couldn't stop myself. "Does Grant know?"

Donnie's dark eyes sparkled above his fixed expression. "You'll have to ask Grant about that. But if you care about him, I wouldn't advise it. He's got a lot on his plate right now."

Geneva seemed more than willing to accept that, but I still chafed to know. It's one of my biggest sins: I always want to know everything, especially stuff that's none of my business.

"Is there anything we can do to help?" Geneva volunteered.

"Just the usual. Work hard and pray harder." Donnie

flexed his shoulders as if to throw off the weight of what we'd been discussing. "You know, it's amazin' how easy I forget that everything is in God's hands, not our own. I put all this stuff on the altar, and the first thing I know, I'm back totin' it again, groanin' under the load."

"But idn't it great that we can just lay it down again," Geneva said, her open features alight.

"Amen, sister." His peace recovered, Donnie headed back to the garage.

"C'mon, Lin." Geneva put her arm around my shoulders and gave me a gentle shake. "Just lay it down, and let's get back to work."

Easier said than done.

If it hadn't been for my upcoming real-estate exam, I'd probably have obsessed for the next three days. I studied instead.

Saturday of the big exam finally came, and I took the test, sweaty-palmed and quaking. The worst part was, Georgia doesn't use the straightforward real-estate test that some states do. It uses the tricky version, with lots of little booby traps in the wording, which pissed me off so badly from the beginning of my course that I wasted a lot of mental energy resenting the nature of the test. I'd have been a lot better off accepting things and moving on, but that was the story of my life.

Anyway, I finished the test along with most of my class and a roomful of young kids, middle-aged women, and male retirees. Afterward, we staged another impromptu celebration at the steak house—the one with a mega-bar loaded down with all the mediocre food you can eat for $8.99—except, ironically, steak.

I drove home at ten with mixed emotions. Huge relief because the test was behind me—now that the course was finished, my time was once again my own, so I could focus on the campaign and really enjoy the final push—but my liberation wasn't total. A sword still hung over me: my test scores.

Common sense told me not to worry. I'd done so well on the practice exams that I was sure to pass. But the old me was curled in a fetal position wringing the bedclothes in anguish over every single question that had given me pause. Despite the progress I had made, my old self still wasn't easy to ignore.

So I was really glad to see Tommy on the front porch when I drove up to 1431 Green Street that night. He stood and lifted a poster that said, "Way to go, Sis!" in one hand and what looked like a bottle of champagne in the other.

Pleased by the surprise but worried about the champagne, I hurried over to give him a big hug.

"Wow. What a neat surprise." He'd used the leftover Desert Sunrise paint from my apartment for the poster.

Tommy proudly presented me with the chilled bottle, which turned out to be sparkling white grape juice. BIG whew. "Strictly legal," he said. "Hope you don't mind."

"The very best kind." I saw that he'd put two of Nana Grainger's etched crystal flutes on the wicker table between the rockers.

"Sit, sit. I want to make a toast." He poured the grape juice, handed me mine, then ceremoniously lifted his glass. "Here's to my big sister and all the new beginnings yet to come, for both of us. I'm proud of you, Sissie-ma-noo-noo."

He looked so strong and sure and full of hope that I truly believed he could make it. I resolved then and there that his dumb Sissie-ma-noo-noo nickname wouldn't bother me anymore.

I stood and bowed, then lifted my glass. "Here's to you and me, Tommy—to all we had and never knew, all we lost and are better off without, and all the Good Lord has in store, one day at a time."

"Hear, hear."

We settled into our chairs. I pulled my thin jacket closer

in the delicious cool of the night. Sixty-eight degrees is my very favorite temperature.

"We'd all planned to stay up and toast you," Tommy explained, "but from seven on, Uncle Bedford kept takin' off his pants, Depends and all, and tryin' to go to bed. And the General was havin' a rough time stayin' awake, so I told the Mame and Aunt Glory you'd understand."

"I do." I nudged his forearm. "But I sure am glad you were here. Sometimes I feel so alone, it almost takes my breath away."

"Yeah. It's really hard after havin' somebody there waitin' for you to come home for so long. Even when the relationship's a train wreck, there's something about havin' that warm body on the other side of the bed. And the stuff that's passed between you, the history. Good or bad, it's a powerful connection that's tough to do without."

Truth, purely spoken, from somebody who had been there. It was a gift. Finally, a man who talked to me about important things. Wouldn't you know he'd be my brother. That nasty little ache of loneliness tugged at my insides. "How about you, Tommy? What's it like being you these days?"

He leaned forward, his arms braced on his thighs. "Still good and getting better, thanks to AA. Hard, but good. I've got a long way to go and a lot of amends to make, particularly to my kids, but for the first time in my life, today is enough, just as it is."

"Is it hard, not drinking?" I thought about the booze and beer in the spare refrigerator.

He inhaled deeply. "Sometimes. Sometimes I get crazy for a drink, whether I know the trigger or not. Experience has taught me to meet my sponsor, or any long-timer I can find, and get as far away from temptation as I can until we ride it out." He shot me a wry glance. "The boat's always a good place for that. My sponsor is a basshole, too." He peered back out over the hedges and the tracks beyond. "But the crazy times are getting fewer and farther between.

The longer I stay sober, the more I work the program, the better things go." He sipped the grape juice. "Not that it's easy. I spent a lifetime running away from things, blaming everybody but myself for the choices I made." He looked down. "Learning to live another way, a better way, takes time, but it's worth the effort. I'm beginning to like the guy in the mirror. And the other people in my life. Even the General."

And me? I could hardly blame him if he didn't.

Maybe because we were on Miss Mamie's porch, I asked the unaskable question that had occurred to me earlier. "The booze in the spare refrigerator . . . does it bother you?"

Pensive, he exhaled heavily. "That's hard to say. When I'm Jonesin' for a drink, I'm hyperaware that it's there. But I also know I could go to the Tote-A-Poke and load up almost as easily. So it isn't really a matter of the stuff being there. Liquor is everywhere. But sometimes when I'm weak, I just need to get away from it." He granted me a wry smile. "My sponsor says that'll change with time and continued recovery. He can sit in a bar all night now without turnin' a hair. His sobriety is so precious to him that all the Jim Beam in Kentucky couldn't tempt him to throw it away." He rolled the glass of grape juice between his hands, staring at it as if it contained the real thing. Then he relaxed into the rocker with that sweet Tommy-smile. "Boy, am I lookin' forward to the day when my sobriety is that strong."

I rocked beside him in the dim light. "You'll get there, Tommy. I believe in you."

When he didn't reply, I looked over and saw his eyes had welled and he was struggling with his emotions. When he came to himself enough to speak, he took a quick swig of juice, then said, "That's awful good to hear, Lin. Especially from you."

"I did so much wrong with us, Tommy. Made your life

so miserable when we were little. Judged you when we were big. I wish I could erase it all.

"I know we have the General and Miss Mamie—they love us both the best they can—but it's not the same. We're family, Tombo; we can help each other. I love you, brother."

He nodded, and a warming peace settled between us, no longer a thread, but now a golden bridge.

Why had it taken so much to bring us to this simple place?

"I saw you with the General," I whispered. "In the kitchen." I eyed him fiercely. "I'm so proud of you, Tommy. And so ashamed of myself. I had no idea. No, that's a cop-out. I wouldn't let myself see—"

He cut me off. "None of that, now. Nobody beats up on my big sister, not even you." He poured me another glass of juice. "You were doing the best you could. We all were." There was real compassion in his face. "Thanks be to God, we both know better now. Be glad for that. Celebrate it. Beatin' yourself up doesn't help anybody, least of all the General and Miss Mamie."

He was right and I knew it, but old habits die hard. We rocked in silence until I had wrestled my self-condemnation into a head-lock.

"What time are we supposed to pick up that truck tomorrow?" he asked with a hint of the old mischief in his voice.

"Ten." Most of my Buckhead friends were not early risers. I'd planned the itinerary to hit the heathens first, then finish up with the churchgoers after they got home from services. "Why?"

"Plenty of time. How 'bout I take you fishin' before-hand?"

Tommy had never asked me fishing, not even when we were kids.

"What time?" I knew perfectly well that the answer would be horrendous.

His grin made it all but a dare. "Five o'clock."

"That's only six hours from now. It's pitch dark at five," I protested.

"Yeah, but by the time we get you a license and have a sausage biscuit at the Dam Store, then get the boat in, it'll be dawn." He let out a contented sigh. "You really gotta see the sun come up over the lake, Sis. It fills your soul."

Who in their right mind would get up at five on a Sunday morning to go fishing, especially with a full day of moving ahead? But then, I had no more illusions of being in my right mind.

And Tommy had never asked me before. If this was a test, I wanted to pass it. "Okay. Five o'clock it is."

"Hot damn." He stood to his feet and took my half-full glass. "Up you go. Bedtime."

I grabbed the poster, having decided to give it a place of honor in my perfect girly apartment. A huge yawn escaped me. "Agh. Five o'clock."

My brother let out a wicked chuckle as he held the door for me. "A word of advice. Don't analyze it. Just do it. When the alarm rings, sit up, put your feet on the floor, and head for the bathroom."

Determined not to let him get the best of me, I resolved to do just that.

Six hours later, I hit the deck. Two hours after that, I sat silent in the boat, semi-comatose despite liberal infusions of hair-on-your-chest coffee from the Dam Store. In silence, we watched the sun rise huge and orange against the black silhouette of the distant shoreline.

Tommy had forbidden me to speak, invoking the "Quiet Game," Miss Mamie's favorite method for putting a lid on our childish back-seat squabbles.

But sitting quiet in our snug cove on the west bank with my brand-new fishing license in my pocket, I didn't mind. Words would have been sacrilege there. Not even a ripple marred the still surface of the cove. You could see all the way down to the mossy stump at the edge of the drop-off beside us.

A single crow called, then soared from a nearby pine. I couldn't remember ever feeling so peaceful. I began to understand why Tommy loved to fish. It gave him a good excuse to search out moments like these, away from all the problems of living.

We drifted at anchor until the sun cleared the trees and the light shifted to set the lake asparkle.

Tommy stood. "Okay, Sissie-ma-noo-noo." He handed me a rod and reel. "Just hang on to this while I attach the bait." He drew an odd gizmo out of his tackle box. It had a painted "head" with a neon orange splotch above red eyes, and a sort of a hula skirt made out of chartreuse-and-white clipped rubber bands that concealed a substantial hook. "I use artificials. This is a spinner bait." A wire angled up from the head, then bent to support a long, gold, leaf-looking thing. "That's the spinner," he explained when I touched it. "It flutters when you're trolling, but when you drop the bait, it helicopters to slow the descent."

Whatever.

Next he showed me how to work the reel. "This line's a little heavy for a beginner, but it's what I had set up. You'll do fine with it." He picked up his own rod and reel. "See that dead tree over there? Now watch what I do." He cast his bait into the shallow water beside it, then started reeling in along the length of the trunk. "Just bring 'er back nice and easy, and as the depth drops, let your bait drop, too. Bass like to hunt down in the branches. Once you clear those, just keep bringin' her in easy." His hook came up empty.

He patted me on the arm, then headed toward the prow. "She's all yours." When he reached the forward deck, he smiled back at me. "Okay. Go to it. And the 'Quiet Game' resumes. Just try not to hook me, okay?"

"Okay." I watched as he cast his baited hook with a graceful flick of his rod into the channel.

The line zizzed through the reel into a perfect arc until it sank and he began to draw it in. "Now," he murmured like a golf announcer. "I'm at depth in the channel, next to the drop-off. There's a lot of dead stumps down there that the big boys like. I'm gonna stroll through 'em and see if I can't tempt somebody with a little breakfast." He nodded toward my side of the cove. "Go ahead. Try casting your hook in over by that tree to get the feel of it."

Supremely self-conscious, I did my best to duplicate his fluid motions but ended up launching my hook like a stone out of a slingshot. It shot out straight, then fell with a plunk nowhere near the fallen tree.

"Drat."

"Sh."

I started reeling in. "*You* were talking." Mr. golf-announcer.

"I know what I'm doing," he chided in subdued tones. It was the backseat all over again, only this time it made me smile. I shut up.

Tommy was grooving with his equipment, playing the reel like a delicate instrument in the hands of a blind man, his eyes intent on the almost invisible point where his line met the water.

I was trying to decide what to do next when my rod almost jerked out of my hand. "Awk! Tommy, I think I got something!"

He backed toward me, still mesmerized by his own line. "Did you hook a stump, maybe?"

"I don't think so." It was all I could do to hang on to the pole. "It was just wham, and the line started to run. Something's definitely alive on the other end." The pole arched.

"I'll be damned." Tommy wound in his own hook lickety-split. "Keep the tip up until I get there. Man, that must be a monster! Keep it up, and whatever you do, don't let go of that rod!"

He stuck his pole in a holster and leapt over to help me

battle the fish. The fish tried to surface, and Tommy made
me put the rod down in the water to keep it from breaking
the surface and maybe shaking loose the hook. But it managed to come up more than once.

"Holy shit! It's a mother!" Tommy yelled at the sight
of flashing gills and fins. Then he settled back to giving me
instructions. I got the fish back down. It fought me hard,
surfacing and running. The next ten minutes were the long-
est and most exciting I could remember. By the time the
fish was finally worn out, I was, too, but at last, I reeled
my very first catch to the surface alongside the boat.

Tommy was waiting with the net. "Damn, Sis! Look at
that thing!" He snagged it and lifted the net over the boat
with both hands. "That's a ten-pounder if it's an ounce.
More. Look how thick he is!"

The bass gave one last, desperate struggle. With perfect
aim, it flipped a glob of scaly fish slime smack onto my
closed lips. I clamped them even tighter over a stifled
scream. "Mmmmm!" Then I raked my mouth across the
sleeve of my jacket, but the smell of fish lingered even after
I scooped up lake water to wash it off.

Tommy laughed. "Hah. You've been initiated!" He freed
the hook, then reverently placed my trophy into the holding
tank. "Would you *look* at *that*. First cast. First cast!"

He got out the instant camera and a hanging scale and
a ruler, then took pictures of me holding the fish from the
scale and along the ruler, then some more shots with his
35-millimeter, never keeping the bass out of the water long.
"Twelve pounds. Twelve fricken pounds! That's a lifetime
fish, on your first fricken cast!"

I was delighted but did my best not to gloat.

Then, after he'd stowed the gear away and placed my
trophy back in the holding tank, Tommy threw his hat
down onto the carpeted deck and proceeded to do a stomping, cussing devil dance on it. "Shit! Damn! And eighteen
colors of hell! Forty years! Forty fricken years, I've been
fishin' this fricken cove, and never caught anything over

six pounds, and *she* throws in a hook for the first time—in the wrong fricken place, mind you—and catches a twelve-pounder! Twelve pounds, three ounces! Biggest fricken fish this sixty thousand dollar rig ever saw! Shit!"

I could tell he wasn't mad at me, just the situation in general, but the $60,000 price tag took me aback.

He started pointing at the trees and ranting about being powerless over the blankety-blank fish in this blankety-blank cove, and the blankety-bank lake, and every pond and stream on the blankety-blank planet. And then he started carrying on about detachment and some other stuff that lost me completely, until at last he wound down and stood with his back to me, breathing hard, for what seemed like fifteen minutes but was probably only five.

Then he turned around and ran his hand down his red, sweaty face like Treat Williams in *1941,* and came up wearing a pretty scary smile. "Disregard that," he panted out. "The old Tommy just paid us a visit, but I convinced him not to stay."

"I think you are amazing." I looked up at him in awe. "Absolutely amazing."

"Yeah, well." His posture eased a little further. "I'm not proud of it, but I gotta admit, it was cathartic."

"I think you probably scared away the rest of the fish, though."

He laughed outright at that and picked up the net, heading for the tank.

"What are you doing with my fish?" I demanded as he scooped it into the net.

"I'm a catch-and-release fisherman," he explained as if that should settle the matter.

I straightened. "Wait a minute. That's fine for you, but who said I was? That's *my* fish. I want to keep it. Or mount it. Or something. Not let it go."

Tommy shook his head. "This is a sport. Real sportsmen do it for the catch, the fight, the experience. A magnificent granddaddy like this one deserves to live and make lots more like him." He pointed to the pictures he'd taken. "You've got all the proof you need. We can have a mounted replica made, or blow up one of the 35-millimeter shots and frame it if you want to."

"No." What was I thinking? The last thing I wanted was a fish hanging on the wall in my perfect girly apartment. Or a picture of one, for that matter. "We could eat it."

"Bass are not *food*," he said with the conviction of a defense attorney pleading for an innocent client facing the chair. "They're magnificent *toys* God gives us to play with."

Still not grown up.

"You love to eat fish," I argued.

"Lin, Lin, were you been?" Another annoying remnant from my childhood. "This is Lanier we're talking about. Sewaged regularly by municipal treatment facilities and poultry farms. Pooped in by every Canada goose from here to Montreal. And home of the world's largest floating trailer park. Everything else aside, are you seriously telling me you want to risk eating that poor old granddaddy fish? He deserves a medal just for staying alive in all that junk."

Sufficiently disgusted, I relented. "All right. You can let him go. But I don't have to like it."

"Good woman."

Another insight left me suddenly weary. "It's all about letting go now, isn't it?"

He nodded. I could tell from the soft sadness in his eyes that he understood.

This insight business could be exhausting, sapping my energy along with my misconceptions.

Tommy lowered the bass into the water, and I sat on the side of the boat to watch the biggest fish I would ever catch disappear safely into the green deep.

"This is a good thing, isn't it?" I asked. It was a rhetorical question, and we both knew I wasn't talking about letting the fish go.

"A very good thing. An important thing," my brother said.

"A first."

"Yep."

We were happy, both of us. And what was, was enough.

Best of all, the memory of my big fish was ours, just Tommy's and mine.

I decided to keep it that way, just between the two of us.

Chapter 17

The next day I dragged my sunburned face and aching bones into the drugstore at eight-fifteen.

Geneva was already checking the Monday morning delivery, so I joined her beside the register.

"Look at you," she fussed when she saw my pink forehead, cheeks, and blotches. "I thought you were going to take that real-estate test and move this weekend. When did you have time to sunbathe?"

"I didn't." I picked up a small case of laxatives and opened it to check the contents against the packing slip. "Tommy took me fishing at the crack of dawn yesterday before he helped me move into the apartment." I continued checking off the other items in the bright red plastic shipping crate. "Who knew you could get sunburned before nine-thirty in the morning?"

"Not me," Geneva said. "But of course, you hadn't had any sun all summer."

"No." She had a point. I held the title of Whitest Woman in Christendom hands down, having forsaken sunning since menopause had gathered up all the melanin so nicely distributed in my once-golden complexion and herded it into embarrassingly situated concentration camps on my upper lip, neck, cheeks, and forearms.

I glanced into the mirror by the earring display and

cringed at the deepening pigment under my nose that looked for all the world like a mustache.

As always, Geneva did her best to cheer me up. "So, you went fishin' with Tommy."

"Yep. It was fun." I didn't say anything further. Hoarding the experience, I'd kept my resolution and hadn't even told Tricia when I'd called for my "Poor Babies" about the move.

Geneva took the hint. "So. Did you put anything on that burn?"

"Yes. Aloe." I glanced back into the mirror. Man, was I a sight. Pink, peeling, and blotchy.

She peered at me, looking deeper than my skin. "Are you okay? 'Cause I can manage by myself here if you need to—"

"No, I'm fine, really. Just a little spacier than usual. If that's possible." Boy, did I miss the organized, clear-headed Lin of old.

I have a theory about that, by the way. See, when you hit middle age, half the hairs that used to be on your head shift into reverse and migrate down through your brain to your upper lip and chin, leaving your thinker like Swiss cheese in the process. I am living proof that this is true. Tricia says it's just the stress, and that I'll get better once my life settles down. I hope she's right, but my flakies feel awfully permanent.

"Whatever you say," Geneva said without conviction. "But if you ever want to start cutting back to regular hours, just let me know. I can always cover the afternoons and Saturdays with teenagers."

Who were more trouble than they were worth, as we both knew. Now that I could run the computer and help with the billing and ordering, Grant didn't bat an eyelash at the overtime he was paying me.

I was pretty pleased with myself about the computer, actually. But I still only knew how to do exactly what I knew how to do. If the slightest thing happened that wasn't supposed to, I had to go running for Grant or Geneva.

Geneva fished some Epsom salts from the bottom of the crate. "So, how did the move go?"

"Fine. We got everything from town." I bent beside her to retrieve more of the items on the packing list I had started. "My friends were very happy to get their basement and attic space back."

Friends.

After seeing them, I wondered if the term really applied anymore. They had all been properly kind and solicitous, and I was grateful for their help, but I had felt a vast gap between their couples world and my single one, a gap that left me with that all-alone-on-the-top-of-a-flagpole-in-the-wind feeling, despite Tommy's reassuring presence.

I'd always had so many friends. Family just wasn't the same.

Feeling sorry for myself, I told Geneva, "But you know how it is. I had a lot more junk stashed away than I remembered, so there's still tons to go through." Why was I whining? I had promised myself last night after Tricia nailed me for it that I wouldn't whine anymore. "There's stuff piled everywhere in the apartment. And the garage—thank goodness that was available for the overflow." So many *things*. We'd moved Miss Mamie's Buick to the porte cochere. "It's cram-full, now. I have no idea where I'll put the stuff."

"Don't worry," she said in that motherly tone of hers. "You'll be in and settled before you know it." She handed me a case of allergy tablets. "Grant wants these shelved beside the house brand. He's already put out the comparison flags."

"Right."

When I returned she'd reached the bottom of the crate. "Okay." She straightened, rubbing her lower back. "All checked in." She handed me a sack of natural vitamins to shelve. "Here. I'll do the stomach stuff."

I liked this part of the job. It was mindless and undemanding enough so that we could visit. Geneva started working across the aisle from me. "So. What're you plannin' to do with yourself now that you don't have class anymore?"

"Get moved in, of course. But after that, I don't know."

Three evenings a week and Saturdays.

A year before, I would have filled those open hours in a New York second with urgent priorities, things that had everything to do with everybody else in my life but me. But after just two months in Mimosa Branch, my perspective had shifted, narrowing in on the immediate with the clarity of a microscope. The stripping away of my old life, traumatic though it had been, had certainly simplified things, and I was beginning to appreciate some of the changes—and the choices, basic though they were.

Before, time had been a restless, insatiable tyrant. Now my three evenings a week and Saturdays had become a gift, one to be savored and spent with considered alacrity, like the twenty-dollar bill my godmother had given me when I turned twelve.

Ironic. I'd been so afraid that coming home would constrict me, rob me of my privacy, imprison me in a living anachronism of outdated restrictions and ideas. Instead, I had slowed down to a saner pace and begun to live.

And let live. BIG change.

"How 'bout I come over after work and help you get settled in?" she volunteered.

My knee-jerk reaction was to decline with profuse thanks, but my new self reminded me that I needed help. So I made a choice and made a change. "That would be great. What time?"

"Seven-thirty? I'll even bring fried chicken."

"Fried chicken? Geneva, that's too much trouble. You don't need to make—"

"I have no intention of making anything but a trip to Mrs. Drumstick. Potato salad or coleslaw?"

"Potato salad." More progress. My old self had

prompted, "whatever *you* like," but I was getting better at ignoring her.

I was feeling very smug until Grant walked in looking so tanned and handsome in his California chic that my willful libido immediately stripped him to his glorious imaginary buff. Well, not so imaginary. I'd already seen everything but what was under his running shorts.

Humiliated by my perverse imagination, I felt my ears go molten and snapped my attention to the vitamin shelf. When Grant reached me, he stopped right behind me, bending to say quietly, "Why is it that you look like a deer in the headlights when you see me lately? I think we need to talk about this. The porch?"

His closeness was so delicious and infuriating that I had to grip the edge of the shelf. "Not tonight. Geneva's helping me move in."

"I could help, too. We could talk afterwards."

The last thing I needed in my current state of frustration was to be wedged into the apartment with Grant while Geneva looked on, gloating. "Thanks, but no. We're doing secret girl-stuff."

"Okay. After the meeting tomorrow then."

My inner Puritan prompted an icy, "No!" but my voice said a disgustingly meek, "Okay."

"Great." He straightened with a chuckle. "I warn you, though, I'm adding secret girl-stuff to my list of woman-questions."

Perfect. I'd have to make something up.

He moved on, leaving only a whiff of Jade East in his wake. Boy, did I wish he hadn't told me he wanted to sleep with me.

It didn't seem possible, but thanks to Geneva, I was able to spend my first night in the apartment that very night. We'd laughed a lot and accomplished even more, and I'd sent her home at ten-fifteen with a box full of doodahs that she'd loved and I'd realized I could do without.

A few chores still remained. Pictures and mirrors stood propped against the walls where I wanted to hang them, but the rest of the boxes and extra furniture had been shifted to the garage below me, and my nesting compulsions were almost satisfied.

I had thought I'd be happier about that momentous passage, but I rationalized that I was probably just too tired.

After George collected Geneva, I locked the new deadbolt Tommy had installed, then pivoted to survey our handiwork. Two exquisite white-on-white ceramic urn lamps from Thebaut's stood regal on matching eighteenth-century Chinese chests that flanked my white Haitian cotton sofa. Underfoot, the muted terra-cotta tones of my antique oriental rug became wall-to-wall carpet. The colors were perfect with the paint, as I'd known they would be. Two comfy floral-print chairs and a tambour table from our old den faced the sofa across the clean lines of the thick-glass coffee table that had set us back $6000.

And to think how guilty I had felt about spending that, when all the while Phil was . . .

Aanh! My internal Phil-alert buzzer sounded. No more Phil regrets allowed!

I leaned down and stroked the coffee table's graceful turn where the side became the top. "Bless every cent of your gorgeous six-thousand-dollar self."

It occurred to me that talking to my furniture was not a good sign, but I dismissed the idea. Yet there was no dismissing the odd emptiness beneath my sense of accomplishment.

I turned my attention to the front wall that faced the main house. The chestnut entertainment armoire from my cozy little lady's study just fit between the two front windows. The white miniblinds I'd gotten for half price at Home Junction looked just fine without draperies. I liked the crispness of the effect. On the wall opposite the sofa, my glass-topped ormolu console sat behind the easy chairs.

My Chippendale mirror would hang over the console, reflecting the sofa and my favorite floral watercolor, a large original of a Charleston garden in full spring splendor.

A couple of plants and pictures hung, my nesting compulsion decreed, and I could hunker down here very nicely.

Truly a perfect girly apartment. And I had what I wanted. I was alone.

So why wasn't I happier about it?

Yawning, I passed my white wicker breakfast set and tiny kitchen on my way to the bedroom. I stood in the bedroom doorway and surveyed my beautiful white cutwork padded headboard with matching dust ruffles, and my comfy king-sized bed that looked like a linens commercial with its down pillows and 500-thread-count Egyptian cotton damask sheets. The headboard and narrow, hand-painted bedside chests were a perfect fit, with not an inch to spare. The gold-framed rhododendron botanical prints that hung above the bed were perfect. The tall alabaster lamps with white silk shades were perfect. So was the white wicker triple dresser that had been in my guest room back in Buckhead.

So why was I crying?

I sagged against the jamb and slid to the perfectly pickled floor.

I'd looked forward to this move for two whole months. Both air conditioners were chugging away at their perches. And I was crying as if somebody had died.

What was wrong with me?

A strong rap sounded at the door, followed by two brisk rings of my $29 wireless doorbell.

Who the hell at this hour? The digital readout on my clock radio said ten-thirty.

Grant?

Surely, he wouldn't.

I didn't want to see anybody at that moment, least of all him.

When the bell sounded again, with more knocking, I

forced myself to my feet. "Go away! I'm in the bathtub!"

"Lin?" My mother's voice held more than a hint of alarm. "Lin, honey, are you all right?"

At least it wasn't Grant. But I didn't want my mother to find me in such a sorry state, either, especially since I'd insisted on doing this.

"Just a minute, Miss Mamie!"

I splashed my face in the bathroom sink, then dried off, only to confront the reflection of a peeling, blotchy me with tear-swollen eyes and a Rudolph the Red nose.

Shit. Shit, shit, shit.

Tossing the towel, I headed for the door.

More knocking. "Lin?"

I took a leveling breath, then opened to find my mother standing on the stoop in her fuzzy slippers and flowered terrycloth robe, with the General's special bottle of hundred-year-old cognac in one hand and a gallon of her neatly labeled homemade peach ice cream in the other.

"I saw your lights still on. May I come in?" she asked with disarming uncertainty.

I had resolved to get a grip on myself, but instead, I stepped back, hung my head, and nodded, unable to speak for the tears that bullied their way back out.

"Oooh, honey," she said gently, enveloping me, ice cream and all. "It's gonna be okay." She closed the door with her foot. Then, to my amazement, she started crying right along with me. The ice cream hit the floor like a concrete block beside us as she guided me to the sofa, then sat down next to me, rocking and crying. "My sweet, sweet girl. I could kill that man for doing this to you. Just kill 'im."

I hated being so vulnerable before her. "Why is this so hard?" I managed between shudders. "I wanted to do this apartment. Spent all my money. Why am I sitting here blubbering like a child?"

"Oh, honey." She rubbed my back the way she used to when I had asthma. "You're crying because it's hard. And it's real. And things will never be the same." Leaning back, she cupped my hair and drew my head to her shoulder. "All your life, you think things are going to be one way, and then, suddenly, through no fault of your own, you find out they aren't anymore, and they never will be. It's sad. So sad you can hardly breathe sometimes."

Sheltered there in her arms, I realized she wasn't talking just about me. It put us on level ground for the first time ever.

"Look what you've been through, are going through still. You wouldn't be human if you didn't grieve." She let go with one hand to fish a Nana Grainger hanky from her robe pocket, then swipe at her eyes and nose. Unlike Scarlett, my mother always had a hanky. "Facing the truth, wishing with all your heart that it wasn't so, that things could be different, but knowing that they can't be. . . ." A shudder rippled through her. "So you cry. And you grieve. But you don't have to grieve alone."

She pulled back to look at me as only a mother can look at a beloved child. "Always so independent, so determined, even as a tiny baby." She smiled, dabbing at her nose. "You never wanted to cuddle. I blamed myself, for bottle-feeding you.

"And then, when you were a little girl, you were so strong and outgoing and precocious. Everyone in your presence was eclipsed, even the General. So strong-willed. 'I do it my byself!' It was that way about everything."

Her voice calmed to a steadier tone. "And after Tommy arrived, it was almost as if you felt we'd betrayed you somehow. You withdrew even further into your own little world, with those deep brown looks."

"I was spoiled." I dragged in a most unmannerly, juicy sniff. "Jealous, probably."

"No. You were my one and only Lin—fierce, stubborn, independent, too smart by half, doing the best you could. Never be sorry for that, sugar. I loved you then and I love you now."

"I love you, too, Mama." It was true, but no wave of sentiment accompanied the declaration.

"You don't have to go through this alone," she said fiercely.

I should have been comforted, uplifted by my mother's acceptance, but instead, I felt only sadness for us both. That damned curse of Eve. *Her desire shall be for her husband.* . . . I didn't want Phil anymore, but his loss left a gaping void in my life. Once we move beyond our mother's arms into the arms of a man, our mother's arms will never be enough again.

I knew the same held true for her. Love of a child might run deeper than any marriage bond, but it was no substitute for what passed between committed partners.

So there we sat, two women doing our best to survive change without the men who had held our hearts.

I remembered a rhyme my Granny Beth used to sing. "If your troubles and my troubles were hangin' on a line, you'd pick yours and I'd pick mine." At least I wasn't having to watch the man I had once loved disappear by degrees, leaving a sad, unpredictable stranger inside the familiar shell. I was luckier. Phil wasn't hanging around ruining my life.

Not in person, anyway, just in past perfect. Given time, though, I meant to see him exorcised for good and all.

Who knew? Maybe that was the reason behind my fantasies of Grant Owens. An imaginary replacement for my obsession with Phil?

Now, there was a recipe for disaster!

I resolved then and there to go to the adult toy store ASAP. Maybe some battery-powered relief could flush Grant Owens out of my system.

"Come on, Mama." I pulled away and rolled up off the sofa. "Let's eat the world's best homemade peach ice cream and drink hundred-year-old cognac."

After a sniff and a blink, she stood with twice the ease I had managed. The "Finger of Judgment" waggled at the bottle I'd picked up off the sofa. "That's the General's special cognac. I'd thought we might just drizzle a little over the top."

I laughed. It was beginning to work, diminishing the tension that had once resonated between us. "Drizzle if you want, but I'm making me a peach cognac shake. A strong one."

She paused, flat-mouthed. "Sounds pretty good, at that. Make it two."

I rescued the ice cream, still rock-hard in its plastic container. "I hope this'll fit in my little microwave."

"Microwave?" The Mame's bosom inflated. "Lin, dear, you don't cook my ice cream."

Happily, "the tone" no longer had the capacity to sting. After all those defensive years, the button it used to push had at long last been disconnected.

That was a good thing. A very good thing.

I laughed again, spontaneously. "I'm not going to cook it, Mama. I'm just going to soften it up enough so we can use it." Lord, how I wished I wasn't so aware of the metaphors in my life. "Then we'll pile up in my bed and watch *An Affair to Remember* on the VCR."

"I don't know, sweetie." Her worried look returned. "I don't think I should leave the General alone for so long. He might—"

"Daddy's probably sleeping like a baby. And even if he isn't, Tommy will hear him."

She peered at me, clearly wondering if I was on to her game with Tommy and the General. But the Mame being the Mame, she didn't bring it into the open, and that was okay.

"All right, I'll stay. But only until the movie's over. And only if we can watch a comedy. I've had enough crying for one night."

"Comedy it is." I had scads of good ones. "I know. How about *She-Devil*?"

"Oh, I love that one. It's so deliciously *mean*."

So I ended up spending my first night alone working with Geneva, then drinking very expensive spiked peach milkshakes and watching *She-Devil* with my cackling eighty-year-old mother.

And I wasn't alone.

Maybe things were working out as they were meant to, after all.

Chapter 18

The next morning Geneva and I had scarcely gotten the drugstore opened up when the phone rang and I answered it.

"May I please speak with Geneva Bates?"

Sally Hester: I recognized the voice.

"Geneva, it's for you."

"I swan," Geneva grumbled as she carried over the coffee pot she'd been pouring. "George knows better than to call me before the Birthday Bunch."

"It isn't George."

Frowning, she took the receiver. "Hello?" I could tell from the way her features congealed that something had happened. "Uh-huh. Uh-huh." Tense silence. "Uh-huh." She turned her back to the Coffee Club, who were listening as intently as I was, but pretending not to. "Good. I hope she stays there, bless her heart. This must be awful, for all of 'em." Pause. "Yes, we have a printout of all the volunteers. I've got one in my car." Nodding. "There's a couple of sheriff's deputies—good boys, worked real hard for us. I'll call them first." More nodding. "Okay."

Her eyebrows rose. "Grant? Why him?" Frown. "Oh. I see. I hadn't thought of that." Worried look. "How soon?" Eyebrows up again. "Yow. I'll warn him, then." Nodding.

"Okay. And thanks for calling." Worried smile. "You've been great."

She hung up and handed me the coffee. "Better make a fresh pot. I'll explain everything in a minute." Then she went into the pharmacy to pull Grant aside for a murmured conversation.

The only thing I overheard as I started the coffeemaker was Grant's, "If she thinks it'll help Donnie, okay."

The Coffee Club sat like crows on a phone line watching a possum freeze in the path of a speeding car.

Geneva emerged through the Dutch door, her pleasant expression forced. "Lin, could you come help me with some stock downstairs?"

"Sure."

Rex Beard touched the brim of his cap. "I'll take care of the refills."

"Thanks." I followed Geneva down the stairs. She motioned me all the way to her car parked in the alley, where she unlocked the back door and rummaged through her crate of campaign files until she found the volunteer printout. Then she crossed to the driver's door and opened it. "Hop in."

My curiosity kicked into high gear. Once the door was closed behind me, I realized she hadn't put the keys in the ignition. "Tell me. I'm dying."

"That was Sally Hester on the phone. The story about the mayor is breaking at noon today. She'd wanted to wait another week, but a competitor got a whiff that somethin' was up with the DA, so she has to go with it now." Geneva nervously scanned the alley. "She said the press would come down like locusts out at Velma's, but as soon as she found out last night, she called Velma and warned her. So Velma took her kids and their families to a friend's home in the mountains to hole up until the worst of this passes."

"Good for her." This was pretty exciting. I only hoped it didn't turn nasty, as these things had a way of doing.

"Sally called Donnie last night, too. She's already taped

a brief interview with him. She said his statement was simple, direct, and dignified. I know the rest of the press is gonna try to corner him, though."

"Donnie can handle them. I mean, what are they, compared to Hell's Angels?"

She nodded, smiling, but her eyes were uncertain. "Anyway, Sally said she's on her way to interview Grant."

"Grant?"

"It's all Mimosa Branch. She said it might help take some of the attention off Velma and Donnie, since Grant's the treasurer of Donnie's campaign. People are bound to assume there's some connection. She said the best way to control that would be to put out what we want said, first."

"Dang." I suddenly realized what this would make Mimosa Branch look like to the rest of the county. Heck, the state. Heck, the *world*, thanks to CTNC. "Man. This town is gonna seem like a hotbed of crime and corruption."

Geneva barked a laugh. "Honey, it *is*!"

That broke the tension.

She opened the door to get out. "I'm gonna go up to the Wee Tots Shoppe to call these deputies and see if we cain't get Velma's sealed off from everybody but our regular workers. I have Velma's private cell phone number. Once everything's set up, I'll call and let her know, just to ease her mind." She got out with a groan that echoed the stiffness I felt from doing the same.

"Do me a favor, would you please?" she asked. "Call George and ask him to bring over the little TV from the kitchen. Grant says the old antenna's still hooked up on the roof, so maybe we'll be able to get the local news, in case something shows up there. Sally said there probably wouldn't be anything until six, but just in case . . ."

"Okay."

When I emerged from the basement stairs into the store, Grant winked at me and grinned. "Listen up, you guys," he announced to the Coffee Club. "Company's coming again. Let's keep this place picked up."

"Not them DEAs agin?" Rex Beard asked in alarm.

"Nope." Grant played on the suspense, revealing as little as possible. "We're done with the DEA."

Heads met in a buzz of excited conjecture.

"Geneva said Sally Hester's coming," I said quietly.

"Yep." Grant peered toward Main Street.

"There isn't any connection between last week and the judge's files, is there?"

He eyed me askance, grim. "What happened last week has no connection with Donnie's campaign. None."

A carefully worded reply when a simple man-answer of "no" would have done just fine. My curiosity shivered to life like a cat's back when you mess with its tail.

"Who's comin', Grant?" Uncle Delton broke down and asked.

"The TV people."

"You just made their day," I told him.

Again, he looked toward Main Street. "Let's hope this makes their next six years, with an honest mayor in city hall."

"It will. It has to."

He turned to me, skeptical. "Do you really think Ham Stubbs is going to take this lying down?"

Of course I did. "Sure. What can he do? They've got him dead to rights." Ah, the ignorance of the innocent. Shows how much I knew.

That night, traffic was backed up for a quarter mile from Velma's gates. Up ahead, I saw at least six remote broadcast vans, lots of lights, reporters crowding the cars as they pulled up to the gates, and uniformed police with yellow flashlights checking IDs as the faithful showed up for our regular work session. Several cars were turned away, which snarled things even more.

As I passed through the chaos, I wondered how many

of our people would take advantage of this shot at fifteen minutes of fame.

I doubted seriously that much work would get done tonight. And I was willing to bet a week's pay that we'd have almost a hundred percent attendance.

Sure enough, when I finally reached the garage, there were no places left in the gravel parking area, so I had to pull up into the bricked plaza in front of the house. Once inside the garage, I found a catering crew presiding over an impressive spread of champagne, iced-tea punch, roast beef, jumbo shrimp, crab dip, and mounds of fresh fruit and cake cubes with chocolate fondue. From the noise above us, everybody else was upstairs.

On the buffet, a small tented note on index paper said in Velma's elegant script: "Eat up. And take the leftovers home. God bless." Another tented note on the opposite side of the table said in neat block print: "Refreshments provided by the Committee for Honest Government in Georgia."

A PAC! We were being wined and dined by a heavy-duty PAC.

I wondered what Donnie would think about that, but it didn't stop me from loading up my plate. Great cocktail food was one of the things from my old life I did miss.

Upstairs, the room was already jammed with people fixated on the big-screen television, where Donnie's weathered features appeared in profile facing Sally Hester in what looked like the den of Velma's house. As usual, he wore black jeans and a white golf shirt.

Grant stood propped against the bookshelves, intent as everybody else. Nobody made a sound. No eating. No drinking.

"Pastor West," Sally began on the screen.

Donnie lifted a staying hand. "Donnie, please. I'm just plain Donnie to everybody."

"All right, then, Donnie. The Gwinnett County District Attorney's office has announced today that preliminary

charges have been filed against your opponent, incumbent
Mayor Hamilton Stubbs of Mimosa Branch. Based on evidence discovered by the heirs of the late Judge DeWitt
Christianson, those charges include, among other things,
misappropriation of municipal funds in excess of three hundred thousand dollars. Do you wish to make a statement?"

"Yes, Sally. I do."

The camera angle switched to a full-face of Donnie from
over Sally's shoulder.

As usual, he radiated intensity and concern. "As a Mimosa Branch taxpayer, I find these charges very disturbing.
I think Mrs. Christianson and her family were very brave
to turn over the evidence to the proper authorities. But this
is America, Sally. People are innocent until proven guilty,
including my opponent. If there has been corruption, it's
up to the courts to prove it. I'm the last person in God's
good earth to be judgin' anybody, includin' my opponent.
I leave that to the Lord."

"And how will this affect your campaign?"

He shook his head, calm as he could be. "There will be
no changes. I started out running a positive campaign based
on honesty and full fiscal and governmental accountability
to the taxpayers of this city. Full disclosure, just like I've
made from the pulpit about my life. None of that has
changed."

Two-shot. "And a colorful life it has been, according to
reports."

Close-up. Donnie met her eyes without flinching, but
also without aggression. "It was a life of sin. I'm not proud
of the things I did before the Lord made a new man of me.
God deserves all the credit for who I am today, not me.
And He's the one in charge of this election. I trust Him
with it, just like I've trusted Him with everything else in
my life."

Power and conviction radiated from the screen.

Two-shot. "So there you have it. Challenger Donnie
West points no fingers concerning the charges lodged

against his opponent, incumbent Mayor Hamilton Stubbs of Mimosa Branch, Georgia."

The network cut to commercial, and somebody muted the sound. A pulse of subdued silence followed, like a collective heart skipping a beat.

"Donnie'll be governor within ten years," Grant breathed out.

"Nope." Fred Martin shook his head. "Never happen. No party would risk it. They cain't control him. Only God can."

"Yeah?" Uncle Delton countered. "And what if God wants him for governor? How 'bout that, huh?"

"I just want him elected mayor," Fred exclaimed in high spirits.

Grant slipped out as the room erupted in speculation amid the laughter that followed.

I found a chair arm to sit on and started eating my goodies. The shrimp were amazingly flavorful for ones so big. And one bite of the cocktail sauce cleared my sinuses.

A few minutes later, Grant reappeared with some food and a plastic glass of tea. He sank to the floor beside me.

"You look tired," I told him.

"Thanks a lot," he shot back. "So do you."

"I have a right to. I worked with Geneva until after ten last night, then my mother showed up at my door with cognac and homemade peach ice cream, and we stayed up until two drinking ice cream toddies and watching a movie."

"Sounds like fun."

"It was, actually. But it left me out of gas. I'm fading fast." I stifled a yawn. "If I fall asleep, just have somebody heave me onto the bed in the back room."

He nodded, blinking.

I studied him. "How about you? Trouble sleeping?"

He colored fetchingly. "Some."

No illumination, of course. Why did I expect any? He was a man. He gave man-answers. Why did I keep hoping he would open up so I could find out who was living in that body that drove me crazy?

Wasn't that somebody's definition of insanity—doing the same things over and over to the same result but expecting them to turn out differently?

While I was quietly eating and obsessing, his head dropped back against my leg, sending a frisson clear up to my waist.

Rrrrrrr. Was I tempted to get hold of that tawny, wavy hair.

"Are you asleep?" I asked louder than I intended.

He straightened. "Maybe."

Danger, danger, Will Robinson! He's touching you!

"What happened to the interview Sally did with you this morning?" I asked inanely.

"It'll be on before too long. The news cycle runs about forty minutes."

"She told Geneva you did a good job with it. Getting used to the camera?" I teased.

He shook his head "no," then stood. "I'm going back to the computer room to work on the mailing lists. Call me if anything comes up."

I nodded.

When the chair emptied a few minutes later, I slid gratefully into the seat and did my best to stay awake. With all the people running up the temperature in the room, it proved impossible. The next thing I knew, the place was quiet, and Grant was carrying me down the hall toward the back bedroom. And he wasn't even straining.

Reveling in the warm security of his arms around me, I pretended I was still asleep until he laid me on the spread and pulled it halfway over me.

"Mmmm." I still didn't open my eyes. "What time is it?" I cracked a peek.

The room was dim, and he stood smiling down on me. "Ten." He brushed my hair from my eyes. "You started snoring, so I brought you in here."

"Oh, shit." So much for romantic moments. I covered my head with the coverlet. "Shit, shit, shit. I can never show my face with those people again."

He tugged at the coverlet. "It was only me and George and Geneva. Most everybody had gone home by the time you started."

"Most everybody?" I was ruined. I'd never live it down. I jerked the spread off my face. "Who else? Who else saw me?"

"Down, girl. There wasn't anybody else. I was just teasing."

"Well, it's not funny."

"Actually, George was snoring louder than you were. Geneva and I found it pretty entertaining. We did critiques, but you won. We both agreed, we'd never run across anybody who could snore just as loud on their side as on their back the way you can, so you got the prize. You shut right up, though, when I picked you up."

"Y'all are cruel. Why didn't you just wake me up?"

"You said if you fell asleep, just to bring you back here, so I did. You didn't say I had to do it right away."

He was loving this entirely too much.

Overheated from breathing back my own wretched shrimp breath, I sat up and got to my feet. Grant should have stepped back, but he didn't.

"Where are you going?" he asked, but that clearly wasn't the question he was thinking. I heard the TV in the living room and the sound of George's even snoring, but all I saw was Grant, way too close and way too appealing.

This time, *he* kissed *me*.

As before, it was hungry and possessive, the kind of kiss that marks a woman.

And this time, I was as greedy as he was.

It had been this way in the beginning with Phil—had stayed that way until he'd stopped kissing me in favor of heavier foreplay. But I wasn't thinking of Phil.

I wasn't thinking of anything. I just went with the fantasy.

Oh, God! I was starting to act like a man!

Chapter 19

Only the presence of George and Geneva saved me from myself. That, and a royal, long-distance dressing down from Tricia after I got home. (I woke her up again. The old me felt personally responsible for ruining her sleep patterns.)

As he had the last time we'd kissed, Grant took three steps back, which suited me fine. I stayed plenty busy with the campaign and tweaking my new apartment for the next week. I even cut back to forty hours at work. (So I could take a day off to go to the adult toy store on Piedmont Road in Atlanta. More about that later.)

Shelia had come into the drugstore for a visit, looking trimmer and refreshed, but she'd assured me she had no intention of returning before November.

Then, on Yom Kippur, the bottom fell out. (After living in Buckhead for so long, I always kept up with the High Holy days. Since so many of our volunteers were Jewish, my charity organizations never scheduled functions that week.)

Geneva opened the plastic bag that held the *Gwinnett Gazette* she always brought from home, then read the headline with an explosive, "Judas, Herod, and Jezebel! That low-down, dirty, lyin' snake!"

The Coffee Club swiveled as one toward the register where she was sitting.

"What?" I abandoned my post behind the soda fountain. When I tried to look over her shoulder, she growled, actually growled, then muttered, "Page eight!" and opened the paper so hard it tore.

Anxious to see what had happened, I grabbed my granny glasses and my wallet from my purse and made for the paper stand out front. There, inside the display window, I saw what had set her off. "Besieged Mayor Cites Clerical Error, Issues Check to Cover Costs."

Why, that low-down, dirty, lyin' snake!

Blood boiling, I dropped in fifty cents and took the whole stack, fully intending to come pay for all of them after I'd gotten change. Back in the store, I claimed one paper and distributed the rest.

A tense silence settled as we read that the mayor now claimed the entire utilities scandal was nothing more than an accounting mix-up, saying he and his undisclosed partners (the judge being one) had fully intended to pay for use of city crews and equipment. Whereupon he had produced for the district attorney a signed, notarized contract between his development company and the city dated three months before the work had started.

It had to be bogus. Otherwise, Stubbs would have come up with it right away.

Not only were his own and Gary Mayfield's signatures on the documents, but also the head of the city works department and his assistant manager.

What pressure had been applied to get those signatures? I wondered. And the notary—Mary Woodard, it said—was she crooked, or had Ham Stubbs extorted her the way he'd once extorted Gary?

Ham Stubbs had made this personal when he'd confronted me at the store, but this opened the door on my infamous temper for the first time in years. Fortunately, Tommy wasn't there to goad me into incoherent ranting the way he used to, so I managed to keep a tenuous grip on myself. But I could feel my blood pounding in my neck and cheeks, and my stomach felt like I'd just eaten Drano.

General exclamations of outrage broke out and escalated through the Coffee Club, with the notable exception of Ottis Wilburne, who frowned at the others in silence.

When Grant walked in, grim-faced, reading his own copy, I looked up only briefly, still held prisoner by the infuriating article. Once inside the pharmacy, he dropped his paper to the pass-through with a disgusted grunt, then donned his white coat.

"Damn." Geneva slapped her open paper down beside the register. "Just damn!"

All eyes turned to her in shock. She *never* cussed.

"What does this mean?" I asked everybody and nobody in particular. "For the campaign?"

"That we're back where we started," Grant decreed. "Trying to unseat a powerful, unscrupulous incumbent." He shook his head. "Donnie predicted something like this might happen. So did Sally. Too bad the story broke early. It gave the mayor enough time to come up with this travesty."

"So what do we do now?" I, the doer, the fixer, asked.

Geneva plunked her forehead to the counter. "I just want to throw up. Preferably all over Ham Stubbs."

"But if he's got the contracts...." Ottis Wilburne ventured. "Maybe he really didn't...."

Geneva, Grant, and I all glared him into silence.

"Aw, wake up and smell the coffee, Ottis," Uncle Delton snapped. "You know as well as I do that those so-called contracts are fake. You gotta ask yourself why it took him a week to come up with 'em."

"Yeah." Rex Beard pointed his spoon for emphasis. "If he'da had 'em in the first place, seems like he'da told the DA right off, when they charged him."

Grant nodded. "And if nobody can come up with concrete proof that those documents aren't legitimate," he said, "I doubt the DA'll be able to make any charges stick, much less get a conviction. The mayor's version of this is incestuous, but probably not a felony."

"So just damn, and double dog-dammit." Geneva sat up with newsprint across her forehead where it had rested on the paper.

"Geneva, if you don't get a grip on yourself," Grant said, deadpan, "I'm gonna have to break out the smelling salts."

"I'll cuss if I damn well please."

I squelched a smile at the thought that Geneva Bates might have just entered the discreet Fundamental Christian equivalent of her own Fuck It phase.

"Those contracts have to be fake," she insisted. "Somehow we've just gotta get the proof. Get one of those people who signed it to talk."

My inner pessimist was dancing with perverse glee. "Once they signed that, they were in for good and all," I reasoned. "Think what charges they'd be open to if they admitted it now. God knows what the mayor did to get them to go along in the first place."

"Somebody could offer them immunity," Geneva protested.

"I think maybe we'd all better just calm down, set some realistic goals for the campaign, and go from there," Grant said with typical male condescension. "Even if we could, I don't think it would be smart to interfere. If anyone from Donnie's camp tries to pursue this, it'll look like a vendetta."

"Well, maybe it oughta be," Geneva said with uncharacteristic venom.

I agreed.

Grant left the pharmacy and came to the register to take Geneva's arm. "Come on. Let's walk up to the Doughnut Shoppe for an ice cream cone. My treat. Boss's orders." He nodded to me. "Cover for us, please. I need to cool

Geneva down before she says something that might come back to bite Donnie."

Jerk alert! Jerk alert!

"She's standing right here," I pointed out. "Is there some reason you're talking *about* her instead of *to* her, because if there is, the women of the world would like to know."

Grant glared at me, then turned to Geneva, "Would you please accompany me to the Doughnut Shoppe? I think a brisk walk might help you cool down"—he shot me another poisonous look—"and I'd like to speak to you in private."

"Sure." Geneva had been so distracted by the exchange between me and Grant that she seemed perfectly fine by that point.

"See?" he told me. "*She* didn't make a federal case out of it, so why do you?"

"Newsflash, Grant," I retorted. "Geneva is not a child who needs to be handled or distracted. Or patronized by you. She's an adult who deserves to be treated with respect and dignity."

Grant rolled his eyes. "Geeze. Here we go. . . ."

"An adult," Geneva finally intervened, "who would like to take you up on that ice cream. C'mon. Let's go."

"Geneva," I called after them as they headed for the front door, "how can we expect to raise his consciousness when you let him get away with stuff like that?"

"Thanks for takin' up for me, sugar," she called back, "but I'm a big girl. I can look after myself."

The Coffee Club snickered.

I aimed the "Finger of Justice" at them. "One more sound out of y'all, and I'm not making another cup."

October rolled in four days later, and things got even worse. Separate polls of Mimosa Branch voters conducted by the *AJC*, the *Gwinnett Gazette*, and CTNC showed Mayor Stubbs with a solid fifty-five percent, fifty-eight percent, and sixty percent lead, respectively.

Our own initial phone canvasses had indicated fifty-six percent support last summer, so that meant the story hadn't done a thing except maybe improve the mayor's standing.

With less than three weeks remaining until the election, this was devastating.

Once again, we at the drugstore pored, fuming, over our papers.

There was no word about any of the charges being dropped yet, but Velma had called us from the mountains, livid, after she'd seen the CTNC poll results on satellite TV.

Geneva turned to Grant. "Three different polls say he hasn't lost a single point of local support from the figures we came up with last summer. He maybe even gained some. How can that be?"

"Beats me. Maybe his supporters are people who don't care what kind of government they have here," he said.

"I can't believe that," she protested. "But it almost seems as if the scandal never even happened."

"There's lies, damn lies, and statistics," I quoted. "You'd have to see how the questions were worded, know who conducted the poll, and analyze the demographics and the size of the sample to get any real feel for how accurate those numbers really are."

"Yeah, but dang," Ottis Wilburne piped up. "Three different polls. Makes you wonder."

"Does the name Clinton ring a bell?" Fred Martin snapped. "This country has gone straight into the crapper, includin' Mimosa Branch!"

"If only there was something we could *do*." I was halfway out of my skin with frustration. "Something. Anything. It's so infuriating just to have to sit here and watch this happen."

"So now what?" Geneva asked, clearly demoralized.

"We work hard and pray harder," the Coffee Club quoted Donnie in perfect Greek Chorus form.

• • •

That night my very own phone rang at ten o'clock. "Hello?"

"Hi. I saw your lights still on." Grant.

I reacted to the sound of his voice like a teenager with a monumental crush, curling onto my side under my perfect girly bed linens and cradling the phone. "I couldn't sleep. Too upset about the mayor."

"Same here." A long pause. "And other things."

"Like what?"

"Like . . . how about I come over so we can talk?"

Sounded like a proposition to me. And despite my new battery-powered love life, I was even more attracted to him than ever. Yet as happy as my libido was with the prospect of having him here, I realized it would be a recipe for regret.

"How 'bout the porch?"

An even longer pause, into which I read disappointment. "Okay. Dress warm. It's cool out there." The nights had finally started dipping below sixty.

"I'm an adult, Grant," my new self said before I could stop her. "I know how to dress."

I could almost hear his eyes rolling the way they always did when I called him on his male garbage. "Whatever. Ten minutes?"

"Works for me."

I leapt out of bed and put on my polar fleece zip-up robe over the light cotton-knit pajamas I slept in. Socks and fleece-lined moccasins completed the ensemble.

L.L. Bean instead of Victoria's Secret, for sure. Maybe I'd done it on purpose, as protection. At any rate, I was nice and warm when I sat down on the porch.

Grant arrived in sweats and a windbreaker, looking devastatingly rugged and tousled. "Hi." He glanced down, shy and more than a little awkward.

"Hi." The air around us was crisp and cool and redolent with chemistry.

He sat in the chair beside me, but didn't settle, leaning forward instead with his elbows braced on his thighs, hands tented to his mouth. A clear signal that he meant to say something important.

I was sorely tempted to fill the dangerous silence with campaign talk, but I remained quiet instead, knowing it was important for him to speak first.

For a man as articulate and opinionated as he was, he sure seemed to be struggling to come up with something to say. My overactive imagination immediately went wild with all sorts of possibilities, all of them extreme.

He nodded his head stiffly, like one of those little bobbing dogs you see in cars' rear windows. "The 'yes, desperately,' is winning."

Ohmigod. A jolt of delirious arousal turned me molten from hip to hip. "Oh, no," I groaned out, bending down to my lap with my hands over my face.

"Oh, no?" His defenses flared. "Would you mind explaining that? Because when a man says he wants to sleep with somebody, and she says 'oh, no,' that sounds pretty bad."

"It is bad, because the 'yes, desperately' is winning with me, too."

I heard him straighten beside me. "Well, that's good, isn't it?" His tone was optimistic, almost boylike.

How could I make him understand? "No. That's bad. Very bad."

Wounded pause. "Oh. The Goody Two-shoes thing?"

"No. It's more than that." I sat up to find him staring at me intently. "We are wrong for each other. So wrong, it isn't even funny."

"No offense, Lin, but I wasn't proposing marriage. I just thought we might need to get this out of our systems."

"There. See?" I shook my head at him in disgust. "A perfect example. I am *not* a 'get this out of our systems' person. I am an old-fashioned girl who hasn't slept with anybody but my husband. Casual sex is not in my vocabulary."

He smiled, but not without compassion. "Has it not occurred to you to try?"

"All the fuckin' time, but my mind tells me it would be a humongous mistake. My body, however, tells me to sleep with you, and it won't shut up." I drew my legs up under my robe, propping my heels on the edge of the seat, and hugged my knees. I couldn't look at him. "I have been fantasizing about you for weeks, and it's driving me crazy."

Oh, shit. I looked over in shock. I hadn't meant to tell him that!

Pleased amusement softened his expression. Then he let out a brief laugh. "Hah! So that explains the deer-in-the-headlights reactions."

He was entirely too smug about it.

He stood and drew me to my feet, pulling me close. Instantly my physical response scrambled my brain and made me fiercely hungry for the taste of him and the feel of his naked body on mine. In mine.

Oh, Lord. I could never be rational with him touching me.

"Take a chance, Lin Breedlove Scott." His voice had the hard edge of desire in it. "Let me make love to you. Ravage you. Pamper you. Tease you. Eat you."

Yum, *eat* me. . . .

Then a jolt of reality hit me like a bucket of slush.

Oh, God! The tattoo!

It hadn't even occurred to me until that moment, because I'd never really thought I might actually go through with this madness.

"What's wrong?" He pulled my stiffened body closer. "Tell me."

How could I tell him that I had a life-sized tattoo of two bright red cherries outlined in black on my ass, captioned "Eat Me" in elegant script? I'd been drunk and eighteen when I'd gotten it. The whole thing had been Phil's idea, actually, inspired by my insatiable appetite for getting and giving oral sex. After we'd both sobered up, it had become the ultimate inside joke between the two of us. The only time I ever thought about it was when I had to go for a physical or to the gynecologist. On those occasions, I'd covered it with a big Band-Aid. Even my obstetrician hadn't seen it.

Now all I could think of was Grant's reaction when he saw something so sleazy graven on my Goody Two-shoes butt. My mind swarmed with pejoratives: lurid, vulgar, slutty, indecent indelicate, improper, lewd, nasty, raunchy—

Why were there so many synonyms for *trashy*?

"Lin?"

"Grant, I have to think about this. Long and hard. It goes against everything I've ever believed." Liar! You were perfectly willing to chuck all that out the window until you remembered the tattoo. "I don't know if I can have sex like a man."

He chuckled, rubbing his formidable erection against my belly, which sent a frisson through both of us. "I don't want you to have sex like a man. I want you to have sex very much like the woman you are."

"Then I would need commitment, and we don't have it. You're going back to California as soon as you can sell the store. And I don't know what I want yet. Certainly not a real relationship. It's too soon."

"A perfect time for some just plain fun, Lin's-a-pin."

"Don't call me that," I grouched. "Only people who knew me when I was a kid are entitled to call me that."

"I humbly beg your pardon, my precious porcupine," he said without a shred of contrition.

"Oh, stop it. Endearments aren't you, even sarcastic ones."

He sobered, then enveloped me in a kiss that was as close to having sex standing up with your clothes on as you could get.

When it was over, he sat me back into the chair, then crouched down facing me with a grin. "Think it over, then.

I want this, but only if you're ready for it as it is. No promises. No ties. No games." He pecked the tip of my nose. "And no pressure. Your job is secure either way until Shelia wants it back." He stood. "Just let me know. I'm long past ready. You see, I've been fantasizing about you ever since you chewed me out on this very porch last July the fifth."

I wish he hadn't told me that. And he'd remembered the date we met. Again, I covered my face with my hands. "Oh, no."

"There you go again," he said cheerfully.

I watched in turmoil as he left.

I had to be crazy even to consider this. Deep down inside, I knew I had made up my mind already, but I couldn't face that. Not yet.

It ended up taking me eight days to say yes. Eight endless, strained, excruciating days of work and obsession.

Chapter 20

Needless to say, I didn't tell Tricia for fear she might arrange an intervention and have me carted away to sexual rehab. I planned to tell her, but not until it was too late.

This was one decision I had to make for myself. I was the only person who would have to live with the consequences, after all. Grant had made it clear that there could be no strings attached.

I wanted to do this. I wanted to see what it was like to have sex with somebody. Not love. Just simple, animal sex. I certainly didn't love Grant. We were both clear on that. But I did like him well enough—his nonjerky half, at least. The jerky part, I had decided, came with the pecker. And minus the pecker, I wouldn't be in this dilemma. Major Catch-22.

Deciding to sleep with Grant was one thing. Telling him, though, was another thing entirely. I tried for forty-eight hours, but finally ended up calling him late Wednesday night.

"Hullo?"

Drat. He was already asleep.

My feckless mind conjured images of him lying tousled in sheets that smelled faintly of Jade East.

"Grant, I've been trying to tell you something for two days, but I couldn't quite bring myself to do it face to face."

"Okay." He inhaled heavily. "Let's have it then."

"I . . ." *Why* couldn't I just come right out and tell him? I'd rehearsed a hundred different ways.

Just do it!

"I want to fuck you till my eyes fall out." Yiiii! Disaster! Where had *that* come from? Definitely not one of the hundred I'd rehearsed.

I buried my horrified face in the pillow, my ears scalding.

Fortunately, he laughed, then said a desire-thickened, "I'll be right over."

"No! God, no. Not tonight."

Pause. "Okay, then. When?"

"Despite my unbelievably crass invitation, I want it to be romantic. Special. Is that all right? I mean, I know we're not—"

"It's the only way I would want it," he said with affection. "You deserve romance. And a better man than me."

The sad thing was, I knew it, but my body was more than willing to settle.

"How about Saturday night?" he proposed. "Does that give you time to prepare yourself?"

He understood about that much, at least. Three more days of alternating dread and anticipation. "Okay. Where?"

"Leave that to me. It'll be just the two of us, and very romantic, I promise. I'll even cook dinner for you."

"You can cook?"

"Learned from the masters out in Brentwood."

I added another item in the plus column. "Cool. I've never had a man cook for me before."

"Maybe you've never had a real man before, period."

Wow, was I hoping he was right.

"Okay. Saturday night it is."

"The whole night, Lin. Not just a date. I want to sleep holding you and wake up with you beside me. I ache for that."

Another plus that melted me on the spot. "So do I."

But my old self rapped me across my psychological knuckles for the seventy-leventh time. *This will be sleeping with a man on the first date! How dare you sell yourself so cheap?*

Don't listen to her, my new self argued smugly. *Between work and the campaign and the porch, you've spent the past two months with this man, night and day. Not a conventional courtship, to be sure, but it counts.*

Grant broke the lengthening pause. "Would you rather I pick you up or meet you there?"

"Meet you," I hastened. The idea of leaving for the whole night with Grant and a suitcase where my mother could see us made the backs of my knees sting. "But where?"

"I'll let you know. If I can work out what I hope I can, it's nearby."

I questioned the advisability of that. Atlanta would probably be a lot more discreet. But after making all the arrangements for so many years with Phil, it felt nice to have somebody else in charge for a change. "Great."

"And you're sure about this?" I couldn't tell if he needed reassurance or was more concerned about the effect this could have on me. Either way, I liked him better for it.

"As sure as I *can* be, Grant." We had promised truth. "I'd be lying if I didn't say that a million doubts have gone through my mind, but I've made my decision. I want this."

"Sounded like it."

I would never live that down . . . *Fuck you till my eyes fall out.* I buried my face into the pillow in shame.

"Till Saturday, then," he said, sounding stiff and formal. "I will feed you and ply you with wine and kiss you and make love to you until you faint, but I want those big brown eyes to stay right where they are."

I had an orgasm right there on the phone.

I finished work early the next day, so I slipped over to the mall and scoured the stores for something sexy, which in my case means opaque, preferably with sleeves. Which raised the whole body issue.

I was old enough to know better, but I, like most of the women in this country, have been conditioned to compare myself not just to other women, but to other surgically enhanced nubile women. So what looked back at me in that dressing room mirror caused an almost mortal nosedive in self-esteem.

Forget the tattoo. What on earth had made me think I could expose my very real-woman body to a good-looking, fit man like Grant? I had stretch marks. And a lateral hysterectomy scar—and an appendectomy scar, and one on the other hip from the graft for my spinal fusion. And a tummy pooch that only a concentration camp or a carving knife could cure.

Serious cold feet set in. I actually hyperventilated, but after sitting down and breathing slowly through my nose for a few minutes, I had the wherewithal to face my body and myself.

Grant had said he wanted me. Not the barflirts or the twenty-somethings who mooned over him in the store. He'd said I was quite a woman. Well, I was. And this was the package I came in.

I tried to see myself with new eyes. The bustline had dropped a bit, but it was still present and very accounted for. I still had an hourglass shape—it held more sand than the one I'd had at eighteen, but I was built like a woman, yes sir.

I decided then and there that my body, at least, would not be an issue. I was going to do this thing, and this was the only body I had. I resolved to wear it as if I was wearing Cindy Crawford's. And that was that.

Except it wasn't. I could make mature, enlightened, self-assured resolutions till the cows came home, but when I looked in the mirror, it was still my flaws that looked back at me. I tried on more lingerie in an effort to find a compromise between caftan and a transparent French-cut teddy to wear.

I settled eventually on a pink jacquard slip of a gown with a matching kimono that was almost long enough, but not quite. It was the best I could do with my budget, body, and time constraints. After much debate and many, many rejects, I also bought black satin mid-rise panties and a matching pushup bra.

I still hadn't resolved the issue of the tattoo, but I did feel a little like Cher getting ready for the opera in *Moonstruck*. Maybe because I was *acting* like Cher did in *Moonstruck*. She slept with a man the first time she met him in that movie. A sweaty man! But oh, was it romantic.

Once my lingerie shopping was done, I spent the rest of the evening online at the library computer, then drove all the way down to the Megadrug in Duluth for one of the more embarrassing errands of my lifetime.

As I had when I was perusing the dildoes at the adult toy store, I picked up a basket and pretended I was a royal duchess shopping for Queen Anne cherries at Harrod's. The last time I'd concerned myself with condoms, they'd been stashed behind the counter where you had to ask the pharmacist to get one. These days, even back at Chief Parker's, they were now displayed openly. Still right under the pharmacist's nose, mind you, but she was too busy to pay any attention to me.

The prices took me aback. You had to buy a whole pack, too. I reconsidered my earlier decision to buy a selection of types and sizes, but after a mental tug-of-war, I used the printouts from my online research to choose a variety, opting for the "ribbed for her pleasure" when available. Then I found the spermicide rated most effective and dropped it into my basket with my "Top Ten" condom collection.

I paid in cash, hugely grateful that the pharmacist was a woman—and a discreet one. She didn't turn a hair at my purchasing ninety-six condoms in assorted brands and sizes, though she must have thought me suicidally promiscuous.

That done, I made a beeline for home. By the time I got there, I was physically and emotionally pooped, but pleased with myself.

Somehow Grant and I managed to get through work on Friday without anybody's noticing how wired we both were. With only six days left till the election, Geneva was so preoccupied with the last-minute push that I doubt she'd have noticed if we were sneaking into the stockroom to smooch, which we certainly were not. Like a lot of things about my relationship with Grant, these days of waiting had been alternately frustrating and delicious.

I told the Mame that I'd been invited to a party in Buckhead and was going to stay with a friend. Fortunately, she didn't ask for details. I still cringe that I felt compelled to tell my mother anything, much less lie like I had in high school when Phil and I wanted to stay out all night together, but there you are. Sure, the Mame and I had made amazing progress, but the last thing I needed was to arrive home to find the police there, summoned by my mother when I didn't come home.

Friday at seven, I finished my week at the store and went straight home to my perfect girly apartment. After a leisurely Lean Cuisine and a couple of glasses of wine, I finally picked up the phone and called Tricia.

"You have twenty-seven minutes of call time left for the number you have dialed." For once, I was glad the time was running low. Tricia was bound to hit the roof, and I wasn't sure how long I could take it.

Of course, there was no guarantee she would be home on a Friday night. The university had lots of faculty events in the fall.

"Hello?" she answered, chipper as ever.

"Hey. Can we talk?"

"Got company. How 'bout later?"

"Okay. What time?"

"Ten." I heard her cup her hands around the receiver,

then she whispered, "The dean of my department and his wife. They always leave by nine-thirty, thank God."

"Okay. Ten." I paused. "It's a biggie." Let her chew on that.

At nine thirty-three, my phone rang.

I grinned. *Couldn't wait, could you?* There went my phone-card excuse, but never mind. "Hi," I said, fully expecting Tricia to reply.

"Hi, yourself," Grant answered.

I almost dropped the phone. "Hi," I repeated inanely.

"I won't see you at Velma's tomorrow. Gotta work. But of course you know that. I always have to work on Saturdays." I wasn't the only one who was flustered, it seemed. "Anyway, I wanted to let you know that I haven't forgotten about giving you directions for tomorrow night. You'll get them."

"Why don't you just tell me now?"

"That wouldn't be romantic at all, would it?"

Smiling, I curled up against my pillows. "No, it wouldn't."

"See you at seven, then. Come hungry, in every sense of the word."

"I will." Oh, yes. I'd be bathed and powdered and perfumed, in my most casually elegant, slimming outfit, with black satin underwear beneath. And a fetching peignoir ensemble in my overnight bag—along with the dozen pills I had to take every darn day and night.

"G'night then," he said.

" 'Night."

I hadn't fully hung up when the phone rang again.

"Hello?"

"Okay." This time, it *was* Tricia. "I got rid of the dean and made John put the food away. So what's the biggie?"

"It's a biggie."

"You said that. We do not beat around the bush, my girl. You know this. So let's have it."

"I'm sleeping with Grant Owens tomorrow night."

"Nooooooo!" she shrieked.

I jerked the phone away from my ear, wincing at the decibel level from my usually gentle, unflappable friend.

"I *knew* this was where you were headed! You cannot do this to yourself!" I could picture her pacing with the cordless phone. "I will not let you! This is the dumbest, most self-destructive thing you could possibly do, and what is more, you have to know that!" She ranted on for several more minutes, during which I heard a door open in the spaces between her tirade, and John say, "Good God, Tricia. What is going on?" to which she yelled, "Shut that door and keep it that way unless you want to die. And go to bed!"

I had never heard her talk to John like that in my life, and I don't think John had either. I heard a slam, and Tricia zeroed in on me again, citing social diseases, Grant's obvious flaws, my lack of both experience and sanity, etcetera, etcetera.

She was hollered hoarse by the time she wound down.

I tried to be as gentle as I could. "Honey, I've decided to do this thing, but I really appreciate your concern for me. I understand that you love me and don't want to see me hurt."

"Or with herpes or genital warts or AIDS!" she flared.

"Well, I'm not a total idiot. I researched condoms on the Internet and bought a selection of the ones with the lowest failure rate. And some spermicide. A little squirt kills lots of germs in addition to the sperm."

"I cannot believe I am hearing you talk this way. You, who told David that there's no such thing as safe sex, because the failure rate for conception with most condoms is thirty percent, and a human sperm is a hell of a lot bigger than an AIDS virus."

"Grant seems very healthy, and we discussed STDs. He says he's clean, and I choose to believe that." Considering the whores Phil had been with while I was still having unprotected sex with him—infrequent though it was—I might very well have been the one with the herpes or the genital warts. Or AIDS. I'd already dodged a bullet there.

"Who are you?" she demanded. "What have you done with my sweet, precious, pure friend Lin?"

"That Lin lives no more," I told her and knew it for the truth, way down deep. "But there is a Lin here, one who loves you just as much as the old one ever did. And values your opinion, really. But this Lin has choices to make that the old Lin never would or could. And right now, I choose to have sex like a man."

"What?" That brought her up short.

"Have sex the way men do, not all tangled up with the cares and commitments of a lifetime. Sex. Just sex. And I want to know what it's like with somebody besides Phil."

A long pause, then a sullen, "So if you'd already made up your mind, why in blue blazes call me beforehand instead of after? That's cruel and unusual and unconstitutional."

"Because I need your advice."

"I gave you my advice. Don't do it!"

"That's not what I need your advice about," I said calmly. "I need help deciding what to do about the tattoo." Did I neglect to mention that Tricia had seen the tattoo?

"Lord, Lin. That's the least of your worries," she grumped.

"Be that as it may, I can't decide whether to let him see it and risk his thinking I was a cheap tart somewhere along the line, or cover it up and risk his wondering what sort of sinister disease might be under the bandage."

"Let me get this straight. You're planning to sleep with a man on your first actual date, but you're worried he'll think the *tattoo* on your ass is cheap?"

"Tricia," I chided, "you have no call to get sarcastic." Yikes. That sounded *way* too much like Miss Mamie's "no call to get huffy" ploy.

"Lin." Tricia groaned. "Please don't do this to yourself."

I took a long, slow breath. "I guess I'll just have to decide about the tattoo on my own, then."

The thing I was about to do now lodged between us like Stone Mountain, and I felt the weight of it in my chest. "Is this going to be too much for you? Am I going to lose you over *this*?"

I'd lost too much already. I could not lose her, too. No man was worth the friendship of a lifetime. " 'Cause if that's the case, I'll call the whole thing off."

She groaned again. "I cannot believe I'm saying this, but no. This will not tear it with me. We're best friends. We've been through chicken pox, bad perms, puberty, childbirth, teenagers, hysterectomies, menopause, and aging parents together. I guess I can survive one wrong man-thing if you can."

"Thanks. Oh, thank you." Tears jumped out all by themselves, which was happening way too often, by the way.

"Don't worry. I'll be here waiting to pick up the pieces." At the sound of my tear-dampened shudder, her tone melted. "It's okay, honey," she soothed. "It's okay."

I knew she didn't think it was, but I loved her for saying it.

I was winding things up just before one on Saturday, planning to leave Velma's for the big "get ready," when who but Gladys Soseby should walk up to me carrying a wrapped gift. "Geneva told me to give you this. Here you go, honey." She laid it on the piles of postcards I'd been stickering with address labels. Then she waited for me to open it.

I did my best to remain cool, but my ears betrayed me. Had Grant arranged for Gladys to be the one who delivered his message, that old bad boy? Very clever, if he had. "Thanks, Gladys. I wonder who it's from?"

"Well, open it and see." She hovered expectantly.

I paused, enjoying the opportunity I'd been given to torture Gladys back a little. "No. I think I'll save it till I get home. More fun that way."

"Whatever." Flatmouthed, she retreated.

I rose to leave, picking it up. The box was cold. Not heavy, not light.

I didn't open it until I got to my car. Inside was a perfect gardenia in a tiny vial of water, a note, and a small bottle of custom-blended perfume. I recognized the label from one of Buckhead's most exclusive scent shops. Opening it, I breathed in an exquisite balance of florals, light spices, and a hint of citrus.

No dithering over what scent to wear tonight.

I opened the note. "1287 Harbor Lane, The Moorings at Lanier."

I knew the neighborhood, one of the lake's most exclusive, near Oakwood.

A lake house. All right! I started up my engine. "I'm a-comin', honey. I'm a-comin'."

Resurrecting one of the rules from my long-ago dating experience, I forced myself to drive around until ten after seven, just so I wouldn't seem too eager. Which was stupid, because I was no debutante and Grant was no panting adolescent.

Games! my new self indicted as I pulled through a shielding allée of crepe myrtles to the elegant, shingled house, a sprawling California ranch right on the water. Tasteful nightscaping illuminated the manicured plantings and recessed doorway.

Should I carry my overnight case myself, or would that be dorky?

I decided to carry it as far as the door and let Grant take it the rest of the way. I was actually quaking as I stood poised to knock or ring. But before I could decide which, the door opened onto Shangri-la, and Grant was standing there with a glad-to-see-you look that made me rock solid and certain.

Behind him waited candlelight, soft music, a cozy fire, and wonderful aromas from the kitchen.

He opened his arms and drew me into the privacy of the foyer for a slow, sensual kiss. "God, you smell good," he said when we came up for air.

"Thanks to you. It's perfect."

He looked at me, really looked at me, and I could tell he liked what he saw. "It's supposed to be. They asked me a lot of questions about you, and I answered them, and they came up with your own personal scent. It's unique, just like you are."

It should have sounded hokey, but it didn't. It sounded like music to a deaf person at long, long last.

"What questions did they ask?" I was fishing, but what the hey.

"How you dress. How you think. What you like. What you don't."

"But you don't know those things about me."

"I beg your pardon. I told them you look luminous in pink, and you like elegant, tailored clothes. And you think like nobody I've ever met. You're naïve one minute and outrageous the next, and always, always honest. And funny and smart and hardworking and very, very brave."

A symphony, and I drank it in like a dazzled thirteen-year-old.

His arm around me, he snagged my suitcase, brought it in, then closed the door and locked it. "As for your dislikes, I told them you don't like beets or cornbread or turnip greens or stuffed shirts or cramped little cars or racism or injustice. But most of all, you don't like people who kidnap your cats."

I laughed, grateful for the humor that freed me just a little from the spell his words had worked. "That's not true. I like you."

"And I like you. Very, very much."

I wanted to lose myself in the depths of those big hazel eyes.

So long. It had been so long since I'd been able to see myself as someone desirable, someone that any man would want, much less a man as gorgeous as Grant.

My libido had completely short-circuited my jerk-alert.

We strolled into the magnificent glass-walled great room that overlooked the lake and the private marina on the opposite shore of the bay. On the coffee table in front of the long, tasteful sweep of white-leather sectional sofa, champagne chilled in a silver bucket alongside a tray of tempting hors d'oeuvres. Fresh flowers and gold-rimmed china and crystal graced the end of the mahogany dining table, set for two.

Mellow classics permeated the room from hidden speakers, just loud enough but not intrusive.

Perfect. Perfect, perfect, perfect.

Beware of perfect, a nasty inner voice whispered. *You thought it was perfect with Phil, and look what that got you.* The cynical words flattened everything, evaporating the warm fuzzies from Grant's welcome.

I sat down on the sofa facing the beautiful nighttime view, deliberately ignoring the inner poison that tried to rob me of the moment. The stubbornest part of me refused to surrender to the condemning voices now arguing inside my head and my heart. And every one of those voices came with a frowning face:

You is the hard-headedest chile I ever saw! Zaida admonished me from the Sweet By and By.

Miss Mamie collapsed in horror.

Nana Grainger had the celestial vapors. *Linwood, remember yourself! You are a Grainger; you have people. Do not shame us.*

Meanwhile, an instant replay of Tricia's reaction wound out behind it all.

Shut up! Everybody! I commanded the many manifestations of my conscience.

But one still, quiet voice remained—my Granny Beth's. Her face came so clear to my mind's eye that I caught my breath. *Well, sugar,* she said in her matter-of-fact way. *You always did have to learn everything the hard way. But I'll give you this: you always took your medicine like a trouper afterwards. God help the parents of a child who's so dead-set on sinnin' that she's willin' to take the licks.*

Bless her heart. She would have understood. I wondered if she had ever considered anything so scandalous herself, but dismissed the idea as unworthy.

Grant poured me champagne and sat an easy distance away on the sofa. For some reason, the space was comforting. I liked that he wasn't rushing things.

I tried a crab angle from the tray. "Wow. These are divine, nothing like the ones at the Chinese restaurant."

He smiled, pleased. "That's because these have real crabmeat in them."

"I'm impressed."

"Wait till you see supper."

We talked of the campaign and Shelia's convalescence and anything and everything but us. Gradually, the din inside me subsided. I'm sure the champagne helped. Then a timer rang in the kitchen, and we moved easily to the table.

Grant brought out dinner and served like a pro. The food was amazing: big, flavorful shrimp in delicate lemon wine/butter sauce over rice, fresh asparagus, broiled Roma tomatoes, and for dessert, two generous individual ramekins filled with fresh raspberries drizzled in framboise liqueur then covered with lightly sweetened sour cream and finished with a crisp brulée.

Excellent quality ingredients, simply and artfully prepared.

"Do you eat like this every night?" I asked as I finished the last scrap of my raspberry brulée.

"No. Only for very, very special occasions," he said. "Otherwise, I eat like you."

"And how do you know what I eat?"

"You said so. It's part of your daily ritual with Geneva." *Ritual?* "What daily ritual?"

"You ask her how her night was, and she tells you what she and George did, and then she asks you about yours, and you tell her what you had for supper and what movie you watched and how you slept, and then she—"

Did I hear *rut*? "I didn't know you were paying such close attention."

"I always pay close attention when it comes to you." He fixed me with a stare so intense it made me wiggle. Then he reached across the table to cup my chin and brush his thumb across my lower lip. "You had a crumb."

He stood, reaching his hand out for mine. "C'mon."

Where? The bedroom? I wasn't ready for the bedroom. I took his hand anyway and rose.

He led me down to the living area, picking up a remote on the way. The music shifted to slow, danceable oldies. "Dance with me." He drew me into position and started swaying gently from side to side.

"I'm afraid I can't follow too well. My knees—"

He leaned his cheek against my ear. "Don't worry. We'll take it slow and easy."

I hoped he was talking about more than the dancing.

We danced for a while, and I felt a growing consciousness of his body against mine. Then his lips moved from my hair to my neck, and then my jaw, and then my mouth. I closed my eyes and soaked in every minute sensation. There was nothing proprietary in these kisses. They were more a gentle exploration, and my skin radiated delicious chills from wherever his lips touched me.

A few more minutes of that, and I'd have to sit down or lie down.

I must have gone a little limp, because I opened my eyes to find Grant looking down on me, he features serious. "I'd like to get off my feet. How about you?"

I clung to him, nodding.

"Take all the time you need to get ready. I'll wait out here."

I nodded again. Then I headed for the bedroom.

Chapter 21

I detoured through the kitchen—maybe in a last, subconscious effort to stall—for a fortifying glass of champagne from the bottle Grant had just opened (our second). While there, I found among the used pots and bowls a pristine dish full of brownies topped by a folded piece of ivory paper that had my name written on it in an unfamiliar feminine hand.

Geneva? Setting it aside, I looked at the name again. No, too loopy for Geneva's writing. Faintly familiar, though.

With guilty pleasure, I snagged the biggest brownie and bit into it. Whoever had made them must have used bran, because it had a strangely coarse consistency, but the taste was sinful and chocolaty, with just a hint of coffee and a spice I couldn't identify.

I carried the flute of champagne and the brownie back to the bedroom . . . and my destiny as a liberated woman.

Grant had put my overnight bag in the candlelit, marbled, master bathroom. After opening the case, I stood there reflected by the mirrored walls and tried not to faint. For some reason, I felt like the "final *Jeopardy*" music was ticking away in the background despite the fact that Grant had told me to take my time.

Why had he stopped making love to me, I wondered, and sent me in here?

To give me another chance to change my mind?

Maybe, but by that point I was determined to follow through, so my practical side got down to business. What to do first?

Condoms.

Completely forgetting the spermicide as I finished my brownie, I got out the assortment of rubbers I'd purchased and placed two of each on the nightstand beside the luxurious king-sized bed. I looked at the haphazard pile of packages and wondered if he'd get the idea I anticipated a marathon. Worried, I weeded out the duplicates and dropped those into the drawer, out of sight. After further consideration, I raked all of them into the drawer, reasoning that by the time he got to them, he might not notice how many there were.

I closed the drawer, then turned down the bed, arranging the pillows artistically. That chore accomplished, I went back to the bathroom.

What next?

My bladder raised its hand. *Yo!* I'd drunk five glasses of water along with my wine at dinner.

When I pulled down my black silk panties, the smell of my new custom perfume blasted from my crotch.

Oops. I'd overdone the intimate application.

After the call of nature had been answered, a quick whore's bath toned the scent down to a demure level.

Demure? my old self sneered. *You have "eat me" tattooed on your butt and you're about to screw a man you barely know, and you're worried about* perfume? *Puh-leez!*

Shut up!

Out of habit, I tucked my silk shirttail neatly into my panties, then raised, buttoned, and zipped my matching slacks before I realized I should probably slip into something more comfortable. The negligee?

That seemed so abrupt, so blatant. But then again, this whole setup was nothing if not blatant.

And what about panties? Panties or no panties under the gown?

Oh, hell. I was no good at this. No good at all.

Maybe my black satin underwear with just the little silk kimono over it.

But what if Grant was the kind of man who wanted to undress me himself?

Shit. Shit, shit, shit.

Why hadn't I thought this part through beforehand?

Still fully dressed, I opened the sliding glass door and headed out onto the balcony for some fresh air to clear my head. I went straight to the rail and gripped it, stretching my calves with a couple of lunges, then arching my back to relax the muscles while I closed my eyes and sucked in the cool air, trying to relax.

Opening them again, I turned to find Grant standing not ten feet from me on the long deck, staring at me with disarming intensity. It hadn't occurred to me that he might go out onto the deck, too. Yet I knew enough about men to understand that our reasons for being out there were universes apart.

I don't know why it embarrassed me to be caught, observed when I'd thought I was alone, but it did. The sensation was another splash of cold water on the fires we'd ignited in the living room.

Before I could dither further, he closed the distance between us and took me into his arms, urgent this time. "I want you. I want to see that body naked. I want to kiss and touch every part of it. And then I want to claim it." He kissed me, hard, and for a moment I forgot everything, even my tattoo.

He guided us into the darkened bedroom. There he kissed me almost senseless, and while he did, he unfastened the buttons of my blouse and slipped it off, then undid my slacks and let them fall to the floor.

Only then did I realize that I'd stupidly worn knee-high stockings. Hastily, I scraped them down with my toes and peeled them free, hoping he was too distracted to see, and worried that they might have left red indentations around my calves.

All the while, Grant was stroking my body with his perfect hands. It was what I had longed for, but for some reason, the reality wasn't anything like the illusion. So far, this was hardly what I would call a breathless assignation. It definitely had its moments, but I was so damned self-conscious. I could not remember ever feeling so exposed and vulnerable.

Now clad only in my underwear, my skin pebbled in the cool air we'd let in before closing the sliding door behind us. "I'm cold," I murmured the first chance I got.

Pulling the linens back further, Grant lowered me to the damask sheets. As I lay back, he drew the covers up to my black satin bra, his eyes never leaving my face. I watched as he stood there unbuttoning his shirt, then stripped it away, revealing the curly golden hairs on his chest. Just enough hair. Not too little, and definitely not, thank God, too much. All summer long, I'd wondered what it would feel like to grip those clean golden hairs in my fingers or nuzzle my face into his chest. Now I was about to find out.

A paroxysm of renewed desire tugged at me deep inside.

Then Grant stripped off his pants, underwear and all.

Yo! my new self observed. *That should do very nicely.* But it was purely a mental observation, lacking the impact of sensation.

He slipped under the covers beside me and kissed me on the mouth, then began to explore with his lips where his hands had already gone.

At first, I thought it was just his chest hairs that tickled me, but when his mouth brushed seductively down the side of my neck, I heard a high, semi-hysterical cackle escape me.

"Agh! Oh, I'm so sorry," I said, appalled. "Guess you

just hit a nerve there. It tickled. Disregard. Disregard." I grabbed his cheeks and planted a kiss on his mouth, this time trying the tongue thing first, myself.

He seemed to like that. We kissed some more, and I felt myself begin to relax and get with the program. His lips left mine, trailing lower to the swell of flesh nicely pooched up by my prone position and satin push-up bra.

Again, I had an instant, uncontrollably spasmodic, ticklish reaction.

We are not talking a laugh here. We are talking berserk, grimacing, tickled-to-the-point-of-torture hysterics. Ticklish on an atomic scale: worse than when they scrub the soles of your feet at a pedicure; worse than when your brother used to clamp you down in a WWF hold and have at your ribs; worse than if someone dragged a feather down the indentation between your hip and your pubic rise.

This reaction was pathological. And the more I tried to squelch my ticklishness, the more extreme it became.

Grant tried to be a good sport about it, really he did, but everything just unraveled from there. I mean, men don't ever appreciate being laughed at, but sex is the one time when any laughter, much less maniacal cackling, is devastating.

Yet he persevered, varying pressure and placement of his hands and his kisses, but nothing helped. Pretty soon the slightest touch of any kind set me off.

It got so bad that at one point I actually lapsed into yelling at my traitorous body. Aloud. "Dammit, you did this to me! I wouldn't even be here if it wasn't for you! And now you sabotage me! I don't get it!"

"What?" Grant reared up and looked at me in anger, his male ego finally forced beyond the pale. "*I* sabotaged *you*?"

My tears of psychotic laughter shifted abruptly to ones of embarrassed frustration. "I'm not talking to you. I'm talking to myself!"

"Do you do that often?" he snapped.

I did, but I was already embarrassed enough without

confessing that. "This hasn't ever happened to me before."

"If you say so," he slashed out with a harsh edge.

"I say so."

He threw back the covers and rolled to sit with his back to me at the side of the bed. "Well, obviously, this isn't going to work." He bent to retrieve his silk shorts, giving me a great view of what I was going to miss, thanks to my treacherous inner Puritan.

I grasped the back of his arm just above the elbow. "God, Grant, I'm so sorry. Maybe we could try again in a while. Watch a movie. Snuggle. Just sleep together. . . . Maybe this was just a little abrupt."

"Maybe this was just a big, fat mistake on my part." He stood, drawing his shorts up over his firm ass. Then he turned and slid his runner's legs into his slacks. "I know you didn't mean to be a tease, but I'm too old for games like these, Lin, including the ones you seem to be playing with that self you talk to."

At first my mind couldn't register what I'd just heard. "A tease? Did you just call me a tease? Is that what you think this was all about?"

"Conscious or not, isn't it?" he said with contempt. "We had a deal, Lin: absolute honesty. Well, I'm being honest now, and that's how this looks from my side."

Every scrap of my humiliation and self-criticism abruptly transformed to a firestorm of outrage. I was tempted to give him a lasting parting gift that would make him sing soprano for a week. "Did I miss something, here?" I said in smooth, *summa cum laude* Southern bitch. "Did we just go through a time warp back to high school? Because that's what your bullshit tease talk sounds like from my side."

"Typical. You women are always dishing out the criticism, but you never can take it, can you?"

You women!

He sat down and pulled on his socks, the thin kind I'd always hated. "And after I spent half a day buying and preparing that dinner. Ninety bucks, not counting the wine. Plus the corsage. And the *perfume.* I couldn't afford it, but you seemed like such a fuckin' aristocrat. I wanted to impress you."

My blood ran cold.

The man I had fully intended to sleep with—unite with both physically and spiritually—had actually called me *a tease,* then totted up the price tag as if it were some kind of investment that was supposed to have a guaranteed return!

Gorge rose in my throat.

Scowling, Grant shrugged into his silk shirt.

You knew he was a jerk, my old self gloated. *I kept telling you, but did you listen? Nooooo!*

Oh, God. What had I almost done?

The truth hit me like a pickup sending a possum to glory on I-85. I had hunted down and almost bedded a man who was another version of my ex-husband Phil at his worst—a charming, selfish, sexist, arrested adolescent. A throwback to the *Playboy* Philosophy. No wonder I'd been obsessed with Grant. He'd been so familiar: attractive, winsome on the surface, but lacking in depth, compassion, or commitment.

Telling moments from our previous conversations flooded back to me. Grant had laid it all out for me—the cold, detached way he'd talked about his marriages, his women, his children; his fixation with only the monetary value of things; his lack of feeling in relating the essentials of his life; his unforgiveness for his father—but I'd been too lonely and enabling to see the elephant in my parlor. Or in this case, on Miss Mamie's porch.

The man just wants a beer.

That same man had just wanted sex, and said so.

Thank God he hadn't gotten it. Thank God!

But at that moment, I wasn't certain I could have felt any more ashamed even if he had.

Grant finished buttoning his shirt. "Why are you sitting

there looking at me like I just turned into a werewolf?"

"You didn't just turn into one," I heard myself say. "You were one all along, only I wouldn't let myself see it. I do now." I hitched the covers higher.

"Whatever," he said as he had so many times before, only this time, the word made my skin crawl. It was emblematic of the way he dismissed anything that might demand more of him than he was willing to give, which was almost nothing.

I thought of the fable of the scorpion and the frog, and realized I had no right to hate Grant for being the sleaze he was. He'd told me who he was, yet I'd still been compelled to sell myself cheap. So I was the only one to blame.

Grant slid his feet into his expensive Italian shoes. "Feel free to stay the night. Just clean up before you leave. I left the dishes. Since I cooked, it seems only fair for you to do those."

If I hadn't still been so angry with myself, I might have given him that lovely parting gift, after all.

He stormed through the double doors that led to the foyer, leaving them open in his wake. As he headed for the entry, my mind cleared enough for me to call after him, "Tell anybody about this, one word, and I'll swear on a stack of Bibles that you couldn't get it up! And everybody will believe me, because I *am* Miss Goody Two-shoes!"

He pivoted in shock.

Bull's-eye!

Clothed in my most autocratic bitchiness, I glared at him, fully prepared to make good on the threat.

He stomped out, slamming the front door behind him.

I waited until I heard him drive away to put on my robe and close the safety latch so he couldn't get back in.

Too furious and shaken to drive back home, I wrapped myself in the white silk comforter from the bedroom, then extracted with trembling fingers my prepaid calling card from my wallet. Too unsteady to dial the requisite hundred numbers, I decided with infallible feminine logic that champagne and brownies would be the perfect cure for my queasy stomach. So, trailing the satin coverlet like a train, I steamed into the kitchen and collected the bottle, the platter of comfort food, and the cordless phone. Then I settled into the soft sofa facing the fire and the lake, ready for some serious therapy.

When I calmed down enough to dial Tricia, though, I couldn't see the numbers on my calling card.

Duh!

Cussing loudly and ranting about the injustice of losing my eyesight, I left the warm satin embrace of the coverlet to retrieve my f—ing granny glasses, slugging champagne from the bottle as I went. Once I was securely ensconced again, though, it still took me four tries to get all the f—ing numbers right.

"You have five hundred minutes of call time remaining for the number you have dialed." (I'd broken down and bought a new card on the way home from Velma's in anticipation of post-coital discussions.)

Tricia's phone scarcely rang before she answered. "Hello?" her voice sounded almost desperate.

"It's me."

"Thank God! I was praying you'd call before you went through with—"

"There's nothing left to go through with. It's over." How could I tell her?

"Damn." A deflated pause, then, "What do you mean it's over? It's not even nine-thirty."

I took a huge, consoling bite of brownie, then chased it with a generous swig of champagne.

"Lin, are you there?" Alarm crept back into Tricia's voice.

"Yes, I'm here. I'm just eating brownies and drinking champagne . . . from the bottle."

"This does not sound good."

"It's not good. I have single-handedly added a new superlative to the Poor Baby Club. This is a sixer."

"Uh-oh."

"No, I take that back. This does not deserve so much as a '*puh*' of a poor baby. This belongs in a new club: the Kick My Ass from Here to Afghanistan Club."

"Ah-ah-ah," Tricia chided sharply. "You know the rules. We do not beat ourselves up. We have the rest of the world for that."

I continued to wallow in self-loathing. "This is an exception."

"Where's Grant?" she asked, trying another tack.

Now *she starts calling him by name*, I grumbled internally. "The Filthy Beast has gone. Left. Phhhht! And a Filthy Beast he is, indeed."

"Good grief, Lin, do you think you could get to the point? What the hell happened?"

"Nothing, you'll be happy to hear. Nada. Zilch," I told her with more of a grudge than I would have imagined. "Well, almost nothing. I am sitting here in my black satin underwear. We got that far. Actually, he got even further. Stripped right down to the old Johnson, and a nice one it was, I must say. Not that I've seen many—only two in the flesh. Unless you count that old man in the park, but that was so quick that—"

"Lin, are you drunk?"

"Just a little. More mad than anything."

"Well, stop swilling champagne and stick to the subject. You know how fast that stuff knocks you out, and I will expire on the spot if I don't hear every detail."

An odd lethargy began to overtake me, one that felt different from the predictable effects of champagne. "I don't want to give you details. They're too humiliating."

"This is me," she countered, "The woman who knows you got swacked and wet the bed at the Kappa house when we went up there for the Georgia game our senior year."

I took another defiant swig. "I still wonder if that girl ever noticed her mattress had been turned. Or if it stank."

"You always did think your pee don't stink," she teased

in the cracker accents of our long-ago childhoods. Then she sobered. "Come on. Let's have it. Everything." Then she backpedaled. "Let me call you back on my nickel, though. It's my turn."

"No. Don't hang up. I have no idea what the number is here, and I'm still too shook up to drive home. And probably way too drunk."

"Where is here?"

"A gorgeous lake place overlooking a marina. Grant borrowed it from a friend—a friend he probably told he was planning to screw me."

Her groan was resonant with the "I told you so," she was far too kind to ever say. "Okay. Spit it out, honey, every scrap. Confession is good for the soul."

Not an easy assignment. My lips and front teeth had already gone numb, along with my twat; unconsciousness could not be far behind. I was feeling oddly floaty, too. But I made a valiant start, employing our time-honored rhythm of tell-a-little, ask-a-little, tell-a-little that reduced the most overwhelming circumstances to manageable bits. Punctuating my confession with lots of chocolate and just enough champagne to wash it down, I offered up all the gory details of my preparation, dinner, and seduction.

I was still conscious when we got to the denouement, but my speech was oddly affected. I felt like my sinuses were on the outside. "So he just climbed in with me, nekkid as a jaybird. I still had my underwear on—"

"The black satin ones?"

"Yeah."

"And?" She tried to keep the alacrity from her voice, but both of us knew it was there.

"And it didn't happen for me. We kissed some, and he stroked me all over, but I was too self-conscious, too guilt-ridden to really enjoy it." Funny, I didn't feel that way anymore. A strange calm had settled through me. "Still, I was determined to make it work."

"You is the hard-headedest chile I ever did see," she quoted Zaida.

"Exactly. So I tried, but then this awful thing happened." I corrected myself. "Or maybe it was the best thing, depending on how you look at it. I guess I'd have to say the best."

"And what was that?"

"I got ticklish. Psychotically ticklish." I started giggling, struck by the silliness of it all.

Silence.

"It got worse and worse every time he touched me. Pretty soon I was screaming with laughter," I went on with growing amusement. My mind was trying vainly to communicate the seriousness of all this, but the rest of me was determined to see it as funny. "He kissed my boob, and I laughed at him."

Tricia missed another cue. She was supposed to ask what happened then.

"I was so humiliated," I said between laughs. "You just cannot laugh at a man under those circumstances. It was a disaster."

More silence.

My silliness faded somewhat. "Are you still there?"

"Mmmm-hmm."

"Well, say something, then," I prompted, mildly annoyed by this breach of time-honored tradition.

"Well, I . . . You—" Her voice sounded strangled, and with good reason, because when she tried to speak again, she burst out laughing, too. It wasn't the creepy hysterics I had suffered with Grant, or the drunken giggles that had just overtaken me. This was a wonderful, cleansing, relieved belly laugh.

After all I'd put her through, I didn't begrudge her a good, long laugh at my expense. Several times it abated only to crank back up again, but at last, she returned to the receiver. I heard two brief chuffs and remembered the way she always puffed a dry whistle in an effort to regain control of her lips whenever her tickle box had gotten tumped over. "Oh, Lin. I am so proud of you," she finally managed. "What a gloriously delicious save from the jaws of degradation."

Ironically, her laughter sobered me. "Yeah, well, there was nothing glorious about it at the time. But the worst was yet to come. Grant finally got fed up and started to dress. And while he was dressing, he accused me of bein' a tease."

"You are joking." No amusement there. "The man is an idiot! A Ncanderthal!"

"Worse." I should have suspected something was wrong with me when I felt almost no anger in telling her, but I was my usual, naïve self. "Then he starts tickin' off what he spent on the evening and bitchin' about the wasted investment."

"Holy Mary, Mother of God!" Our ultimate childhood explctive—since we knew no Catholics, we'd figured it wasn't as bad as our brothers' "Goddammits." And no self-respecting small-town Southern girl would ever utter the name of Christ or Jesus in vain. "He did not!"

"He did." What had happened to my shame? I'd felt it so keenly only half an hour before, but it had left me almost entirely, replaced by only a minor tug. "And suddenly, I realized what you'd been trying to tell me, what I should have seen from the very beginning. What a selfish, uncaring person he really was."

"Honey, I had no idea he was *that* big of an asshole," Tricia said. "I was just afraid he'd use you and lose you. What he did, though . . .that qualifies Grant Owens for the Seven Jerks of the World."

A life-changing revelation shaped itself inside my consciousness. "Tricia, I almost hopped right back into bed with somebody just like Phil. Same shit, different bucket."

"Man." A gravid silence stretched between us.

Calm now, I was feeling remarkably philosophical about the whole thing. "But you can't blame a shark for being a shark, as my Granny Beth used to say. I brought this on myself." I took another bite of brownie. "Can you believe I was so stupid and self-destructive?" I asked with my mouth full. "Grant told me what he was. Told me, but I was too needy and blind and obsessed to hear it. How could I have been so *stupid*? I talk behind my hand about women like that."

"No you don't," Tricia countered.

Not out loud, but I did it in my mind. *Judge not, that ye be not judged*, I remembered Granny Beth saying whenever I'd been critical and self-righteous—which was far too often, I now realized without a shred of guilt, which made me wonder if I'd finally evolved to a higher plane of consciousness. Maybe tonight's disaster would cure me of being judgmental, if nothing else.

"At least you came to your senses before it was too late," Tricia offered with loyal compassion. "That's all that really matters here."

I sat up to rearrange myself, and the world tilted on its axis. "Whoa! Steady, boy."

"What?"

"The weirdest thing, Tricia. Suddenly I feel like I'm not even touching the sofa, sort of floating. And when I turn my head too fast, everything leaves behind this kind of rainbow aura in its wake. Rock-video special effects, in real life. Or did I pass out, and is this a dream?"

"I told you to stop drinking that champagne," she scolded.

"I did. I will." I swung my head from side to side again. "Oh, way cool. Wow."

After a short pause, she said in an ominous tone, "I know the sound of that *wow*; I have heard it many times. But never from you." Another pause. "Where did you get those brownies, Lin?"

Totally sidetracked, I relaxed against the cushions. "Found 'em in the kitchen."

"Mmm." I could tell she was working up to something,

but I was so relaxed, I didn't care. Heck, I was so relaxed, I didn't even care what had happened with Grant anymore.

"There was a note," my voice told her. "With my name on it. Writ by a girl."

"Go get the note."

"Well, we're certainly gettin' bossy, aren't we?" I said as I stood. The room started spinning, so I braced myself on the sofa until it stopped.

"Sorry," she answered without compunction. "Take it slow and easy. I don't want you to fall."

"Takin' it slow." I worked my way to the kitchen on the curiously slanting floor. "The note, the note, the note." I braced myself on the counter, but it shifted like a boat bobbing gently at anchor beneath me. The note. Ah. There it was. I picked up the folded paper. "Okay. The note says Lin, L-i-n."

"Nothing else?"

"Ah, nope. Well, yeah. Here's some more. It was on the inside."

"What does it say?"

I knew she was dancing on tiptoe to know, and I found it highly amusing. "It *says,* 'Eat up and have fun. You'll thank me in the morning. Cassie.' " A flood of affection welled inside me. "Wadn't that *sweet* of Cassie to send me some brownies?"

It didn't occur to me at the time that the presence of the note and the brownies meant blabbermouth Grant must have told Cassie what we'd been planning.

Tricia sighed. "No, honey. I'm pretty sure it wasn't sweet. Knowing Cassie, though, it wasn't evil, either. But it is trouble."

"Trouble? How?" Funny trouble, if you asked me.

"I'm pretty sure those brownies are laced with pot."

"Ooooh. So that was the magic spice." I didn't mind, not in the slightest. Come to think of it, I didn't mind anything. "Cassie won, after all. She finally got me stoned." Some distant pulse of outrage tried to sound, but my overwhelming sense of well-being instantly snuffed it out like a sumo wrestler sitting on a singing frog.

"How many brownies did you eat?" There was genuine concern in Tricia's voice. Looking back on it now, I can't blame her. I was at an undisclosed location, too intoxicated to drive, and I'd just ingested God knew how much pot, in addition to the equivalent of an entire bottle of wine.

"Only three." I adored her for being so caring. Simply *adored* her. "No, four."

"Okay. I want you to put the rest down the disposal."

"Ahhhh. Really?"

"Yes, really. If you love me, do this thing."

"Oh, sweetie, I love you better'n I love my old selfish self. Of course I'll do it."

It took a while (the spiked brownies jumped right off the plate halfway to the sink), but I eventually accomplished the task as ordered. She made me drink several glasses of water, then walked me through locking all the doors. By the time I finished, gravity felt like Jupiter.

"I'm headin' for the sofa. Gotta lie down."

"Okay. Lie down and go to sleep. And *don't* let anybody in. You'll have a hell of a hangover in the morning, but it'll go away eventually. And just keep telling yourself, sweetie: You didn't do it. You did not sleep with that bottom-feeder of a man."

I collapsed on the cushions, drawing the satin comforter over me. "And another thing!" I told her before I passed out. "He never saw the tattoo."

For that, I was *truly* thankful.

Chapter 22

I didn't wake up until after ten, but Tricia's dire hangover prediction didn't hold true. I was hungry, extremely thirsty, mortified, and looked like Tammy Faye Bakker on a bad day, but I didn't have a hangover. After gathering my things, I fled for home, leaving Grant's mess for *him* to clean up.

As soon as I got my own front door locked behind me, I called the Mame and told her I'd come down with the flu at the party, so she'd better not risk visiting for a while. The way I sounded, it wasn't hard to convince her. Then I dug in.

With the election only days away, I knew I should be at campaign headquarters, but there was no way. Instead, I soaked and scrubbed until the water got cold, then slathered myself with lotion, dried my hair, and holed up in the bed with my mother's peach ice cream watching *Ben Hur*.

About two o'clock, I heard a car drive up outside, the door slam, then heavy, labored footsteps up my stairs.

The last thing I needed was company.

A chill went through me. What if it was Grant?

But he wouldn't be driving, would he?

I knew I'd have to face him eventually, but I wasn't ready. Not today.

Rapping sounded on my door. Insistent ringing of my bell.

Then a voice from heaven. "Lin, would you open the door? I'm afraid this stoop is gonna fall off with me on it."

Tricia!

I raced to let her in. "You came! You really came!"

She hugged me fiercely. "I thought I ought to deliver these in person: poor baby, poor baby, poor baby, poor baby, poor baby, poor baby!"

A sixer! "Thanks. I needed that." We parted, both of us choked up despite our smiles. I dragged in her enormous suitcase. "Oh, boy. You packed for a month!"

"A week," she corrected as I closed my front door to the world again and locked both of us safely inside.

"Oh, Tricia!" I caught her in another hug. "I'm so glad to see you."

"I should hope you are," she said with her usual dry wit, "'cause it took some doing to bust loose on such short notice and hop on down here." She broke the embrace and stepped back to look around. "This is precious, Lin. A jewel." She dropped her purse by the door as if it hadn't been five years since we'd seen each other. "This color's perfect. And your things look great." She pointed to the coffee table. "I'm so glad you saved that; I've always coveted it."

"Take it home with you. It's yours."

We both chuckled.

Oddly formal, she pointed to the bedroom. "May I?"

Why did it always take some time to warm up in person, regardless of how intimate we'd been on the phone just the night before? "Lord yes." I motioned her to go ahead of me, launching into my standard hostess spiel. "Open all the closets, ramble through my drawers, eat my food, drink my liquor, read my mail, whatever you want. All I have is yours, Patty-ricia." I hadn't used her playground name in decades.

It chipped away a little of the awkwardness.

The phone rang, and I wasn't surprised to hear Miss

Mamie on the other end. "Lin, honey, there's a strange car out front of your apartment."

"I know. Tricia decided to surprise me with a visit."

"Oh, and you with the flu. How sad."

"Actually, I'm feeling a lot better. Maybe I just had a reaction to something I drank, but I'm okay now."

"Oh. Then why don't I just bring y'all something to eat?"

"Thanks, Mama, but we're just fine."

"Well, if you say so." She brightened. "How about dinner tonight, then? I know Glory and Bedford would love to see—"

Again, I felt compelled to set her straight. "We're already booked for tonight," I lied. "I know Tricia wants to see all y'all, but later in the week, okay? Thanks anyway, though, about tonight."

"Well, if that's what you want," she sniffed, "bye."

I hung up. Tricia did her best Stan Laurel look, which she did very well. "The Mame?"

I nodded.

Moving right along, I motioned her to my bedroom with that same odd formality that felt like a shoe a half-size too small.

"You always were the best hostess I ever knew," she said as she entered my private retreat. "Oh, how cute. I love this. You were right. Perfect girly in the extreme."

I rescued the ice cream from the bedside table. "You can either sleep in here with me, or on the sofa—I'm afraid it's not a foldout. And there's always one of Miss Mamie's guest rooms, of course."

She made the sign of the cross in the direction of the main house. "I pick here."

"I have to warn you. I wear a bite guard"—I gritted my teeth so badly I was wearing them down to nothing. Wonder why?—"and I snore, even on my side."

"Then I'll feel right at home. John snores like a two-cylinder outboard low on oil."

"Perfect. I'll change the sheets."

"Don't you dare. You're the cleanest person I know."
She bent closer to the ice cream and inhaled the summer
scent. "Is that what I hope it is?"

"Miss Mamie's homemade peach. I've been eating out
of the container, but if you don't mind that, we can split
the rest."

"You've got a deal. But only if you let me pay for pizza.
I heard they deliver now."

"Yep. It's a brave new world in Mimosa Branch."

"So I saw driving in." Tricia hadn't been back since her
mother's stroke. When was that? '91?

A pulse of silence resonated with all the changes both
of us had witnessed.

"Okay." She rubbed her hands together. "Let's get me
unpacked, then we can order a large thin-crust all the way."

"With extra mushrooms and tomato sauce," I remembered from our adolescence.

"Thank God some things don't change," she said, hugging me again, the distance between us gone.

"Thank God they don't." I still had my faith and my
best friend. And a cute, cozy hidey-hole of my own. And
my grass-widow virginity. That was a lot.

The next morning dawned cool and rainy, perfect sulking
weather. I woke with the weight of Saturday night heavy
in my chest, worsened by the dread of facing Grant—a
dread even Tricia's comforting presence couldn't dispel.
Unlike Atlanta, there was no avoiding someone in Mimosa
Branch. I had to see him, and soon, but the thought of it
made me ill. I was chicken, I know, but facing his peckerheaded attitudes would force me to revisit how blind-
stupid I'd been about him. Not a pretty prospect.

Yuk. Major yuk.

I fully intended to take my medicine like a trouper; I
just needed a brief reprieve.

I removed my plastic bite-guard, then dialed the drug-store, praying Grant wouldn't answer.

My prayer was granted; Geneva's voice said, "Chief Parker's Drugs. May I hep you?"

I came right out and asked for some time off, starting immediately.

"The Good Lord sure has a way of workin' things out," she said with audible relief. "I didn't know how I was gonna tell you, but yesterday at church, Shelia asked me if she could come back to work early, the sooner the better. She's feelin' fine, and their hot water heater exploded Saturday. The new one cost almost seven hundred dollars, installed. With that and all the medical bills they're still tryin' to get straightened out, she told me she sure could use some hours."

Tricia sat up beside me sporting a serious case of bed-head rendered even more comical by the elastic band of her sleep mask. She shoved the mask up to her forehead, then headed for the bathroom, yawning and scratching.

"That's perfect," I told Geneva. "The job's Shelia's in the first place. Tell her I appreciate her sharing it for as long as she did."

"Are you gonna be okay?" Geneva asked with genuine concern. "How will you manage without—"

"I should be hearing from my real-estate test any time now. And thanks to all the overtime . . ."—I couldn't bring myself to say Grant's name—"y'all gave me, I've saved up enough to get by for several months." All I had to pay for were my utilities, food, gas, and car insurance. Assuming I didn't get sick. "This works out perfect. My best friend Tricia came down to visit on the spur of the moment, so I could use a break."

"Tricia Canfield, the cheerleader?"

"None other, but she's Tricia Long now."

Speak of the devil, Tricia drifted in with a cup of coffee in each hand. "Two Sweet'N Lows," she mumbled as she sat mine beside the phone.

"Law, she was the sweetest girl," Geneva said.

"Still is, and better lookin' every year, doggone her." It was true. Even without makeup, Tricia's flawless skin set off her classic features and thick, dark hair. "She has a son in college and another who's a senior in high school."

"Well, bring her by if y'all get out today."

"If we get out," I said, knowing full well that I had no intention of crossing Grant Owens's threshold until I absolutely had to.

"Will we see y'all tonight at Velma's?" she asked. "Things are windin' down, but I know there'll be tons of people there who'd love to see Tricia."

"Am I needed?" If I was, I'd bite the bullet and go, Grant be damned. "Really needed?"

She paused, alerted by the reserve in my question. "Honey, you've already done more work than any three other people put together. You lay out and visit with Tricia. But I'm countin' on havin' both of y'all at the victory celebration Thursday, and that's an order."

There was no avoiding that. Win or lose, Donnie deserved our support, even if Grant was there. And Grant would be there.

Mega yuk.

At least the victory celebration would provide plenty of distractions. And Tricia could be my bodyguard, so I wouldn't end up alone with him. "Count on us," I assured Geneva. "Tricia and I wouldn't miss it."

I hung up and turned to find Tricia propped beside me sipping coffee, half-asleep with her mask still on her forehead.

"Mission accomplished," I announced. "I'm free for the week. Maybe forever."

She came alert. "Did he fire you? 'Cause if he did, you can file a sexual harassment suit. If he dares to—"

"Down, girl. Shelia wanted to come back to work early. She needed the money." I snuggled back under the covers. "If you ask me, it's divine intervention. When I think of working in that store with him . . ." I shuddered.

Now that that prospect had been eliminated, I felt the weight inside me lift at least a little. "How about we get dressed, head for Buckhead, and spend whatever money you have left after paying for those last-minute plane tickets?"

"I thought we were going to stay in bed all day and eat destructively and watch old movies."

"We can if you want to," I said, hoping she didn't. "I just thought you might like to play Buckhead."

She yawned and pulled up the comforter. "Okay. But I want two more hours of lolling before I get up. It's barely eight."

"You got it." I could use a few more hours myself. How delicious, to hunker back down in bed.

"Buckhead it is, then." Tricia yawned hugely. "But only if lunch is on me! 103 West."

My favorite—elegant, expensive, and delicious.

After the humiliating auction of my home, I used to be afraid of running into my friends. Now that Grant had established a new benchmark for shame, my previous fears paled by comparison. It might be fun to pretend for a day that I belonged to that charmed world I'd left behind—a world Tricia was still very much a part of, thanks to her decision not to "look under rocks"—even though I now knew it was all a carefully groomed illusion. Grown-up make-believe.

"Remember when we used to play store?" she asked as if she'd read my thoughts. "How we raked the leaves away to make little 'rooms' in the store, and all the things we came up with for merchandise?"

"Acorns. Pine cones. Leaves. Our toys." Sitting there beside her, I realized with bone-deep clarity that I was glad I'd chosen truth and reality over a life based on playing pretend. I didn't blame Tricia for choosing otherwise, not one bit. But I didn't envy her either, not one bit. My new life wasn't easy, but it was honest.

We lolled till ten, then went to town, had a sixty-dollar lunch—yum—and afterwards shopped till we dropped, seeing not a single familiar face. A good time was had by all, especially Tricia's Visa Gold.

Try as I might to get around it, Tricia and I were forced to accept at least one of Miss Mamie's invitations. We picked dinner on Tuesday night, to get it over with.

I tried to prepare Tricia for what she'd find, but she couldn't conceal her anguish when she saw Uncle Bedford. People as tenderhearted as Tricia rarely have poker faces, and she was no exception. But a glass of sherry and a heavy dose of Miss Mamie's brittle conversation, punctuated by the General's booming non sequiturs, soon brought back her self-control. Still, she sat perched through dinner, nervous as a Pentecostal in a nest of Papists.

Fortunately, the little cannibal didn't materialize, but Uncle Bedford mumbled in irritation throughout the meal, ignored by the rest of the family. Tommy asked about Tricia's husband and the boys, a topic that would have been safe except for my father's continued well-meaning interruptions that had nothing to do with what we were talking about. Eventually Tricia got so rattled that Miss Mamie rescued her by asking Aunt Glory to tell about the girls. Since the General was used to tuning Aunt Glory out, he lapsed into welcome silence and concentrated on his food.

But I ended up grateful to the General in the end. No sooner had Miss Mamie and Aunt Glory cleared away the dessert dishes, than the General stood up and slapped his belly. "Good supper, Mame. I'll sleep well tonight." He scanned the table. "It's past my bedtime. Who hasn't gone home yet?"

"Thomas!" came my mother's outraged response from the kitchen. "Have you lost your mind?" She burst through the swinging door with a fresh pot of coffee in her hand. "Where are your manners?"

Tricia and I leapt to our feet so we wouldn't miss the golden opportunity to escape.

"This has been lovely, Mrs. Breedlove," Tricia said. "Just lovely, but I wouldn't want to keep the General up. Or Uncle B. Lin told me they retire early. And I'm pretty tired myself. But thank you for the wonderful meal. It's been so good to see y'all again."

"Bedtime," Uncle Bedford announced as he teetered up out of his chair.

My mother looked like she might burst into tears, and my heart went out to her, but I knew if we stayed, things would only escalate between her and the General. I walked over and gave her a hug. "It was great. Thanks for having us."

Aunt Glory emerged from the kitchen, took one look at Uncle Bedford from behind, and blanched.

Depends alert.

"Let the girls go, Mamie," she said with more than a hint of desperation. "I'm sure they have lots to do. You know young people."

Outnumbered, my mother relented. "Well, it sure was good to see you, too, Tricia. Don't be such a stranger."

"I won't." Tricia stepped closer to the General and hollered, "It sure was good to see you again, Mr. Breedlove."

"Good to see you, too."

We were almost out of the front door when we heard my father blare, "Pretty woman, Mame. Who the hell was she?"

I folded my lips in an effort to escape without laughing, but by the time we reached the privacy of the porte cochere, I heard not laughter, but suppressed tears from Tricia.

She stopped behind the Confederate jasmine. "Oh, Lin," she whispered, "I had no idea it was so bad. I could cut my tongue out for the things I said about your family."

"It's okay. You were right. It *is* a loony bin." I gave her a brief hug, then drew her toward the apartment. "Come on. I don't want you to waste another tear on this."

"How can you bear it?" she asked as we walked down the graveled driveway. "It's so sad."

"Yes, I guess it is. But I didn't just walk in on it after three decades. It happened gradually. Maybe that blunted the impact. But crying over it accomplishes nothing. Everybody in that house is there by choice. They might not like the circumstances, but they're getting on with things the best they can."

"Like you've been doing," she said, her voice steadier.

"Yeah." When had I stopped being embarrassed by them? I wondered. "It was pretty hard to take when I first came back, I must admit. But over these past few months, I've come to appreciate the courage and the optimism Miss Mamie and Aunt Glory bring to each new day. Daddy and Uncle Bedford are doing the best they can, too. For now, they're cared for in familiar surroundings. It's enough.

"Even Tommy. He's worked so hard to get his life straight lately. I'd be the Witch of the World not to support him now."

She took my arm. "Is this the same perfectionist who's been calling me all these years?"

I grinned. "No. I told you, she's dead and gone."

"I loved her a lot," Tricia said, "But I think I like her big sister even better."

"Her big sister's glad."

"Let's call Cassie," Tricia proposed out of the blue as we climbed the stairs, "and ask if she wants to have lunch tomorrow. She and Sharon."

I look back now and wonder if she had a premonition.

But then, I experienced only a small, unworthy resentment that Cassie's lover would be included in our first reunion in decades. Gay or not, it wasn't fittin'. "We don't have dates. Why should Cassie?"

"Ah. So the old perfectionist *isn't* dead, after all." Tricia fixed me with a look of indictment.

Zinger! I drew an imaginary javelin out of my chest. "She is, she is. She just rises like Dracula on occasion. But a stake in the heart like that one is all it takes to put her down again."

She chuckled, heading up the stairs. "Come on. Let's watch *Shirley Valentine* and drink Kool-Aid cocktails."

We did just that, but not before we invited Cassie—and Sharon—to lunch.

Tricia and I had been waiting at the Fireside Café for almost a half-hour when one of the cooks pushed open the swinging door to the kitchen and hollered, "Is there a Lin Breedlove in here anywhere?"

All conversation stopped, leaving only the rattle of the kitchen fans.

Lin Scott, my old self corrected in annoyance.

So much for anonymity. I raised my hand only to be scowled at by every overweight subcontractor in the place— at least a dozen.

The cook pointed the receiver to the front counter. "Phone! Pick up at the register."

Cassie always had been pathologically late, but it wasn't like her to call. Maybe she'd matured.

Like you did? my new self said, popping that particular condescending balloon.

"I'll be right back, Tricia. Gotta be Cassie."

Even after months at home, it never occurred to me that it might be an emergency with my parents. They'd been there forever; I guess I believed they always would be.

It was an emergency, but not my parents. "Oh, God," Cassie practically panted into the phone. "I am so glad I caught you. We were afraid you might have left. Lin, we've got to meet right away. Someplace safe. Not in town."

"Where are you? What's the matter? Cassie, are you all right?"

"Fine. Great. Better than great, actually. At least, if we can pull this off."

"Pull what off?"

The sound of heavy traffic behind her almost drowned her out. "I've figured out a way to beat the mayor at his own game. But we have to get hoppin'. We need Tricia, too. And maybe a couple of others we can trust. But for now, just y'all."

"Cassie, the election's tomorrow."

"I know it," she said, exasperated. "So why are you wasting time?"

"Tell me where you want to meet, then."

"Dunwoody. That twenty-four-hour Copy World near the Magnolia Tea Room."

"Can we grab a bite first?"

"Probably a good idea. We might not have time to eat tonight."

Fortunately, the Fireside was a meat-and-three place. We could be out in fifteen minutes if we bolted our food. I looked at my watch. "Okay. My watch says one-thirty. Why don't we say an hour at Copy World in Dunwoody?"

"Check. Two-thirty in Dunwoody."

I hung up the phone and flagged the waitress. "We need to order."

I sat down beside Tricia, the backs of my knees tingling. "Cassie has come up with something big. We need to meet her in Dunwoody. But first, we should eat. We may not have another chance later."

"Lin, what is going on? I haven't seen you look this diabolical since that time we rigged that séance when we were seniors." Tricia remained impatient while the waitress came over and took our orders.

"And we're in a hurry, please," I told the waitress. "We just got called back to work."

As soon as she was out of earshot, Tricia leaned close. "What's up? Tell me."

"If Cassie's right, this could be big. But I don't dare talk about it here. Let's just eat, then I'll tell you in the car."

She sat back, arching her eyebrow like Mr. Spock. "You're enjoying torturing me with this, aren't you?"

"Only a little. But we really can't talk about it here."

Our food arrived. "Fast enough?" the waitress asked without rancor.

"Blazing." I handed her two ones. "Thanks."

She smiled. "Here. Let me get y'all some more tea. Unsweet, right?"

"Right as rain." Boy, but was it fun to have some genuine excitement in my life that didn't involve strippers or Uncle Bedford's shoes. Or Grant Owens.

Forty-five minutes later (I drove like the wind down Peachtree Industrial, scaring the bejeebers out of Tricia), we pulled into the Copy World and went inside.

Cassie was waiting at the entrance, wearing a broad-brimmed straw hat circled with sunflowers, and clad in a baggy, bright yellow shift embroidered in brilliant yarn tulips. "Aaaaghhh! Tricia, Tricia, Tricia!" She swooped down and enveloped her. "I can't believe you're really here. It's *so* great to see you."

"You, too." Tricia pushed her to arm's length. "Would you look at that dress, a dead ringer for the seventies."

"Dead ringer, nothin'," Cassie informed us. "It's the real thing. Bought it in Haight back in '71. It's my good luck dress, has a wonderful aura. That's why I wore it. We're gonna need all the positive karma we can get."

I feigned seriousness. "I shouldn't be talking to you, you know. I unwittingly ate four of those lethal brownies of yours."

Cassie had the decency to look sheepish. "You're okay, aren't you? No bad reactions or anything?"

"Not really. Except I parted company with my body and gained two pounds."

A tall, stylish knockout of a woman in a power suit strode toward us with purpose, carrying some printed ledger-sized paper.

Tricia and I exchanged surprised glances. I guess we'd expected some fey New Ager, not this cross between a cover model and a CEO. But Cassie had said Sharon worked for a major accounting firm. Maybe opposites do attract.

"They've got the first batch copied," Sharon said in a crisp New York accent, showing Cassie the paper, which was printed, on closer inspection, with several long facsimile ballots, each topped by a traced circle. "How does it look? They didn't have the exact same stock, but this comes damned close." Against the copies, she held up a single long facsimile ballot with a hole cut above the printing so it could be hung on doorknobs.

Cassie compared the paper. "Perfect. You'd need a magnifying glass to tell the difference." She stood on tiptoe in her Birkenstocks (not an easy thing to do). "If anything's gonna blow our chances, it'll be the marking, not the paper, anyway."

She caught Sharon by the arm. "Sharon, honey, these are two of my oldest and best friends, Tricia Canfield Long and Linwood Breedlove Scott."

"You Southerners sure are big on those long names, aren't you?" Sharon said as she shook our hands with a firm, businesslike grip.

The "you Southerners" opener raised a red flag, but in deference to Cassie I let it lie.

"Well, you know what they say, honey," Tricia drawled. "The longer the name, the bigger the bitch. So watch out."

Sharon chuckled. "I like her."

"Then you'll *love* Lin." Tricia might be laid back, but she did enjoy getting the last word.

"Okay," Cassie said with the enthusiasm of a camp counselor, "Now that we've all sniffed each other's asses, what say we get to work? We've gotta cut the ballots apart on that big paper cutter over there, then we have to hand-cut all the circles—all four thousand. After that, find people we can trust to help us distribute them in the wee hours." She led us toward the work tables by the copy center while Sharon went for more copies for us to work on.

"Whoa, whoa, whoa," I said. "Cassie, would you mind explaining what we're doing here?"

She giggled her burbly laugh. "Oops. I got so excited about all this, I clean forgot." She motioned us close, glancing from side to side to make sure nobody was within earshot.

Cassie tried to whisper, but her version was as loud as most people's regular speaking voices. It was, though, softer than her usual voice. "Remember when you said I should work for Donnie, and I said that would sink him for sure, and you said maybe I should work for the mayor, then?"

Tricia swatted me. "Lin!"

"I was only kidding." I rubbed my arm.

"I know you were," Cassie said, "but the more Sharon and I talked about it, the more we thought it might just be a good idea. Not the way you suggested, though. We decided that Sharon could be a mole in the mayor's campaign. Nobody knows what she looks like. She leaves early for work and doesn't get home until late. We never hang around together in Mimosa Branch; we do our socializing in town. So we figured she'd make a perfect spy." Cassie shot her an indulgent look. "She's always wanted to be a spy, ever since *The Avengers*."

"She does look a little like Mrs. Peel," Tricia observed.

"Oh, doesn't she?" Cassie rhapsodized, then sobered. "Anyway, she started quietly working at the mayor's election headquarters in his basement. Just doing what they told her to, until they discovered she knew all about computers. Then she became indispensable. There were lots of red flags pointing to something shady going on, but she never found any proof. She suspected it had something to do with this locked closet that nobody but the mayor or Gary Mayfield ever went into, but it wasn't until she went in really early this morning that she stumbled on the truth."

All three of us checked the aisles to make sure nobody was listening.

"Nobody heard her come in. She'd left her car for an oil change down the street and walked over. The mayor and his cronies were meeting in the mayor's study with the door closed. She heard him raisin' hell because their liquor supplier had decided to blackmail them by jacking up the cost of the payoffs."

"Payoffs?" This was the most linear I could ever remember Cassie's being, so I didn't want to spook her, but I was dying to get to the meat of the matter.

"Sharon hid in the storage area and got an earful. Then after everybody left for work, she used a screwdriver to pop the pins on the locked closet. Idiots had left them on the outside."

"And what was on the inside?" Tricia prompted.

"These." Cassie held out the facsimile ballot. "Or ones just like 'em, all cut out and ready to hang on doorknobs in the poor sections tonight at the witching hour."

"And?"

"And, tomorrow morning, the same rented vans that carried people to register last summer will make their circuits through the same poor neighborhoods to carry people to the polls. The only trick is, you have to have your facsimile ballot, marked the way the mayor wants you to vote, to get a ride."

"Can he do that, legally?" Tricia asked.

"I can't imagine it's illegal to take people to the polls. And you can bet he doesn't actually pay for it. He probably funds it with some sort of PAC with an innocuous-sounding name," I surmised.

"Then it really gets good," Cassie said. "Once you've voted, you turn your ballot in to the driver and receive a special token, redeemable out the back door of the liquor store for a six-pack of beer or a bottle of cheap wine."

"Holy crow," Tricia exclaimed. Then she dropped her voice. "That's major election fraud. Shouldn't we go to the secretary of state? He's the one over the elections."

"Right," Cassie said with uncharacteristic sarcasm. "Before tomorrow?" She shook her head. "And we don't have any hard proof. Sharon said there were no receipts for the liquor anywhere."

"Ah, yes. The old raincoat full of cash," I said in memory of our notorious Georgia senator of yore whose scorned wife blew the whistle on his affinity for raincoats stuffed with illicit hundred-dollar bills.

"Oh." Tricia deflated.

A cheerful thought occurred to me. "Ooooh. After paying off those construction costs for the subdivisions, I'll *bet* he didn't like having the booze price hiked on him."

Cassie grinned and wrinkled her nose. "He was so mad, Sharon hoped he'd stroke out, but no such luck."

"Yeah," I agreed. "Like Granny Beth used to say, 'The Good Lord wouldn't have him, and the devil's getting too much use out of him to take him.' "

"So now?"

Cassie handed me the facsimile ballots. "Look closely."

Tricia and I did. It took us both a second look to notice what Cassie and Sharon had done. "I'll be damned. You kept everything the same except the mayor's race."

They had changed the blackened column to Donnie West. It was a single change, almost unnoticeable amid the local referenda, council race, and school board elections, but it was there.

And it had taken Tricia and me two good, hard looks to notice it.

"Oh, Cassie," Tricia breathed out. "Do you think this could work? I mean, what if somebody notices the change? All it would take would be one person to put them wise."

"That's where the Good Lord comes in," I said with conviction. "And we know whose side He's on."

Cassie and Sharon rolled their eyes at me on that one.

"So now," Cassie began.

"We work hard and pray harder," I finished in Donnie's immortal words.

"My naturopath is channeling us lots of pink and spiritual protection," Cassie offered. "I didn't tell her what it was about, just a major crisis between light and darkness." Her middle fingers circled to her thumbs, she raised her arms overhead with a deep breath to touch hands, then lowered them. "Can't you just feel the energy? We're at the intersection of yin and yang. Draw power from it, not fear. Feel the wind of destiny blowing through us."

Tricia cocked a skeptical eye at our favorite unreconstructed hippie.

"Here we go, my little space cadet." Sharon approached us with an armful of ballots. "Isn't Cass adorable when she does all that New Age stuff? Completely over the edge, but she's so darn sincere, you gotta love it."

She handed me half the stack. "Let's get cutting. And keep it neat. Theirs are die-cut, but we'll just have to do the best we can."

"Who's paying for all this?" I felt obliged to ask.

"I am." Sharon smiled, transforming her austere face to almost pretty. "And it's worth every penny to get to be a part of dirty Georgia politics, especially when it benefits the good guys."

"Well, you go, girl," Tricia said. "For this, we might have to make you an honorary Southerner."

"Okay," she replied, deadpan. "But do me a favor: don't tell my mother. She's had enough shocks, as it is."

We all laughed together.

I sat beside Tricia and started cutting. Four of us. That was a thousand apiece. One down, nine hundred ninety-nine to go.

Four thousand ballots later, the commando corps met at Cassie and Sharon's at eleven. I'd done the recruiting in person, quietly pulling people out of campaign headquarters, then briefing them in "the conference room." Every one I asked agreed without hesitation—in most cases, with alacrity. Velma, her daughter, all four of her sons, and two of her daughters-in-law (the other two had to stay at the mansion to baby-sit all the kids), plus Geneva and her daughter, plus the four of us made fourteen altogether. As instructed by Sharon, we'd all worn comfortable, light-colored clothing.

Once we were assembled in Cassie and Sharon's living room—a hodgepodge of nouveau fortune-teller and California Mission décor—Sharon opened a huge bag from the SportsPlanet at the mall and started handing out fluorescent joggers' vests. "These are the closest I could find to the ones the police wear. Here's hoping they'll keep us safe. But don't put them on until you're actually going out into the neighborhoods." She paused, looking us over. "You do know this is going to be dangerous, don't you? We'll be skulking around in some pretty rough places."

She'd told us earlier that we'd be concentrating on the neighborhoods that showed up most frequently on the mayor's list of supporters. Her brow furrowed. "If anybody wants out, we'll understand."

"I can see the headlines now," Velma's oldest son joked. " 'Prominent Local Attorney Slain in Midnight Raid on Pebblestone Subdivision.' "

Velma's whole crew thought that was pretty funny, but Geneva winced. "Y'all, I know Donnie wouldn't want us to do this if even one person might get hurt."

"So why are you here?" Sharon challenged with typical Yankee brusqueness.

That got Geneva's dander up. "Well, I'm not Donnie, am I? And *I'm* willin' to take that risk to get rid of that crooked son-of-a-gun of a mayor. We tried it the right way, and that snake just slithered right out of trouble."

"You know what they always say," Velma chimed in. "The way you do thangs *ain't* the way you do thangs." Half the room finished the axiom with her, then broke into more laughter.

"I thought that was just Granny Beth's saying," I told Tricia.

"Where did you think she got it?" she asked me.

"Seriously," Velma's son said. "I don't think we'll have any trouble. Apparently, this has been going on for years. The people in those neighborhoods are expecting the ballots to go out. And I imagine the troublemakers are looking forward to their booze. Why would they bother us?"

Applause and "hear, hear's."

Sharon started distributing maps and the printouts she'd made that morning. "I sorted the names by neighborhood and printed them out. We'll work in teams of two, for safety's sake. We counted out the ballots for each team, with a few extras thrown in. Each team has been assigned three neighborhoods, marked on your maps. Just make sure the mayor's people are long gone before you swap the ballots. And take care not to get ours mixed up with theirs."

She distributed shopping bags full of our ballots, with empty plastic bags for the mayor's. "As soon as you're done, we'll meet back here to make sure everybody's safe. Don't forget to come back, or we'll send out the Marines, which will blow this whole thing sky-high."

No wonder she was a partner in a Fortune 500 firm.

"Back here, it is," we all confirmed.

Charged with excitement, we went to our cars and headed for Mission Impossible.

"Are you scared?" I asked Tricia as we drove toward the public housing development on the west side of town.

"Heck, no." She rubbed her hands together. "You?"

"Are you kidding? I've been begging God to take me home for two years, now." I waggled my eyebrows. "I can't think of a better way to go than in a commando raid."

"Well, you're just gonna have to go some other way, my dearie," she told me, "because this operation is gonna come off smooth as silk. I can feel it in my bones." She grinned at me. "Anyway, you told me weeks ago that you thought the Good Lord needed you to help pull this off."

"That was the height of hubris," I admitted with more

than a pang of superstitious fear. "He can do it on His own just fine without me. Without any of us."

"Maybe He's doing it just fine *with* us. Did that ever occur to you?"

"Ask me after the results are in."

Chapter 23

True to Tricia's prediction, the "Great Swap-out" went off without event. The only hitch was, the mayor's people didn't get finished with their rounds until almost one, and there were a lot more of them than there were of us.

Sharon and Cassie finished first and picked up doughnuts on the way home, then made lots of strong coffee. Most of us met back there at about four, but when four-thirty rolled around with no sign of Velma and her youngest son, we all waited anxiously to make sure they were okay, stuffing our faces and toking up on caffeine in the meantime. We were ready to start searching when the two of them finally drove up. They'd gotten lost in a mobile-home park and had to walk around for more than forty minutes before they finally found their car. Once we'd welcomed them back, we all got ready to leave.

"Thanks so much, everybody," Cassie told us as we clustered near the door.

"No," Geneva said. "We should be thanking you and Sharon. None of this would be possible without y'all. I wish I could think of something wonderful enough to do for you."

"I can," Sharon said quietly. "Just treat us the same way you'd treat anybody else, and leave it to God to judge who we are. Like Donnie does."

Geneva hugged her. "Honey, as Lin's precious Granny Beth used to say, 'Christianity is a little-red-wagon religion. Anybody who ain't mindin' their own little red wagon ain't been readin' the Book.' I think you'll find just as many good folks in this town who believe that as people who don't.''

Everyone present nodded, and I stood convicted by my grandmother's words. Cassie was my friend. That hadn't changed, nor had the things I loved about her. I'd never let her reckless heterosexual behavior come between us before—or her affinity for pot. Why should this?

It was freeing, letting go of the need to judge her.

"Okay," Cassie said, beaming. "Y'all go get some sleep. You've earned it. But don't forget to say your prayers before you do. And don't forget to vote."

"How about you?" Velma asked. "What'll you be doing today?"

Cassie held up both hands with fingers crossed. "Vote, crash, and pray this works."

"It'll work," Tricia declared. "It has to."

Velma turned to Cassie and Sharon. "I'm expecting the two of you at the victory celebration tonight."

The two of them looked at each other, apprehensive. "I don't know, Velma," Cassie said. "Frankly, I'm not sure we're up to bein' whispered about and glared at."

"If you want to be treated like everybody else," Velma said with kindness, "you ought to do the good things everybody else does. We want you both there, and I won't take no for an answer. When Donnie finds out what you did for him—''

"Whoa. Back up, Jack." Cassie pushed out both hands. "We swore y'all to secrecy, and I'm holdin' you to it. For Donnie's sake, he shouldn't know anything about this. If it works, he doesn't need to. If it hits the fan, we'll take the heat, not him."

"She has a point," Velma's oldest son said.

"Yep. He shouldn't know, and neither should anybody

else," Geneva said emphatically. "Not even afterwards, if it works." She suppressed a yawn. "Boy, am I glad Shelia's workin' today instead of me."

Velma headed for the door. "Okay, everybody. Polls close at seven tonight, so we'll see you then."

Sharon sent Cassie a questioning look. When Cassie nodded, Sharon smiled with pride. "We'll be there," she told Velma, "but not until later. I still have some moling around to do at the mayor's tonight. As soon as I find anything out, I'll come straight to you with it, Velma."

If she had the courage to go back into the demon's lair, then face Mimosa Branch with Cassie at Velma's, surely I could face Grant.

After what our commando crew had just accomplished, my situation with Grant now seemed like a tempest in a teapot. I believe it's called perspective, but I was just beginning to get acquainted with it.

Tricia went straight to bed, but I stayed up so I could vote when the polls opened at seven. Election day dawned cool and clear, perfect fall weather. As I pulled into the middle-school parking lot to vote, I saw that the rental vans were already unloading their passengers, some of them with our ballots in hand. A flood of adrenaline shot through me. It was all I could do not to stare.

Inside, everything seemed to be moving smoothly, but I was nervous as a toy poodle in an arcade, convinced that somebody would wise up to the altered ballot and point immediately to me, shouting, "There she is! She did it!"

Have I mentioned that I tend to overdramatize and project preposterous scenarios?

Nothing happened, of course. Everything just went along as usual. After I voted, I sat in my car and watched the vans pull away as others arrived.

Had they collected the ballots and given out the tokens? Only time would tell.

"Not my will, but Thine," I prayed briefly, then headed home.

When I got there, Miss Mamie was waiting on the front porch of 1431 Green Street. She flagged me down with a FedEx envelope. "Oooh-hoo! This just came for you! I knew you'd want to see it."

What I wanted was to go to bed, but I parked and trudged up the stairs to fetch my letter, too tired to realize what it had to be. When I saw the sender, though, I perked right up: the real-estate testing service. Heart pounding, I opened the cardboard envelope and drew out the letter inside. A number "96" in a blank at the middle of the page jumped out at me. I scanned the contents just to be sure. "I passed! Mama, I made a ninety-six!"

We hugged each other good and proper.

"Of course you did, sweetie. We all knew you would." After we'd hugged, she took the letter and pored over it herself. "Gracious. A ninety-six. How impressive." She handed it back to me. "And I know you'll be a top-notch agent, too."

"I hope so." A giant yawn overtook me. "But right now, all I want to do is go to sleep."

"I saw y'all didn't get in till dawn," my mother couldn't resist telling me. "Work or play?"

"Work." Another yawn. "Last-minute campaign stuff."

She gave me one more hug for the road. "Well, Donnie's lucky to have y'all, that's all I can say."

Back at the apartment, I found Tricia sleeping so soundly I didn't wake her. I just crashed and slept until five on the other side of the bed from her.

"You look terrific, Miss Real-Estate Agent," Tricia said under her breath that night as we approached campaign headquarters. "Stop acting like you're going to your execution. I told you, I am not leaving your side. You do not have to do this alone."

She'd loaned me one of her sensational dresses, a red one, that I still couldn't believe I could get into. I had to admit, it looked great. I should have been sassy, but I was cotton-mouthed at the prospect of seeing Grant. My new-found perspective had deserted me. "Why do we have to get here at seven? Why not eight?"

"Coward." Tricia pushed me by the small of my back. "The sooner you get this over with, the better you'll feel. I tell you, it's not gonna be nearly as awful as you think it is. You'll do it, and it will be behind you. That simple."

We entered the open garage door together. Inside, red, white, and blue bunting hung everywhere above the fifty or so people already there. The worktables had been covered with plastic red-checkered tablecloths and shifted to the edges of the room, making space for dancing to the band from The Bluegrass Barn in Suwanee who were plucking out a toe-tapper. Two huge-screen projection TVs sat up on tables in the corners. Tricia and I cruised a terrific spread of barbecue, slaw, potato salad, chocolate cake, and Brunswick stew that was set up on the far wall beside a podium where Donnie would make his speech when the time came.

Our candidate was the first one to approach us. "Lin! Tricia." Donnie took my hands and stepped back. "Man, you look like a million bucks. Both of you." Then he leaned close to inspect my eyes. "A little tired, though." I could see the wry sparkle in his own. "You been gettin' enough sleep lately?"

I stopped cold. Did he know?

Of course not, I told myself. *How could he?* "Not lately, but I plan to sleep well tonight. After you win."

He grinned. "I sleep good every night, 'cause my conscience is clear, praise Jesus."

Was that a subtle chastisement? Could he know?

"Yeah, well, not all of us are as good as you are," Tricia observed dryly.

"Every person here is as good as I am," Donnie responded. "Most of 'em, better." There was definitely something behind his smile. "Oh, by the way, Sally Hester's here," he told me. "She's upstairs. Said she'd like to speak to you in private for a few minutes."

Sally? What could she be wanting with me? "Okay."

Tricia followed me up the stairs. At the landing, I paused for a moment with my hand on the knob, hoping Grant wouldn't be on the other side of the door with Sally. I pushed it open to find not Grant, but Velma, chatting with Sally in the living room.

I let out a relieved breath.

Tricia excused herself with, "I'm going to get myself some of that Brunswick stew. Can I bring y'all any?" When both Sally and Velma demurred, she left us alone.

I sat in a comfortable chair. "Donnie said you wanted to talk to me."

"Yes."

Velma started to rise. "I think I'll get some of that stew, myself—"

"No, stay, please." Sally pulled Velma's arm. "I want you to hear this, too."

We both sat poised.

"I've been working on the judge's files and the Gordon case with the local authorities, the DEA, and the State Attorney General's office since this whole thing started. Interagency friction set in early. Now the feds are involved."

"I know," Velma volunteered. "We already gave them the originals. They couldn't seem to settle on who should get what. Georgia politics being what they are, we decided the Justice Department would be safest."

Sally sighed in exasperation. "There's been way too much territoriality going on about all this, but that happens when everybody from the county DA to the feds want a piece of the action." She shook her head. "I know you were disappointed when the mayor wiggled out of the corruption charges, but he's not out of the woods, not by a long shot."

We both perked up.

"I wanted you to know that I discovered Dr. Gordon is a silent partner in the subdivisions. Since the DEA is prosecuting him on drug charges, they cooperated with the feds and the state attorney general to investigate the connection as a money-laundering scheme. My sources tell me the good doctor and the mayor are in deep manure. So even if Donnie loses, which he probably will, it's not the end. I don't know how long it will take to bring charges, because after the debacle with the paving scheme, the prosecutors are being really careful to nail things down. But charges will be made, and this time they'll stick. A grand jury is already subpoenaing witnesses, but that's strictly on the Q.T."

"Maybe you *can* fight city hall," I said, encouraged.

"I wouldn't be here if you couldn't," Sally said. "And this time, Ham Stubbs will be not only tried, but convicted. They're also looking into some serious allegations of election fraud."

My chest felt as if a huge fist had reached inside and clenched my heart. Velma and I shared a pregnant look. Would our whole commando unit end up subpoenaed? Or worse?

Then Velma smiled benignly, the very picture of innocence. "Who knows, Sally? Maybe Donnie might win. By a landslide."

Sally's journalistic instincts sharpened her features. "I've just told you something confidential. Is there something you might like to tell me in return?"

"Not a thing," Velma said. "But if God could free the Israelites from Egypt, I'm sure He can arrange to have Donnie West elected mayor of Mimosa Branch, don't you think?"

Sally narrowed her eyes, shrewd. "You haven't by any chance got a Moses hiding in the bulrushes somewhere, have you?"

"No," Velma lied with convincing sincerity. "But as

Donnie often says, 'The Lord worketh in mysterious ways his wonders to perform.' "

Heart pounding, I went back downstairs to tell Tricia that we all might be in the soup. I was sidetracked, though, when I stepped out of the stairwell to discover that my parents and Aunt Glory and Uncle Bedford were sitting at a corner table near the open doorway—doubtless so they could beat a hasty escape if Uncle Bedford got out of hand.

To my surprise, I was really happy to see them there. The Mame and Aunt Glory looked wonderful, both in tasteful church attire, but my father was wearing an ancient Madras sport coat with clashing seersucker pants, and Uncle Bedford was decked out in mismatched plaids accented by white patent leather shoes. One could only imagine the fracas there must have been over letting them out of the house dressed like *that*.

I crossed over to welcome them.

"Hey, y'all." I beamed at my parents. "I sure am proud y'all could come."

"Tommy's comin' later," Miss Mamie said. "He had one of those fishin' meetin's, but he said he'd be here by ten."

Aunt Glory leaned forward. "We brought two cars just in case Bedford takes a spell, but I sure am tickled to get to go to a real party after so long."

"Glory drove us all to the polls today," the Mame declared with pride. "We all voted for Donnie. Even Bedford."

Now *there* was a scary prospect for democracy.

I leaned close to ask, "How could you be sure he voted for Donnie?"

"Gracious, you know perfectly well he couldn't have managed on his own," Aunt Glory said openly. "I had to mark his ballot for him, of course, but don't worry. Nobody seemed to mind."

Another scary prospect for democracy.

The bluegrass band struck up a lively number, and Uncle Bedford rose abruptly, taking Aunt Glory's hand. "Come on, sweet stuff. Let's cut a rug." It was a glimpse back to happier days, and the first time he'd recognized her since I'd come home.

Teary-eyed with joy, Aunt Glory allowed herself to be led by her tottering husband to the dance floor where, to everybody's amazement, he proceeded to dance almost as well as he used to, which was well indeed.

Not to be outdone by his little brother, the General pulled Miss Mamie onto the dance floor and did a passable two-step also. Everybody in the room watched and clapped, and the band kept playing until Uncle Bedford tired and began to falter. When the music ended, he grinned his old, wonderful grin and gave Aunt Glory a big hug.

Weeping openly into her hanky, she helped him back to the table to rest.

"By damn, Bedford," my father said, giving Uncle Bedford a substantial clout on the back. "It sure is fine to see you two dance again. Just fine." He seated my mother. "Tell ya what I'm gonna do. I'm gonna get us some lemonade."

Miss Mamie started to rise. "Here, let me help you with that."

"Sit down, bride." I hadn't heard him call her that in ages, and his staying hand on her shoulder was more of a caress than a gesture of control. "If my little brother can dance, I can get my woman a lemonade, and that's all there is to it."

My mother looked up at him with pride. "Why thank you, Thomas."

It was enough for them, and I no longer had to make a judgment about that.

"Oh, and Thomas," Miss Mamie added, "while you're up, how 'bout bringin' me some more of that stew?"

"There you go, takin' advantage of me," he grumbled without resentment. He was, after all, still my father. "Typical. Just like a woman." He headed for the refreshment table.

In the absence of music, Uncle Bedford had lapsed back

into his distant, unapproachable daze. I saw Aunt Glory look at him with such loss and longing that I took her hand and squeezed it in consolation.

She turned to me. "I live for those precious moments when the door opens inside him and we find each other again," she said. "But afterward, losing him . . ." Her eyes welled with pain. "It gets harder and harder. Sometimes I wish those moments didn't come, so I could let him go."

My heart broke for her. "If you need anything, Tricia and I are right here. Don't hesitate to ask for help, Aunt Glory. You're family just as much as Uncle B."

She nodded in gratitude.

As I stood, I caught the Mame looking at us with an odd expression. Was it longing? Jealousy? Whatever it was, I could see she was hurting, too.

Before I'd come home, I would have used any excuse to avoid such an emotionally charged situation, but that night, my own wounded heart propelled me to give her a big hug. My arms around her, I said the words I'd longed to hear her say to me. "I love you, Mama. And I'm so proud of you. I don't know how you do it, stay so strong for all of us."

She clung to me as if I were about to go away forever. "I love you, too, Lin," she said in a broken whisper. "And I am so, so proud of you."

I held on, savoring the healing grace of that moment. A lifetime of unresolved issues remained between us, but it dawned on me that I could let them go—cast them off like Marley's chains. Miss Mamie would always be Miss Mamie, and I would always be me, yet I had the choice to release my hurts and simply love her. My soul felt instantly lighter.

It was a revelation that brightened my whole perspective of the future. For thirty years, I'd run away from the craziness in my family. But only when I'd been thrust back into the heart of it had I begun to see things clearly, and to forgive.

My mother broke the embrace, dabbing at her eyes with a paper napkin. "I sure am glad you came home."

"So am I, Mama." And I was. I didn't know what the future held for me, but I now believed, down to my toes, that it would be good.

The band resumed playing, and Uncle Bedford perked right up. Maybe music was the magic key to that inner door.

I left my family and found Tricia over by the buffet line pigging out (pun intended) on barbecue and Brunswick stew.

I watched her drop a spoonful of stew onto the slice of trash white-bread she was holding, as Brunswick stew was meant to be eaten. She took the bite, her eyes closed in bliss as she savored it. "I swear, that's heaven. Nobody north of Charleston knows how to fix Brunswick stew the way it should be."

I leaned close. "Never mind the stew. Major news bulletin. We need to go to the conference room."

"Where's the conference room?" she asked with a longing look at her plate.

"Out by the pasture gate." I pointed to her supper. "Bring that with you."

We passed Grant on our way out the open garage door. I was so preoccupied that I said, "Hi, Grant," and walked right past him before I realized what had just happened.

When I did, Tricia grabbed my arm to keep me from turning around. "Don't you dare. That was perfect. Just perfect. Now keep on walking, and no matter what you do, do not look back. It would ruin everything."

A delayed pulse of . . . something—not fear, not anger, not regret—lobbed a heavy beat inside me, but in its wake, all I felt was devilish delight. "Oooh, that *was* perfect, wasn't it?"

"And it'll stay perfect as long as you're too busy having a good time to pay any attention to that scumbag."

"I think I can manage that," I said with a new confidence. Why had I made such a big deal out of it? Seeing Grant just brought home how very *over* my obsession was.

"I'm serious," Tricia told me. "There will be hundreds of other people here tonight. All you have to do to pull this off is focus on them, not Grant. You don't have to ignore him. Just treat him like you'd treat any old pharmacist."

Any old pharmacist. I had to chuckle.

Then I remembered why we'd come outside, and sobered. "Well, there's good news and bad news," I announced.

"Give me the bad news first."

"I really have to give you the good news for you to understand the bad news."

We were interrupted when several cars bearing Franklin Harris and a crowd of his neighbors drove up. Franklin's niece Jacey rolled down her window as they approached us. "Hey, Lin. Hey, Tricia."

We all knew why they had waited to come, and it saddened me, but Tricia responded with her usual dry humor. "Where y'all been?" she hollered in mock exasperation. "We were beginning to think you didn't like us."

Laughter came from their car and the others who could hear us.

"Well, here we are," Jacey responded, "So now we can party *down!*"

"How's the wildflower garden?" I called to Franklin.

"Doin' just fine. Just fine," he said out the open window.

"Great. Let me know if you need anything, now." I waved them on. "Y'all get that party rolling. We'll be right there."

We reached the pasture gate just about the time the last of them entered the garage, leaving us alone. "All right, already," Tricia said, impatient. "Let's hear it."

"Sally Hester told me and Velma that she found a connection between Mack Gordon and the mayor's subdivisions, so the feds are investigating the whole mess as a money-laundering operation. She said both of them will do time, for certain. There's even a grand jury investigating it."

"That is good news."

"Yep. Now for the bad news: That same grand jury is also looking into serious allegations of election fraud. Apparently, somebody talked."

Her eyes widened, and she rubbed her arms against the chilly breeze that gusted across the pasture. "You don't think they might have been watching last night when *we*—"

I motioned her to silence. "Who knows? But I doubt it."

"How come?"

"Wishful thinking, maybe," I admitted.

"Whoooo." Tricia pivoted, then sagged, unseeing, against the gatepost. "Maybe I'm not so sorry to go back to Alexandria on Sunday after all."

I scanned the dark pines and rolling pastures, then raised my eyes to the cobalt sky where bright stars shone. It was such a perfect night, and the sound of the bluegrass band wafted to us on a cool breeze. "You know what? I am not going to let this ruin my night. I am going to go back in there and have myself a celebration." My spirit lightened, just saying it. "I mean, look how I agonized over seeing Grant, and that was nothing. *Nothing*, because I was too busy having a life to let it throw me.

"And what good would it do to go into a tailspin about the feds?" Even as I said it, I couldn't believe this was me, Lin, who even had to *think* about "the feds," much less have good reason to worry that they might come after us. "What's going to happen is going to happen. We might as well enjoy ourselves in the meantime." I gave Tricia's shoulders a consoling squeeze. "You're in the clear, anyway. None of us will give you up."

None of us will give you up? How very cinema noir, and I'd actually gotten to say it—me, Miss Goody Two-shoes!

Cool. Cool, cool, cool.

Tricia eyed me with an unconvincing smile. "Oh, I don't know. It might raise my stock with the boys to be subpoenaed by a grand jury. Not convicted, mind you, just questioned."

"Even if the law saw us, which I don't think they did, they'll never indict us, much less convict us. All we did was swap the ballots. It's a civil matter. The mayor could sue us, but *that's* not gonna happen. We cheated the cheater. Who's he going to tell?"

"That's the best part." A wide, smug smile spread across her face. "The whole operation is so diabolically, deliciously elegant that I almost can't stand keeping it a secret." At my look of alarm, she hastened to say, "But I will. Not a word. Not even to John."

"*We'll* know," I consoled myself as much as her. "Heck, this is ten times better than our Theta Alpha oath"—which was so secret I couldn't remember a word of it—"So cool it's rock-solid."

"Yeah." She dragged the word out, her features relaxing. It was a truly delicious moment, one we stood and savored until both of us got chilled.

"Brrr." Tricia scrubbed her arms. "Let's get inside. I could use some decaf."

"Me, too." We started back in. "You don't need to worry about being my bodyguard anymore. Grant doesn't bother me. As a matter of fact, I'm grateful to him."

"Grateful?" Tricia recoiled in alarm. "Are you nuts?"

"No. I think I'm finally a little bit sane." I smiled, at peace within myself. "Thanks to him, I found out that I wouldn't let myself do anything that destructive. And I finally saw Grant for who he really is. It made me realize I'd rather have no man than settle for one like him." I chafed my own arms, not from the cold, but from the shiver that ran through me at the thought of my own wrongheadedness. "You know, I've sworn I didn't want to settle lots of times, but now I *mean* it. Maybe if another man comes along, I'll look for what I really need to see."

"Good thinkin', Big Sister," she said with pride. "And it's not *if* a man comes along, it's *when*." She nudged me to move faster. "Step lively. Let's party down."

"I may even shake my bootie," I said, feeling free, way too big for my britches, and dangerous. "Regardless of the fact that it could end up costing me thousands at the orthopedist's."

We rejoined the party. After properly welcoming Franklin, Jacey, and their group, we ate, danced, talked with old friends, and had a great time. I even managed to keep from watching Grant out of the corner of my eye.

The dumb schmuck sulked, all alone, around the edges of the festivities. He wasn't sulking because of the campaign budget; we'd finished with almost a thousand dollars left in the till. He was sulking because I wasn't paying any attention to him, one way or the other. Thanks to Saturday night, I also knew why he was alone, and I hoped, for the sake of the women of the world, that he stayed that way. But I wasn't mad at him anymore. And I wasn't afraid.

Oh, but it was a good night—one that got even better when Cassie and Sharon arrived. The entire "commando squad" rushed to embrace them, while only a few people scowled and whispered behind their hands.

Cassie had been right about facing derision. There were some dirty looks, but when Donnie made a great show of welcoming the new arrivals, even those subsided.

Tricia and I couldn't wait to get Cassie and Sharon alone so we could find out the news from behind enemy lines.

We hijacked them on their way to the buffet. "So," Tricia said to Sharon. "What's up at the mayor's?"

Sharon beamed. "Nothing. Absolutely nothing. I swear, they're clueless." She shook her head. "Stubbs, Mayfield, all of them. They're all kicked back, smug as capos and twice as slick. The mayor even had a new body wave just for his acceptance speech."

I hugged her. "That is too, too great."

Across the room, Miss Mamie and Aunt Glory ignored us, opting to whisper and stare at the pierced, spiked punkers instead. It was progress of a sort. At least she wasn't bending my father's ear about my "shaming" them in public with "those perverts."

After Cassie, Sharon, and I had gotten our food, we all settled down to eat and visit while the last of the election results were being tallied. Geneva, Donnie's head deacon, and four influential supporters had each stood watchdog over a precinct, then followed the ballots back to city hall to make sure everything was on the up and up. Anticipating his usual landslide, the mayor had even allowed them to witness the counting along with the regular election monitors. The results would be made official and released to the media just before eleven. We would hear about it on the news just like everybody else.

Donnie had set the big-screen sets to CTNC, whose crew arrived at ten with none other than Sally Hester.

My old paranoia flipped faster than a cat shot in the butt with a BB gun. Lord, how I hoped she wouldn't get wind of the commando raid. *Get real*, my new self sassed. *There is no way she could know anything. We've got the drop on even the famous Sally Hester. Enjoy it.* I resolved to do just that.

To our surprise, crews and reporters from all three Atlanta stations arrived, too. We figured it must have been a slow news night. Win or lose, we had great coverage.

Tommy arrived at ten-thirty. "Sorry I was late, Sis," he told me as he hugged me. "I was with my sponsor."

I pulled back to face him. "You don't have to explain. I'm just glad you're here." He piled a plate, then joined the family. My father and Uncle Bedford were both sound asleep in their chairs, so I'm sure the Mame and Aunt Glory were glad for somebody to talk to.

Grant kept drifting into my vicinity, but every time I saw him, I was more convinced that he and I were *so* over.

Despite my resolution to enjoy myself, though, my stomach knotted harder and harder as the time passed, while the news crews—at Donnie's invitation—scarfed down all that was left of the buffet except the trash bread. Some of them even buck-danced a little to the bluegrass.

But everybody was in position well before eleven, though we knew our story was such small potatoes that it would probably get relegated to the end of the news segment. Still, an atmosphere of electric tension subdued the talk among us as we gathered before the podium. Finally, eleven o'clock arrived, and Wayne Burnette—TV repairman extraordinaire and designated holder of the official remotes—turned up the volume on the sets. CTNC's theme filled the room.

Silence fell. Everybody watched the screen except the crews focused, at the ready, on Donnie, who stood holding his wife's hand behind the forest of microphones. He didn't even look nervous, and neither did she.

That's faith for you.

"This is CTNC with all the news, whenever it happens," the anchor said. "Tonight's top story, the mayor's race in Mimosa Branch."

Lead story! We gasped collectively, holding our breaths, then let them out again as the anchor put the election in context by recapping the stories about Dr. Gordon, the results of his divorce trial (all charges against Reba had been dropped, but the jurors must have gotten wind of it, because they awarded her almost nothing), and the mayor's paving scam.

Midway into the last, the crews' lights brightened to solar intensity.

"And now, with all precincts in and tallied, a surprising upset by reform candidate Donnie West. A staggering seventy-five percent of the vote has made Pastor Donnie West, *Mayor* Donnie West of Mimosa Branch for the next six years."

Pandemonium! Even the normally reserved Christiansons went bonkers.

"We did it! We did it!" Tricia and Cassie grabbed hold of each other and bounced the way they used to at pep rallies. Even Sharon, looking a decade younger in the broad grin she was wearing, started hugging perfect strangers and shaking hands.

Donnie kissed his wife, then kept watching the screen with a grateful, relieved expression. Then he saw something that caused him to blare, "Listen up!" over the PA system.

Everybody quieted down enough for us to hear, "In a related story, the Mimosa Branch race to fill the seat vacated by Councilman Fred Waller has put residential contractor Price Robinson into office by a five percent margin over longtime city employee Alvin Winters."

Pandemonium times two.

We'd broken Ham Stubbs's hold on the city, made a difference. *I* had made a difference. And the sweetest part was, the evil little bastard had footed the bill. His vans had driven the voters to the polls, and his money had paid for the liquor now being consumed by the clueless automatons he'd counted on to keep him in office.

Sweet. Sweet, sweet, sweet!

Surrounded by joyous chaos, I reveled in the elegant irony that only a few of us, commandos all, would ever know.

Suddenly, my hometown was looking like a pretty great place to be.

"We go now to Mimosa Branch, live at the victory celebration for reform candidate and mayor-elect Donnie West."

The whistles, shouts, and applause escalated to deafening levels. Donnie raised his hands. "If y'all could just quiet it down a minute, I'll say my piece, then y'all can go back to celebratin', and my wife and I can go home to *bed*."

At the roar of laughter that followed the double entendre, his weather-beaten complexion colored brightly, but it didn't show on the screens.

"First, I'd like to thank a gracious Heavenly Father and my dedicated supporters for gittin' me elected." Amid the cheers, he paused, grinning straight at Cassie and Sharon, who were linked, their arms around each others' waists.

"It's mighty humbling to see what lengths my loyal friends have gone to to make this possible."

Tricia and I looked at each other in shock. He knew! It was sparkling in his eyes.

Donnie went on. "It does me good to know the citizens of this community are willin' to put a minister of the Gospel in a position of civic authority."

More cheers, punctuated by fervent "Amens."

"And I want to pledge to you tonight," he said with the compelling intensity of divine inspiration, "that my first two official acts as mayor of Mimosa Branch will be to order a complete audit of financial records, and to make certain that the municipal services to the neglected neighborhoods of this town are brought up to standard."

Everybody but Franklin Harris went wild. Franklin just closed his eyes, lifted his face toward heaven, his hands clasped in prayer, and mouthed, "Thank you, Jesus."

The reporters all shouted questions on top of each other, but Donnie didn't answer any of them. Instead, he waved to us again. "Thank you. Thank you. Now if you good folks will forgive me, I'm going home. I'm so tired I had to let my wife drive me here instead of comin' on my Harley. Now *that's* tired!"

The happy twosome left the dais and started working their way though the gauntlet of handshakes, hugs, and backslaps.

The cameras immediately focused on their reporters, who gave recaps while the TV screen switched to a live shot of the grim-faced mayor leaving his own podium without the courtesy of a concession statement. As he passed his wife, I nudged Tricia. "Look. That's his wife."

"You mean that woman who looks so smug?"

"None other." The cameraman focused in on her smiling face for several seconds before cutting back to the mayor. "She's positively gloating."

"Well, who can blame her, married to *him?*"

"Eeeeeyew!" we said together the way we had in high school.

On the screen the TV crew goaded the mayor with inflammatory questions until he slammed the door in their faces. The picture cut back to the anchor, who introduced Sally Hester's wrap-up, complete with glowing predictions for Donnie's administration and political career.

If anybody could keep from getting fleas, it was Donnie.

I looked over to see him and his solemn, always-seen-but-never-heard wife approach us. When they reached us, I confronted him with a pointed look. "You knew."

Tricia, Cassie, and Sharon froze.

That mischievous sparkle twinkled in Donnie's eyes. "Not much goes on in this town that I don't know about. My congregation is spread out all over. Why, I'd be willin' to guess you've seen most of their neighborhoods."

He did! "And it's okay with you?" Cassie asked.

"The Lord worketh in mysterious ways His wonders to perform." Donnie's tired smile was beatific. "Who am I to criticize His methods?"

"Anyway," his wife said, exposing horribly crooked teeth, "everybody knows, the way you do thangs ain't the way you do thangs." She trusted us with a broad grin that revealed even more dental wreckage while Donnie looked on her with absolute adoration.

And I had thought her slow witted and servile because she never smiled or spoke.

Wrong. Wrong, wrong, wrong.

"There's another saying my old granny used to tell me," I told them. "The way things seem ain't usually the way they are."

"Amen to that," Donnie responded, "and goodnight ladies. We're gonna say good-bye to your folks, then head home."

Despite the afterglow of this day's victory, I could see how exhausted they both were. They left the four of us grinning like mules eating briars.

I turned to Sharon and Cassie. "What now? This must be marked by something momentous."

Just then Wayne, shifting the TVs to a local station in search of more coverage, came in on the local weather forecast. In the brief interval before he moved on, we saw the weather map that indicated clear skies and highs in the low eighties for the whole Eastern Seaboard.

"I know!" Tricia punched the sky. "Road trip!" She drew us into a huddle. "The weather's perfect. The beach will be deserted, and there's room for all of us at my beach house. Let's do it! We can be there in eight hours. The rest of y'all can sleep while I drive. Y'all can come back on Sunday. I'll either fly home or get John or one of my boys to come get me. It's perfect. Say you will?"

It *was* perfect. "I'm in," I said. Have I mentioned, I'm impulsive?

Cassie looked at Sharon and hesitated. "Guess y'all better count us out. Sharon has a big presentation tomorrow at work."

"After all you did last night?" Tricia was as awed as I was.

"She never leaves things to the last minute," Cassie explained with pride. "I told you, we're exact opposites. She's brilliant and organized."

Sharon waved off the compliment, turning to Cassie. "Cassie, I want you to go. The three of you have been friends all your lives. This may be your last chance to run off together. I want you to go." It was not the ploy of a martyr. You could see that she really wanted Cassie to be happy.

Cassie's brow wrinkled. "Really?"

"Yes, really. It's what you want to do. Admit it."

Cassie hugged her. "Oh, I do, I do, I do!"

"Then go." Sharon pushed her toward us. "Y'all have a great time. And don't let her corrupt you. She can be very persuasive."

Acting like kids, the three of us did our old pep-rally

hop until my knee went out. Fortunately, no lasting harm was done.

"We shall drink and eat chocolate and sing songs and tell stories and stay up late and sleep until two," Tricia crowed.

"Road trip!" we said in unison, then departed to pack.

Chapter 24

I packed only the essentials: my two favorite pillows, a few comfortable outfits and sleep shirts, and (at Tricia's insistence) my bathing suit and sun blocker. Plus two gallons of the Mame's peach ice cream that she had sleepily, but happily, donated even after I told her Cassie was going with us.

"Honey," she said as she handed me the small cooler filled with iced-down precious cargo, "after what Cassie and that woman of hers did for Donnie, she can have all the ice cream in my freezer."

My jaw literally dropped open. "What are you talking about?"

"Swappin' those ballots on the mayor." She shook her head. "How Ham Stubbs managed to get away with all that liquor nonsense without anybody findin' out is a mystery to me, but I sure am glad y'all turned it against him." She studied me with concern. "Why do you look so shocked? Surely you didn't think y'all could pull off somethin' like that without people findin' out." The Mame smiled indulgently. "Mimosa Branch might have grown, but it's still Mimosa Branch."

So that was why she hadn't turned a hair when Cassie and Sharon had entered the victory celebration. She'd known.

"We're all real proud of you," she went on. "Especially Tommy. He said this would go down in the lore of Georgia politics forever."

"Tommy knows?"

"I believe he heard it at his fishin' meetin'." She dropped her voice confidentially. "Since it's a secret, we didn't say anything at the party."

I knew perfectly well that if the Mame was privy to the facts, the entire Old Guard of Mimosa Branch probably was, too. Plus the AAs at my brother's meeting, but from what Tommy had told me, *they* knew how to keep a secret.

I couldn't believe the turn this all had taken. "Thanks for the ice cream." I handed her a slip of paper on which I'd written my cell-phone number and the one at Tricia's beach house. "I'll call you when we get there. Cassie and I will be back home before midnight on Sunday."

"Try to make it as early as you can," my mother requested as she headed toward the back stair. "I hate waitin' up real late."

A lot of surprising things had happened in that most exceptional day, but I was further surprised by my own realization that she spoke from genuine concern. "If it gets late Sunday," I said without a scrap of resentment, "I'll call you from my cell phone so you won't have to worry."

With that, the dreaded mommie-net evaporated. Poof, it was gone. Hallelujah, hallelujah, amen.

"Thanks, honey," she said, visibly moved. "I'd really appreciate it. I get so scared thinkin' somethin' might have happened to you."

"I know." It had taken me fifty years to understand that love was behind all the things she did that drove me crazy, but better late than never.

On the way back to the apartment, I stowed the ice cream in the trunk beside my shopping bags and Tricia's expensive luggage. Inside, I found her fortifying herself for the long drive ahead with strong coffee. When I told her our deep, dark secret wasn't as deep or dark as we'd thought, she reacted first with shock, then amusement. "Lord, I'm glad I moved away from here. You can't get away with anything."

"I guess it only matters if you're doing things you need to get away with."

She looked at the clock. It was already past midnight. "Wups. We're supposed to be at Cassie's right now." She stood and picked up her purse. "Let's get this show on the road."

I grabbed my pillows and my purse, then double-checked to make sure everything was turned off and locked up tight.

On her way out ahead of me, Tricia paused for a last affectionate look at my new home. "Good-bye, perfect girly apartment. I'll be back soon, I promise."

I followed her onto the landing, then closed the door and locked it. This really was my home, even more so because she had been there. And it would be a good place to come back to on Sunday.

Eight hours later we arrived at Tricia's and crashed.

At two o'clock that afternoon, we got up, ate, then headed for the beach with chairs, towels, lotion, and paperbacks. The long, hard-packed stretch of gray sand was deserted.

We settled in our chairs just beyond the reach of the cold, lapping waves and meditated in companionable silence for at least thirty minutes. A perfect sea breeze kept the sun from being too hot. I sat there, soaking up the warmth, and started reading my best seller. For the first time in three years, I was peaceful enough to get right into the story.

Then Cassie piped up with, "I've got an idea." (She never had been much good at sitting still.) She looked up and down the deserted beach. "We've got the place to ourselves. Why don't we sun topless?"

Tricia laughed. "Cassie! This is still a public place. We're way too old for such silliness."

"Yeah," I seconded. My inner Puritan pruned up, scandalized, affixing dire homosexual motives to Cassie's suggestion.

"Phhht. Y'all were too old when you were ten." Cassie pulled her bandeau down to her waist, exposing her large, sloping breasts. She started slathering them with lotion.

"Cassie! What if one of my neighbors sees you?" Tricia protested.

Cassie looked back at the row of houses, giving whatever neighbors might be watching an even better view of her middle-aged boobs. "Doesn't look like anybody's home." She giggled. "Even if they are, they'll get over it."

I couldn't help but laugh, which delighted my new self and sent my Puritan sulking. Cassie was so unselfconscious about her body. I wished I could be the same.

"Come on, you two," she urged. "Are you true women, or wimps? I double-dog-dare you." The ultimate childhood challenge of the TLC (Tricia, Lin, Cassie) Club.

Tricia waved her off, but I decided that life was too short not to try it. So before I had time to change my mind, I dropped the straps of my suit and lowered it to my waist. Flesh that had never seen daylight tingled in the sun's warmth.

As I'd suspected, the world kept right on turning.

"Lin!" Tricia did her best to look outraged, but she ruined the effect by laughing. "I cannot believe you are doing this."

"Actually, it feels great." I shot Cassie a pointed look. "But this is as far as I go. And if anybody comes, I'm covering up."

Cassie grinned. She shoved some megablocker at me. "Better put plenty of this on those nipples. Trust me, you do *not* want sunburned nipples." She winced in remembered pain. "Oooh. Very terrible. Trust me."

I lotioned as instructed, then the two of us relaxed, our faces to the sun, eyes closed, for several minutes.

"Oh hell." Tricia slapped her book down onto the sand.

"Y'all are crazy, you know that? But if I'm gonna have to sit out here between the two of you *nature girls*, I guess I might as well do it, too." She closed her eyes tight and jerked down her suit, revealing a long, angry scar on the side of her right breast. Cassie, applauding, couldn't see it, but I could.

Tricia cocked one eye open at me. I frowned, questioning, at the scar.

"I knew this would happen," she grumbled.

"What?" Cassie leaned over.

Tricia turned so she could see the scar. "This." Her voice hardened. "It's from my lumpectomy."

"Lumpectomy?" My stomach dropped five feet. "Tricia! When?"

"Last year." She averted her eyes to the unending line of the horizon.

"You never said a word." How could she have kept something like that from me? *Why* had she kept it from me? "Why?" I didn't mean for it to sound like an indictment, but it did.

Her eyes were guarded, defensive. "You had enough to worry about. And I'm fine, really."

"Oh my God, Tricia," Cassie anguished. "Was it malignant?"

"Yes." My stomach dropped another five feet. "But it was contained," Tricia said, matter of fact. "They got good margins and there was no cancer in the nodes. I didn't even have to take chemo. Just some radiation."

Topless or not, I fell onto her shoulder and cried. "Oh, honey. I am so, so sorry that I was too caught up in my own selfish stuff to be there for you."

"There you go again, overdramatizing," she said in that dry way of hers, patting my bare back. "You were there for me, silly. Every time I started to feel sorry for myself, I talked to you and ended up feeling better. At least I wasn't in your shoes."

I laughed through my tears and retreated to my own chair. "Thanks a lot."

"Yeah," Cassie interjected with all good intentions. "At least your husband wasn't screwing around on you."

I froze, but Tricia looked at Cassie with an odd smile. "Actually, he was, and still is, but he hasn't run us into destitution."

"Oh, fuck!" Cassie covered her mouth with both hands. "Tricia, I didn't mean. . . . I mean, I didn't know. . . . Oh, shit. I am so sorry."

"Don't be. I've known for a long, long time. This is just the first time I've said it out loud. Frankly, it's almost a relief to admit it."

I took her hand, her image blurring through tears of pride and sympathy. "You are so brave. I'm so proud of you."

Cassie took her other hand and we sat there, topless, staring across the wide green Atlantic.

"So now what?" Cassie asked. It was a question as huge and open as the sea before us.

"We stay friends forever," I answered with absolute conviction worthy of the Mame, "and we go on."

"To where?" Tricia asked with a catch in her voice.

Cassie repeated the answer I had given her what seemed like years ago. "Tomorrow. That simple. Just tomorrow."

One of Tommy's favorite AA sayings came to mind. "Yesterday's gone, tomorrow's always a day away, but today's a gift. That's why it's called the present." I inhaled the expansive breath of the sea. "God, it took a lot to teach me how to live the gift, but I wouldn't change a bit of it, because it got me here."

I looked at Tricia. She was crying quiet, necessary tears. "You'll make it, Patty-ricia," I told her. "We've been where you are; we can help, I promise. And it will get better."

She squeezed our hands.

I closed my eyes and lifted my face once more to the

cleansing brightness of the sun, savoring its warmth on my bare skin.

Amazing what three short months had accomplished. I'd come home in desperation, yet here I sat, half-naked with two lifelong friends, content and hopeful in a way I never would have understood unless my life had played out exactly as it had. My circumstances had changed very little, but I had changed a lot. I'd finally outgrown my fuck-it phase.

My new word was *joy*.

Joy, joy, joy.

About the Author

Atlanta native Haywood Smith lives on the shores of Lake Lanier, joyously anticipating the new lessons life as a single woman of faith will bring her. "As an old-fashioned Southern girl, I'm facing my 'suddenly single' life with the same anticipation as Lin, wide open to the positive possibilities, not the least of which, I hope, will be a grandchild or two (hint, hint)." One of the things she enjoys most is getting fan mail from her readers. If you enjoyed Lin's story, please take a moment to let her know by writing Haywood Smith c/o St. Martin's Press, 175 Fifth Avenue, New York, N.Y. 10010. She cherishes every single positive letter.

Watch for her next book, *The Red Hat Club*, the funny, touching adventures of six women, friends since high school, which captures the unique cachet of North Atlanta then and now.

Swan Coach House. Wednesday, January 9, 2002. 11:00
A.M.

After a brief, nonproductive swing through the gift shop
and gallery in search of some "thinking of you" trinket to
brighten up my son Jack's bachelor apartment or my daughter Callie's dorm room, I went downstairs to the sunny
main restaurant, cheered by the familiarity of its dark wood
floors, chintz tablecloths, and padded walls bright with
tastefully garish tulips. As usual, I was the first to arrive,
still clinging to the illusion that punctuality was possible
with the Red Hats despite more than three decades of evidence to the contrary.

"Table for five, please," I said to the lone waitress, a
plump, nondescript woman I didn't recognize.

She didn't blink at my red fedora, ancient sable car coat,
and tailored dark purple pantsuit. The Red Hats were such
a fixture here that our eccentricities had become part of the
basic orientation for the staff. "Sorry, mah-dahm," the waitress said in thick Slavic accents, "must wait for all here to
be seated." Clearly, she had no idea she was dealing with
a Buckhead institution, one that was allowed to bend the
Coach House's ironclad edict. With the exception of private
parties, mere mortals were never seated until everyone in
their party had arrived. But owing to our longstanding pres-

ence, the Red Hats were the exception that proved the rule—provided we were discreet about it. Clearly, this new waitress hadn't gotten the message.

I looked for her name badge, hoping the personal touch would thaw her out a little. She wasn't wearing one, but I tried anyway. "My name is Georgia," I said in my most approachable manner. "What's yours?"

She arched an eyebrow in disdain. "You could not say it. Too hard."

Serious attitude.

My master's in Southern Bitch kicked in, smoothing my voice to honeyed ice. "What a lovely accent. Where are you from?"

"Romania," the waitress answered with a defensive shrug.

Great. This was going to be a challenge for both of us.

"Please get the manager," I said distinctly. "Tell her it's the Red Hats."

She scowled again.

I pointed to my red fedora. "Tell the manager that the Red Hats are here, and I want to be seated."

She disappeared into the back, then returned with the apologetic manager du jour. "Sorry," the young woman whose name tag identified her as JOSIE said in unctuous tones. "We were shorthanded, so we pressed Vashkenushka into service from the kitchen. I forgot to tell her about y'all. Please forgive us." Despite the fact that we were the only ones in the cheery yellow foyer, she glanced about, her expression clouded with concern as she lowered her voice. "I really appreciate your continuing discretion about this arrangement, though. We'd have mutiny if the other customers found out."

"Trust me," I reassured her. "No one will ever hear it from us." As if everybody who was anybody didn't already know.

The manager's brow eased. She motioned the waitress toward our regular banquette in the back corner near the kitchen door. "Seat the ladies in red hats as soon as they come in. Just this one group, no one else," she instructed, "and treat them well. They're very special guests."

"Yes, madam," Miss Romania said, but her manner bristled with contempt as she led the way across brilliant slashes of winter sunshine that slanted through the white plantation shutters.

I sat down in the shady corner, but kept my coat on. The room was chilly, and I hadn't been warm between November and April since 1989.

When our little group had first started meeting there— long before we were Red Hats—the waitresses had been Junior Leaguers working their required service placements. Back then, the bigger the diamond, the worse the waitress, and Atlanta's well-to-do young matrons were seriously solitaired. The League had eventually hired paid staff, but the joke was on everybody for a while: the quality of service hadn't improved for a long time. For the past decade, things had been much better, though still a little slow from the kitchen. But that was an accepted part of the mystique, along with the limited—but excellent—tearoom menu.

The Red Hats didn't come for the service, anyway, or for the food. We came because the Coach House was an Atlanta institution, a link to our past with a great tea party quotient. I couldn't count the bridal showers, baby showers, luncheons, and receptions we'd all attended there.

"To drink today?" the waitress asked with a decidedly aggressive note.

"I'll have unsweetened tea, please," I said. "No lemon." I like iced tea, and I like lemon, but nowhere near each other.

"No coffee?" she challenged. "Isss cold today. Maybe hot tea?"

"No, thank you." I suppressed a blip of irritation. She would learn. "Just plain iced tea, please, no lemon." It's a Southern thing, drinking iced tea at lunch even in the winter. Shrimp salad just doesn't taste right with coffee. "And

I'll need lots of refills," I said, smiling in an effort to lighten things up. "I'm a heavy drinker."

Not a flicker of amusement crossed her broad face, prompting me to wonder if she didn't understand, or if total lack of humor was one of the main requirements for working there, as I had long suspected.

"My friends will be here soon," I told her. "We usually stay until closing. If you'll keep our glasses filled, we'll give you a big tip." It was only fair, since she wouldn't be able to turn the table.

"Big tip," she seemed to understand, but she didn't break a smile. "I get your tea."

A Romanian waitress at the Coach House. What next?

I still wasn't accustomed to Atlanta's being crowded with people from other countries.

Outwardly, I had met the onslaught with resolute enlightenment and Southern hospitality, but inwardly, a lingering part of me wanted to circle the wagons. Gone were the narrow social boundaries of my childhood—Crackers, Blacks, Catholics, and Jews, Mainlines and Pentecostals— erased by this new invasion that made unlikely allies of anybody who'd grown up here.

Maybe that was why we Red Hats clung even tighter to our little group as we grew older. It was the one solid connection to our past.

"George!" Diane called to me from across the room. She must have just had her hair colored, because her white roots were not in evidence below her red beret. She'd worn contacts since she was nine, but today the thick glasses I hadn't seen in years contorted her attractive face into a peanut shape, reminding me of the momentous day we'd met so long ago.

Lord, I'd forgotten how blind she was without her contacts.

"I lost a lens and almost didn't even come." Even more flustered than usual, she muddled her way between the tables, poking through her enormous Vuitton shoulder bag as she bumped the chairs. "Dad-gum it. I put that paperback you loaned me in here somewhere, but now I can't find it."

Considering the shape the paperback would probably be in, I quickly reassured her, "Well, don't worry if you can't." She was notorious for loving whatever she read nigh unto death—breaking the spines, slopping coffee on the pages, sometimes even baptizing them in the tub with her—so I only loaned her the ones I could live without.

I changed the subject. "Did you remember your joke? It's your turn, you know."

She flopped dramatically into the seat beside me. "Yes. But it's getting harder and harder since Sally"—her good ole girl hairdresser—"had that stroke. She was my only source."

"What about the new girl?"

Diane grimaced. "She weighs eighty-seven pounds, has black lips, piercings, and a fuchsia streak in her 'bedhead' hair. I don't think she would know a joke if it bit her."

I laughed. Diane was naturally a stitch, but she could not tell a proper joke for beans. "How many times have I told you?" I said. "You need to get e-mail. People send me jokes all the time. You should try it. Lee's been dying to set it up for you." Her only son, Lee, had graduated in business with a minor in Japanese from Harvard and a master's from Wharton. Now he made big bucks consulting for a major Japanese company in Asia.

"Lee?" she scoffed. "From Tokyo?"

"He comes home every three months, and you know it." We baby boomers might be dragged kicking and screaming into the Age of the Internet, but not our grown sons and daughters; they were all computer-savvy.

Diane, on the other hand, seemed to consider it a matter of honor to hold out. Very passive-aggressive, which was definitely her style. I loved her, but you had to be careful or she'd store up hurts, then bite you on the ankle when you least expected it.

"I swear," I harped, "once you get on-line, you'll love it. Instant gossip, honey. And Lee would probably e-mail you every few days from Tokyo, instead of just calling once a month."

"Right. And what about spam and viruses and upgrades and expense?" She adjusted her thick glasses.

I stifled the urge to laugh.

She peered at me earnestly from the depths of distortion. "I haven't got time or energy for one more thing in my life. But since you're so hot about the Internet, why don't you just find me some jokes next time it's my turn?"

"No. That defeats the purpose."

Diane straightened the rich purple-and-red paisley of her challis skirt. "I thought the purpose of bringing a joke was for us to laugh," she grumped.

"It is. But it's also important for us to have to find the joke," I reminded her. "Finding the joke requires positive personal interaction outside the group. It's good for you. For all of us."

"Lord." Flat-mouthed, she sagged. "Like I said, I have enough to do without having to prod people for jokes."

Game called on account of pain.

We both knew the secret sorrow she was talking about, but Sacred Red Hat Tradition Five (Mind your own business) kept me from prodding. If she ever decided to talk about it, she would. Frankly, if John had done to me what Harold was doing to her—after she'd put him through law school and remodeled their houses and been the perfect corporate wife for a quarter of a century—I'd have jumped off the top of Stone Mountain long since.

But then, I was the only one of us who hadn't finished college and worked. I'd met John my junior year and taken the June Cleaver track.

Diane deflected the pregnant silence that had fallen between us by scanning the Ladies Who Lunch now filling the room. "Where's our waitress? Are you sure we have one?" she asked, reminding both of us of the long-ago meeting when we'd finally realized that nobody wanted to wait on us because they couldn't turn the table. We'd triple-tipped ever since, and a good time was had by all.

I wasn't so sure about today, though; Miss Romania had a chip the size of Bucharest on her shoulder. "I don't see her. She's new—Romanian, doesn't speak much English. She took my drink order and promptly disappeared completely."

Diane opened her napkin, then snagged another waitress on her way to the kitchen. "Excuse me, miss. Could you get our server, please? We need drinks and muffins and rolls and lots of plain butter."

We didn't need the rolls and butter, of course, but some of us wanted them.

"Right away, ma'am."

I looked past her to the entry, saw a small red pillbox hat bobbing through the waiting patrons, and waved. "Oh, good. There's Teeny."

Teeny nodded in acknowledgment, doing her best not to attract attention in her tasteful black reefer coat and impeccable purple wool sheath as she skirted the room in our direction. When she reached us, she slipped gracefully into a chair, her blue eyes less shadowed than they'd been in a long time.

"M-wah, m-wah." Hats grazing, Diane did that fake Euro kissy thing on either side of Teeny's delicate features. "Look at you, Teeny girl, gorgeous as Audrey Hepburn in that new dress. I swear, you don't look a day over twenty in that outfit."

As always, Teeny responded to the compliment with awkward pleasure. "Thanks." She shrugged off her coat, revealing tapered sleeves in a rich bouclé wool. "I made it."

"You are joking." I reassessed the simple, elegant creation. The cut was sophisticated and beautifully tailored. "I'm gabberflasted. It looks like you paid a fortune for it." Teeny hadn't sewn since our boys were in T-ball, but her rotten, rich husband kept her on such a short leash financially that she might have been forced to take it up again. The possibility annoyed the poo out of me, but no way would I let on. Teeny was allergic to conflict of any kind. "That tailoring. I can't believe you actually made it."

Teeny's eyes glowed as she looked down and to the right. "Thanks."

Diane gave her a sideways hug. "Worthy of Old Miz Boatwright's Home Ec class."

"Miz Boatwright," I mused. "Now there's a blast from the past. How in this world did you remember her? You didn't even go to Northside."

"SuSu and Linda bitched about her enough." Diane mimicked Linda's dead-on imitation of the woman we had tortured for trying to teach us to cook and sew. "No spiders, ladies. Tie and trim those loose threads, or it's ten points off for every one of 'em."

Teeny giggled behind her hand, prompting me to wonder yet again if she ever let loose and laughed aloud like she used to. Our monthly jokes were no way to tell. She never "got" them. And she was even worse than Diane at telling them.

"Miz Boatwright," I repeated, nostalgic. "Ruling duenna of Northside's domestic arts." Her image sprang vividly from three decades ago, surrounded by cutting tables, arcane kitchen appliances, and sewing kits in the Home Ec lab. I could still remember the faint underscent of sewing machine oil mingled with the aroma of the muffins she baked every morning for her friends on the staff. "A blast from the past," I repeated.

"Who's a blast from the past?" Linda approached from behind a group settling at the table beside us. Her wide face was framed by soft, shiny silver curls that only she, among us, had the courage to wear. She looked ten years older than we did, but didn't care, secure in her doting husband's love. Her red knit waif-hat and bulky purple sweater earned a few curious glances before she plunked into her usual chair.

"Miz Boatwright in Home Ec," I informed her. "Diane actually remembered her name."

"Ah," Linda nodded. "The poor soul who tried unsuccessfully to make proper homemakers of us." She looked to Diane. "Thank your lucky stars you didn't have to suffer such nonsense at Westminster."

"I'm sure they assumed you'd hire all that out," I said without malice. It was true.

Linda looked at me. "Miz Boatwright succeeded with you, George. You can cook like Julia Child and sew almost as well as Teeny."

"My sewing days are long gone. The last thing I made was a Nehru jacket for John." Then a sobering thought struck me. "Oh, gross. Do you realize that when we were in her class, Miz Boatwright was probably younger than we are now?"

Linda groaned. "Thanks a lot for that cheerful little observation."

Teeny jumped in with a prim, "Perhaps you'd like to follow it up by counting crow's feet. If so, I suggest you start in the mirror."

"Teeny!" I perked up, hoping she'd intended the zinger. But she simply blinked back at me with her usual wide-eyed innocence. Teeny didn't have a hostile bone in her body; she just said whatever she thought without considering how it might sound.

Uncomfortable at the mere hint of conflict between Teeny and me, Diane invoked the first of our Sacred Red Hat Traditions: "Do over."

Tradition One (Do over): Any one of us, at any time, can simply ask for a fresh start and get it. Change of subject, change of attitude—no matter how bad we might have screwed things up (in which case, immediate apologies are in order).

Diane peered in her best ex-schoolteacher manner at

both of us. "I'm in no mood to be reminded of my middle-aged shortcomings, even by Teeny."

"Oh, for cryin' out loud, Di," Linda chimed in, "Teeny didn't mean anything by it." She never did.

Frankly, any one of us would have been delighted if she had. She hadn't stuck up for herself since 1974, the one and only time. (More about that later.) We all longed to see her stand up to that sorry, good-looking, good-for-nothing husband of hers. But Teeny would steadfastly keep up appearances, hanging quietly on her discreet, tasteful martyr's cross until the day she died, and we'd love her anyway.

"So." Linda steered to a topic we could all safely complain about. "Where's the waitress? Don't tell me you've scared her off already, George."

Did I mention that George is my nickname? It's short for Georgia, but not my native state. That would be too redneck. My mama was very artistic and forward-thinking, so she'd named me after the infamously liberated artist Georgia O'Keeffe, a fact that has always given me a clandestine sense of scandalous satisfaction. But only the Red Hats and my husband are allowed to call me George.

Miss Romania finally appeared with my tea—with lemon despite my request otherwise, dad-gum it—and a small basket of bread with strawberry butter balls.

I removed the wedge from the side of my glass, then wiped the rim with my napkin, but the damage had been done. That first glass would taste faintly of disinfectant to me, even with plenty of Sweet'N Low.

Typically straightforward, Linda took charge of the bread basket and assessed its skimpy contents. "I'm afraid we're going to need lots more than this."

When the waitress frowned, clearly confused, Linda clarified, pointing to the tiny muffins and fat rolls. "More bread, please. Now. And much plain butter. Plain butter."

Still scowling, Miss Romania disappeared—without taking the drink orders.

Linda helped herself to a muffin. "Yum. Poppy seed."

"Well, keep 'em down there by you," I grumbled. "Don't tempt me. I have to save my calories for the main course."

"Tradition Twelve," Linda invoked. (No mention of weight or diets.) Passing the rolls to Teeny—whose metabolism, unlike the rest of ours, kept her rail-thin no matter what—she promptly shattered the same tradition. And Tradition Five. "I'm tellin' you, George, as long as you walk at least four times a week and give up on trying to look thirty again, fat's like dust: it reaches maximum thickness pretty quickly. Then you can eat whatever you want within reason without gaining any more."

Easy for her to say. Her devoted little urologist husband was as barrel-bodied as she was. But my husband had grown increasingly thinner and more distant in recent years, working out and working late with driven compulsion. I dared not risk letting myself go.

Of course, I was still operating then under the illusion that if you "did it right," your marriage would be safe from the plague of infidelity that had wiped out most couples we knew. It had started slowly with our parents, then spread like some immoral ebola through our own generation, with Bill Clinton as its poster boy.

At the sound of a familiar smoker's cough over the polite din of female conversation, we all turned to see SuSu hurrying in, her freckled face overtanned and her once-red hair a strangely greenish hue. She never wore a hat, red or otherwise; flatly refused.

She could have used one, though. One look at her hair, and I didn't have to see the others' reactions. I knew that another of our sacred traditions was on its way as soon as she got settled in.

"Hey, y'all," she said in her husky smoker's voice as she shucked her jacket, revealing the khakis, sweater, and white shirt that were her flight uniform. "I've gotta leave early to work the six o'clock to Houston, so let's get this show on the road."

Essence of SuSu: arrive at least half an hour late, then cause a scene trying to hustle everybody up.

None of us wasted any emotional energy being annoyed by it anymore. We did, however, compensate by teasing her about being the world's oldest stewardess.

"You manage to get to the airport on time," Linda chastened. "So we know you can teach an old dog new tricks. How 'bout spendin' some of that newfound punctuality on your best friends for a change? Don't we deserve it?"

"Punctuality is precious," SuSu shot back. "What little I can muster up, I have to save for matters involving money."

Still, I kept hoping she might eventually apply some of it to her social engagements.

"Where's the waitress?" SuSu asked with a familiar, dangerous glint in her eye, scanning the menu as if she actually might order something besides her usual. "I've gotta be out of here by two."

She closed her menu decisively, rose, and headed for the foyer. "I'm gonna tell the manager we need some service."

"Our poor waitress," Teeny murmured, her gentle soul always pained by confrontation. "She doesn't seem to understand much English. I don't think it was very wise of them to assign her to us."

Linda cackled. "God, no. We're something you work up to."

"Yeah," I chimed in, "like waitress boot camp: a shared ordeal that bonds the staff together."

Diane let out her throaty chuckle. "Somebody gets to be the Princess and the Pea. It might as well be us."

"Princess? Hah," I said with more than a hint of bitterness. Princesses, indeed. We had all had our tantalizing taste of happily ever after, but only Linda's had lasted. The rest of us were living in denial or running scared. SuSu had lost everything, forced to support herself after two decades of wife-and-mothering.

"Oh, dear." Teeny peered toward Josie, who, standing beside a haughty SuSu, was searching the room for our invisible server. "I hope SuSu doesn't get snippy this time."

There was a heartbeat of silence; then the four of us— even Teeny—burst out laughing, loud enough to draw stares and muffle the herd-of-birds roar in the room.

Of course SuSu would get snippy. She always did, but we loved her anyway, just as we overlooked her chain smoking (thank God the restaurant was smoke-free), her drinking, her stubbornly disastrous taste in men, and her persistent failure to wake up and smell the coffee.

Diane motioned her back over. Before SuSu reached the table, our favorite waitress, Maria, emerged from the kitchen with warm rolls, plain butter, and her pad. "Sorry about the hang-up, ladies. Seems Vashkenushka just up and left without telling anybody."

"Oh, gosh." Teeny grimaced, quick to take responsibility and drag us along with her. "Now see what we did. We ran that poor woman off."

"Well, good riddance if you did," Maria said matter-of-factly. "The devil owed this place a debt, and he paid it with that woman." She lowered her voice conspiratorially. "The manager only put her out front because the cook threatened to quit if she didn't get her out of the kitchen." She poised her pen. "How about drinks? Water for everybody, plus the usual?"

Linda considered, buttering a roll. "Could you make us some more of that hot lemonade you did the last time, Maria? It was so-o-o good."

"Certainly. How about a couple of pots for the table?"

The room was still cool, and the hot lemonade sounded wonderful. "Good with me."

The others nodded.

"All right, then." She knew without being asked to take our orders right away. "The soup of the day is clam chowder, and the fish is pan-seared tilapia with a lemon-butter sauce." She patiently endured the cosmic compulsion that causes Ladies Who Lunch to complain about the delay while waiting to order, then dither like they've never even seen a menu when the waitress finally arrives with pen in hand.

I won't even discuss the thing about splitting checks and the havoc wreaked by to-the-penny purists. In the interest of time and global tranquillity, Maria also knew without being asked to do separate checks.

After allowing a decent interval for consideration, I went first, as usual. "I'll have the shrimp salad plate, please."

Maria scribbled away, flipped the page, then waited through the lengthy passive-aggressive pause of indecision that followed.

I kept myself from getting annoyed at the others' dithering by checking for familiar faces across the room, but found none. An office luncheon of twelve, six Talbots-y, white-haired quads, lots of upscale duos, and a corner table with three women in tennis sweats, which was so not done these days.

Not a soul I knew. It just wasn't our town anymore.

Finally, Diane got things rolling again by ordering her usual. "I'll have the Favorite, no pineapple, please."

"Same here," Teeny followed on cue. "But pineapple's okay for mine."

Linda muttered over the hot entrées, then ordered what she always did. "I'll have the French onion soup and chicken salad croissant."

"Very good." Maria removed their menus, waiting for SuSu to make up her mind.

"A glass of Chablis and the combination plate," SuSu finally declared. "But bring me regular coffee, too, please." She turned to us. "I need the caffeine. The flight goes on to Arizona, then Salt Lake City, so it'll be morning before we make the layover."

Coming from SuSu's mouth, the term layover was a

double entendre of galactic proportions, but the four of us managed to keep straight faces.

We waited until Maria was gone before we all leaned in toward SuSu and whispered, "MO! Big-time."

Red Hat Sacred Tradition Two: Anybody can call a makeover (MO) when it's warranted.

"What is with that hair color? Shades of senior green," I said sotto voce, referring to the summer I'd worked as a lifeguard in high school and ended up with olive drab instead of bleached blond hair.

"The color's not nearly as awful as George's was that time," Teeny was quick to soothe, "but it definitely has a cast of that same green."

"You didn't resort to drugstore hair color, did you?" Linda asked, aghast. " 'Cause that's what happened to my cousin's friend. The salon color interacted with the cheap stuff, and she went bald within a week. Had to wear an Eva Gabor wig for more than six months while her hair grew back out." Sounded like an urban myth to me, but Linda clearly believed it.

"Of course I didn't use that junk," SuSu said, indignant to be accused of one of the most alarming signs of impending poverty or personal neglect in a Buckhead girl. "Charles still does my color, just like always." She clearly wasn't taking the MO in the spirit of sisterhood. "Granted, I'm a little late getting to him this month. I had to cover for a flight on my regular appointment day. But I haven't sunk to shampoo-in."

Diane peered at her uncovered coiffure. "Kinda that pool-green color we got as kids."

"Pool." SuSu's eyes sharpened as the truth sank in. "Shit."

"Ha. Mystery solved." I drove the point home. "Those layovers in Cancún and Arizona and New Mexico. Pool hair."

At least SuSu had the good grace to look sheepish. "I've been swimming laps." She pulled a thick shock of her stylish bob toward the front for a closer look. "Double shit. It is green." She flicked it back into place. "Oh, well. Charles'll fix it next week."

The rest of us exchanged glances.

"Speaking of Charles, Suse," Diane ventured, "maybe this might be a good time to try somebody else. He hasn't done you any favors for the last few months."

SuSu scanned our faces for confirmation and got it. "Why didn't you say something sooner?"

Ever the peacemaker, Teeny leaned forward, sympathetic. "It just happened sort of gradually. Today's the first time it's rated an MO."

"Okay. I'll consider it, but next month. I don't have time to go hunting."

"Try Joanna, at Athena on Buckhead Avenue," three of us said in unison.

"You can have my appointment next Tuesday," Linda volunteered. "You'll love her, and she can fit me in anytime."

"Okay. Enough. I'll go." Uncomfortable, SuSu glanced toward the kitchen. "Where's my wine?" She turned back. "Enough about me. I call a do over. Who's got the joke?"

Diane raised her hand. "Me, but remember, joke-telling is not my forte."

"We live in hope, Di," Linda said as always. "Go for it."

She pulled out a paper from her purse and unfolded it to reveal her loopy, inflated handwriting. "A Buckhead housewife and her husband were having an argument about sex," she read, dropping her voice on the last. " 'You never tell me when you're having an orgasm!' the guy yelled.

" 'How can I?' she yelled back. 'You're never here!' "

Linda and SuSu laughed. I'd heard it ages ago, but laughed anyway.

"Good one," SuSu ruled.

"I second that." Linda.

Teeny smiled politely, a quizzical expression on her

face. We'd long ago given up on trying to explain the jokes to her. We loved her as much because of her naïveté as in spite of it.

Suddenly Diane looked as if she might burst into tears. "Okay, now that that's out of the way," she said, leaning in to keep anyone beyond the table from hearing, "I've got major trouble, and I need y'all to help me."

That got our attention, pronto. Spring-loaded with concern, four red hats and one green head huddled up as she reached into her pocket and produced a tidy little note that she smoothed out next to the bud vase where all of us could see it.

"Buy sheets—310 thread count. Paint the kitchen," it said in a precise male hand.

"I found that in the pocket of Harold's suit last night."

"So?" Linda asked.

"We don't need any sheets," Diane growled in a tone I'd never heard her use before. "And he sure as hell isn't painting any kitchens at my house!"

At last. She'd finally acknowledged the truth that we had long since known. The question was, what was she going to do about it?

My mind swirled with possibilities. I was great at analyzing my friends' problems—almost as great as I was at denying my own.